A RESPECTABLE MARRIED WOMAN

Published by
LACUNA
www.gbapl.com.au/lacuna
An imprint of
GBA Communications
PO Box 278 East Melbourne
Victoria 3002
Australia
Web www.gbapl.com.au

National Library of Australia cataloguing-in-publication entry:
Banks, Glenda.
A Respectable Married Woman/author, Glenda Banks.
ISBN: 978-0-646-56969-7

Text design by Peter Maddigan
Cover design by Design Immersion
Printed by BPA Print Group Pty Ltd Burwood VIC

A
RESPECTABLE
MARRIED
WOMAN

❖

A story of passion, prejudice and triumph set in Victoria's
mid-19th century goldfields

by
GLENDA BANKS

LACUNA
An imprint of
GBA Communications

Author's note

A Respectable Married Woman is a story about passion, prejudice, violence, heart-break and triumph, affirming the strength of the female spirit against seemingly insurmountable odds.

Set in Australia's Victorian goldfields during the second half of the 19th century, it begins in England in 1848 and follows the fortunes of three women who typify settlers of the day, leaving the only life they know to face the unknown on the other side of the world.

Retracing their footsteps I became absorbed by the history of Victoria's goldfields and the women who raised families there in conditions so primitive as to be beyond our comprehension today, but still found the will to set up schools and hospitals, and challenge the prevailing social structure to become leaders of style and substance.

I came across echoes of their lives in city archives and country cemeteries; in the crumbling remains of slab huts and carefully preserved boom-time build-ings; in one-room museums in once thriving ghost towns now bypassed by high speed freeways and on bronze plaques mounted incongruously on urban high-rise monoliths.

Although Martha, Charlotte, and Connie – central characters in this story – will not be found in official archives, they are carefully researched composites of the passionate, compassionate and achieving women whose spirit shines brightly through the folklore and legends of Victoria's goldfields and the clear, confident eyes of their descendants.

While houses borrowed for the settings of parts of this narrative still exist the action taking place in them is entirely imagined.

Unless otherwise noted, I have used placenames by which Australia and its states and territories are known at the time of publication.

Acknowledgments

The Golden Age: A history of the colony of Victoria, 1851-1861, by the late Dr Geoffrey Serle AO, Reader in History at Monash University, is acknowledged to provide one of the most comprehensive records of this definitive decade of growth in Victoria's history. *The Golden Age* was the first book I read while researching Victoria's goldrush era. It proved an invaluable and inspiring resource through each phase of the development of this narrative, as did Jennifer Hagger's *Australian Colonial Medicine* – a moving reminder of conditions faced by women in the goldrush era, as well as a record of medicine in the bush. I would also like to acknowledge the contribution of the many librarians, curators and family historians who generously offered information drawn from memoirs, journals and other artefacts to help shape the life and times of the characters portrayed in this story.

Glenda Banks has a mainstream media background as a journalist, editor and publisher. She has a PhD in historiographic metafiction and is the author of seven nonfiction books exploring contemporary social issues. This is her first novel, set in the framework of Australia's mid-19th century Victorian goldfields. She lives in Melbourne surrounded by many of the historic markers bearing witness to the people and events that shaped this story.

For

Judie, John and Sarah

Chapter One

THE HIRING

I never thought when my time came, that I would be buried in a land of searing sun, half a world away from the lush green hills of my beloved west country. I always assumed I would end up lying in the shadow of the tiny, windswept church perched high above the River Lynn. It is an odd thing, too, to watch them shovel the rich, red earth onto the coffin that holds my own lifeless body. But I had always imagined death would be like this, with me watching the rituals required to dispatch me decently.

I know people were often shocked when I talked about what I thought happened after life. I daresay there were some who would have thought Martha Wootten a heathen. Indeed, plenty crossed themselves when I said I didn't believe there was such a place as heaven. I just couldn't see as how if nobody has ever been there and come back to tell of it, anyone could be so sure there is a place we all float up to when we give up the Ghost. It seemed much more likely to me that our souls linger on, around and about the cadaver for a while, to make sure, as it were, there is no twitching nerve on which to hang the hope of life. After that, they hover somewhere, to dispense wisdom and advice when called upon by those they leave behind.

I have seen something like that happen for a few moments when a woman gives birth. Many's the babe I've helped into the world and I've had plenty of opportunity to notice things while I watched and waited.

They say a woman is closest to death at the moment she gives life to her child, and I'll vouch for that. Often, when the pain reached a peak, I would see a woman smile a very peaceful sort of smile. When I'd ask her about it, later, she would tell me it had seemed she was floating, high above the pain, watching her own body giving birth as if she were merely an observer. At that moment, I believe a woman is suspended between life and death. And if the good Lord deems she should live, He sends her soul back down into her body again.

Now I can see my beloved Charlotte leaning forward to drop a spray of wattle onto my polished box. She knows it is my favourite blossom next to the tough gorse on the hills around the cottage, cruelly torn from me, so long ago. Dear love, don't weep for me. Old Martha's happy to rest in peace knowing you have someone else to stand beside you now in the land we have both come to love.

There, there, sweeting. Take comfort in Richard's arm around your shoulders, holding you safe and warm against the chill of death. And Mistress Jade, so pale and still. Not a bit like your naughty sister, Kate, who pouts and stamps her dainty foot when all is not as she would have it.

And you, young master Dickon ... although I suppose we cannot call you Dickon for much longer now that you are near a grown man. What would your grandfather have given to know you now, lad? Had he allowed your mother stay with him, as she'd begged, he would have known a far greater happiness than pride in his precious name.

I remember the first time I set eyes on your mother, Dickon. It was in the middle of what passed for a summer in England, all those years ago in the year of our Lord, 1848. She was then just barely eighteen, thin and pale, her blue eyes dark ringed from sleepless nights spent weeping. My whole body ached from the long and wearisome journey by coach from the schoolhouse in Lynmouth to Bristol. But I managed a stiff bob as the footman announced my arrival to the grey haired gentleman standing with his back to the great marble fireplace in Hatfield Hall, and a slightly more painful, deeper one in the general direction of the two ladies seated on a fine brocade settle across the room.

Glancing up, as I held the dip a fraction longer than necessary, I noticed the elder woman had a high colour, as if she would faint from stays too tightly laced, and that she fanned herself, feverishly, with the pages of a letter, while the younger woman wept silently into a wisp of white lawn.

"Your references, Wootten?" thrusting forward his open hand, Sir Ian Hatfield, baronet, and master of the grand manor house in which I now stood, held my eyes fast to his, as if to keep them from straying to the weeping young woman across the room.

"If you please, sir," I responded promptly, presenting the folded letter, secured by red sealing wax bearing the imprint of the Revd Aloysius St John, vicar of the parish in which I had, until recently, thought to remain for the rest of my life. There was silence, save for the sound from a huge grandfather clock as it relentlessly counted off the seconds, while Sir Ian absorbed every syllable on the closely penned sheet he held at arm's length. As he read, I allowed my mind to wander back over the weeks before I had read the notice which had brought me to Hatfield Hall.

Two months ago, I mused, I would have been sitting secure and content in a small cottage beside the River Lynn, servant to none and mistress of the home I had bought and paid for out of earnings hoarded over a lifetime of maidservant positions. My home was just half a mile from the edge of town and within easy walking of the market and church, yet far enough from the noise and bustle for me to enjoy a restful retirement. The gooseberries I grew and the eggs from my fat, brown Lohmans would have supplemented my savings until my time ran out.

But I never reckoned on the rain. None of us did. Oh, we knew it could rain in Somerset – especially along the north coast from Minehead to Lynmouth. But the long periods of drizzle and mist only served to keep the rolling countryside lush and green, far greener than that of the warmer, drier south.

But on May Day, at the exact moment Maizie Smallridge's youngest was about to receive her crown of cowslips and apple blossom, the heavens pulled apart and the deluge began, swelling the rising river until its banks could hold no more. Maizie's farm was washed away and her eldest son went missing for days. Everyone lost something, I lost my little refuge, saw it swept away as I watched from the top of a grassy knoll where a few of us had gathered with what scant possessions we had managed to salvage and haul up the slippery slope. The last I saw of my comfortable retirement was my thatched roof bobbing away out towards the Bristol Channel.

Lynmouth was devastated. As the flood waters receded, the blacksmith and a small band of bold souls offered to rebuild our homes at the top of the craggy mount overlooking what was left of the town. They said they would call it Lynton and everyone would be safe from the floods up there forever.

But I had nothing left with which to purchase foothold on the mountain. For safe keeping, I had sewn my savings into my horsehair mattress, and that had been washed away with the rest of my belongings. All I had I held in my hands – the egg money in my purse and a knee rug recovered from the lower branches of a leafless yew hanging out over the swollen river.

It was while we survivors sat huddled in the safe shelter of the church hall, some days later, that I saw my salvation. A notice, pinned on the vestry bulletin board, offering accommodation and a small stipend in exchange for a temporary position as a lady's maid.

As I scanned the words I thanked the good Lord for putting a stern mistress in my way when I had first started out in service at the age of twelve years. Although I was a far from willing student when the notion was presented to me, I had bowed to her authority and learned to read, write and reckon from the butler. An unforgiving man, he taught me my letters and numbers not from a love of learning but the master's port. A full jug, drawn off the house keg, for lifting the future prospects of his underlings and putting one more feather in the cap the mistress wore to the charity meetings.

"These seem to be in order." Sir Ian's rich and resonant voice broke into my review of the near and distant past and brought me back, abruptly, to the present. I looked up quickly, searching his eyes for the hint of a welcoming smile.

"This is your new mistress, my daughter, Miss Charlotte Hatfield," he intoned, indicating the younger woman on the far side of the room with a nod in her direction.

"Her mother, the Lady Margaret, will inform you of your daily duties later. But before you agree to accept the position offered you must be prepared for all it entails – for there can be no going back on your word once it is given. That, as you will learn, will be quite impossible.

"My daughter ...' as he glanced at the girl she turned her beautiful face to him with such an imploring look I had to turn my own away, for such emotion openly displayed embarrassed me.

"My daughter," Sir Ian began again, sadly, "has brought disgrace and dishonour upon her family. The eldest of my three daughters, she abused the privilege of my affection by meeting secretly with the son of our local coach builder. Believing herself to be in love, and knowing I could never give my blessing to such a union, she ran away with him to London, where the unlikely couple effected an irregular marriage by a jobbing priest. I traced them to rooms close by Temple Inn, and there the matter might have ended, with the future prospects of my two younger daughters, Miss Beatrice and Miss Melanie, as promising as one might expect.

"But God had ruled my errant daughter should be further held accountable for her fall from grace. It would appear she is to bear the coach boy's child."

Here, the poor lass who had held herself so bravely throughout the ordeal of public disclosure fainted clean away.

I was across the room and down on my knees in a moment, searching for the small bottle of salts I always carry deep in one of the pockets hidden by the folds of my workaday skirt.

"I'll hear the rest after I have put Miss Charlotte to bed," I announced grimly as the young woman stirred – purposely leaving off the customary sir or madam.

Lady Margaret allowed herself a sigh of relief and found the strength to pull the bell cord and summon a footman to carry her daughter to her bed chamber. There, tucked to the chin with white linen, soft blankets and a down filled quilt, the poor lass gave over sobbing at last. I felt for the pulse in her wrist and satisfied myself the blood was coursing normally again before I deemed it safe to leave her and return to complete my contract with her father.

Finding my way down the back stairs I tapped on the oak-panelled door of the library, where Sir Ian waited to finish reciting the terms and conditions of my employment, and paused for word to enter. The command came swiftly. Sir Ian stood alone, now, before the fireless hearth in which any butler I'd worked under would have ordered the housemaid to build a blaze, for the house was cold despite the pale sun filtering through the leaded panes of its large bay windows. There was no more warmth in my response as I answered Sir Ian's inquiry after his daughter's health.

"She is as well as can be expected," I replied, as curtly as I dared, for I was not averse to giving a body the rough side of my tongue if I felt it was deserved. But I was careful not to put too much of an edge on my tone because, Lord knows, I needed the position. And although I had long since made it a rule never to become attached to the gentlefolk I served – I'd seen too many loyal servants sent away to be forgotten once they had outlived their usefulness – I knew Miss Charlotte was in dire need of someone to show compassion as well as care for her.

"But as you suggested, sir," I ventured, boldly, although I was already committed to the position, "I need to hear the rest of the story before I can commit to Miss Charlotte's long-term care."

"Yes, indeed," Sir Ian replied, brusquely. "But listen carefully for I must lower my voice to ensure none of the other servants are privy to my plans. Damage enough has been done to our good name already, without giving those below stairs more to gossip about in their cups."

Quietly, but enunciating each word so clearly that his voice carried with the clarity of a choirboy's, he continued, "I intend to send Miss Charlotte on a long journey. A voyage to the other side of the world, in fact, where her condition can be hidden from her sisters and the circle in which the Hatfield family moves.

"I love my daughter, dearly, despite her recent transgressions. She has always been a free spirit and I feel I am, in part, at fault for indulging her eccentricities.

"She would have none of the restraints imposed upon her by her class, and mixed freely with the tenants and workers on the Hatfield estate. But marriage to a coach boy and the birth of a bastard will close doors in her face forever. And in those of her sisters.

"For her own sake, and theirs, I have decided to send Charlotte to Her Majesty's colonies in Australia. Once there, a marriage will be arranged to a suitable candidate by one of my contacts in the area – in all likelihood an officer of good breeding but poor prospects.

"This will ensure my grandchild will have a name, and with the dates of the birth and marriage clouded by time and distance, my daughter will be able to rejoin the family as a respectable married woman. Thus, the family honour is preserved, she will have a future, and the prospects of her two younger sisters will no longer be compromised by their sibling's situation.

"As Miss Charlotte's maidservant, you will travel with her to Australia, see her safely settled into her marriage and delivered of her child, with the expectation of returning to England at some time within the next two years.

"My cousin, Sir Giles Chalmondly, left England for Port Melbourne a twelve-month since, to oversee the establishment of a private banking facility. I have written advising him of my daughter's situation and requested his assistance in the search for a suitable husband. Until such time as that happens, you will live under his roof.

"My esteemed brother, Captain Hugh Hatfield has command of the

Chetwynde, flagship of a line which regularly carries settlers and supplies to Australia," he continued.

"Concerned for Charlotte's future happiness, he knows the colony well and believes that, with the acute shortage of women of our class in Port Melbourne, my plan is likely to succeed.

"He has agreed to take his niece with him on his next voyage, and to arrange the safe transfer of both my daughter, and the generous dowry I intend to settle on the prospective new husband, into Sir Giles' safe keeping.

"In the meantime we shall let it be known that Miss Charlotte is preparing to visit Australia at the request of a distant relative, to lift the spirits of his childless wife who yearns for companionship.

"Eventually, word will filter back that she has met, and wishes to marry, a young officer serving in the colony, and although I will be, at first, surprised, I will quickly find it in my heart to approve the union and in due time, its somewhat precipitous issue.

"If you think you can meet the conditions and responsibilities of the position for which the Reverend St John has so highly recommended you, you will receive a stipend of twenty guineas a year for the rest of your life, commencing from the moment you sign this agreement," he concluded, glancing down at the vicar's character reference.

Reaching for the document he slid across the satinwood surface of a small console table set between us, I responded without hesitation.

"I accept the position, sir, and you may rest assured that as God is my witness, I shall discharge my duties to Miss Charlotte with all care and diligence," I replied – adding, under my breath, *and the good Lord help us both.*

Looking back on what followed, it is as if Miss Charlotte and I were characters in a story scripted by some unseen hand . . . plucked from our everyday lives and placed in the middle of a work of fiction, our destiny controlled by the writer's fertile imagination. Perhaps events would be easier to recall in such a form . . .

16

Chapter Two

DEPARTURE

The sun had not yet risen when the Hatfield carriage drew to a halt. Thin streaks of grey lightened the heavy cloud that hung over the scene unfolding before its occupants, and a cold northerly keened along the walkway between the holding sheds and the ships rising and falling at dock's edge. Although it was still dark, the walkway was lit by fires heating smoking tar pots, and already crowded with porters and seamen swarming around the vessel *Chetwynde*, set to sail out of Plymouth on the midday tide.

Searching the basket Cook had prepared for their journey from Bristol, Martha thanked God for the good woman's kindness and foresight as her questing fingers found a small silver flask hidden in the snowy folds of a damask napkin. Unscrewing the cap, which served also as a miniature cup, she passed the flask under her nose to ascertain its contents and allowed the flicker of a smile to lift the corners of her grimly set mouth. In the two short weeks prior to their departure, Cook had become a friend to Martha – and a valuable source of information about her new charge.

Much loved for her genuine interest in the comfort of below-stairs staff, Charlotte had taken a spirited stand to improve conditions for all of the men and women working on the Hatfield estate. Widows and orphans were her special concern, and the Hatfield larder was often raided to provide nourishing treats for women and children without a man to care for them. Such was their affection for her that Cook and Leicester, the butler, colluded to hide such indiscretions from the housekeeper and the estate manager by entering them in the daily records of food consumed as 'picnics for Miss Charlotte and the misses Beatrice and Melanie'.

When the coachbuilder's son began turning up at the kitchen door to carry the baskets of food Charlotte took to the village, Cook had at first thought nothing of it. But others watched with growing concern as the relationship blossomed from friendship to love.

"We had known young Richard since he was a babe," Cook told her. "He was a happy child, willing to run an errand or chop wood for anyone who needed help, and he grew into a strong and capable craftsman when his father took him into the business.

"He and Miss Charlotte made such a pretty couple, so right for each other in every way – except, of course, for the question of class. Miss Charlotte knew she could never gain her father's consent to their marriage, and when she came to kiss me goodbye the morning they ran off to London it was far too late to persuade them to reconsider.

"When her father found them and brought her home, we all feared Charlotte would die from grief at being separated from Richard. Sending her so far away now is the cruellest blow of all – especially under the circumstances," and here she looked directly into Martha's eyes.

"You may be new here, Mistress Wootten, but you are one of us – we have witnessed your kindness to our dear girl, and know you will come to care for her as much as we do."

"Drink this, my lady," Martha said, pouring a measure of Madeira wine into the miniature silver goblet. "It will warm your blood while we wait to board our vessel." Martha did not add that the wine might also fortify Charlotte for her meeting with her uncle, Captain Hugh Hatfield, the ship's master.

Lifting her hand in a fluttering gesture of refusal, Charlotte shook her head. As she did so, the fox lined hood of her travelling cape, held until that moment to half cover her face, slid back to reveal dark ringed eyes and cheeks as pale and translucent as alabaster.

"You must, my dear ... for the baby," Martha coaxed. It was the first time she had spoken of the infant carried within her new mistress's fragile frame, and she had done so only to prevent her young charge fainting away in the face of cruel events to follow. The instant the words had passed her lips she regretted having said them. As their impact registered Charlotte raised her eyes to Martha's with a look of such suffering that the older woman, forgetting her position, drew her mistress to her as if she were a child of her own. But as the tears flowed freely, Martha sensed Charlotte's relief that she could at last acknowledge, without censure, the living reminder of the lad she had loved so unwisely, but so well.

For a few moments, mistress and servant rocked wordlessly together, Charlotte's soft, wet cheek against the rough texture of Martha's woollen cloak. Had Charlotte glanced upward she might have seen that tears were also welling in her servant's eyes, as memories of the child the woman had carried within her own body broke through the barrier she had erected in her mind to ease the pain of his premature loss. But Martha's moment of self indulgence was short lived. Remembering her position she drew back and again presented the tiny cup to the young woman's mouth. This time Charlotte sipped obediently. Building on this small victory, Martha spread a damask napkin on the seat between them and set down one of Cook's still-warm pasties.

"Here, child, try to eat a little of this," she said, noting another small victory won in the shape of a smile that teased her new mistress's tremulous mouth. But she found the win came at a price, as Charlotte took the west-country envelope of flaking pastry filled with meat and vegetables and, breaking it in two, offered half to Martha.

"I will eat if you will eat, for the morning chill affects us equally," said Charlotte, the sadness in her eyes giving way to a glint of spirited challenge.

"Then I suppose I must, my lady, although I am sure I don't know what your father would say if he saw us supping together," Martha replied, shaking her head and taking the proffered food from the hand held out before her.

Charlotte also insisted they share Cook's Madeira and, as the women ate and drank, Martha, uncomfortable with her sudden social elevation, focused her attention on the vessel they would board as soon as there was light enough to step safely from the carriage.

Not a soul had come forward from the ship to meet them, and in light of events so far, Martha felt it was unlikely anyone would. Charlotte had broken her fast alone in the family dining room that morning. The room had been cold and unlit, except for the meagre warmth and light from last night's candles, sputtering indignantly at being rekindled to burn so low to light such a meagre spread.

It was the custom for the family to take their first meal of the day at nine each morning, when Sir Ian would join the ladies in the dining room and take his place at the head of the table. As soon as he was seated Leicester would leave his station by the door and, with measured stride, traverse the polished floor boards to the mahogany sideboard against the far wall of the long, rectangular room. Charlotte and her sisters would count out his steps until, with military precision, he would halt, turn and lift the lids from each of the silver tureens set out on silver burners, inspect the contents, and call out the names of each of the dishes Cook had prepared. Neither the ritual nor the menu varied. There were always kippers – herrings smoked and served in a sauce made from reduced brine and herbs grown in the manor garden, eggs – scrambled and placed upon hot, buttered oat cakes, kidneys – sautéed and covered with thick port gravy; succulent pork sausages and thick, curling slices of estate-smoked bacon.

First Sir Ian and Lady Margaret would murmur their preferences to the footmen stationed behind their chairs. Their daughters, Charlotte, Beatrice and Melanie, would then follow suit. In sequence, each of the five footmen would whisper the orders to Leicester and plates – properly warmed – would be filled and set before the family with servings of their choice.

This morning had proven to be no exception for any of the family or servants save Charlotte, Martha and Cook. Neither Sir Ian nor Lady Margaret had risen early to bid their daughter farewell as she took her leave of Hatfield Hall. Beatrice and Melanie had also kept to their rooms, although they had made tender farewells the previous night, aware only that their sister was leaving to spend some months as companion to a distant relative.

There was no butler or footman present, either, to break the silence with a squeaking shoe or discreet cough, as Charlotte shared her last meal in her father's house with her maidservant. In their place, Cook had made a flustered, brief and unaccustomed appearance in the dining room, bearing a tray upon which she had set a dish of freshly coddled eggs and toasted white bread, two warmed Minton plates and sterling silver flatware. Setting the meagre offering down in front of Martha she made a bob in Charlotte's direction before backing out, clicking her tongue against the roof of her mouth to cover the fact that she had no idea what she was supposed to say in such unusual circumstances. Seconds later, the performance was repeated, as Cook again entered the room, this time bearing a smaller tray holding a small silver tea pot, milk, sugar and two china cups and saucers so thin as to be almost translucent.

It was scant repast compared with the usual family breakfast but Martha knew that Cook had risked her position treading the boards above stairs to present a hot meal to the departing women. The worthy woman had risked yet another brief appearance as Charlotte and Martha took their leave of the sleeping manor house. Emerging from the shadows at the far end of the front hall, well forward of the stairs that led to the kitchen, she had thrust a wide wicker hamper into Martha's arms.

"Take this, Mistress Wootten," she had said. "It is all I can do for the poor lass, now. Although under the circumstances, she cannot stay here, it breaks all our hearts to see our lovely girl sent so far away.

"Take care of her for us, and send word of her safe delivery when you can."

So saying, she had then abandoned all consideration of the consequences of her actions. Taking hold of Charlotte's silk gloved hand she brought it to her lips, murmuring, "God love you, my lady," before turning away to disappear down the kitchen stairs, dabbing furiously at her eyes with the corner of her starched, white apron.

Rising as swiftly as the cold and cramps in her joints would allow, Martha packed away the remains of Cook's parting gift, drew the travelling rug from her mistress's knees and turned to rap smartly on the ornate panel covering the boards behind her head.

"We'd best be making a move, now, Miss," she said, as Barker, the young footman sent with them to handle their baggage, hopped down from his seat behind the driver to peer inquiringly through the carriage window.

Nodding in answer to his unspoken question, Martha moved forward as Barker opened the door and unfolded the carriage steps to hand her down onto the freezing footpath. Taking a tentative step to test her foothold, Martha had her back to the carriage as Barker handed Charlotte down from the carriage. Even allowing for the likelihood of some, if not all, of the below stairs household knowing of Charlotte's condition, Martha sensed intuitively that it was taking him longer than it should to perform this simple task.

Turning to look for the cause she was amazed to witness the young footman in the act of pressing something into his mistress's hand. Balfour, Cook's husband, who doubled as both driver and head groom, averted his eyes from Martha's questioning glance as it swept towards him, making a showy display of reining in the perfectly still horses. Thrusting the cheeky young footman aside, Martha took a firm hold on Charlotte's elbow and began to walk purposefully towards the tall ship tied up to the wharf in front of them, steering her mistress as quickly as possible through the rough crowd that thronged around and about the three-masted barque.

Barker followed at a safe distance, laden with the comparatively few pieces of cabin baggage they were to be allowed to draw on during the long voyage ahead of them. Clothing and comforts were restricted to the bare essentials, with only occasional access to baggage stored in the ship's hold. Bounty emigrants were allowed access to only personal possessions they, themselves, could carry onboard, their meagre home-building tools stowed in the deepest part of the hold until they disembarked. Poor orphaned Irish girls, despatched as housemaids and, if they were lucky, apprenticed seamstresses, were provided with a tin plate, a mug, knife, fork and spoon, a drawstring calico bag containing just one change of clothes, and a blanket to cover them as they slept.

Barker met the challenge of transferring Charlotte's large leather trunk, small wooden chest and four round hat boxes from the carriage onto the *Chetwynde* by hoisting the trunk onto his back, tucking the chest under one arm, and stringing the hat boxes together on a strong webbing belt looped through the handles and buckled diagonally across his body. The fact that he whistled, cheekily, while struggling under his load, provoked a wry smile from Martha. Given the circumstances, she had decided to overlook his familiarity with Charlotte as an expression of the obvious concern shared by all the Hatfield servants for their soon-to-be exiled young mistress.

If Barker had slipped something into Charlotte's hand, it was more than likely some token of their remembrance, or another of Cook's comforts to sweeten the sorrow of leaving her homeland – as they had most probably surmised – in disgrace.

Martha had packed wisely and well for her mistress, selecting from Charlotte's vast wardrobe six morning dresses of varying weight, two pairs of soft, calf-skin ankle boots and two pairs of embroidered silk slippers; six afternoon dresses and two hand-spun cashmere shawls; four satin evening gowns with matching feather hair pieces and three velvet cloaks; an assortment of silk and cotton hose, a soft silk dressing gown and under-garments and nightwear to suit each of the two extreme seasons passengers had been advised they would encounter during their many long weeks at sea.

In one of the drawers which followed the curve in the top of the travelling trunk Sir Ian had purchased to ensure his daughter arrived with a wardrobe befitting a baronet's daughter and, hopefully, an officer's wife, Martha had packed Charlotte's silver backed brush, hand mirror and comb and a set of four small crystal decanters containing her favourite fragrances. In another, she had secreted three sets of swaddling clothes, a cashmere shawl and three tucked gowns against the possibility that Charlotte's baby, quite possibly the new Hatfield heir if it was a male child, might be born before the end of the voyage.

The matching set of crimson, crocodile-skin hat boxes carried Charlotte's favourite *chapeaux*, each stuffed with chamois drawstring bags filled with duck down, and packed into individual calico sacks secured with French frogging.

Martha's only hat, made of serviceable black felt and steamed into the shape of an inverted bowl flaring out into a narrow brim and secured by a pearl-handled hat pin, caught through her thick, greying hair, sat squarely on her head. Her all-purpose, black woollen cloak covered a jacket and skirt made of fibrous tweed, the colour of tarnished pewter. Her feet and ankles met the challenges of both elements and terrain encased, as they were, in stout black boots, oiled and polished to a degree that rendered them impervious to wind or water, and laced high enough to lend support to ankles which ached, increasingly, as her long days in service rolled over into years.

A single portmanteau, which she carried herself, contained her entire wardrobe: two black serge skirts, three white cotton blouses, two knitted shawls, six pairs of cotton stockings, two sets of long, white drawers, two bodices, two white cotton petticoats, a dozen hand-rolled blue cotton handkerchiefs, and her best black leather boots. Around her waist she also carried a small leather satchel containing a selection of dried herbs, salts, crystals and seeds, a bottle of laudanum, two small jars of ointment, and several rolled strips of linen.

The locked wooden chest which completed Barker's load carried documents entitling Charlotte and Martha to enter Australia under the protection of Her Majesty Queen Victoria and the Government of Great Britain, Charlotte's jewellery, and sufficient currency to cover the

24

purchase of such comforts as could be found in ports they might visit while the ship took on new supplies to sustain them as they sailed half way round the world.

Several larger boxes had been dispatched to the docks the previous day, and were already on board. One, containing items deemed necessary to ensure a reasonable degree of comfort in cramped quarters, contained down-filled comforters and hand-sewn sheets, satin-bound towels and bath sheets. Another held Minton china, silver flatware, and delicate lace-edge table linen for their personal use, should they wish to take their meals apart from the rest of the passengers.

There was also a selection of books, journals and water colours for recording the journey, and a portable secretaire complete with bottles of ink, embossed ivory writing paper and envelopes. An elegant *rococo* sewing box filled with packets of precious pins, needles, silver thimbles, wooden reels of fine white and serviceable black thread, twisted skeins of coloured silk, squares and rectangles of starched white linen, and a number of different sized embroidery frames completed the inventory of items considered essential to Charlotte's on-board amusement.

Two beds and chests of drawers, hastily crafted by Hatfield carpenters from age old elms grown on the estate, were already installed in the limited space allotted to Charlotte and Martha aboard the *Chetwynde*, along with a scaled-down campaign table and folding chairs.

Boxes stowed below contained sufficient furniture of good quality to set up a home fit for an officer in Her Majesty's army serving in the colonies. There was also a fine hunter, strong enough for the rumoured rough terrain, but mannered enough for the wife of a gentleman of standing, penned on the foredeck along with other livestock bound for plate or paddock. A bronze chest, containing the generous dowry Sir Ian had instructed his brother to offer as an inducement for an eligible suitor to wed his wayward daughter, had been delivered to the ship by an armed messenger well before first light.

Although only small in stature, Martha had always been sturdy, withstanding all manner of trials and tribulations without calling up a warning from that most vital of human organs. But her heart began to beat with unaccustomed vigour as the moment to board the *Chetwynde* drew near. Try as she might she could not quiet its loud and quickened beat. Nor could she subdue the uneasy voices in her head, whispering of the dangers of the deep and the threat of savages said to inhabit the greater part of the vast new continent for which they were bound.

For a fleeting moment, fear caused her to falter. Her eyes played tricks upon her mind, presenting false images of familiar scenes ... a village green, dotted with young girls in their summer cottons, drifting like blossoms on a soft, summer breeze ... a graceful spire rising above the church where she had been baptised, married, and had expected to be buried.

"Martha, dear?" Charlotte was looking back, her glance reflecting the anxiety in the older woman's eyes.

"Hurry along now, Miss," Martha replied, recovering her resolve, and motioned her charge towards the long, narrow planks sloping up to the deck above them.

Raising her skirts above the muddy water pooled in front of her, Charlotte placed one foot tentatively on the boards rising and falling with the gentle swell. Pausing, she lifted her travelling veil and turned to take one last look at the world she was leaving behind. Her pale, beautiful face, lit by thin rays from the rising sun, was momentarily shadowed by such anguish that it silenced the strident voices of dockside workers milling around them.

At that moment, as if to break the unbearable tension, a sudden surge lifted the ship and lowering it again almost immediately, so that the gangway rose and fell away, creaking alarmingly. With her weight balanced on the foot she had placed upon it, Charlotte's expression turned to horror as the angle of the incline increased, then dropped away ahead of her.

Separated from Charlotte by the crowd surging between them, Martha moved forward, frantically, to catch her fragile charge. But a swarthy seaman, balanced precariously on the ship's rail as he worked to free a snarled cargo net, had foreseen the likely consequences of the swell and, leaping down onto the gangway, caught Charlotte in his arms and lifted her safely back onto firm ground.

In the confusion that followed, neither Martha nor Charlotte noticed the nod of recognition exchanged by the seaman and Hatfield's heavily laden young footman.

As the swell settled, the seaman glanced in Martha's direction, a broad smile puckering the livid scar scoring one side of his weather-beaten face. Turning back to Charlotte, he gently lowered her veil, tugged his forelock and motioned toward the heaving gangway. Stepping on ahead, he turned and, walking backwards, held both her hands in his, leading her slowly up the groaning boards to be met at the top by one of the ship's officers.

Bounding back down again, the sailor tugged his forelock once more, reached for Martha's portmanteau with one hand and placed the other firmly under her elbow as she traversed the distance from dock to deck to join her mistress. Retracing his steps once more he pulled the cabin trunk from Barker's back and, heaving it onto his own, motioned the young footman to follow him.

The officer to whom Charlotte had been entrusted stepped forward as she paused, uncertainly, in front of him. "Captain's compliments, Miss Hatfield, ma'am. Ensign Frobisher at your service. If you will permit me to escort you to your quarters, the Captain will join you there as soon as we are safely underway."

His expression of well-mannered concern changed to unguarded admiration as Charlotte lifted her veil once more, acknowledging his greeting with a brief smile. Witnessing the exchange, Martha mused on the possibility that this personable young man might be a contender for Charlotte's hand. But as soon as the idea entered her head she dismissed it. If Charlotte were to wed a ship's officer he would expect to take her home to England after the return voyage, where speculation would undoubtedly arise on their precipitous issue.

27

A sigh escaped the older woman's lips as she considered the portents for a happy outcome to Charlotte's predicament. Perhaps it was the sigh or the sudden droop of her shoulders that invited attention, but a gnarled hand fell on Martha's shoulder, and she found the devilish face of the sailor who had helped them to board safely, close to her own.

"Begging your pardon, missus, but if you're needin' a hand in the coming weeks, Newbold's the name. Tom Newbold. It can be hard leaving home for the first time ... and I be more than willin' to fetch and carry and do whatever I can to make the young lass comfortable."

Martha's immediate reaction was to show him the sharp end of her elbow for his familiarity. But she sensed genuine compassion in his warm, burred voice and found herself nodding acceptance instead; and as if a pact had been sealed between them, she allowed her unlikely ally to lead her along the narrow walkway between the ship's rails and the cargo lashed to the decks against the surge of the turning tide. Ahead, the young officer had requested, and been granted, permission to place an arm securely round Charlotte's slender waist to hold her safe against the swell and, two by two, the women and their escorts, followed by the footman, reached the safe haven of the Captain's quarters.

Barker deposited the chest and the hatboxes inside the door of one of the two staterooms in the aft deck reserved for first class family passengers and set off in search of the trunk, abandoned by Newbold in favour of ensuring Martha's safe passage forward. On his return, Barker set it down beside the other pieces and walked back through the saloon to the Captain's quarters. After requesting permission to enter, he braved Ensign Frobisher's raised eyebrows to ask if he could be of further service before returning to Hatfield Hall. Turning toward Charlotte as if he was about to speak to her he raised his hand in a half salute before wheeling smartly through the door to rejoin Balfour for the long drive home.

Saluting the officer and nodding to Martha, Newbold, too, took his leave, tapping the side of his nose conspiratorially as he walked past her on his way through the door.

Ensign Frobisher was the last to leave. Glancing cautiously at Martha he turned towards Charlotte, settled securely on the window seat with her back towards the expansive view aft. Uncertain if he should kiss Charlotte's hand or salute her before departing, military ritual prevailed and he saluted smartly, if somewhat reluctantly, before returning to his duties, meeting and greeting other first class passengers.

Shaking her head to mask the hint of a smile, Martha leaned across her charge to draw the heavy curtains against the chill permeating the wide expanse of green-tinted water glass behind them.

"Ah, Martha, that helps," said Charlotte, as Martha knelt to loosen the laces holding fast the leather encasing the younger woman's ankles. Gently, she freed each foot before wrapping them both in the knitted knee-rug drawn from a side pocket of the worn portmanteau. "What happens now, I wonder ...?" Charlotte whispered.

A tap on the cabin door provided the answer – at least, for the time being. Martha rose as it swung inward and Tom Newbold ducked his grizzled head under the lintel, smiling roguishly.

'I clapped the cabin boy in irons for being so tardy, and brought this up here to you myself, missus," he announced, carefully sliding aside rolled charts to set a carafe of fortified wine and platter of fresh bread and thinly sliced beef on the heavy oak table in the centre of the room.

"Your bags are stowed in your quarters, ladies, and young Robbie will be let out of the brig on condition he has a jug of boilin' water waitin' for you when you are ready to wash your hands." Making a courtly bow to Charlotte, he motioned Martha to accompany him to the door.

"Remember missus, if you need help with the lass, I'm your man," he whispered.

"A common fellow!" Martha muttered, just loud enough for Charlotte to hear. For although she had warmed to the sailor and his efforts to help, she was not about to permit such familiarity in the presence of her mistress.

But Charlotte had not noticed the exchange. She was reading, ashen faced, from the scrap of paper held tightly in her hand since Barker had pressed it into her palm while handing her from the carriage at the end of the journey from Hatfield Hall. Wordlessly, she passed the note to Martha.

Beloved, it read, *I have learned of your fate from Barker. His uncle, Tom Newbold, is aboard the vessel in which you sail. He will look after you and send word to me of your safe passage. Fear not, for I will never forsake you. One day I will come to claim you as my wife. Ever your own loving Richard.*

Chapter Three
THE VOYAGE

Martha was at a loss to know whether to be relieved or angered by the communication. On one hand, the note Charlotte had passed to her held a promise of hope she knew could sustain her charge through the trial of separation from all she knew and loved. On the other, holding onto the hope that she might one day be reunited with her young lover, and father of the child she carried within her, would almost certainly prevent Charlotte from ever returning to England and resuming her rightful place in the family that meant so much to her.

Folding the note carefully back into its original creases gave Martha a few sorely needed seconds to formulate a response to the unspoken question in Charlotte's tear-filled eyes. Then, slowly shaking her head, she moved forward to sit beside the young woman slumped on the settle before her.

"Miss Charlotte," she began. "My dear, this is happy news, indeed. For you know that the father of your child has provided you with a guardian for the duration of our voyage, someone who has a connection with Hatfield Hall and can communicate with him on your behalf.

"But you must think forward, beyond the duration of our journey, to the new life that awaits you if you are to prepare a secure future for yourself and your newborn. Although it will distress you almost beyond bearing to hear what I must now tell you, I beg you to listen carefully, for it may help you to find the courage to see this through.

"I may have been a servant all my working life, but I am a woman, older and wiser than you, my lady. I, too, have known great happiness with a young man, when we were much the same age as you and your Richard. I, too, have held a child within me for a few precious months, and known great sadness when I had to relinquish the one, and lose the other even before he lived.

"I know how you suffer. For while I carried my son within me I had to let go of the love I had for his father, and plan the best future I could for our child without him – as you are now required to do.

"In my case, the man I loved was the son and heir of the titled gentleman in whose house I was employed as a parlourmaid. I was young, pretty and eager to accept the love offered to me so artlessly.

"My young gentleman was handsome and honourable – for it was his intention, from the outset, before we even suspected the inevitable had happened, to make me his wife. But we had neither the experience nor the means to overcome the objections of his family.

"Looking back, we were foolish to even think we might be accepted together in his world – and he certainly could not live in mine. To shorten a long and predictable story, we were separated as cruelly as you were from your Richard.

"The very day he informed his father of his intention to marry me, my lover was dispatched to London with a letter in his pocket purchasing a commission in the Guards, and I was sent packing with a small purse of sovereigns in mine, to sustain myself and the child I carried until I was fit enough to work again.

"But it was while I was walking away from the house in which I had known such happiness and such sorrow, that I was offered a chance to redeem myself in the eyes of the world, and give my unborn son a chance to escape the stigma of being born a bastard.

"Walter, a young footman who was employed by the same family came running up the driveway behind me, calling my name and begging me to stop – for I was a fast walker then, as now, and even three months gone I could outpace most men I had ever met. So I slowed my stride and as he drew level with me, Walter passed me a piece of paper with a name and address scrawled hastily upon it.

" 'Take this, Martha,' he said, breathlessly, going on to tell me that it bore the name of his sister, and directions to her cottage in the village. And that she was a midwife, and would look after me until my time came.

" 'You will not be a stranger to her as I have talked of you often', he said. 'She knows that I hold you in the highest esteem, and if you will do me the honour of staying with her until you get your bearings, I know you will find her a true friend'."

Pausing to walk across the Captain's cabin to the chart table, Martha poured a glass of the wine Tom Newbold had thoughtfully set down for them a few moments earlier, and handed it to Charlotte.

"Drink this, my dear, for there is more to my story, and the lesson you learn from it will require inner fortification.

"I had nowhere to go, I was racked with grief, and I accepted the young footman's offer of help, most gratefully,' Martha continued. "Together, we walked on along the winding drive with its tall green poplars sighing above us, until we reached the great iron gates bearing the family crest – a standing bear with sword and shield, and a crouching deer. As they swung open, my self appointed escort made me promise to go straight to his sister's cottage, vowing to meet me there the next day, on his weekly entitlement of one afternoon off.

"I found my way to his sister's tiny, thatch-roofed cottage just as Mistress Mary Wootten was pouring a brew of rich, dark tea from the enamel teapot she kept refilled in the centre of her kitchen table to refresh the steady flow of visitors who crossed the threshold. Some came to seek advice and guidance on their condition, others bringing with them the latest of the infants she had delivered so she could see how well it thrived.

"Mary had never married, dedicating her life, instead, to nursing her ageing parents until they passed away, and then turning her skills to new lives coming into this world. She had, indeed, heard of me …and of my lack of wisdom in selecting what I thought would be the love of my life. Her brother, it seemed, all unknown to me, had appointed himself my unofficial guardian. On his behalf, she made me welcome and bade me stay as long as I wished.

"True to his word, Walter arrived the following day, bringing messages of comfort from our fellow servants, and a basket of clothes from the housekeeper – a kindly woman with a practical streak. She had put together a whole wardrobe for me, for I had nothing but the uniform in which I stood when I was summarily dismissed by my young lover's father.

"Over the ensuing weeks, Walter was a regular visitor, bringing more messages and practical gifts from below stairs at the manor house. Gradually, a friendship was formed, and when I was six months along, Walter asked me to marry him. It was the most touching proposal of marriage a woman in my circumstances could ever hope to receive. He told me he had always admired me but had neither the courage nor the words to acquaint me of his feelings. When word had filtered down below stairs about the young master's feelings for me, he put all thought of speaking of his own hopes from his mind. But when word of my dismissal – and the reason for it – became known, he decided to offer what help he could and leave the rest to fate.

"With evidence of my unfortunate love affair now apparent to all the world, he wondered, without wishing to cause offence in any way, if I would do him the very great honour of becoming his wife, and in so doing, also allow him to become father to my child."

Here, Martha paused and poured a glass of the robust liquid for herself. Touching the glass to her lips she allowed herself respite from the painful task of reliving old memories while the warmth of the wine coursed through her body.

"In the moments following Walter's proposal," she went on, 'I realised the good Lord had blessed me with an opportunity to provide my child with not only a name but a kind and generous father. Young as I was, I knew I had to make a decision that would both break my heart while, at the same time, start to mend it.

34

"And, Miss Charlotte, it did break my heart to put the past behind me. Close the door on it, knowing I could never open it again. But there is truth in the old adage that as one door shuts, another door opens. I accepted Walter's proposal and we were married quietly, just as soon as the banns had been read for the third time, in our local parish church.

"My new life lasted just two weeks. Walter had been allowed a weekend off while the family was in London for the season, and was spending it building a room onto his sister's cottage for us to call our own.

"He was raising a large beam with the help of a stout rope hooked to the roof truss and tied to the harness of a horse that pulled the hay cart for a farmer who lived close by, when the animal stumbled and the rope slackened, releasing the beam as it was positioned above him.

"The weight of it crushed his chest as it fell across him and Walter died in my arms, whispering my name with his final breath. The shock of the accident brought on the birth of my baby three months before my time.

"My son took leave of this world before he was christened, my only consolation being that his kind and loving stepfather would be there ahead of him, waiting to take his hand and lead him into the light.

"Some months later, I received a note, conveyed to me by one of Walter's friends at the manor house. The paper bore the images of a standing bear, brandishing a sword and shield, and a crouching deer. Walter's friend had been instructed to bring it to me by the housekeeper who, in her wisdom, sought to set me free from futile hope. The note was, in fact, an announcement. One of many duplicated by a calligrapher's careful hand, and destined to be sent to friends of the manor house family who lived at a distance from events shared by their immediate circle.

"Arthur, Earl of Almsforth, and the Lady Caroline Almsforth, take great pleasure in announcing the marriage of their son, Charles, to the Lady Davinia Wells. The marriage took place on ....'That was all I read before I crumpled the parchment on which the announcement was written, and threw it into the fireplace where it flared briefly, blackened, and turned to ash.

"I resolved to build a new life for myself from that moment. I buried

35

my pain in the deepest reaches of my heart and vowed to shed no more tears for what might have been. Instead, I would rejoice in the knowledge that I had been loved, albeit briefly, by two decent, honest and worthy men, and had known, for a while, the unutterable joy of impending motherhood.

"I remember standing to face the unhappy bearer of bad news with what I hoped passed for a warm smile, and thanking him for taking the time to deliver the housekeeper's communication.

"Please tell her Mistress Martha Wootten thanks her for this and her many other kindnesses, and that I have apprenticed myself to my husband's sister to learn the noble art of midwifery so that I shall be well able to look after myself from now on," I said, sending him on his way with a precious farthing for his trouble.

"Oh, Martha,' said Charlotte, setting down her glass and reaching for the older woman's hand. 'Oh, Martha, dearest friend, I have been so blinded by my own grief that I have failed to look into the hearts of others around me. How my situation must have pained you. How bravely you have borne the resurgence of your own bittersweet memories while trying to comfort me as I live with mine.

"I shall take courage from your fine example. I, too, will endeavour to shed no more tears for what might have been, but rejoice in the memory of Richard's love, and do the very best I can to ensure a secure future for his son."

The room in which Charlotte and Martha found themselves, later, was one of two staterooms positioned on the aft deck in accommodation set aside for the most privileged paying passengers. Each stateroom measured an exceptional nine feet by nine. Mullioned windows afforded a view of sea and sky in the ship's wake which could be enjoyed from a window-seat furnished with soft cushions, or hidden from the alarming prospect of foul weather by heavy velvet drapes. A small door set in the panelling of the external wall led into an *en suite* privy built out over the sea far below so that effluent could be easily and efficiently sluiced away.

Smaller cabins lined each side of the first class quarters, separated by a saloon housing one long table, a serving board, two settles, scattered chairs and a small grand piano. At the far end, two cabins providing sleeping quarters for the senior ship's officers flanked the doorway to an observation deck set aside for the exclusive use of persons of quality.

The Captain occupied one of the two forward staterooms, fitted out with a surprisingly small, utilitarian wooden bunk, hanging space for his uniforms and a tall, narrow chest of drawers holding his personal possessions. In the other, the table – now cleared of the refreshments he had ordered for Charlotte and Martha – dominated, while racks containing charts, journals, log books and telescopes lined the caulked oak walls.

While Charlotte, as the Captain's niece, had been allocated one of the prized aft-facing staterooms, Martha was to be accommodated in an adjacent cabin, afforded immediate access to her mistress through a curtained doorway, hastily contrived by the ship's carpenters just hours before the Captain's niece and her maidservant arrived on board. In each area, the narrow beds fashioned by Hatfield carpenters had been bolted to the floor for their comfort and safety against inevitable rough weather. Each bed held deep storage drawers built into the framework below.

The stateroom being large enough to allow such consideration, Charlotte's bed was positioned behind the swing of the door leading out into the walkway, allowing privacy in the unlikely event of unexpected access. Her sleeping form could be further shielded from view by muslin drapes which could be drawn to enclose the bed entirely. Martha's simple but adequate bunk was set hard against the back wall of her accommodation, its head and foot touching the walls on either side.

Settling Charlotte on the window seat with her feet elevated and covered with her fox trimmed travelling cloak, Martha worked quickly to unpack the drawers under both beds. To her surprise, the contents of each were of identical quality. Down-filled mattresses, comforters and pillows, damask quilts, light-as-air merino wool blankets and monogrammed linen promised a measure of comfort Charlotte had lived with all her life but Martha had never previously known.

Scaled-down chests of drawers, also fashioned from the Hatfield elms, were held fast to the walls in both the stateroom and cabin by moulded metal cleats. The top of one at the foot of Charlotte's bed had been covered with a slice of fine Italian marble, so that it might also serve as a wash-stand. To that end, Martha placed a shallow silver bowl in the centre of the marble slab, together with a matching water jug. Both jug and bowl could be stowed in a drawer below, fashioned deep enough to hold the filled jug standing upright. A hinged panel just two inches wide, running the width of the chest, allowed for a small mirror to be drawn up, turning the chest of drawers from wash-stand to dressing table. A folding stool stowed in another narrow compartment built into one side of the miniature masterpiece ensured Charlotte could complete her toilette in comparative comfort.

Martha's chest of drawers had been crafted to replicate Charlotte's in terms of size, shape and quality, but as no servant save a housekeeper had the time or inclination to reflect upon her appearance, the panel at the back of her chest held an exquisite, inlaid rosewood tray for carrying refreshments from galley to stateroom, should her mistress prefer to dine in private. There was, however, a hinged side panel which opened to reveal a folding stool, on which Martha could sit to record events and accounts in a journal to be presented to her employer upon her return.

In Charlotte's quarters, curtained hanging space was provided to conceal day and night clothes needed during the voyage, and a storage space below the window seat revealed a collapsed campaign table. Positioned against the window seat, occupants of a state-room could, if they wished, dine, paint, or play cards upon it. Above the table an ornate oil lamp swung alarmingly as the ship rose and fell on the rising tide.

In Martha's cabin, hooks positioned on the wall at each side of the door opening onto the internal walkway provided hanging space for her all-weather cloak and felt hat. The makeshift robe also served as hanging space for garments hand-washed for herself and her mistress in the small pewter bowl atop her chest of drawers. A shelf along the wall on one side of Martha's bed held a James I bible and an eight-inch oil lamp which could be lit to augment the natural light filtering through the porthole.

"Madam," said Martha as she walked back through the curtain separating her space from Charlotte's. "Before we venture out against the chill on deck, which is all noise and bustle while the crew makes final preparations for us to put to sea, might I suggest you take to your bed while I select the garments you will wear for the rest of the day. It is my understanding that on the day of departure one does not dress formally at the Captain's table, but we need time for the creases to drop from your day dress before luncheon."

"No Martha, dear, I have done nothing but sit since first light. I am now thoroughly bored with inactivity, and need to exercise my mind and my body or I will just lie there, thinking.

"Instead, I will help you select and hang the garments I shall wear until we sail into warmer climes. Look, I am on my feet already."

Moving quickly, Charlotte stood beside the ornate travelling trunk standing open to reveal hanging space for gowns and wraps, and drawers for hats, shoes and gloves. 'See, I will select, and you shall hang!'

Martha, at odds to know how to reply to her mistress's bold response, found her mouth forming shapes but issuing no sound. Recovering from her surprise, she shook her head slowly from side to side, and fixed Charlotte with flinty eyes.

"Miss Charlotte, you know as well as I do that it is unseemly for you to act as if you were your own maidservant. I suspect it was just such defiance of convention that gave rise to the circumstances we find ourselves in today.

"I have been charged with your care. It is my understanding that your father, Sir Ian, had high expectations of my ability to encourage you to remember and preserve your status in the time we are together. I am entirely sure he would not approve of your intention to challenge the established order in this manner."

"Tush, Martha! Who is to observe us within this confined space?

Besides, I shall go quite mad if we are to spend the coming months in such close quarters, sleeping, eating and communicating with each other, and all the while endeavouring to maintain such an absurd sense of propriety. You have already proven yourself a caring friend and confidante. If you wish to separate our stations in public, that is your choice. In private, we are companions. I shall have no more discussion on the subject."

Standing before the older women, hands on hips, Charlotte gave Martha flinty stare for flinty stare, then throwing back her head, burst into peals of laughter. Sensing this was most probably the first time her young mistress had found reason to laugh in the last few months, Martha threw up her hands in defeat, whereupon Charlotte made a great show of selecting, extracting and holding garments against her body for Martha's opinion and approval, before handing them to the older woman to hang on the ornate brass hooks, hitherto hidden behind drawn damask drapes.

Within an hour, working together with much head-shaking by Martha and wide smiles from Charlotte, the two women had created an orderly space in which they would spend the coming days, weeks, months together, while the *Chetwynde* sailed across the oceans between England and Australia.

"*Now* will you rest, my lady?" asked Martha drawing aside the curtains to Charlotte's bed, more sure of compliance after such intense activity.

"Indeed, I will, Martha; in truth, I am quite spent, and have no wish to venture on deck when we sail at high tide. My goodbyes are done with. I have shut off my tears and intend to concentrate on the moment I catch my first glimpse of Australia. I am firmly set on recovering my strength, along with my spirit, so that I will be well prepared for the birth of my child. I will rest until we are underway, and then we can take a turn round the saloon where, Ensign Frobisher informed me, we will be introduced to the other first class passengers over a light lunch."

So this is how it is to be, thought Martha, pulling up the quilted coverlet to insulate her charge against the chill air which would soon begin to cool her pulsing blood.

Slipping through the curtain separating her space from the stateroom, Martha sank slowly onto her own bed. From a pocket secreted by the heavy folds of her rough serge skirt, she withdrew Walter's fob watch and, leaning towards the porthole, squinted to read the time in the wintry morning light.

The *Chetwynde* was due to stand off from the dockside at noon, pausing for a final farewell from families and friends before adjusting the rigging to ride out into the open sea on turning tide. The ship's bell would ring at fifteen minutes to the hour, signalling fair warning to passengers who wished to frame the faces of their loved ones for the last time as the crew unfurled the sheets to fill with wind.

It seemed she had barely closed her eyes when Martha was woken by the sound of the ship's bell, accompanied by a great cheer from passengers, the crew on deck and those lined up dockside to farewell them. Drawing on Walter's assurance, given in the dark days before she came to know and love him, that in times of uncertainty she could always draw strength from the prospect of something wonderful waiting for her, just around the corner, Martha allowed herself to acknowledge the thrill of the moment. But before she could speculate on what that something might be, the voice of her mistress, newly woken from the deep sleep into which the young seem to fall so easily, brought her back to the moment.

"*Bon voyage*, Martha! Come, let us link our hands and hold fast to the memories of home and loved ones, together, while we salute the future."

As Martha walked through the curtain to join Charlotte on the window seat, the *Chetwynde* swung round to face the open sea, affording them a picture book view of coast and country which would be engraved on the memory of all aboard who could bear to look. Propped on the narrow ledge below the sill of the aft window, Martha noticed, were images of Charlotte's younger sisters, Beatrice and Melanie, their faces thrown into sharp relief against the retreating coastline, slowly fading into the mist still clinging to trees and hedgerows.

Performing the rituals required to make their first public appearance since boarding the *Chetwynde* took an hour before Martha was satisfied that Charlotte would 'do'. A large jug of scalding water had been left outside Martha's door for Charlotte to freshen her face. Lotions, scents and a light dusting of face powder had been applied with a swansdown puff, lips glossed with the faintest smear of rose oil on the tip of a slim sable brush.

Helping her into a dove grey gown of the softest silk and wool, and lacing her feet into matching antelope ankle boots, Martha at last pronounced her mistress fit to leave the privacy of her stateroom. Pausing to glance swiftly into the mirror above the cleverly contrived chest, Charlotte wrapped a short, fox trimmed wrap around her shoulders, and dropping a light kiss on Martha's weathered cheek, stepped through the stateroom door into the corridor leading to the saloon. There, waiting patiently was Ensign Frobisher, deployed to escort Charlotte from her stateroom to the Captain's table, where first class passengers were gathering in anticipation of the first of many meals to be taken together.

"Ma'am," said Ensign Frobisher, offering Charlotte his arm.

"Ensign Frobisher," she replied, with a radiant smile, causing the bewitched young officer to pause mid-stride and Charlotte to lose hold of his arm, reaching for the hand-rail running along the walls on each side of the walkway for support.

Naughty girl, thought Martha, her lips twitching at the mischief occurring two steps ahead of her; but she saw the flirtatious moment as a healthy sign of recovery on Charlotte's part, and let it pass.

"Miss Hatfield. Ma'am," Frobisher mumbled, the colour rising above his whiskered cheeks as he struggled to recover his composure, reposition his arm and draw level with Charlotte again. "My apologies, ma'am, I am to inform you that the Captain sends his compliments and awaits your arrival in the salon."

The first person to introduce himself to Charlotte was Major Roland

'Rollo' D'Arcy. Standing on the far side of the heavy oak table set to accommodate the twelve first-class passengers, the newly appointed Surgeon General to the new colony, and Captain Hatfield, D'Arcy's eyes brightened with interest as Frobisher handed her to her seat.

The *Chetwynde*, a relatively small and compact six-hundred ton barque, was an unusual emigrant ship for its time. Built to exacting specifications to accommodate the owner of a small but successful shipping line when he decided to transfer his family, along with the headquarters of the Weymouth Shipping Line, from Plymouth to Port Melbourne in the heady days of the land boom along the south east coast of Australia, it was superior in every aspect to most of the vessels then transporting settlers from England to its most distant colony.

Edward Allen Armstrong had insisted upon a high degree of comfort and exclusivity for his family and wished to fit out his vessel accordingly. He had been to America to inspect the stylish, made-to-order clipper ships owned by wealthy northern east-coasters there, many of whom made regular business trips across the Atlantic taking their families and friends along for the ride. The stylish facilities provided for first class and privileged paying passengers impressed the class conscious Englishman. Made massively rich by the recent increase in traffic between England and Australia as word spread of opportunities presenting to opportunistic gentlemen, artisans and farmers in the 'new America', he sought to make his own mark with an unparalleled show of style and substance when he sailed through Port Phillip heads.

Selecting the finest English oak, he commissioned his new vessel to be built with luxurious accommodation with opulent fittings for his family and friends. Two unusually large staterooms aft of the other cabins would be occupied, separately, by Edward Armstrong and his wife, Ethel, who shared nothing in common except their children – all six of whom were to be accommodated two-by-two, along with their nannies, in the three smaller cabins on their mother's side of the ship. The three cabins along Edward's side of the ship were fitted with single bunks and reserved for Edward's unmarried brother and business partner, George, his childless, widowed sister-in-law, Elaine, and his general business factotum, Willoughby Isaacs.

There was also impressive accommodation for the fare-paying passengers who would underwrite the cost of the voyage. Family cabins, in which the upper of four, two-tiered bunks could be folded up to provide comfortable sitting space during the day, ran along either side of the ship on the lower deck. Single men and women were to be accommodated in smaller, two-bunk cabins, the sexes segregated from each other at either end of the family area.

Amidships, a central saloon afforded space to meet, eat, socialise, worship or attend one of a number of educational lectures devised to familiarise them with the ship's protocols and the opportunities awaiting them on arrival at their destination. A small, wedge-shaped room forward of the single women's cabins on the port side of the ship, reached by a narrow central corridor and entered only through a stout locked door, served as the ship's hospital. Its mirror image on the starboard side accommodated two small stool-rooms.

Even the few steerage passengers they were obliged to carry, availing themselves of free passage offered by Government in response to the growing demand for domestic workers, farm labourers, builders and artisans of all kinds to consolidate settlement in the colony, would be accommodated in quarters vastly superior to those endured by their counterparts on most other ships. Tiered bunks were fitted with mattresses filled with fresh sweet-smelling straw, burnt and replaced at the end of each run, fresh air shafts were built into the crawl space between the upper bunks and the bulkhead above, and four stool rooms, two at each end of the steerage deck, reduced the risk of disease from spilled slop buckets. Food came from the same galley that served the crew and paying passengers by way of a box-like device, raised and lowered by rope pulleys, from which meals were doled out by a crew member overseen by one of the officers to ensure equitable distribution. An innovative and astute businessman, Edward Armstrong read everything he could find about improvements in the shipping industry – including reports in The Times of the endeavours of activist, Mrs Caroline Chisholm, to engage the British Government's attention to the need for improved conditions for assisted passengers, in particular, those travelling aboard British ships on the lucrative Australia run. He learned of her outrage at the casual attitude to the spread of disease aboard almost all emigrant ships. Having observed, first hand, the appalling condition of the many men, women and children who had barely survived long months at sea on disease-ridden ships, Mrs Chisholm told of passengers cooped below decks, hatches battened down for days, depriving them of daylight and fresh air, forced to eat rotten food. She described how illness spread through mattresses, saturated by the natural consequences of sea-sickness, consumption and dysentery, being dried out and re-used on voyage after voyage; of lower decks described as swirling cesspools as chamber pots and buckets were left rolling around the floor in rough weather. And she told of whole families dying at sea for lack of medical checks prior to boarding and adequate medical care once their vessel was underway.

Seizing the opportunity to take the high moral ground – and engage the interest of potential passengers – Edward Armstrong announced that from the time Weymouth Shipping Line opened its doors in the new Port Melbourne headquarters, every man, woman and child who boarded one of his ships could expect a much higher standard of care and accommodation than any of its competitors. To that end, he promised, in a letter penned to The Times, the company's flag ship, the *Chetwynde*, would stand open for inspection on arrival in Port Melbourne at the completion of its maiden voyage, by not only Port authorities, but Mrs Chisholm, herself.

Given the challenge of transporting his business, his family and their entire estate to a new and largely unfamiliar environment, Edward addressed the need to provide adequate cargo space by planning to have the *Chetwynde*'s hold accommodate, in addition to the possessions and personal effects of the proposed one hundred and twenty passengers and crew, sixty-eight boxes of Mrs Armstrong's clothing and personal effects and forty-two boxes of linen, eighteen chests of china, silver and flatware sufficient to entertain small parties of important expatriates at ports along the way. There were also two other important items – the company's massive steel safe (never far out of Edward Armstrong's reach), and an impressive, claw-foot, cast-iron bath, complete with decoupage screens, which could be erected to allow members of the family to bathe as often as water could be spared between provisioning ports.

In the event, a month before their scheduled departure, Edward's youngest son, Charles, aged six, contracted smallpox from an itinerant worker while the family was vacationing at their country retreat in the flatlands. The disease spread rapidly, wiping out Charles' father and siblings leaving Edward's only brother, George, to take over the running of their business and responsibility for Edward's widow, Elaine. George, however, had never really warmed to the idea of relocating abroad but, as had been the case since they were children, he had acceded to his elder brother's wishes rather than have to deal with the consequences of opposition. A farmer at heart, he loved the calm, orderly seasonal rhythm of life in England – particularly from the perspective of living on the land in rural East Anglia. He also loved his sister-in-law, Elaine, who shared his preference for a quiet and predictable country life.

Not known for taking great leaps of faith, George decided to stay with the life he knew, and within weeks of his brother's death, as sole heir, had divested himself of the Weymouth Shipping Line and the Westminster town house, married Elaine and settled into the family mansion to breed cattle, hunt foxes and raise, in very quick succession, five robust, country-loving children.

The *Chetwynde*'s life under the Weymouth Shipping Line's new owner, William J Holloway, of Holloway Shipping, had begun two years before

Charlotte and Martha found themselves on board, as the flagship of the fleet at the upper end of the Atlantic run. But it soon found itself outclassed and outrun by the new American clippers boosted by auxiliary steam engines, whereupon it was reassigned to its originally intended route transporting fare-paying passengers from England to Australia, and filling up on the highly lucrative home run with wealthy expatriates returning from other British colonies including Hong Kong, India and Africa, and grand tour ports in Italy, Spain and the south of France.

Holloway had selected Charlotte's uncle, Captain Hugh Hatfield, as master of the *Chetwynde* from among several ranking captains commanding other impressive vessels in his newly acquired fleet. His outstanding record of seamanship and the high esteem in which he was held by his cohorts in the close-knit seafaring community struck a chord with the younger man, who recognised in Hugh qualities that reminded him of his own, late, seafaring father. No formal contract was ever drawn up between them. A simple handshake served to seal the agreement and proved a portent for enduring friendship.

The *Chetwynde* became Hugh Hatfield's permanent home, replacing the cottage he had shared with his beloved wife and daughter – now a crumbling ruin on the side of the hill overlooking a small fishing village a few miles along the coast from the Port of Plymouth, since fire had swept up the valley and taken them from him. Now, he eagerly anticipated sharing his new home with family, if only for a few precious weeks.

Charlotte occupied a private and very special space in Hugh's heart, for both his own wife, Katherine, and his brother's wife, Margaret, had given birth to daughters in the same month of the same year. His darling Rose, had she lived, would have been the same age as Charlotte. When he was informed by his brother, Sir Ian, of Charlotte's predicament, Hugh's heart went out to her. While accepting the necessity of the only recourse thought possible in their rigid, class-conscious society, having known true love, himself, he was devastated by the prospect of encouraging his niece to enter into an arranged and, predictably, loveless marriage.

The younger of the two brothers, Hugh had chosen the sea over the army or the church – the only options available to men who lacked independent means when an elder brother inherited entailed estates. He had established his own independence by rising through the ranks to command some of the finest ships in the British merchant fleet. Finding his love for the woman he adored returned and rewarded with an enchantingly beautiful daughter filled his cup to overflowing. His long weeks at sea were never lonely, for he had only to close his eyes and picture Katherine, hand in hand with Rose, running out of the cottage to greet him on his return.

Though the tragedy that curled the edges of that image had occurred almost twelve years ago, on still nights, in oceans around the world, he would map the milestones they might have passed in Rose's life on her way to womanhood. Now, standing before him, Charlotte, Rose's contemporary, provided him with another chance to be a loving father – if only *in loco parentis*.

Forswearing protocol, Hugh drew Charlotte into his arms and kissed her face so tenderly that Martha expected the tears to start flowing again. Instead, Charlotte returned her uncle's embrace, smiling delightedly. She was still clinging happily to his arm as he delivered a short speech of welcome to the rest of the passengers gathering round the table, proudly informing them of his great joy at being able to introduce them to his brother's eldest daughter and his own favourite niece.

Relinquishing her uncle's arm only to take her place immediately to his left, Charlotte viewed the tall figure, as he stood behind his chair at the head of the table, with gratitude as well as affection, knowing she could count on his understanding as well as his wise counsel. When all the ladies were seated and the gentlemen had taken their places, Hugh explained that formalities were relaxed on the first night at sea, and invited his guests to introduce themselves to their fellow diners. Charlotte, sensing Martha's apprehension, stood to be the first to invite attention.

"As my uncle has already informed you, I am his niece, Charlotte Hatfield,' she said. Then, turning to smile at Martha, "And this is my dear friend and companion, Mistress Martha Wootten."

The gentleman seated next to Martha rose to his feet and introduced himself as the Reverend Giles Stockwell, Church of England priest. *By the look of him newly ordained, newly wed, and undoubtedly a second son,* thought Martha, smiling sympathetically, as the young man blushed and stumbled over his introduction of, "my wife, Mrs Stockwell," seated to his left.

Next, came banker, Winston Leaumont and Mrs Leaumont, seated to the right of the Surgeon General, Dr Francis Trowbridge, who had taken his place at the far end of the table.

On Dr Trowbridge's left, at the extreme diagonal of Charlotte, Major Roland D'Arcy (please call me 'Rollo') rose to identify himself. The Surgeon General's beautiful but pale and fragile daughter, Helen Trowbridge, occupied the seat next to D'Arcy and, following Charlotte's lead, introduced her dear friend and companion (in fact, nurse), Madame Thérèse Bardot.

Mrs Trowbridge, the Surgeon General's wife, had thoughtfully positioned herself next to her daughter's nurse and opposite Reverend Stockwell, both of whom, she felt, might need a little help keeping the conversation going in the middle of the long table. A rather portly and pretentious middle-aged gentleman who introduced himself as Master of Music, Orwell Blake, was seated on her left. Next to him, filling the last chair to Captain Hatfield's right, sat the internationally renowned tenor, Signor Orlando Minelli, who informed the assembled company that on arrival in the colony, accompanied by Master Blake, he was to perform in front of the new Port Melbourne Music Appreciation Society in the vaulted hall at Customs House.

The introductions over, Captain Hatfield invited Reverend Stockwell to say grace, and the meal commenced. *If this is a taste of what is to come then we shall not waste away for want of sustenance,* thought Martha, as pheasant followed fish, and a succulent sirloin of beef followed the pheasant, with fine wines to complement each course. Custards and poached pears, trifle and fresh cream were then spooned, carefully, into exquisite crystal dishes, and finished off with sweet dessert cordials. Explaining that lack of available space prevented the gentlemen retiring, the Captain, with permission from the ladies, passed the port around the table while a fragrant assortment of steaming tisanes was offered to cleanse their delicate palates.

While the guests were savouring the port and tisanes, card tables were set up for those who wished to remain in the saloon and test their skills – some against their better judgement – as the free flowing wine diminished caution and loosened pockets. D'Arcy, in particular, seemed keen to throw down a challenge to banker Leaumont and the Surgeon General, breaking open the first of two packets of playing cards placed ready on the surfaces of each of the exquisite walnut tables, their tops opened up to reveal their green baize lining.

Charlotte, seated on one of two velvet *chaise longues* on the opposite side of the room, soon found herself in conversation with the charming Helen Trowbridge, while Martha and Miss Trowbridge's nurse-companion, Thérèse – women of similar age and disposition – engaged in gentle discourse around the treatment of *mal de mer* and other debilitating assaults upon the digestive system likely to be experienced at sea.

The Stockwells retired to their cabin, explaining somewhat hastily that the Reverend needed to prepare his sermon for the service on the foredeck the following morning. Mrs Trowbridge and Mrs Leaumont linked arms companionably to take a turn around the foredeck, while Master of Music, Orwell Blake, tested the tone of the Bechstein by playing a selection of chords sympathetic to Signor Minelli's robust delivery of a suite of voice-warming scales pursuant to forthcoming performances . . .

The pattern established and friendships formed on the first day under sail, Charlotte and Martha soon settled into a regular routine of rising, dressing, reading, eating and – wind and weather permitting – taking turns around the deck with their sailing companions. Besides the ever changing sea and sky-scapes, the most amusing distraction for passengers of all classes was the shed-like structure lashed to the foredeck, open on all sides in fair weather, and battened down when wind and water were on the rise. Sectioned off by straw bales it housed, as well as Charlotte's hunter, two black and white Hereford cows with calves at foot, a fat sow with eight squealing, suckling piglets, two goats, twelve cages of rabbits and a coop of chickens, their purpose on board to supply passengers with both milk and meat – as well as entertainment. The cows would likely see Australia, their thick, creamy milk rationed according to need among infants, children and expectant mothers. The chickens would last as long as they kept on laying, and the calves, pigs, goats and rabbits provided a living pantry, supplementing the sides of salted beef hanging in the hold beside crates of potatoes, turnips, onions, cauliflowers and essential oranges.

Next on the list of things to see and wonder at were the life boats, strung high off the deck so they could be swung out and lowered unobstructed into the sea in the event, God forbid, the *Chetwynde* should be at risk of sinking. To allay fears, and plan ahead in order to minimise loss of life if such an event should threaten, Captain Hatfield required passengers and crew to present themselves for evacuation drill three times in the first week of the journey, and weekly thereafter until they reached their destination.

Rollo D'Arcy, the only single, and therefore eligible, gentleman among the first class passengers – Signor Minelli and Orwell Blake, who seemed quite absorbed in each other, notwithstanding – dutifully divided his attentions between the only eligible single women, Charlotte and Helen. Each morning, on rising from the breakfast table, he would linger to engage them in conversation about their plans for the rest of the day, presenting options which, although absurd considering they were at sea, amused and entertained them.

Precisely at noon, cutting a dashing figure in white drill breeches and gleaming boots, white silk stock and dove grey tail coat, he would present in the saloon to escort either, or both, of the young women according to their inclination and availability, on a stroll around the deck to view the animals, marvel at the 'flying' long boats, or search for sea creatures through the long glass he had won from the banker, at cards late one night.

Helen, who tired easily, spent long periods resting on her bed, reading in companionable silence under the watchful eye of Thérèse, while the older woman recorded her patient's condition in a pocket-sized journal, examined daily by her employer, Dr Trowbridge. Helen's 'delicate' condition was revealed to Martha by Thérèse one morning while the two women walked at a discreet distance behind their charges, both chattering happily as they negotiated ropes and winches, one on each of D'Arcy's elegantly tailored arms. Dr Trowbridge, Thérèse confided, had accepted a two-year posting as Surgeon General to the new colony in the hope that year-round sun and gentle sea breezes flowing in off Port Phillip Bay would have a remedial effect on his daughter's 'weak chest' – which none of the family could yet bring themselves to think of as tuberculosis or even consumption as the condition was more commonly known.

It was while Martha walked alone behind D'Arcy and Charlotte, one morning when Helen was too breathless to rise from her bed, that Tom Newbold fell into step beside her.

"Begging your pardon, Mistress, but I must speak to you," he murmured touching an index finger to his forehead. "I have been given an account of events back home which might well be expected to have a direct bearing on Miss Charlotte's future. Sad news, indeed, mistress, and I would not be in your shoes when you tell her what you must, knowing that it will surely break her heart."

Alarmed, Martha slowed her pace so that Newbold's words could not be overheard by Charlotte, who was laughing delightedly as D'Arcy drew her attention to a pod of dolphins leaping in and out of the water as they sped along beside the ship.

"Continue, please," she whispered, anxiously.

"Well, mistress, as you know, Miss Charlotte's husband as was – young master Richard – grew up with my nephew, Luke Barker, footman at

52

Hatfield Hall, who asked me to look out for your mistress and your kind self while you were at sea. I was to be of use to you both in any way I could, which is why I am now obliged to recount a story told to me by one of the passengers travelling on the lower deck.

"It was late; I had finished my watch and wandered down between decks to listen to a fiddler playing for the amusement of the other passengers. The man standing beside me had recognised my west-country way of speaking as I called out to encourage the fiddler. Recognising it as his own he thought to strike up a conversation, asking me where I came from and who I knew there, in the hope we might have some common connections. I obliged him by naming my village and some of my friends and acquaintances, my friendly passenger nodding and smiling until I came to coachbuilder Arthur Trevorrow, whereupon he stopped me abruptly, his voice charged with concern.

"'I believe I might have met his son,' he told me, explaining that he had been a clerk of the court of Assizes at Bristol, and going on to say the name had stuck in his mind because it had come up in the lists relating to the unusual crime of abduction, brought against one Richard Trevorrow, apprentice coachbuilder from the Hatfield estate.

"All ears then, for the rest of the story, I bade my fellow west-countryman stretch his memory for the outcome of the trial and its consequences for young Richard. He then revealed the trial never took place; struck out when the defendant died from the typhus scourging the cells where prisoners were held until a circuit court judge arrived to hear the plaintiff and question the witnesses.

"Each of the prisoners held in the cells below the old court house died from the disease in rapid succession, their bodies carted away to be burned and the court house fired to stop the spread of the disease, thought to be carried into the area by a sailor who had jumped ship and stolen a horse to put a wider distance between him and his pursuers." Here Tom turned away to dash a gnarled hand across his eyes and gaze intently out to sea.

"You are a brave soul indeed, Tom Newbold, to bring this awful

53

story to my attention," Martha said, laying a hand upon Newbold's arm. "Although I fear this is the worst news Miss Charlotte could hear in her condition, she must be told, God grant me courage."

In the moment before he slipped away to return to his duties, Martha felt Newbold's large, capable hand cover hers, sending a mute message of friendship and support. The gesture left Martha, long used to dealing with issues of life and death alone, both surprised and grateful.

Brought lower by the news of Richard's death than Martha had ever thought to see her, Charlotte took to her bed, refusing to leave it even to eat until, alarmed by his niece's continuing seclusion, Captain Hatfield sent the Surgeon General to her stateroom, to report on her health.

Arriving unannounced, armed only with the limited information Hugh had seen fit to share with him – a story, concocted in concert with Martha, to explain Charlotte's absence from meals and common areas, that she was in deep mourning for a distant but much loved relative – Dr Trowbridge came across the young woman still in her bed, dressed only in a muslin wrap. Asking leave to examine her, if only to be able to reassure her uncle that she was not falling into a life-threatening decline, he bade Charlotte test her strength by rising to stand beside the bed, eyes closed and arms outstretched for balance. Silhouetted thus, against the sunlight beaming through the wide aft windows, it took the wise doctor no time at all to note the contrast between the young woman's swollen breasts and abdomen and the delicate structure of the rest of her body.

Glancing at Martha for confirmation as she helped Charlotte climb back onto her bed, the wise and kindly doctor looked thoughtfully into Charlotte's eyes before delivering his opinion and advice. Gently but firmly, he told Charlotte that she must end her seclusion and build the strength required to survive confinement and nurture a newborn – expected, by his reckoning, in two to three months. He then prescribed good food, consumed at regular intervals in the company of others, and gentle exercise – preferably out on deck where she could benefit further from fresh air and sunlight.

As soon as Dr Trowbridge had withdrawn from the stateroom, Martha selected a lightweight gown and low-heeled pumps from the hanging wardrobe and white silk under garments from the chest of drawers, laying them across the window seat, before pouring cooled water into the silver bowl on the chest's marble slab. She dampened two damask face cloths, folding one and placing it over Charlotte's eyes to reduce the redness and swelling occasioned by too many unchecked tears. She took up the other to cool Charlotte's wrists and hands. Allowing no protest, she then eased the younger woman to her feet and into the clothes she had selected, to prepare her for ending her isolation at lunch.

Charlotte's first step towards recovery from the devastating news of her lover's death, which put an end to the fantasy she harboured that one day she might be reunited with Richard – with or without Sir Ian's blessing – was to acknowledge that he was now lost to her forever. The next was to commit to the survival of the enduring legacy of their love, the child she could feel moving within her.

And so it was that Charlotte appeared in the saloon, pale as the ivory gown Martha had selected for her earlier that morning, a cashmere shawl, so fine it could be drawn through a woman's wedding ring, tied loose and low to camouflage her condition.

Accepting the murmured expressions of condolence offered by the other diners with a resolute smile, she forced herself to swallow some of the food and wine the Captain had drawn from his own cellar to celebrate her recovery.

As soon as the meal ended, Martha, conscious of Charlotte's pallor, suggested a spell on the observation deck. Reserved for first class passengers this elevated, sheltered space behind the bridge held folding chairs placed to catch the afternoon sun. To Charlotte's immense relief, Helen and Thérèse were the only other occupants. In the moment Martha had taken to arrange a pillow behind Charlotte's back, Helen had reached for the slim volume of poetry lying in her lap, and the two fragile young women were soon lost in gentle discourse around the respective merits of Yeats and Browning.

While they were thus engaged, Martha and Thérèse, who had continued to meet, if only fleetingly, since Charlotte had taken to her room, cast practiced eyes over each other's charges. The changes they noted might not have been obvious to others, but to them it was heartbreakingly clear that Helen's breathing was even more laboured and that Charlotte's smile had lost its spontaneity.

As the spread of British colonisation increased the distance women travelled to join their menfolk in postings overseas, it had become the custom for English women of style to adopt a more relaxed mode of dress in tropical climes, especially on increasingly frequent voyages to and from colonies established in Africa, India and Hong Kong. Fabrics were lighter and corsets were laced less severely. Through varying climes, cashmere and muslin shawls fell softly across shoulders and breasts to protect them from the sun, and straw brimmed bonnets replaced felt, silk and feathers to ensure complexions remained interestingly pale. The custom and the climate as the *Chetwynde* sailed across the Indian Ocean allowed Charlotte to conceal her pregnancy as it continued to swell her slight form. If the other women gathering in the saloon at mealtimes, or to listen to the mellifluous voice of Signor Minelli as he rehearsed for his forthcoming concert, had their suspicions, in deference to her relationship with the Captain, they set them aside.

Major D'Arcy, however, had long been intrigued by the overly protective attitude of both Charlotte's maidservant and her uncle to their enchanting charge. While he regarded any woman of marriageable age a potential asset, and Charlotte both beautiful and beguiling from the outset, he thought it prudent to proceed with caution when it came to the challenge of attempting to secure the affections of the Captain's niece.

Like many of his establishment contemporaries, D'Arcy's predilection for games of chance – with both cards and women – had a significant influence on his social and financial security. And he knew that a 'good' marriage was considered a trump card with the power to purchase both.

Good breeding, good looks, fine clothes and an excellent education, combined with natural charm, had set him up for success with women at an early age. At twenty-five he had married well and seemed secure for life. But the generous allowance paid by his young wife's father to support the couple while D'Arcy waited to inherit his father's considerable estate was abruptly withdrawn when the chase he was driving at breakneck speed overturned, killing the new Mrs D'Arcy and leaving her husband with serious debts.

Since then, he had sought to cover his losses by investing further in games of chance and heart. He had played to win on the horses, and for a place in the marriage stakes, and lost heavily on both counts. The horses he fancied turned out to be slow, and, on hearing the news that his father had disinherited him after covering his debts for the third time, the father of the eighteen-year-old heiress to whom D'Arcy was by then engaged, withdrew his consent for the impending nuptials.

With his debtors at his heels, D'Arcy took the only option left to him. Presenting a letter of credit, signed by his father to purchase a commission in the highly regarded Royal Dragoons, he avoided persecution by volunteering to take up a temporary posting on the other side of the world. Further, his voluntary exile would position him well either on arrival in the new colony, or upon his return, for marriage with a wealthy young woman who knew nothing of his duplicitous past.

To his surprise, just such an opportunity had presented itself at the very beginning of the journey. There was little doubt that a baronet's daughter, travelling with all the trappings of a woman of substance – including the fine hunter he had seen her fondle affectionately on the foredeck – was an 'appropriate' marriage prospect. But he knew, instinctively, that if he were to capture the heart, mind and money of Miss Charlotte Hatfield, something more would have to be offered than good breeding, good looks, fine clothes and an excellent education. Somehow, he would have to find a way of making himself indispensable to her. D'Arcy had begun to build the connection with Charlotte almost as soon as they left Plymouth, hovering attentively when she took her seat at meal times and thinking up new games to amuse her on the long hours in between; making sure he was available to escort her when the first class passengers toured ports they visited when the *Chetwynde* pulled in for fresh food and water. And, cleverly, he congratulated himself, also wooing the maidservant as well as the mistress in his endeavour to earn acceptance and trust. Should he fail, however, he could subtly turn his attention to Charlotte's friend, Miss Trowbridge, for the companionable young women were frequently to be found together and she was, by reason of the close proximity, also a recipient of D'Arcy's elegant attention.

Indeed, the prospect of courting the Surgeon General's daughter had seemed less of a challenge than pursuing the Captain's niece, on first consideration. But although equally appealing in appearance and charm, Miss Trowbridge had no titled connection and was clearly delicate, and he simply could not risk losing another wife – and sorely needed income.

There was no doubt in D'Arcy's mind that Charlotte had warmed to him as an agreeable friend as the weeks went by. It was only when she emerged from her stateroom following her period of deep mourning that he recognised her vulnerability, and how it presented the opening he had been looking for.

Coming upon her seated alone on the observation deck while Martha had returned to their quarters to fetch her journal, D'Arcy begged permission to join her, casually drawing a slim volume of sonnets from his jacket pocket as he lowered himself into the wicker chair beside her. Poetry being her passion, Charlotte was drawn to inquire about its contents, whereupon D'Arcy urged her to accept the beautiful hand tooled, leather bound book as a gift. Well practised in the art of gentle persuasion, he overcame her blushing protestations with the assurance, eyes downcast, that nothing could bring him greater pleasure than knowing she would share verses held as dear to his own heart, as he believed they might be to hers. When he raised his eyes to meet Charlotte's he saw his implied intimacy had not caused offence. In fact, her smile signalled a hope it had been most favourably received.

Subtly changing his literary focus from love to loss over following 'chance' meetings in the same secluded setting, D'Arcy, acting on instinct, told Charlotte about his own experience of love, most cruelly lost. Haltingly, tears clouding his pale grey eyes, he described the accidental death of his young wife, insisting no-one could appreciate the depths of despair in which it had left him unless they had experienced such a loss themselves.

"My dear Major D'Arcy," Charlotte whispered, through her own tears, raising her hand to cover his. "Dear friend, how brave you are, and how solicitous of another whom you have been told is suffering the loss of a mere distant relative.

"But I feel I must reveal the depth of my own despair if I am to comfort you in yours.

"My dear uncle, out of concern for my feelings and honouring his promise to my father that he would help to shield me from further shame and censure, told our fellow passengers but half my story when I took to my stateroom to grieve in private. The loved relative I mourned was, in fact, my own beloved ..."

Scarcely daring to breathe, hiding his triumph behind a mask of concern, D'Arcy listened intently as Charlotte revealed the rest of her story, culminating in her blushing confession that it was further complicated by her soon-to-become-apparent condition.

Raising the hand Charlotte had placed over his own to his lips D'Arcy gently kissed it, noting that rather than being surprised by his action, she accepted the gesture as an involuntary act of compassion.

From that moment, D'Arcy was never far from Charlotte's side. Martha, ever watchful of Charlotte's health and disposition, attributed the improvement in both to D'Arcy's constant and ever-more solicitous attention.

During one of her regular meetings with Captain Hatfield to report on Charlotte's recovery, Martha remarked on the effect D'Arcy's companionship seemed to be having on his niece, and was agreeably surprised to learn that he, too, had observed the growing friendship and the resulting change in Charlotte's health and demeanour with interest. In fact, the Captain mused, the widowed major might well be considered a most fortuitous possibility in the matter of the redemptive marriage Charlotte's father had planned for her.

"Indeed, the young gentleman in question approached me two days ago, seeking my permission to make his feelings known to Charlotte when he judged the moment to be appropriate," he revealed.

"He then told me of his own heartbreak over the death of his young wife and their unborn son: a tragedy from which he thought never to recover. However, upon meeting Charlotte, he believed time and circumstances had conspired to put love in his path once more.

"Furthermore, having heard from her own lips of the predicament in which she found herself, he wished – if he were to find his feelings returned – to provide Charlotte and her unborn child with the love and protection he had expected to invest in his own two lost loved ones."

Pausing, Captain Hatfield leaned back in his chair and looked intently into the eyes of the older women on the other side of the chart table.

"Although we have known him for only a short period of time, I have observed young D'Arcy's bearing, and, given his prospects as a commissioned officer in the Royal Dragoons, his family connections, and his concern for our dear girl, I believe he could well be considered a serious suitor," he continued.

"If Charlotte accepts his proposal, her father should be more than willing to welcome home, in due course, the wife of the eldest son of General Sir Wellington D'Arcy, whose holdings include an estate in Scotland and grand houses in London and Bath.

"All things considered, Mistress Wootten, he could be the perfect choice to restore Charlotte to her rightful place in society, and her position as the cherished daughter of an established county family. But in light of recent news concerning her first love, we must ask ourselves if she is ready to consider such an opportunity."

"Indeed, Captain Hatfield, I do believe she might be, now that her condition can no longer be hidden, and she has lost all hope of ever being reunited with her first love. She appears to have accepted her situation as that of a grieving widow who must plan for the future of her child. I believe that has opened her mind, if not her heart, to the prospect of marriage in the relatively near future, and there can be little doubt that she finds the major's attentions agreeably sympathetic."

"Well then, Mistress, let us observe things for a few days longer to see how our dear girl receives D'Arcy's approach to put their friendship on a more formal footing."

So saying, Captain Hatfield rose from his chair to hold open the door for the woman he confidently believed cared for the future happiness of his niece as much as he did.

Late the following evening, with first-class passengers gathered on the observation deck to admire a full moon as it rose to flood the sea around them with silver light, a scuffle broke out on the deck below.

A child's voice, raised in fear, followed by raucous laughter, caused the small group on the observation deck to move forward as one to witness events unfolding below them. But D'Arcy knew, instantly, the meaning of the moment, and recognised it as presenting the perfect opportunity to prove himself indispensable to Charlotte.

Vaulting the guard rail to land on the deck below, he pulled a swarthy farm hand away from a terrified girl backed up against the side of the grain shed in the shadowed space beneath an overhanging lifeboat. Holding the child protectively close with one arm, he laid her assailant low with the other. It was all over in a moment, with crew members hauling the man off to face the rest of the voyage in irons.

Lifting the girl, scarce more than a child, into his arms, D'Arcy carried her up onto the observation deck and through to the first class saloon where he placed her gently on one of the velvet settles.

Hurrying to his side, Charlotte reached for the girl's hand.

"What is your name, child? Where are your parents? We must bring them to you, immediately."

"Connie, ma'am. Connie McCormack. Me ma and pa have gone to God. I'm by meself." The girl replied.

Shocked that someone so young should be travelling such a distance alone, Charlotte insisted the girl be taken immediately to her own stateroom where she might be examined by Dr Trowbridge away from prying eyes, and her situation for the rest of the voyage considered. As D'Arcy reached down to gather up the girl again, he glanced behind him to see Charlotte gazing upon him with such pride and affection that he knew, in that instant, his future was assured.

Two days later, Captain Hatfield, who had also observed the major's dashing rescue of the Irish orphan girl, gave his unqualified consent to D'Arcy's petition to approach Charlotte with a proposal of marriage.

Chapter Four
A FORTUITOUS CHOICE

The ceremony took place in the saloon the following morning. Ensign Frobisher stood up, bravely – considering his own feelings for Charlotte – beside the groom who appeared in full dress uniform. Orwell Blake sobbed silently as he played the bride in with a faultless rendition of Mendelssohn's Wedding March. Connie McCormack, one of a complement of twenty three Irish orphans destined to populate the new colony in service to settler families, and now temporarily assigned to Charlotte following her rescue by the brave major, presented as bridesmaid. Charlotte, her ice-blue gown enhanced by a head-dress fashioned by Martha and Thérèse working long into the night turning the skirt of a silk petticoat into a wreath of artificial orange blossom, presented as a happy, if not radiant, bride.

The oaths were taken in front of Captain Hatfield who performed the ceremony according to the rules relating to births, deaths and marriages at sea, with the Reverend Stockwell offering a final blessing. The breakfast which followed served to fittingly celebrate the occasion, ending in spontaneous applause when D'Arcy drew his ceremonial sword to cut the wedding cake, pausing dramatically before plunging the blade into the elegant confection to kiss the lace-gloved hand of his blushing bride.

However, D'Arcy had one more card to play which stilled any last minute concerns Martha might have about the character of the man they had known for such a short time. Accompanying his new wife to her stateroom, he put his integrity beyond question when he brushed her lips with his and retired to his own quarters, vowing, with a reluctant smile, to do so every night for the rest of the voyage in consideration of her delicate condition.

The run across open water from Hong Kong, their last port of call en route to Melbourne, was expected to take less than two weeks. Instead, the *Chetwynde* was blown off course by strong winds off the Cape, and then becalmed, approaching the tiny British colony just as the clouds were gathering to herald the start of the typhoon season.

The weather turned in the dark of night just south of Lantau, causing the barque to run for cover on the leeward side of the island. But rather than finding a safe haven, it was blown back out to sea by gale force winds whipping around the wall of the storm to encounter the full fury of a force five typhoon, screaming in from the south east. Rolling and pitching, the *Chetwynde* found herself poised on the crest of a wave twice as high as its mizzen one minute, only to fall down the wall to crash into the broiling black water below, the next.

While the crew worked frantically topside to pull in the sheets and secure the rigging, below decks the passengers in more crowded accommodation clung to their bunks, sheltering their children as best they could from flying objects and the swirling mix of vomit, effluent and food, and water pouring in through shutters ripped from the portholes.

First-class passengers found the aft deck bore the brunt of the weather. High above the water it was exposed to the elements as well as the best views. The sound of screaming winds assaulting shutters securing windows and portholes was punctuated by the noise of furniture and flying objects crashing into fixtures and fittings like cannon balls and musket shot.

In Charlotte's stateroom, Connie McCormack was thrown from her makeshift bed on the window seat, rolling helplessly with the rise and fall of the ship. Martha, clinging to ropes looped hastily through brass rings on each wall as she tried to reach the terrified child, watched in horror as Charlotte rose from her bed with the same intention.

"No, mistress, No!" Martha screamed as Charlotte pitched forward and fell, her head glancing off the corner of the marble slab on top of the chest of drawers. At the precise moment Charlotte fell unconscious to the floor, the stateroom door burst open to reveal D'Arcy. Dropping to his hands and knees he crawled across the pitching floor to reach his wife, now thrown hard up against the opposite wall.

Martha reached her at the same time, and together, cushioning her with their own bodies, they waited out the final moments of the storm until it moved on over them, conserving the full force of its fury for the crown colony, due north. As the seas subsided, Connie crawled out of the cupboard under the window seat in which she had frantically sought refuge. D'Arcy, now on his feet, bent down to pick up Charlotte and lay her carefully back onto her bed. As soon as he had set her down, Martha thrust him aside to hold a bottle of pungent salts to her mistress's nose.

"Breathe, my lady," she urged frantically, her free hand searching for Charlotte's wrist and throat seeking a pulse.

The oldest of six siblings, all lost to the potato famine, Connie had witnessed the births of all her brothers and sisters, and recognised the signs of Charlotte's imminent confinement. Moving quickly, she ran through the curtain into the adjacent cabin to return with the small black satchel containing the essential elements of Martha's profession. Charlotte, now into her seventh month, let out a low moan, prompting Martha to send D'Arcy to fetch Dr Trowbridge as soon as ever he could be found.

Edging forward to take her place at Martha's side, Connie worked swiftly to remove Charlotte's white linen skirt, her stockings and her undergarments, while Martha took instruments wrapped in white linen cloths, thick gauze pads, and two blue bottles of clear liquid from her satchel.

D'Arcy returned, visibly shaken by the scene before him. Dr Trowbridge would come as soon as he could, but was attending to life-threatening injuries suffered by members of the crew, fighting to save the ship at the height of the storm.

Sending him out again, this time to the galley for boiling water, Martha set to work to deliver a child born well before its time.

Charlotte and Richard's son was small, as was to be expected given his premature arrival. A high forehead and long limbs marked him as his father's child. Protesting loudly at his untimely ejection from the warmth and security of his mother's womb signalled his determination to fight for his place in the outside world.

"Your son has strong lungs, my lady," Martha smiled, as she ran an expert finger around the inside of the newborn's mouth in search of a sound palate, counted fingers and toes, and satisfied herself there was no evidence of port-wine stains on his otherwise perfectly formed body. Satisfied, she wrapped him tightly in a swaddling cloth and positioned him gently in the crook of his mother's arm.

A tap on the door signalled D'Arcy's return with a jug of boiling water. Scrambling to her feet, Connie ran to collect it before sending him away with the news that his wife had been safely delivered of a healthy son. Retiring to his own quarters, relieved that his prospects were still assured, D'Arcy was happy to leave the women to complete the rituals of Charlotte's unexpectedly early confinement.

In the state room Martha and Connie worked feverishly to ensure the recovery of both mother and son from the traumatic circumstances of the birth. They knew the next few hours would be critical. While conscious and seemingly relaxed, Charlotte had been weakened by injuries sustained immediately prior to delivery which, being so premature, presented a greater than usual risk of blood loss and infection. And the baby, although appearing robust, would need time for his heart and lungs to gather strength to ensure the rhythm of life was sustained.

By first light the following morning Martha, having sat beside Charlotte throughout the night, was satisfied that both mother and son were in no further immediate danger. Leaving them both sleeping peacefully, she roused Connie from her bed on the window seat to fetch tea, bread and coddled eggs for their breakfast. She had also sent Tom, who had knocked on the stateroom door as soon as he could be spared from his duties topside, for a large jug of stout to stimulate lactation. For with the need to avoid revealing the arrival of a child so soon after Charlotte and D'Arcy's wedding, Martha had to reconcile convention with necessity and put the baby to Charlotte's own breast, rather than seek out a wet nurse from among the bounty passengers.

"Major D'Arcy was in the saloon when I passed through on my way to the galley," Connie ventured, addressing both Martha and Charlotte when she returned with their breakfast. "He said I was to inform you that he hoped to visit his wife at her earliest convenience."

"Let us fortify ourselves, first, Connie, and then you may inform the major and her uncle, Captain Hatfield, that Mistress Charlotte will be pleased to receive them in one hour," replied Martha, as Charlotte, woken by the exchange, stretched and smiled.

With the *Chetwynde* nearing her destination, it was agreed that Charlotte, Martha and Connie would remain in their quarters for the rest of the voyage. This might not be seen as strange by the rest of the passengers, as others were recovering from *mal de mer* and injuries sustained during the typhoon the night before. Besides, the ship's stay in Hong Kong would be necessarily brief. Captain Hatfield was eager to be well to the south when the next hurricane blew in from the east. Only the Reverend Stockwell would be informed of the birth, to ensure the child would be named and welcomed officially into Australia in accordance with Christian rituals and British regulations.

There was also the question of Connie's status to be addressed. Officially one of a group of Irish orphans destined to be allocated to established families as indentured servants, she would be separated from Charlotte and Martha on arrival in the colony unless Major D'Arcy agreed to register, officially, as her employer. D'Arcy who had no interest in the domestic arrangements of his household, made the required declaration to Captain Hatfield, witnessed by the Reverend Stockwell, and the girl's future with a loving mistress and caring mentor was assured.

Questions raised by other first class passengers when the family eventually emerged on deck to disembark could be avoided by the Captain's niece and her entourage remaining on board a day longer than the others for a lingering family farewell.

Young and resilient, Charlotte recovered swiftly from her confinement and appeared on D'Arcy's arm within a week to take meals, while her son – baptised Richard Trevorrow Hatfield D'Arcy, by the Reverend Stockwell with Martha, Captain Hatfield and Dr Trowbridge standing up as godparents – remained in the stateroom in Connie's care. Connie, now assured of her place in the family, fell naturally into the role of devoted nursery maid, taking little Richard –soon known by the endearing derivative, Dickon – to her heart as she had once loved her baby brothers.

D'Arcy, charmingly solicitous of Charlotte and his stepson, first refused, then reluctantly accepted the dowry that went with Charlotte's hand in marriage, assuring her uncle they would both be safe and secure in his keeping.

The *Chetwynde* sailed past the Otways lighthouse, through Port Phillip heads and into the calm waters of Hobson's Bay without further incident, dropping anchor off Williamstown.

A sand bar at the mouth of the Yarra River prevented larger ships sailing on up river to the Port of Melbourne, and the *Chetwynde*'s passengers were required to clamber onto a fleet of flat bottomed steam-driven vessels to complete the last short leg of their voyage. Cabin and hold baggage were loaded onto punts standing off from the ship to be loaded onto bullock carts lined up on shore for the overland journey to Port Melbourne.

Leaving Dickon in Connie's care, Charlotte and Martha joined D'Arcy on deck to farewell their fellow first class passengers. The Trowbridges were among the last to leave, Helen and Therèse lingering behind the doctor and his wife to allow Helen and Charlotte to embrace, promising to visit each other often once they had settled in to their new accommodations.

The delight the two young women expressed at the prospect of continuing their friendship prompted Martha to take Thérèse's hand in silent recognition of the realisation that a long-term friendship was unlikely to eventuate. For it was clear that Helen's condition had deteriorated during the last weeks of the voyage. This was confirmed by Thérèse, who drew her new friend to one side, ostensibly to present her counterpart with a small remembrance of their time together.

"Mistress Wootten, dear friend, I have been grateful for our discourse and your support these past months, and sincerely hope we may meet again, soon, during what I fear may be the short duration of my position in the colony.

"We hold onto the hope that the Port Melbourne climate might work some miracle but, as you can see, the rigours of a long voyage have taken their toll on our dear girl.

"As we might have expected from the closeness of their friendship, early in the journey Charlotte entrusted Helen with the story of events leading to her marriage to Major D'Arcy. Your news of the precipitous arrival of her son, imparted to us in confidence and held close to both our hearts, has given Helen great joy.

"She has asked me to convey to Charlotte, through your good self, an expression of deep affection and the hope that you, Charlotte and the blessed infant will visit us at the house of the Surgeon General as soon as you are settled in your new home." Here Thérèse paused to brush the back of her gloved hand across her eyes.

"My dear Madame Bardot," Martha replied. "Charlotte has told me of her great affection for Helen and wishes me to assure you that it is her dearest wish that little Dickon should meet his aunt Helen as soon as possible.

"For myself, I would be glad of the opportunity to continue our association, for I fear we shall both be in need of a trusted friend in the weeks and months ahead. Rest assured we shall send word, soon, of our intention to call on you at your earliest convenience."

Dinner that night was a sober affair, with Captain Hatfield presiding over the long table set for only three guests: Charlotte, Martha and D'Arcy. Connie remained in Charlotte's stateroom with Dickon, content to sup from a plate, delivered by Tom Newbold, piled high with choice cuts from the last of the chickens, and steaming vegetables sourced from the markets in Hong Kong.

"Here child, eat well, for you will need all your strength to care for our little Dickon over the next few weeks, if I am not mistaken," he said, with an encouraging nod. "But you are a brave girl, and it is clear you love this family as if it were your own. So, if you ever need a friend, leave word at O'Shaunessy's hotel, hard behind Customs House, and Michael O'Shaunessy will know where to find me."

Forward, in the saloon, the meal concluded with the customary port and cigars for D'Arcy and the Captain, and tisanes for Charlotte and Martha. Rising to embrace his cherished niece before adjourning to his quarters, Captain Hatfield drew a small leather case from inside his jacket.

"Dearest girl, I want you to accept this trinket as a token of the bond we share and my hope for your future happiness. It was meant for my darling Rose on her sixteenth birthday. I had purchased it on my way home from the voyage after which all hope of seeing her wear it was lost."

Lifting the delicate gold locket from the satin folds lining the jewel case, he took Charlotte by the shoulders and, turning her gently, fastened the fine gold chain around her slender neck. Wordlessly, Charlotte turned back to bury her face in his braided jacket, conscious of words left unsaid, leaving concern as well as love hanging in the air between them.

Their farewell mid-morning the following day was necessarily brief as the Captain was required to meet with port authorities to complete the customary inspection of all vessels entering the newest of Queen Victoria's colonies.

Final farewells were left to Tom Newbold who, having overseen the loading and despatch of their furniture, boxes and belongings onto a waiting bullock cart at first light, whistled up one of the steamers that would ferry the Captain and his family on to the Port of Melbourne. Charlotte's hunter had been swung off the *Chetwynde* and punted to shore with the rest of the standing livestock even earlier, to spare its mistress the sight and sound of the poor animal, blindfolded, squealing and struggling, plunging into the sea if the harness holding the sling gave way – as happened on occasion. Thankfully, the terrified animal had ended up safely ashore, and after allowing Tom to tie it securely to the back of the bullock cart, trotted off happily behind the rest of Charlotte's belongings as the night gave way to a new day.

Impatient with tearful farewells, D'Arcy carried Charlotte off the barque and onto the small boat taking them to the shore line where they would board the steamer; Ensign Frobisher and Connie shielding Dickon from sight between them, Tom and Martha bringing up the rear of the party.

Before returning to the *Chetwynde*, Newbold thrust a slim package into Martha's pocket. "A parting gift from a true friend, Mistress. It will keep you safe until we meet again, for I fear you may have need of its protection before that time arrives."

Putting a finger to his lips to silence the question in her widened eyes, he raised his hand in salute and vaulted the steamer's safety rail to land back on the boards covering the mud flats below. Looking up as the steamer pulled away, he raised one hand to his forehead before heading back to the *Chetwynde*.

The carriage requisitioned by the sergeant sent to meet Major D'Arcy and his family at Coles Wharf suffered greatly from comparison with those built for the family from whom Charlotte was now disenfranchised by deed and distance.

The discomfort occasioned by worn springs challenged by mud-filled pot-holes was exacerbated by the speed with which they traversed the dirt road leading away from the wharf. For, although as yet unfamiliar with the domain, D'Arcy had insisted on taking over from the driver and tickled the horses along at a fast clip, regardless of the crowds populating the markets clustered around the docks. In the small space between the wharf and the Yarra Hotel – the first stop for those who had yet to arrange permanent accommodation – more than a hundred stalls sold a bewildering array of items from oil lamps to chamber pots, garden forks to guns, billy cans to baby cribs. Picking up speed, they travelled on past narrow lanes running off wide unmade roads where hotels, banks and churches dwarfed lesser structures selling provisions, furniture, carriage wheels, haberdashery and gowns. There was even a post office and an apothecary, Martha noted, for future reference.

Ridged and rutted roads caused the carriage to bound and lurch alarmingly all the way, leaving its occupants bruised and breathless. Even the hardened soldier who spent the journey sitting rigidly at attention beside the major, offered up fervent prayers that the wheel shafts would hold until they reached their destination.

Clattering across the approach to the Princes Bridge – a wooden structure recently built over the Yarra River to withstand the weight of bullock carts which often upended the floating punts which previously ferried people and goods across the city's main traffic artery – the fragile passengers arrived at their destination.

In the centre of a cluster of bluestone cottages, built on the east side of the river in Jolimont to house serving officers and their families, the neat, double fronted dwelling allocated to Major D'Arcy was just marginally larger than the steward's cottage in the grounds of the Hatfield estate. But it was clean and cool, thanks to foot-thick bluestone walls and floors made of polished hardwood, rather than the wooden walls and earthen floors in the cottages that housed the families of other ranks in nearby Collingwood.

The boxes unloaded from the ship's hold, and the cabin baggage Martha and Connie had carefully repacked while Charlotte and D'Arcy had taken breakfast in the saloon, had arrived earlier; the precious hunter having been stabled at the army barracks with the other officers' horses on the assumption it belonged to the major, not his wife.

Without waiting for the carriage to come to a halt, the sergeant leapt down from his perch to pull up the lead horse and secure it to the front fence. Looping the reins over the corner post, he called to one of a group of young soldiers who had been squatting, smoking, on the front porch until the carriage drew up, and were now standing rigidly to attention at the gate. The summoned soldier snapped a smart salute and, ramrod straight, listened intently to his orders which ended with a directive to hand Major D'Arcy's wife, her maidservant and nursemaid down from their carriage, and then put himself and his men at their disposal for as long as it took to establish them comfortably in their new home.

D'Arcy, making no effort to climb down from the driver's seat and help his wife alight, himself, pointed the long carriage whip in the sergeant's direction and then over his shoulder at the passengers seated behind them. "Get a move on, sergeant. I must report to the Colonel as soon as possible. Unload the women and let them work out the rest for themselves."

Exchanging confused glances, the three young soldiers waited for their sergeant to hand Connie, clutching Dickon, down from the carriage, then Martha, alert to steady Charlotte should the need arise.

"Ma'am, Sergeant Reginald Baxter, at your service, ma'am," the sergeant intoned before saluting and handing Charlotte down the carriage's two folding steps to the tamped earth outside the front gate.

"Sorry to hurry you, ma'am," he continued, under his breath, "but you are left in safe hands. These are good lads and will serve you well."

Charlotte, sensing the sergeant's reluctance to keep the major waiting, acknowledged the man's concern and, accepting his proffered arm, allowed him to lead her through the gate, along the tessellated path and up onto the veranda.

"Thank you for your concern, Sergeant Baxter," Charlotte replied. "Please do not worry about us. We have faced greater difficulties than this. You had best not keep the major waiting."

"Ma'am. Your servant, ma'am," the sergeant responded. Then, hesitating, as if he wished to say more, he turned away to rejoin D'Arcy – now looking questioningly in his direction – double-timing it back down the path to leap up beside the major as he set the horses smartly on their way back to the city.

By early afternoon the soldiers had completed their assigned tasks.

"Beggin' your pardon, missus ..." Private Edward 'Fast Eddy' Jackson, known for his ability to talk his way out of almost any situation, poked his head round the kitchen door and flashed a perfect set of shining white teeth at Martha, in what he hoped would pass for an obsequious smile. Formerly a barman at The Angel, Islington, and now a foot soldier in Her Majesty's 99th, Eddie was one of many of his soldier mates recruited from London's notorious East End to be stationed at the 'arse end of the earth'. At the time it had seemed an expedient alternative to a spell 'inside' if a little matter of misrepresentation came to light – as seemed likely to happen sooner rather than later. But now he was not so sure. Moving furniture was hard work and Eddie was anxious to establish himself doing what he did best – organising supply and distribution for the owner of a sly grog shop – before he was due to report back to barracks.

"If there's nothin' more you be needing, missus, p'raps you'd be kind enough to sign this here little chitty, so me and me mates can toddle along and get ourselves cleaned up for evening service."

Not fooled for a moment, Martha looked him up and down through half closed eyes and sniffed, disparagingly. "Well, you certainly smell like you've done a decent day's work, boy. But Jackson, lad, I am older and smarter than you will ever be. I'm not signing anything, and you're not going anywhere, until I've been through this place from front to back and inspected every stick of furniture for scratches, scuffs and finger marks."

As soon as D'Arcy had driven off, Martha had directed the soldiers to unload the bullock cart and break open a crate containing an elegant wicker chaise, and place it on the tiled terrace under the bullnosed veranda shading the front of the house. Taking Dickon from Connie's arms she had settled Charlotte and her son on the chaise, covered by a travelling rug she had sent one of the lads to retrieve from the side pocket of her portmanteau.

While Dickon took nourishment under cover of Charlotte's cloak, Martha had overseen the unloading of items piled high on the bullock cart and passed over the fence into the front garden. She had then set the soldiers to breaking open the rest of the crates and supervised the distribution of their contents. The house, although small, comprised four main rooms, two opening off each side of a central hallway which led to the back door, through which one passed into a covered breezeway leading to the servants' quarters.

Work started first on the matrimonial bedroom situated at the back of the house before the breezeway, and shielded from the noise of the night cart grinding along the back lane by a high fence. Although generous by comparison with most bedrooms in the officers' married quarters, the main bedroom in the D'Arcy residence only just accommodated the curtained, four-poster bed, matching wardrobe, mirrored dressing table with its buttoned silk stool, and marble-topped wash stand, all of which had previously taken up no more than a quarter of Charlotte's spacious bedroom at Hatfield Hall. The commode that completed the suite had to be accommodated in the second bedroom across the hall, now set aside for D'Arcy's dressing room. This already housed a valet-stand and armoire for the major's uniforms, morning suit, evening clothes and riding gear, a small walnut campaign table and a narrow bunk – all standard officers' issue sent over from the barracks the previous day.

As soon as Jackson and his men had put the frame of the four poster together and heaved the wardrobe into place, Martha had sent them back outside to locate the dressing table. Sorting swiftly through the cabin trunk which, for the time being, had been left in the breezeway, she had unpacked and set out on the hastily polished table top a collection of tiny porcelain figurines – birthday presents through the years of Charlotte's childhood from her late grandmother – and the silver backed brush and mirror set engraved with the words, *To Charlotte, from your loving sisters, on the occasion of your 17th birthday, 21 September, 1847*, on the reverse of each piece.

Next, she had set Connie to shaking and spreading out the duck-down mattress across the taut wire springs, covering it with hand-stitched linen sheets, a light merino blanket, a quilted comforter, and four goose-down pillows, piled high against the ornately carved bed head. Drapes, packed in the deep wooden drawers built into the base of the bed, although far too long for windows set under much lower ceilings than those in Charlotte's former bedroom, served well enough to ensure privacy when looped midway and pooled on the polished floor boards. Nodding her head in Connie's direction, Martha had sent her out again to bring Charlotte and Dickon in from the veranda and settle them more comfortably behind the four-poster's fine muslin curtains.

The sitting room and dining room situated on either side of the wide hall were the next to be filled. Working as a team, Martha, Connie and the three soldiers had soon established order as exquisite pieces of furniture were unpacked, positioned and polished to restore the patina which enhanced the mellow tones of seasoned timber expertly fashioned by English craftsmen. Fringed rugs, soft as silk and patterned in muted blues and reds, adorned the waxed wooden floors between button-backed fireside chairs and the oval console table. Oil paintings depicting English gardens were hung throughout the house and a black marble clock was positioned in the centre of the mantelpiece over the sitting room fireplace flanked by tall Georgian candlesticks.

The bunks and chest of drawers from their accommodations on the *Chetwynde* were then installed in the servants' quarters, annexed to the rear of a wide breezeway which served as a kitchen attached to the back of the main house.

Martha claimed the bigger room, as was her right, happy to have somewhere warm, dry and still to call her own, again. Dismissing the stubborn memory of her comfortable three-quarter bed, now washed up on some Welsh or Irish beach, if it hadn't been commandeered by a mermaid and taken down into Davey Jones' locker, she was not displeased with her new accommodations. Truth to tell, she mused, looking at the comfortable, if narrow bed, Charlotte's onboard elegant, if small, chest of drawers, velvet arm chair and matching foot-stool, the room offered a level of comfort beyond her imagining in the two-roomed cottage she had lost to the river Lynn.

Connie, never having known a space she had not had to share with siblings, poor-house inmates, or – before moving into Charlotte's suite – shipmates stacked above and below her aboard the *Chetwynde,* was thrilled with the box room. A proper bed, the very same one Martha had occupied on the *Chetwynde*, all to herself – even though it was wedged hard against trunks and storage shelves leaving almost no room to open the chest of drawers from Martha's cabin – was something she had simply never expected to experience.

There was also just enough room for Dickon's crib at the end of the bed. Put together, secretly, by the *Chetwynde*'s carpenters on Tom's orders, it was a work of love as well as art. For even without the promised bottle of rum they received in exchange for keeping their mouths tightly closed about the job, each man involved had put their best effort into tooling, gluing and polishing, as much for the babies they had left at home as for the one for whom it was destined.

By now the afternoon heat had settled like a shroud over the cottage, despite doors and windows opened wide in the hope of catching a breeze to stir the air inside. Inspecting each room with Fast Eddie hopping anxiously from foot to foot by her side, Martha recalled how the soldiers had laboured uncomplainingly throughout the heat of the day, sustaining themselves with only strips of beef jerky and hunks of bread, stowed in a satchel hanging off the back of the bullock cart, and scoops of water from a bucket set on the stone floor in the breezeway. Martha had marvelled at their energy and good humour, their determination to get the job done, and the care and consideration such young and boisterous lads had shown for Charlotte and Dickon. Making as little noise as possible they had hoisted and heaved heavy pieces of furniture through narrow doors and windows without disturbing sleeping mother and child.

Slipping away to her room, Martha retrieved her apothecary case from the locked bottom drawer of the chest beside her bed, and took out the largest of three blue bottles. Pushing it into one of the wide pockets of her all-enveloping apron, she searched deeper in the old leather satchel until she found a paper roll containing the set of six small marble cups she used for mixing draughts to aid the recovery of the ague. Some people still used wooden cups, but Martha had been given the marble cups by gypsies when she had saved one of their women from certain death by successfully delivering a breeched birth. The gypsies swore that the coolness of the marble increased the effectiveness of the draught and over the years Martha had come to believe this to be true.

Pausing to look in on Charlotte and Dickon she made her way back through the breezeway and along the hall to the tiled front terrace where the soldiers waited for her to complete her inspection. Keeping her face carefully composed, Martha folded her arms and looked long and hard at each man. Clearly apprehensive, they expected a less than perfect report – and quite possibly, a good ticking off, followed by a sentence of tedious rearranging, waxing and buffing. Instead, Martha gave the assembled group a curt nod, and passed one of the marble cups to each of them. Drawing the bottle from her apron pocket, she proceeded to pour a measure of the crystal liquid into each one – including her own.

Sniffing the contents, Jackson let out a low whistle. "Christ, missus – begging your pardon – but where did you lay hands on this?" he asked, exchanging broad grins with his mates.

"It was given to me by a friend aboard the *Chetwynde*," Martha replied. "He said it was a good drop and I think we have all earned a little reward."

Taking a tentative sip of the highly prized pure white rum, undeclared contraband smuggled on and off Her Majesty's ships trading in the West Indies, Martha was amused to see the jubilant soldiers each toss back the whole shot, whereupon the realisation of its potency registered in their watering eyes. With heaving chests they shook their heads from side to side like wet dogs. Looking up through tears of laughter they eventually managed to draw breath and croak their thanks.

"A good drop indeed, Missus," said young Jackson, running a hand through his tousled yellow hair and attempting a mock bow. "We'd be at your service again, no worries, should you be thinkin' of movin' on anytime in the future! Now, though, me and the lads'd best be on our way or we'll be doing without our supper."

In turn, each man fronted up and nodded respectfully to Martha, muttered his name and repeated the offer of help should she need strong backs and willing hands.

"Bill Tiler, by your leave, missus."

"Charlie Wills, by your leave, missus."

"Edward Jackson, by your leave, missus, and our respects to the major's lady."

Martha responded to each lad with a firm handshake, thanking them for the speed and efficiency with which they had carried out their assignment. She also thanked them for the concern they had shown for her mistress and the baby, treading as quietly as their loads would allow on the echoing wooden floors.

"No worries, missus," Jackson replied. "We're getting young Charlie in practice for creeping in late after a night on the tiles without waking his twins, delivered last week."

Smothering spontaneous laughter, the young soldiers tiptoed, pantomime style, across the terrace and down the front path, vaulting the closed gate to take off at a run for the barracks or more likely a sly grog shop, Martha thought, wryly.

Inside the makeshift kitchen, Martha carefully rinsed the marble cups in the water bucket, and put them back carefully into her apothecary case, together with the half-empty bottle of Jamaica rum. Setting Connie to prepare a meal of cold meats and vegetables from the camp kitchens, delivered by the soldiers sent to see them in, Martha walked back into the main house and gently eased open the door of the main bedroom. There, in the long shadows of late afternoon Charlotte lay with Dickon in the crook of one arm, still sleeping. Soon, she would have to wake them so Charlotte would have time to make her toilette and dress to greet her husband on his return.

Withdrawing from the room, Martha set about laying the table in the dining room in readiness for the dinner she would serve to the major and Miss Charlotte (she still could not think of her charge as Mistress D'Arcy), later that evening. While their first meal together in their new home would be a simple one – Martha was yet to engage a cook – she wanted it to be memorable. Polishing and placing two exquisite Gallet crystal wine glasses beside the gleaming silver flatware framing the couple's plates on the Honiton lace cloth, Martha allowed herself a small smile of approval. Their new situation would suit quite well, given the family's domestic circumstances and the comparatively short time they would have to stay in the colony.

Chapter Five
TRUE COLOURS

The front door, which Martha had propped open with a dining chair to let in the late evening breeze, slammed shut, causing her to slop the water she was scooping into a crystal pitcher from the bucket set down on the slate pantry floor to keep the contents cool. Major D'Arcy had returned from the barracks earlier than expected, and although she had anticipated his return around sundown, the sound was intimidating.

Smoothing her apron, she rallied her senses to walk up the steps from the breezeway into the hall and through to the sitting room to greet the head of the house with a salutary bob.

"Bring your mistress to me!" D'Arcy ordered, freezing the words of welcome on Martha's lips.

"My lady is resting, sir," she replied. "She thought to recover from the disruption of the day in order to be able to sit with you at dinner."

"I require my wife's presence *now* Wootten!" the major ordered, feet planted firmly apart, his baton beating an insistent tattoo on the side of his highly polished boot. Turning away, Martha trod swiftly across the polished boards and onto the oriental runner gracing the length of the hall. A wedding present from Captain Hatfield, it had been taken up from his own quarters and pressed upon them as they took their leave of him earlier that morning. Gently, Martha tapped on Charlotte's bedroom door.

"Miss Charlotte ... my lady. Are you awake?"

"Is that you, Martha dear?" The response came, thin and reedy. Hurrying to Charlotte's side Martha felt her mistress's brow for signs of a fever. Dickon's birth had been a difficult one; the loss of blood was severe and had taken all Martha's skills to staunch. Charlotte's recovery, although surprisingly quick, was not yet complete and Martha knew there was a risk of fever and fatigue for some weeks yet. One thing she hadn't had to worry about for long was Dickon's health. The baby was gaining weight rapidly, thanks to an abundant supply of his young mother's milk. Unlike many women of her class, Charlotte had not baulked at the prospect of putting her baby to the breast as soon as she had sufficient flow to feed him – which, with no other new mother on board to act as wet-nurse when the birth occurred, was nothing short of a blessing.

"I am glad you woke me, dearest Martha. I have need of Dickon to relieve the tightness in my breasts. Thank heavens he is a hungry baby."

Opening her eyes slowly against the last of the sun's rays as the hot orange ball sank slowly down behind the hilly horizon, Charlotte smiled the slow, dreamy smile of a woman well content with her showing as a mother. Reaching for her son she smiled again as, disturbed in sleep, his mouth made soft sucking sounds. Put to the breast he suckled noisily, causing his mother to exclaim, "Piglet, piglet," and, laughing, raise and kiss his tiny clenched fist.

The pretty picture was framed in time for only a few seconds before D'Arcy's raised voice summoned Martha to return to his presence so loudly, and in such a peremptory tone, that it startled Dickon, causing his hands to flail, anxiously. Backing from the room, Martha closed the bedroom door behind her and hurried back into the sitting room to answer the major's summons.

Standing before him she felt a frisson of fear tease her spine, held rigid by his icy stare.

"If my instructions were unclear, woman, let me repeat them. Convey my compliments to your mistress, and tell her I desire her presence here in this room with me *immediately,*" he said, enunciating each word

82

with exaggerated clarity. The words were delivered softly, but with such underlying menace that Martha found herself turning to comply, until her protective instincts prevailed and she paused to put the case, on behalf of her mistress, for a few minutes grace.

"Sir, by your leave, Mistress Charlotte is resting while the infant takes nourishment," she replied. "I will convey your request and she will be with you as soon as she has completed her toilette and dressed for dinner."

Smiling thinly, D'Arcy pointed his baton toward the open door, and raised his voice to a level that left no prospect of further delay.

"Now!" he said. "I will tolerate no more mewling excuses."

Alarmed by the urgency in Martha's voice as she delivered D'Arcy's message, Charlotte rose from her bed with Dickon still at her breast, and pausing only for Martha to drape a concealing shawl across babe and breast, hurried into the sitting room to stand before her husband.

"Rollo," she began, hesitantly, "is there something wrong, my dear?"

"Yes, madam. Something *is* wrong," he replied, looking at Charlotte coldly. "But I am about to put it right."

Walking out of the sitting room and into the arched passage leading to the front door, he returned with a wide-hipped woman of serving status in his wake.

"This, madam, is Florence Wills, wife to one of my corporals. She has recently given birth to twins, one of whom has failed to survive. She has enough milk for two infants and will now take on the responsibilities of wet nurse to your son. Do I make myself clear, Mrs D'Arcy?"

Before Charlotte could answer, D'Arcy had pulled Dickon from her breast and thrust him into the arms of the astonished Florence Wills. The woman had been waiting to make her bob to the major's lady, and was so taken by surprise at D'Arcy's action and the cruel way in which it was executed, that she almost dropped the infant pressed against her ample bosom. She had time only to clasp Dickon securely before D'Arcy ordered her from the room.

"On your way, mistress, you will be contacted on the morrow, with your instructions on the terms of your employment, and an advance on your monthly stipend."

Mother and wet-nurse had glanced at one another only briefly during the exchange, but each recognised the anguish of one and the compassion of the other. Martha sent up a fervent prayer to a higher being, thanking Him for providing Florence Wills, wife to Charlie Wills, one of her willing helpers earlier in the day, as Dickon's wet nurse. Intuitively, she knew the infant would be in safe hands. Running out through the open door, she caught up with the woman and replaced the apron Florence had drawn up to cover Dickon when she was unceremoniously dismissed, with the shawl which had slipped from Charlotte's shoulders when the baby was snatched from her arms.

"To guard the baby against the chill night air," she whispered urgently to Florence. "Care for our little Dickon as if he were your own."

"I will, missus, I will," the good woman replied, slipping a screw of paper into Martha's hand. "This here's directions to where I live. Visit me when you can and you'll see how the infant thrives."

"No, Rollo! No! Please husband, please don't take Dickon from me so soon," Charlotte cried, as Martha re-entered the house.

"The Wills woman has her orders," D'Arcy replied, unmoved. "She will keep your son in her quarters until he is weaned. She will bring him to visit you for one hour, each month until that time comes. My decision has been made. It is not fitting for an officer's wife to suckle her own child like some common serving wench. That is all I have to say on the subject.

"Besides, my dear, you have me to care for now," he concluded, smiling.

Following the line of D'Arcy's eyes, Martha crossed the room swiftly to button Charlotte's bodice securely.

"Come, madam, please," she whispered, leading Charlotte gently back into the bedroom where the dazed young mother sat, immobilised by shock, on the bed where only moments before she had reclined so happily with her beloved son.

In the sitting room D'Arcy seated himself comfortably in the fireside gentleman's chair, one of the many wedding presents from his unknown father in law. Selecting a pipe from the rack the soldiers had fitted to the wall at one side of the fireplace, he filled the bowl with fine-cut Virginia tobacco and tamped it down hard with the ball of his thumb. Rising to touch a taper to a candle burning brightly in one of the candlesticks Martha had placed there, earlier in the day, he sat back down, fired his pipe, and drew back the fragrant smoke, contemplatively.

"We must bind your breasts at once, my lady," said Martha, tearing strips of equal width from a sheet snatched hastily from the linen press.

"It hurts, Martha ..." Charlotte whispered, her voice muted as if she were unwilling to acknowledge the pain and so give currency to the unimaginable events of the past few minutes. Her fingers explored the bindings, tracing the contours of her new shape. The real pain, Martha knew, would come later, as Charlotte's breasts filled without any prospect of relief during the long night ahead. The younger woman looked down to follow the pattern traced by her fingers, and as she did so Martha saw that her expression acknowledged the impact of the glimpse she had been given of her husband's true character, and the likely consequences of her hastily arranged marriage. Raising her eyes imploringly to Martha, Charlotte turned to reach out to her. As she stood, her head fell back and she crumpled wordlessly to the floor.

Calling for Connie, Martha raised Charlotte's head and slid a pillow beneath it before plumbing her pocket for the ever-present smelling salts. Motioning the bewildered girl to close the door and pull the quilt from the bed to cover her mistress, Martha held the small blue bottle to Charlotte's nostrils and was relieved to see she responded swiftly to its pungent contents.

"Is it true, Martha, or did I dream the awful events etched upon my mind?" she asked, attempting to rise. "Has Rollo really sent my baby away? Am I only to see my darling Dickon when he says I may?"

"All that is true, my lady," Martha replied. "But Florence Wills seems like a good woman, and her husband, we know, is a decent fellow. I believe they will care for young master Dickon as if he were their own." As soon as she had uttered the words, she regretted them.

"But he is mine, Martha, not theirs! I want my baby back, I want my baby back ..." Charlotte keened, with such longing that Martha knew she had to put an end to such futile pleading with cold common sense.

"For the love of God, my lady, hold your tongue! Do you want your husband to forbid Florence to bring the baby to you *at all* until he is weaned? It has been done before, cruel as it sounds, and if you were still at home, occupying your rightful position, you would have had your baby wet nursed from the moment he came into the world.

"Had there been another new mother on the ship when Dickon was born, I would have recruited her myself – although I believe we never should have been so lucky as to find a Florence Wills among them. So bear the separation bravely, my dear, lest you lose the little time you may expect to have with your baby while he is in Florence Wills' care."

The threat of being denied the opportunity to see her baby for the next twelve months quietened Charlotte immediately. Putting her hands over her mouth she stifled her sobs until she had control of them. As they subsided, she took Martha's hands and squeezed them until they hurt.

"Promise me you will see Dickon is settled with Mistress Wells before the week is out, Martha. You can call in on your way to the market. All I ask is to hear that he is still alive and thriving."

Martha nodded assent immediately, anxious to appease her charge and settle her down with a draft of laudanum. But Charlotte was not yet ready to sleep. She raised Martha's hands to her lips and kissed the roughened fingers.

"You are my closest friend in this God forsaken place," she said, "We will survive this terrible time together, whatever it takes, until we can return home, knowing that my son will then be able to take his rightful place in his grandfather's house."

Telling Connie to stay with Charlotte until the laudanum took effect, Martha returned to the parlour and, prepared for another outburst, informed D'Arcy his wife was in no fit state to present herself at his table. To her amazement, he nodded sympathetically, as if he had nothing to do with his wife's indisposition, and announced he would take a light meal, alone, at the console table.

As soon as D'Arcy pushed back his chair, Martha cleared the table and joined Connie in the kitchen for a cold supper before reassuring the anxious child that although she would no longer be required to perform the duties of nursery maid for the next twelve months, she would remain a member of the household, learning the role of parlourmaid.

While Connie washed the dishes and swept the brick floor, Martha informed her she had learned from the soldiers, earlier that day, that it was necessary to clear away all remnants of food and drink so as not to attract the crawling insects that invaded every dwelling in the colony – not to mention the rats that ran out of the produce containers as they were unloaded from the ships.

Leaving Connie to complete her tasks alone, Martha re-entered the main house, tapped on the sitting room door and waited for permission to enter. When the response came, she ventured inside only as far as needed to bend the knee and ask D'Arcy if she might retire for the night. He nodded, smiling absently, as if the tense and turbulent events of the late afternoon had never happened. Exhausted at the end of such a long and eventful day, Martha made her way to the outhouse to relieve herself and sluice her face, hands and arms with water dipped from the rain barrel, before she exchanged her day clothes for a comfortable flannel nightgown. Feeling all her fifty-two, years she climbed wearily into her narrow bed on her first night in her new home and, like the twelve year-old in the box room, fell immediately into a deep and dreamless sleep.

The scream stopped abruptly – as if a hand had been placed over an open mouth. Fighting her way up through layers of consciousness Martha strained to gauge the direction from which it had come, wondering if she had perhaps dreamed she heard someone screaming. But the sound came again, this time muffled, and ending in a stifled sob. Reaching for her robe, Martha leapt from her bed and ran into the kitchen where she was sure she would find Connie, transfixed by the sight of some giant spider, or worse, a snake, as she dipped into the water pail to quench her thirst.

But the kitchen was empty and the wooden lid still sat squarely on the water pail. Martha turned her attention to the box room, surprised to find Connie sleeping soundly, nestled deep into the goosedown mattress and quilted comforter she had unpacked earlier that same day. Shaking her head, Martha marvelled at the seeming reality of dreams.

Within seconds a low moan emanated from the direction of the main bedroom and Martha's knew she had not been dreaming; as the pieces fell into place inside her head, she realised that it was Charlotte who needed help. But given the hour, and her place in the household, especially when the major was at home, this time she could not run to comfort her anguished mistress.

Nevertheless, she crept up the breezeway steps and into the hallway to stand before the bedroom door. Pressing her ear against the polished wood, she heard the sharp sound of an open hand being brought down sharply on unprotected flesh. Then, the major's voice, in a measured tone ….

"Never again, madam, if you wish to see your son before he is sent away to school, will you question my decisions regarding his upbringing – or anything else, for that matter.

"You are fortunate, indeed, that I did not have him taken from you as soon as he was born. But then, in your weakened state you might not have survived, and that would have done me no good at all – would it, sweeting?

"As we are both aware, in the eyes of the law a marriage is not a marriage until it has been properly consummated. And unless our marriage is legally sound, should you lose your life as a result of some unforseen accident or illness, I cannot be properly recompensed for giving you and your bastard my name. So, I determined to see you recovered sufficiently from the rigours of childbirth to ensure you were capable of enjoying the true delights of married life, to which I am now about to introduce you..."

Transfixed, Martha's eye found a narrow gap in the panels which, made of local wood used too soon, had shrunk tongue from groove to allow a narrow view of D'Arcy standing to one side of the bed, Charlotte held close beside him by her hair, wound tightly around his left hand. With his free hand he slowly untied his white silk stock and, unbuckling his wide leather belt, made to unbutton his uniform breeches.

"But it is too soon, sir. . .it is but weeks since Dickon was born. And as you can see, I am not yet fully recovered." Helplessly, she gestured to her bound breasts. His eyes following the sweep of her hand, D'Arcy smiled and, taking a step back, turned to leave the room.

Terrified of discovery, Martha melted into the shadows behind the half open doorway into the dining room. From her hiding place she watched, silenced by fear of discovery and dismissal, as D'Arcy strode through the breezeway, across the kitchen and into the box room, to emerge, a moment later, pushing Connie, stumbling and still half asleep, in front of him.

Standing in the wide open doorway of the marital bedroom, he used his free hand to lift the child's chin, forcing her to look directly at Charlotte. Letting go of her arm, he hooked his fingers into the top the servant girl's nightgown and tore the garment from neck to hem, exposing her budding breasts and knee-length drawers.

"It is your choice, madam I *will* have my pleasure this night. Will it be with my wife, or with her kitchen maid?"

With the dream of Charlotte settling happily into the role of a respectable married woman, content to serve out her period of exile for the term of her husband's posting turning into a nightmare, Martha snatched Connie's hand as the bedroom door slammed shut in the terrified child's face, and led her back through the breezeway to hold the child close in her own bed until Connie gave over sobbing and fell asleep. But there

89

was no sleep for Martha, lying there considering their options.

With no family or friends to call on for help now that the *Chetwynde* had sailed on up the coast bound for Sydney and the return run home, it was clear Charlotte's father should be apprised of their unexpected circumstances. But with a child delivered only weeks after meeting the man she had married it was unlikely he would countenance Charlotte's early return. And even if he did, what would become of Connie? Neither Charlotte nor Martha would consider abandoning the child they had both come to regard with genuine affection.

Rising at first light from the narrow bed in which she had spent the sleepless hours until dawn with Connie curled close, Martha reached for her shawl and slipped out of her room and into the breezeway. Sounds emanating from D'Arcy's dressing room reassured her that he would soon be leaving to take his first meal of the day with his fellow officers. This was confirmed by the sound of the sergeant sent to collect him, talking softly to still the impatient horses, his own and Charlotte's hunter – now considered D'Arcy's and liveried at the barracks – as he waited outside the house for the major to emerge.

Freshening her face and hands from water drawn from the rain barrel outside the breezeway, Martha stirred the embers in the small woodstove and set a pan of water to heat for the eggs she would later coddle for Charlotte's breakfast. Retracing her steps she returned to her room to wake Connie; within minutes they heard D'Arcy's heavy tread in hallway and the slam of the front door as he left the house.

Moving swiftly back through the breezeway and up the two steps leading into the hall, Martha set Connie to cook the eggs and prepare a tisane while she cautiously opened the door to Charlotte's bedroom.

"Come in, Martha dear," Charlotte called, in a surprisingly clear and steady voice considering the events of the previous night.

Pushing open the door Martha stood open-mouthed as she took in the image of her mistress standing calm, if pale faced, beside the smoothly made bed, neatly attired in her riding skirt, boots and a high-necked blouse with the collar unbuttoned and the sleeves rolled up.

"Madam … Charlotte, dear, I feared to find you indisposed and here you stand so …."

"Resolute, Martha. A surprise to you, I am sure, dear friend, after my husband's unforgivable behaviour yesterday and last night. But as it turned out, he was too far in his cups to fulfil his intentions and spent the rest of the night in his dressing room. I filled the sleepless hours reviewing events in my life which led to our current predicament, and considering how we might turn them to our advantage."

Striding past Martha, Charlotte turned left and down the steps into the breezeway, instead of right into the dining room, where Martha had expected her to wait for Connie to serve the morning meal. Setting plates and cutlery onto a large tray, Charlotte then led the way to the wicker table and chairs set out on the back veranda, where the rising sun warmed the chill air of the early spring day. Bewildered but intrigued, Martha and Connie followed, bearing, between them, a large dish of eggs, a plate of toasted bread, condiments, and a silver pot of green tea – a refreshing concoction to which they had been introduced by the much travelled tenor, Signor Minelli, who carried his own supply of the precious leaves aboard the *Chetwynde*.

Spooning eggs onto Charlotte and Martha's plates, Connie made to turn back into the breezeway, to eat her breakfast at the scrubbed pine table where meals were prepared and servants ate after the family had been served.

But, "No Connie, you sit with us. The only meals I take separately from you and Martha from now on will be when I am required to dine with my husband," said Charlotte, rising to draw out a chair for the girl to take her place at the wicker table.

"We have now all been abused by the one person we should have been able to trust with our lives," she continued. "We must acknowledge the indisputable fact that my husband is a cowardly bully who trades on the weakness of those who are not in a position to defend themselves from his abuse.

"In other circumstances, although one marries for better or worse, a woman in my position might expect to be able to turn to her father or some other close relative for protection from a violent spouse.

"Distance and the events leading to the situation in which we now find ourselves have disenfranchised us from that expectation – although I shall, of course, write to my father to inform him of our predicament in the hope that he can exert some influence over my husband's behaviour while we are here.

"Meanwhile, we must manage our situation as best we can until the *Chetwynde* returns. By then we will have been away from England for long enough to allow for the dates of my marriage and Dickon's birth to have lost clarity and relevance. When Captain Hatfield is made aware of our circumstances, he will surely remove us from D'Arcy's reach and take us home where we belong."

Round eyed and mute, Connie wiped her plate with the last of the bread and looked to Martha for help to interpret the meaning of Charlotte's brave new stance, and what that might mean to her own future – for she was beginning to feel safe at last from the consequences of poverty and loss she had experienced at home. Before Martha could respond, Charlotte had taken hold of Connie's roughened little hand and, speaking to them both, hastened to divulge the rest of her plan.

"I am resolved to ensure that we remain together, dear friends, come what may, until we are brought safely back to England – and beyond that time, if that is your wish, for I consider we are now a family, and cannot contemplate losing either of you.

"So let us go forward together, and find out what our new home has to offer. Let us begin right now, by exploring the markets we passed through all too quickly on our arrival. It is a fair day. The sun is up and not yet too fierce. It will be our first adventure in this strange and puzzling place."

Connie signalled her enthusiasm for an outing of any sort, given the time she had spent confined first on the *Chetwynde*, by scrambling to her feet, stacking the breakfast things onto the tray, and scurrying off with them into the kitchen.

Martha took a moment longer to consider Charlotte's proposal while the notion of an adventure took shape in her mind. Reaching into her pocket, her fingers found the small scrap Florence Wills had given her as she left the house with Dickon in her arms.

"A fine day for an adventure, indeed," she smiled, slowly.

Chapter Six

FORGING THE FUTURE

C losing the door behind them, Charlotte, Martha and Connie walked in procession down the tessellated path to the wrought iron gate slung between crennellated posts holding fast to Westminster railings. From there they stepped straight out onto the unmade road – for there was, as yet, no footpath separating the row of neat bluestone cottages from the narrow carriageway on the lower slopes of Eastern Hill.

Pausing to find their bearings, they turned left to follow the wide rutted road that paralleled the Yarra River as it led round to the rough hewn bridge that spanned the murky water. From there it was a leisurely stroll, albeit a dusty one, to the produce markets which had sprung up like field mushrooms around Customs House, hard up against the holding sheds on Coles Wharf.

As they walked, now three abreast along the wide thoroughfare, their progress was stalled by the need to pause and turn away from the choking dust sent up from the churning wheels of six-team bullock carts. Laden with angular blocks of bluestone and nut-brown builders, they passed by at a cracking pace, intent on an early start on a long, hot day striving to complete the new stone bridge being built to replace the old one.

Reaching for the large linen kerchief she habitually carried in her pocket to wipe her eyes, Martha's fingers brushed against the screw of paper Florence Wills had thrust at her as wet-nurse and baby were unceremoniously bundled out of the house the previous day. Although she knew the information it contained would provide Charlotte with the will to endure the long separation from her infant son, Martha also feared the consequences if she took advantage of the opportunity it presented too soon or too often.

However, all thought of risk and consequences were thrust aside by the need to scurry, again, into the hedgerow as a milling mob of sheep surged past, driven in from stations to the north-east with much yelling and whistling by drovers on sturdy mountain ponies, and barking from working dogs weaving in, through, on top of and around the closely bunched, bleating mob. Past their prime, these poor breeders were bound for sheering sheds, abattoir and market as mutton for the stew-pot. But the diversion served to provide a few moment's thinking space and end Martha's dilemma. She decided to risk making the small detour to the workman's cottage that was to be Dickon's home for the first year of his life, confident that knowing her son was within walking distance would serve to shore up Charlotte's new resolve yet temper it with caution.

Drawing the kerchief across her eyes while the last of the sheep, dogs and horses surged past, Martha beckoned to Charlotte and Connie to come close.

"Miss Charlotte, Connie," she said, raising her voice above the noise of the following drovers, urging the stragglers on with whip cracks and whistles. "The morning is yet cool and the markets can wait for our patronage a while longer. Let us learn more about this conundrum of a city in which we find ourselves. I have been given a map and directions to a village across the road on which we stand."

"But Martha is that wise?" Charlotte countered, eyebrows drawn together in a worried frown. "We have yet to learn how safe it is to wander out of our way without first seeking advice. Indeed, I had thought to make a call on the local constabulary this very morning to determine the prevalence of footpads in the city environs."

"Fear not, Mistress, for I have it on good authority that we may expect to be treated with courtesy and respect on our tour of the precinct known as Collingwood. I believe it is likely we might even be offered refreshments," Martha replied, mysteriously.

With the prospect of food and drink, Connie darted forward, looking anxiously from Martha to Charlotte and back, again, to the older woman. Charlotte, herself now clearly intrigued, followed Martha across the wide expanse of tamped earth and crushed rock to a cluster of shops, taverns and livery stables sitting cheek-by-jowl on the other side.

Pausing to shake the dust from their skirts, their senses were immediately assaulted by the aroma of baking bread. Drawn to its source, Connie looked beseechingly at Martha who thrust a token into the girl's hand instructing her to purchase two cottage loaves and three Eccles cakes. Round-eyed at the prospect of biting through the heavenly layers of sugared sponge, rich, syrupy jam and flaking pastry, Connie scurried inside the bakery to emerge, moments later, mumbling through bulging cheeks, that their future loyalty had been assured by 'makeweights' – one of which she had felt obliged to sample while she waited for her purchases to be wrapped and tied.

It was fortuitous, Charlotte remarked later, as she and Martha reviewed the momentous events of the day, that the shop next door sold willow baskets – dozens of them hanging from wires suspended from extended eaves overhanging the open-fronted workshop, wedged between the bakery on one side and a bootmaker's on the other. A hasty purchase enabled them to relieve Connie of her load before temptation again got the better of her.

The bootmaker's next door also provoked their interest. From the state of the roads, only Martha's stout hide lace-ups would withstand the challenge of venturing beyond their own front gate on more than an occasional basis. Charlotte's doeskin riding boots held up well on horseback or springy English turf; but they were no match at all for the unmade streets of Melbourne. Connie had already outgrown the ill-fitting ankle boots issued to the contingent of Irish orphans along with one dress, one shawl, two sets of drawers, a nightgown and a blanket, as they were dispatched, by the British Government, to populate or perish on the other side of the world; and while two new dresses had been stitched from lengths of material purchased in ports en route to their new home, it was now clearly time Connie, too, had a new pair of new boots.

Sitting at his bench at the front of the shop where the light gave his tired old eyes new life, the moment Charlotte, Martha and Connie paused in front of his bench the proprietor scrambled down from his high wooden stool and ushered them inside. Rushing ahead he made great ceremony of wiping the dust off a worn wooden bench before motioning them to sit.

"Spasiba, spasiba, ladies," he effused delightedly, wiping his forehead with the same rough rag he had used to clean the bench. "It is pleasure, it is pleasure."

In the time it took to have their feet measured, select patterns and finger samples of locally tanned leather, they had learned that the bootmaker, who introduced himself to them as Mishka, and his wife, Iris, were also in voluntary exile from their respective homelands. Mishka had fled summary justice in Tsarist Russia when he was identified as a member of a movement representing the poor, dying in their thousands from cold and starvation. He had met his wife, Iris, when an overloaded, London-based cargo ship dumped its excess unfortunates onto the deck of another ship bound for Australia. Iris, dismissed from her position as parlour maid in a London hotel after rejecting unwelcome advances from her employer, had answered an advertisement in *The Times* promising employment in the antipodes, and found herself aboard the same vessel as Mishka.

By the time their measurement and preferences had been recorded in Mishka's curling Cyrillic script, and a cleansing tisane had been offered and accepted in a ritual reminiscent of earlier times in a more civilised setting, a friendship had been forged that transcended that of customer and craftsman. Charlotte, in particular, looked forward to returning for their first fitting, and made a mental note to bring with her the journal in which she had decided to record impressions of her time away from home, the better to illustrate her story when sharing it with family and friends on her return.

Bowing them out of his tiny shop, Mishka stood outside long enough to see them safely to the end of the street where, referring again to Florence's map, Martha led her companions down one of the narrow laneways linking the grid of streets which formed the nucleous of the new city.

The lane in which the three explorers found themselves next consisted of facing rows of diminutive dwellings, front doors opening directly onto shared space little wider than that of the alleyways designed to accommodate night carts sent around the city to collect and carry away human waste.

"Here we are, then," Martha announced, pausing before a faded front door set close against a single window to form the face of a single-fronted weatherboard cottage. In defiance of the dust kicked up from passing foot traffic and the occasional hand held barrow, a pot of bright red geraniums sat to one side of the bluestone slab that served as a front step.

Charlotte, walking ahead and viewing the workmen's cottages with an artist's eye, stopped sharply in her tracks and turned to look back, questioningly, at Martha.

Stepping up onto the bluestone slab, Martha rapped sharply on the sun-worn door before stepping back down onto the tarred blocks edging the shifting dirt road. Instantly, it seemed, the house came alive with the high pitched squeals and dancing steps of excited children, wails of protest from newly woken infants, and the futile protests of a woman attempting to quell the raucous response. Seconds later, the visitors heard the sound of heavier footsteps and, almost simultaneously, the door swung inward to reveal Florence Wills, drying her hands on the end of her apron and casting a knowing smile in Martha's direction.

"Come in, ladies. I was expecting you'd call on us, sooner rather than later," she beamed, reaching forward to help Charlotte through the narrow portal into hall. "Welcome, Mistress D'Arcy, Mistress Martha, and you child – Connie, isn't it? I heard Mistress Martha call your name as we left the major's house, yesterday.

"Let us go straight into the kitchen. There is no parlour, I am afraid. Babies and children occupy the front room. Charlie and me sleep in the other room, and we've built in the breezeway which is where we cook, eat and live. Cosy it is in winter, and Charlie put in a door on each of the side walls so we get a good cross breeze to cool us off in summer."

Two shining-faced toddlers, Little Charlie and Molly May, were duly introduced and sent back into the garden to finish planting a paper screw of pumpkin seeds. Calling through the open door of the children's room to soothe the babies, Florence motioned Charlotte, Martha and Connie to the benches set against a scrubbed pine table filling a quarter of the floor space in the lived-in kitchen. On the table, thin slices of damper spread with butter and preserves had been set out on an ironstone plate, under a wire mesh dome, in anticipation of unexpected guests or the children's tea, whichever came first.

An open fireplace occupied most of the far wall beneath the lower end of the sloping tin roof. A wire-sided meat safe pushed up hard against a tiled wash stand with a large enamel basin on top and a water bucket below filled the far corner. Shelves holding cooking pots, plates and small glass jars containing homemade preserves, which owed their existence to prudent planting in the Wills' tiny garden, lined the walls above the meat safe and wash stand.

The Wills' one concession to comfort was a well-worn leather armchair positioned to one side of the fireplace. Smiling broadly, Florence informed her guests that Charlie had won it from a second-hand furniture dealer setting up on the docks. For want of something better to relieve the tedium of a slow day waiting for incoming bargain hunters to buy what he purchased for a pittance from immigrants on their way home, the dealer had made an impulsive wager on the comparative speed of two cockroaches Charlie had tipped out of his tinder-box onto the boardwalk. The chair was proudly borne home by the soldier on a borrowed hand-cart as a gift for his then heavily pregnant wife, serving to provide a much appreciated resting place in the time leading up to each of her confinements, ample space for nursing newborns and, as it turned out, a haven in which to grieve when the smaller of her newborn twins gave up his struggle to survive a second day.

Once her visitors were seated, Florence excused herself briefly, to return minutes later with two identical bundles clasped to her bosom. Hardly able to breathe, Charlotte rose from the table, arms outstretched to reach for the noisy one, recognising the lusty cry emanating from the depths of one of the bundles as the voice of her son.

Smiling and nodding, Florence insisted Charlotte made herself comfortable in the armchair. Connie, perfectly balanced on a bench, reached her arms out, happily, for the other bundle – identified by his mother as the surviving twin, "Albert, after the dear Queen's husband, of course."

"Oh, Martha. Oh, Florence. What can I say? However can I thank you for giving me these precious moments with my darling Dickon," Charlotte whispered, smiling delightedly through her tears. "I thought to be denied sight and sound of him for at least a month."

Shaking her head in the absence of words to articulate such a bleak prospect, she turned to Florence, imploring impulsively, "May I come here again, so he will come to know me well through the coming months?"

"You may, indeed, my lady. But we had best be careful to keep it our secret, for if Charlie were ever questioned about your visits, he must be able to say, truthfully, that he has no knowledge of them," Florence replied, leaving the consequences of a soldier lying to a superior officer to her guests' imagination.

"Of course, of course, I understand perfectly," Charlotte hastened to reassure the woman. "I share your concern as my visits would be cruelly curtailed should my husband learn of them."

"I think we may be making many visits to the baker, the basket weaver and the bootmaker over the coming months," Martha observed, dryly.

"Let us make a plan, then," said Florence, lowering her voice conspiratorially. "Mornings are best, as Charlie will likely be in barracks or deployed outside the city. If by chance he is at home, I will move the geraniums from the left to the right of the front step. Send Connie on ahead to see where they are before you knock on my door."

Settled on their signal, Florence heated the tea kettle and found a board for the bread, and a plate for the Eccles cakes Martha had taken from her new willow basket. The older children were called back into the house for a thick slice of bread, spread with tasty dripping, half an Eccles cake each, and a quick kiss before being shooed back outside to finish their planting so that the grownups could talk. Connie, swayed first by the urge to relive her childhood, her hands once again deep in the soil, and then by the mouth-watering thought of a slice of bread and dripping, agonised over the choice until Florence resolved her dilemma. Pasting another slice with the precious spread, she retrieved Alby from Connie's arms and sent her out into the garden to supervise the planting project over which Little Charlie and Molly May were arguing to the point of tears.

With Charlotte unable to concentrate on anything other than her son, the two older women spent a mutually agreeable hour exchanging news of the old country and views of the new, and forming a friendship that would hold fast long beyond the time when Dickon was weaned. But all too soon, it was time to leave. The sun was now suspended like a giant egg yolk almost immediately overhead, and Florence urged them to hurry home before the heat settled over the sprawling city and brought on the heat sickness with its headaches and hives.

Retracing their steps along the nameless lane in which the Wills dwelling stood, back past the bootmaker's, the basket weaver's and the bakery – all now shielded from the burning sun by canvas blinds made from old ships' sails hanging limply from hooks attached to the eaves – Charlotte, Martha and Connie walked back to Jolimont in companionable, contemplative silence.

For Connie, the morning expedition had been an amazing adventure. So many experiences compressed into such a short time – the breathtaking parade of bullock carts, horses, dogs and sheep; the mouth-watering aroma of baking bread; the prospect of new boots! And then there was the dripping. Real dripping like she remembered, long ago before the potato crop failed and everyone died. And for a few magic moments, Little Charlie and Molly May brought back the fun and laughter she had once shared with her own small siblings; and she was no longer teetering on the confusing edge of womanhood but a happy laughing child again, not caring if her dress blew up and her drawers showed when she leaned forward to push down the pumpkin seeds. Looking in her apron pocket she discovered three were stuck under the edge of a run-and-fell seam which had frayed at one end – treasures to plant in a kitchen garden she would create for Dickon to play in when he came home.

Martha, ever resourceful, used the journey back to Jolimont to consider her options for protecting Charlotte, as far as she could, from the consequences of her new husband's malevolent mood swings until Sir Ian consented to end her exile.

The first step had already been taken. Her impulsive decision to reunite Charlotte with Dickon by visiting the Wills home had been a risky but positive move. But there was still the need to find a way to deal with D'Arcy's unpredictable anger and unconscionable physical demands. What she needed was an ally, someone close to the major who could provide the practical support she had come to rely on from Tom Newbold aboard the *Chetwynde*. But who …?

And then she remembered the contempt and compassion flashing, in turn, across the eyes of the sergeant sent to meet the major and his family on their arrival in Port Melbourne. It was Sergeant Baxter, rather than D'Arcy, who had briefed the soldiers waiting there to unload the bullock cart and see his family safely settled into their new home. And it was Sergeant Baxter who paused long enough to hold Martha's anxious glance and touch his forehead when he arrived to escort the major back to the barracks the following morning.

Then and there Martha made a mental note to have a quiet word with the soldier when he returned with D'Arcy, later in the day, to lead Charlotte's hunter back to the barracks.

Charlotte's thoughts took her no further forward than her next visit to the cramped cottage where she could see Dickon regularly and, as she held him, reflect upon happier times with his father.

After a late lunch and a short rest, Charlotte and Martha sat together at the dining-room table and worked on the practical aspects of the future management of the Jolimont household, and a calendar of social visits and excursions necessary to establish their social standing as a newly settled military family. D'Arcy had, as was to be expected, assumed responsibility for the disposition of Charlotte's dowry, and while it was evident he would consider any expenditure relevant to his own social standing in the community essential, Charlotte judged his support for anything else would be unlikely to be accessed easily.

"I will speak with my husband at supper, tonight, to request an allowance for housekeeping," Charlotte announced. "He will understand that lists must be drawn up and provisions purchased to stock the larder and put up preserves.

"We can then program our visits to the markets. We already know where to purchase the best bread, in the closest proximity." Here the two women exchanged knowing smiles. "We now need to establish a relationship with provedores who will keep us supplied with quality meats, game and vegetables, milk, flour and eggs, and such delicacies as we might reasonably expect to relieve the tedium of a subsistence diet."

"We should also start putting up fruit, jams and pickles," Martha opined, laughing openly at Charlotte's bewildered expression as she compared the bare back yard of the Jolimont cottage to the orchards and vast kitchen gardens that supported the Hatfield estate.

"We'll buy in as much as we can at first, before the end of the fruiting season," Martha continued. "In the meantime, we will put in vegetables to see us through the coming winter. And that means purchasing seedlings.

"I looked over the fence into our neighbour's yard early this morning. They've gooseberries, rhubarb, tomatoes and strawberries ready to pick, and according to their help, they have been here only a twelve-month. They have also given a quarter of their garden over to herbs and green vegetables. I will have a quick word with Sergeant Baxter when he brings the major home, later today, to see if he can persuade a couple of soldier boys to turn the earth against the back fence so we can prepare the soil for a late summer planting."

The practicalities dealt with, Charlotte turned to planning a social agenda.

"Let us start with visiting Helen and Thérèse," Charlotte suggested. "I long to see Helen, and the Surgeon General's wife will be well placed to advise me of social obligations in military circles.

"And you, dear Martha, found a true companion in Thérèse. You will doubtless be pleased to converse with her again. While you are speaking to the sergeant about help with our kitchen garden, you must ask him for directions to the Surgeon General's House, and what transport might be available to take us there.

"Then there is my Lady Chalmondly, wife to my father's cousin, Sir Giles Chalmondly, proprietor of the Union Bank. Although my uncle would have sent word to her of my changed status, before the *Chetwynde* sailed on, it was the intention that we should reside with the Chalmondlys until a suitable husband could be found for me. She will also be able to advise us of the location of her husband's bank. We must make ourselves known there so that we may present my father's letter of credit for your stipend, Martha dear."

Folding their list of things to do and people to visit, Charlotte rose from the table to lift her late grandmother's treasured Georgian candlesticks from the polished mahogany mantel on which they resided, and placed them either side of a deep silver rose bowl in readiness for the evening meal.

"Come, Martha," she said. "Let us dress the table as we would for a celebration. My husband might not realise the significance of the occasion, but we shall ever remember it as marking the day I took a firm hold on the future direction of the rest of my life."

It was well past dinner time when Charlotte and Martha, catching the cool night breeze on the front veranda, heard the sound of approaching horses and two figures rode into view. The first, clearly identified by the bright light of a low moon as Sergeant Baxter, pulled up his horse, disengaged his feet from the stirrups and swung a leg over his mount to execute a perfect cavalry dismount. The other, slumped across his horse's withers, slid from his mount to collapse over the front gate. Turning towards Charlotte and Martha, the sergeant raised his right hand in a sharp salute before leaning forward to pull his superior officer off the gate, and hoist him over his shoulder in a textbook fallen-comrade-retrieval lift.

With his free hand he lifted the latch and the gate swung in a wide arc allowing access to the front path which he covered easily, despite D'Arcy's dead weight, to stand, back ramrod straight, heels locked together, boot-caps the regulation nine inches apart before the open-mouthed women.

"Ladies ..." he began. "Major D'Arcy is somewhat indisposed. Permission to enter the house and deposit the major on his bed? He will need to sleep undisturbed if he is to be well enough to take Parade in the morning."

"Of course, sergeant," Charlotte replied, smiling in an effort to overcome the discomfort of the moment for Baxter as much as herself.

Rising to her feet before Charlotte could make a move toward the front door, Martha led the trooper along the hall to D'Arcy's dressing room. Standing to one side, she met the sergeant's questioning glance with a telling nod and watched as he deposited his load, none too gently, onto the narrow bed, pausing only long enough to remove the major's boots and throw a blanket over his supine body.

"Sergeant Baxter," said Martha, thoughtfully, as he turned to leave the room. "My mistress would be disappointed if you left unrewarded for your duty of care to her husband under such taxing circumstances.

It is late, and it would appear the major made several detours on his way home, which will have deprived you of the opportunity to return to barracks in time for your evening meal. Won't you take a moment to step into the kitchen and partake of a light supper, and perhaps a mug of ale, before you journey back to your quarters?"

It had been less than a month since their fellow passengers aboard the *Chetwynde* – Dr Trowbridge, his wife, Alice, their daughter, Helen, and Helen's nurse-companion, Thérèse – had settled into the gracious residence which went with the appointment to Surgeon General. But in that time, Charlotte had established a routine which took her out of the Jolimont house for some part of almost every day that her husband was on duty.

Determined to make the best of a bad situation from which, for the time being, there could be no escape, she sought to balance the impact of D'Arcy's dark and dangerous moods by creating another life for Martha, Connie and herself outside the officers' married quarters.

Visits to Florence Wills and little Dickon aside, a woman of Charlotte's social standing was expected to pay her respects not only to her peers but to the wives of city dignitaries and local business leaders as soon as she established herself in the colony, so it would be quite in keeping for her to be seen out and about almost every day, with a companion to carry sundry purchases. While provisions such as food, fuel for the oil lamps, and wood for the stove and fireplaces were delivered, Charlotte knew that shopping for purchases of a personal nature would be considered a perfectly acceptable indulgence for a woman in her situation.

Their first of such outings was to locate a pharmacy to replenish the contents of Martha's apothecary case, depleted at sea in the aftermath of the typhoon. The apothecary case replenished and, on the pharmacist's advice, now also stocked with a goodly supply of heat-stroke powders and calamine lotion to cool the sting of sunburn and insect bites, a printer had to be found. Visiting cards were an essential part of the social protocol for women of a certain station – even between friends.

Creamy vellum writing paper and envelopes were also selected from the display counter at the front of the shop at the top of the hill at the far end of Collins Street, along with string and sealing wax, and purchased with the promise of delivery by runner by the end of the day – earlier if the printer's ink dried sooner.

Charlotte's next purchase was a parasol for herself, and wide-brimmed bonnets for Martha and Connie. Several yards of French tulle were then measured off and carefully wrapped in layers of black tissue paper – essential in the colonies to protect coloured fabric from fading in the strong sunlight and whites from 'greying' – to be fashioned into veils to protect their faces from flying insects that landed on every inch of exposed skin.

On their return to Jolimont, Charlotte, Martha and Connie shared mealy bread and slices of a delicious pork terrine, retrieved from the coolest corner of the blue-stone larder where it had hung, wrapped in muslin, suspended over a bucket of water to keep it cool and moist. In the late afternoon, while Martha put her feet up for a while, and Connie stitched lead shot into the hems of muslin curtains hung across the open sides of the breezeway to screen the kitchen from wasps and flies, Charlotte spent an hour at the ornate walnut *escritoire* which once faced the wide bay window in her bedroom at Hatfield Hall.

Opening the box of deckle edged cards, writing paper and envelopes delivered, as promised by the printer, while it was still light enough to read the elegant raised script, she took a moment to recognise the name on the cards and note paper as her own.

Mrs Roland D'Arcy,
24 St Agnes Close, Jolimont

It was as if Miss Charlotte Hatfield, of Hatfield Hall, in the county of Somerset, no longer existed. Not for the first time, she allowed her mind to drift back to the halcyon days she had spent growing up in the west of England manor house, the cherished first daughter of a loving father and doting mother, and darling of the villagers working on the family estate. And falling in love with Richard. The coachman's son and childhood playmate with whom she shared a love of horses and of the countryside, riding through fields and forests together like wild things, never dreaming for a moment that the happiness they shared would one day turn into love and separate them forever...

Pulling her thoughts back to the present, the first note she wrote was to her dear friend and shipboard companion, Helen Trowbridge, inquiring after her health and signalling her intention to call on her at the Trowbridges' earliest convenience. Adding that Martha also hoped to be received, to exchange with Thérèse the latest thinking about new treatments for illnesses and injuries endemic to their new locale.

The second, to the Hon. Lady Chalmondly, was more formal – introducing herself as the daughter of Sir Giles Chalmondly's second cousin, Sir Ian Hatfield, and wife of Major Roland D'Arcy, serving officer in the Royal Dragoons temporarily attached to the 40th Somerset Regiment now serving in the Port Philip District, and inquiring if she might attend Lady Chalmondly's next 'At Home'.

Connie was primed to loiter at the front gate when the sun dipped and Sergeant Baxter escorted the major home, to ask him, as she flat-palmed apple cores and carrot scraps to the horses, loving the feel of their velvet muzzles as they lipped the treats off her outstretched hand, if he would be so kind as to deliver both notes on his way back to the barracks.

Less than an hour after D'Arcy and his escort rode away the following morning, there was a discreet tap on the front door. A tense housemaid from the Surgeon General's household held out an envelope, begging Martha's pardon for presuming to come to the front door, explaining she could see no way through to the back save the night cart lane, and she was forbidden to enter night cart lanes for fear of bringing infection into the Surgeon General's residence, what with Miss Helen in such poor health.

Martha, nodding approval, took the proffered note from the visibly relieved girl and told her to wait on the veranda for an answer. Returning minutes later, she instructed the girl to carry a note back to Miss Trowbridge, accepting her invitation to call the following Thursday.

The cobalt blue door, set between Corinthian columns reaching up to a sculptured portico on the second floor, was opened by a wing-collared butler who ushered them into the foyer of the Surgeon General's Collins Street home with a twinkle in his eye that belied his formal greeting.

"Mistress D'Arcy, Madam, Miss Helen is expecting you," he intoned as Charlotte placed her calling card upon the silver salver held out in front of her. "If you and your companion would kindly follow me, we shall find our young lady in the conservatory."

Folding her parasol, Charlotte handed it to a parlour maid hovering at the butler's elbow, and with Martha in her wake followed the portly figure in measured procession across the circular, domed foyer and along one of three arched hallways leading off it, through to French doors beyond which was the conservatory. Before opening the doors, the butler – who they later learned was most aptly named Porter – paused to inform Charlotte that 'Miss Helen' had been pulling the bell rope to quiz him on the anticipated time of their arrival every five minutes for the past hour. He said he also wished to prepare them for the temperature and humidity of the conservatory, kept at a level best suited to not only the tropical plants it housed but also his young mistress's delicate condition.

"Charlotte, dear friend, what a pleasure to see you again!" The slight figure reclining on a wicker chaise, eyes bright and her alabaster complexion flushed with the exertion of rising to a seated position, tossed aside the light cotton throw covering her lower body to clear a space for Charlotte to sit beside her. "Just like our time together reading poetry aboard the *Chetwynde*," she exclaimed, happily.

Charlotte, arms wrapped around Helen's emaciated frame, intercepted the glance exchanged between Martha and Thérèse which confirmed her own observation that her friend had failed to thrive, as hoped, in her new environment.

"Dearest Helen, how good it is to see you again. And looking so … bright," she replied. "Look, my dear, I have brought another volume of Keats for us to share. I have discovered the most charming book shop, close by the Post Office, owned by a former professor from the university of Cambridge."

Aware that in her haste to cover her dismay at Helen's appearance she was speaking too quickly and overwhelming her friend with information, and regretting, for a moment, her poor choice of an author who died so young from a similar affliction, Charlotte was grateful for the opportunity to regain her composure provided by Porter, inquiring if they could stay for tea.

She kissed Helen, again, on both cheeks, and rose to embrace Thérèse, who had walked from where she stood beside her charge, to sit beside Martha on a wide wicker settle framed by Kentia palms. Before they could exchange more than pleasantries, the French doors opened wide to admit Helen's mother, and in her wake, Porter with the tea trolley. As soon as he had seen Mrs Trowbridge settled in her customary high backed chair set close beside her daughter, he proceeded, with great ceremony, to pour a fragrant amber tisane from a silver samovar into eggshell cups which he handed, white gloved, to his mistress and each of her guests.

Helen's he placed on the cherry wood wine table to one side of the chaise longues on which she reclined, so as to diminish the risk of spillage occasioned by the young woman's shaking hands.

Pleasantries exchanged, their visit was, in consideration of Helen's evident fatigue, concluded within the hour, with promises of repetition on the Trowbridge family's next At Home day.

The response to Charlotte's request to call on Lady Henrietta Chalmondly arrived a week later, when major and Mrs D'Arcy were invited to a select gathering to celebrate the completion of works at St Peter's Church on nearby Eastern Hill: the event to take place at the end of the following month.

Lady Chalmondly, a devout member of the Church of England (despite the fact that her faith had not been rewarded with longed-for children) had selected her guests for the occasion carefully. Catholics as well as Protestants were nicely balanced, as were engineers and artisans – second tier on the social scale, of course, but a valuable source of inside information leading to new business for the family Bank. New faces were always highly sought after – providing, of course, they were well-connected – and there had been a dearth of those in recent weeks.

It was opportune, therefore, that the daughter of Sir Ian Hatfield, a knight of the realm holding title to untold acres in England's bounteous south west, wished to pay her respects. The young woman's husband, described in *The Port Phillip Gazette* in its *New Arrivals* column as 'the elder son of a Lord Wellington D'Arcy, Bart., said to be one of Her Majesty's closest advisors', could reasonably be relied upon to hold a knife and fork correctly and keep up his end of a conversation. As for the wife, she had been described by those who had seen her shopping in Collins Street, as 'young, quite a pretty gel, reserved and well spoken'.

His well-honed instinct for recognising a useful connection when he saw one, and already bored with the constraints of military life, D'Arcy responded positively when Charlotte apprised him of this most fortuitous invitation. Having secured his future by marrying the eldest daughter of a titled, well-connected family, and by so doing acquiring a considerable sum which, if invested wisely, would provide a comfortable income for the foreseeable future, he had now lost interest in his wife – except, of course, for the occasional urge to exercise his conjugal rights – and had as little to do with her as possible.

However, given that it was Charlotte's relationship with Lady Chalmondly, albeit a tenuous one, which offered him *entrée* to the establishment in this dull city, he became, again, the caring and considerate husband she had known aboard the *Chetwynde*.

111

Excusing his erratic behaviour since their arrival as an aberration occasioned by the rigid and demanding routine to which he was subjected in the service of Her Majesty, the unaccustomed heat, the filthy food, and the lack of companionable male company when he was off duty, he took Charlotte's hand, kissed it contritely, and vowed to make amends.

The change in D'Arcy's behaviour over the weeks leading up to the Chalmondlys' *soirée* raised Charlotte's hopes of repairing the marriage and returning to England the happy and respectably married woman her father had envisaged. He showed interest in new furnishings for the house and increased her allowance, insisting she visit Collins Street, where gowns imported from London and Paris would mark her as married to a gentleman of some substance. For the same reason, he also insisted she engage a couple to manage the house and garden.

D'Arcy himself made a special trip to the Military Tailor in nearby Bridge Road to order a new dress uniform so he, too, looked his best when presented to the Chalmondlys and their circle.

But best of all, as far a Charlotte was concerned, were the evenings. No longer late home, surly and the worse for the grog supplied in dockside gambling dens, D'Arcy took his place at the dinner table and made an effort to charm and amuse his wife.

The Chalmondly's soiree was an elegant affair, as was to be expected, following the traditional form for informal occasions in which persons of significance entertained in their own homes when royalty was not expected to attend. Gleaming chandeliers hung from the ceilings in rooms in which their guests were received before flowing through to the dining room. There, a long table was set with gleaming silver candelabrae, flatware for five courses, and Stuart stemware sufficient for appreciating the varieties of wine served to complement each stage of the meal that followed.

Charlotte had prepared carefully for her first social engagement of consequence in the colony. Drawing on the wardrobe she had brought with her from Hatfield Hall, she had selected the shimmering violet silk gown she had worn to the coming-out of one of her closest friends, held in the family's London residence. The feathers in her hair replaced the tiara she had worn on that night, and she had removed the diamante buckles from the satin slippers which matched the colour of her gown exactly. It was better, she knew, remembering the mantra which governed the dress code for all women of good families, to be safely under-dressed than over-dressed, thus risking censure for 'flamboyance'. D'Arcy, who excelled in presenting himself on such occasions, knew the appeal of a military uniform, particularly a perfectly tailored dress uniform, on a man who knew how to wear one.

Lady Chalmondly was well pleased with the 'pretty couple' as she later referred to the newcomers, agreeing with her closest women friends that, 'breeding is everything'.

More invitations to events held by the Chalmondlys and their connections followed, including one to the official opening of the new theatre where their shipboard acquaintances, Signor Minelli and Master Blake, received a standing ovation for their performance of a selection of well-known operatic arias.

Building his portfolio of promising opportunities, D'Arcy continued to invest in his relationship with his wife, trading on her blooming youth and his own family's good standing in the community at home, to charm influential representatives of her father's generation. But three months after their introduction to the Chalmondlys' social circle, Charlotte felt the quickening of D'Arcy's child, and when her condition became apparent they were, of course, obliged to politely decline such invitations for the time being.

Without the need to keep up appearances, D'Arcy soon returned to his old haunts. Now, more often than not, he missed dinner, returning home when Charlotte, Martha and Connie were asleep in their beds, whereupon Sergeant Baxter would catch him as he slipped off his horse, hoist him over his shoulder and leave him, snoring loudly, on the narrow dressing room bed where he would bother no-one.

For Charlotte, this became the preferred pattern, for whenever he was sober enough to be able to walk unaided up the path to his front door, Baxter would be sent on his way and D'Arcy would slide between the sheets next to his apprehensive wife. But, thankfully, when that occurred he would usually fall into a sound sleep, for he found Charlotte's once lithe body, now swelling with child, unappealing.

For this, Charlotte was inordinately grateful. His indifference to the other occupants was of little consequence to Martha and Connie who saw his infrequent appearances at dinner as something of a respite from his boorish behaviour, and an opportunity to spend more time with Charlotte sewing new dresses for Dickon's anticipated sibling.

There were also the occasions when the major was required to take a detail out into the bush to quell some skirmish between settlers and the natives or hunt down absconding convicts, still serving out their time on farms in the Western District. There were even longer trips escorting teams of surveyors sent out into the bush to stamp Queen Victoria's imprimatur on yet more indigenous land. Then everyone relaxed, and Charlotte spent most of her time under a shade tree in the back yard, now a garden with flowering shrubs, gooseberry bushes and a small vegetable plot planted by Connie, thanks to heavy digging by Elias who, together with his wife, Nellie, looked after the house and garden.

Hired on the recommendation of Sergeant Baxter when D'Arcy was building on the Chalmondly connection by playing the part of a caring husband, they had soon become indispensable members of Charlotte's household. As, indeed, had the sergeant who, when not required at the major's side, had taken to dropping by for a mug of cider and quiet chat with Martha.

With no family of his own, the concern he had felt for the major's family had brought its own reward – a sense of belonging he had thought never again to experience. Trusting him completely, Martha had shared with him her fear that Charlotte's condition would soon force her to forgo her visits to Dickon in Collingwood; the long walk would prove too much of a risk, even if she could be seen out in public at this stage. Within the week Baxter arrived at the gate with a coach and pair, ostensibly to exercise the horses, but in truth to facilitate the first of regular, carefully contrived visits to Collingwood, followed by a gentle drive along the leafy banks of the Yarra River.

Trusting Florence Wills completely, Charlotte planned to relinquish the infant she was carrying to her care when the time came. By then, Dickon could be taken off the breast completely and Florence could continue as wet-nurse to his new brother or sister. Then, joy of joys, Dickon could return to Jolimont where Connie would resume her duties as nurserymaid while Charlotte taught him his manners and, eventually, his letters and numbers, as the Lady Margaret had taught Charlotte and her sisters theirs.

With the sun losing some of its heat, and the days becoming shorter, Charlotte spent her last weeks of pregnancy in blissful anticipation of the new baby's imminent arrival. But as one life waited to be born, another drew to a close. Late one day, as the molten sun sank behind gathering indigo clouds, Porter, the Trowbridge's butler, appeared at the front door bearing devastating news. It was with deep regret that the Surgeon General and Mrs Trowbridge begged to inform Mrs D'Arcy that their daughter, Charlotte's dear friend, Helen, had slipped away early in the forenoon.

Martha ushered the poor man inside where, mopping his eyes with a large, damp handkerchief, he went on to explain that although the event was not entirely unexpected, the dear girl had seemed to rally over the past few days. And that he, Porter, on taking a refreshing tisane into the conservatory – now sanatorium – had found her lying on her long wicker chaise, Charlotte's open volume of Keats pressed to her breast, apparently sleeping peacefully. And how, when she failed to respond to his greeting, forgetting his position, he had run through the house, calling for Dr Trowbridge, who confirmed Porter's worst fears.

Chapter Seven

NEW BEGINNINGS

N ow in her final month, Charlotte was unable to attend the funeral of her beloved friend, sending notes of condolence to Dr and Mrs Trowbridge, and to Thérèse. Apart from a deep sense of personal loss, Charlotte rightfully surmised Thérèse must also be wondering what the future held for her now that her services as Helen's nurse were no longer required.

On the day of the funeral Charlotte sent Martha to represent her and support Thérèse, insisting that with Connie by her side, and Nellie and Elias within easy reach, she would be well cared for in Martha's absence. And so it was, resting in the garden while Connie and Elias weeded the vegetable patch and the church bell sent its mournful message down from the hill, that Charlotte was roused from contemplation of the solemn requiem by a scuffle in the breezeway, followed by an anguished yelp as a tumbling ball of black and white fur flew out off the end of a stout straw broom. Falling to the ground, the furry ball revealed itself to be a small dog, feet flailing and ears flapping wildly, with Nellie hot on its heels vowing to 'flatten the varmint'!

Going to ground in the cover of gooseberry bushes too precious to be bruised by Nellie's broom or Elias' rake handle, as he, too, joined in the chase, the shivering pup was eventually rescued by Connie. Positioning herself on her hands and knees between the Smallridges and their quarry, she persuaded the pup to trade the prickly security of his temporary hiding place for the sanctuary of her apron. Perched on the end of Charlotte's wicker chaise, Connie cautiously allowed the animal's thrusting snout to emerge from its impromptu pouch, followed immediately by its soft black muzzle, brindle face and outsized ears. The rest of its quivering body she held tightly between her knees until its struggling ceased and Nellie gave up her scolding.

"Looks like a gun dog, to me," Elias announced dubiously, pulling a length of rope from around his waist and looping it over the animal's head as it shook itself free of Connie's skirts. "A young'n, too, and a runaway I'll wager."

"Head in the water bucket, and then tried to get to the meat pie cooling on the table top!" Nellie exclaimed, arms akimbo. "Needs gettin' rid of, quick smart, if you ask me. Toss him over the front fence, Elias. Send him on his way with a flea in his ear."

"Oh no, he's tired and hungry – he'd never survive! Oh Charlotte, can he not stay?" begged Connie, who by now had a firm grip on the animal's makeshift leash while holding him protectively in her arms.

As if understanding the tenuousness of his situation, the trembling pup fixed liquid eyes imploringly on Charlotte, who instinctively reached to caress his velvet face and still the shaking.

"We have this day farewelled a dear friend who brought nothing but light and love into our lives," she replied, thoughtfully. "Let us welcome another. We are indeed in need of something to lighten this day. And he has the look of love about him. Yes, Connie, we shall keep him, but he must mind his manners and learn to respect Nellie's house rules, and Elias's hard work in the garden.

"And he shall be named Scamp. For in a lifetime surrounded by gun dogs at Hatfield Hall, I never did see a young one scamper away so smartly as this one did from Nellie's flailing broom!"

Looking around the garden where, moments before she had been reflecting on her isolation so far away from her sisters, Beatrice and Melanie, and her mother, Margaret, to whom she could have turned for comfort at such a sad time, she became aware of the sympathy and kindness expressed in actions, if not words, by those around her. Even the newly acquired help had gathered, silently, to work around her as she grieved for her friend. And she was inordinately grateful, touched by their tacit support and needing to acknowledge it.

"Nellie, dear. Please take a moment from your chores and put up the tea trolley with the Minton for six – and let us have some of your delicious shortbread as a special treat. Elias, please be so kind as to find the loose paling that allowed our new friend access to the garden and secure it so he will not stray and lose his way, again. And Connie, as soon as Elias is done, let young Scamp loose to wander freely, for he is quiet now and needs to find his way around his new home."

Pleased by the sudden lift in her mistress's spirits and the prospect of unexpected company, Nellie nodded in Elias' direction and made her way back into the breezeway. Water always simmering on the hearth, she returned within minutes, pushing the laden trolley ahead of her along the brick path into the shade of tree ferns, transplanted from the forests covering the mountains to the east of the city to the far corner of the D'Arcys' narrow garden. At almost the same moment, Martha emerged from the breezeway with another surprise.

"Charlotte, dear, look who I've brought back with me," she said, sweeping aside the curtain to reveal Thérèse.

"Thérèse, dear, welcome, welcome," exclaimed Charlotte. "Let me first say how devastated we are at the loss of our dear friend and your precious charge.

"You bear this terrible misfortune bravely, but thought to come to comfort us when I am sure you wished only to grieve in seclusion. But please forgive me if I say that I hoped Martha might be able to persuade you to come back with her."

In less time than it took Martha and Thérèse to peel off their black silk mourning gloves, Elias had repositioned a long Luton bench from where it sat in full sun for Thérèse and Martha to share the pool of shade in which Charlotte rested. Behind the trolley Nellie waited respectfully for Charlotte's other guests to arrive, while Elias pulled forward another

118

bench so they would not have to stand for long when they eventually materialised. Expecting to be summoned to the front door to admit them, he rolled down his shirt sleeves before reaching for the jacket required for his other, lately acquired, duties as sometime butler.

"Thank you, Elias. But for your own comfort on this warm day, please remain as you are, and kindly take your place beside Nellie on the seat you have just drawn up. Nellie, you may pour now, for we are all assembled." Charlotte said, indicating the end of her chaise for Connie to sit down also.

Never in all their lives had Nellie and Elias been invited to take tea with the gentry who employed them, let alone in the company of their friends. Having recently completed the period of indenture imposed upon each of them on transportation – Elias for shooting a field rabbit and Nellie for collecting kindling on titled land – they had been immediately recruited by Sergeant Baxter at the behest of Major D'Arcy, and were only just getting used to their new-found freedom.

But Baxter had chosen well. The Smallridges were both temperate and committed – not only to each other but to building on their newfound freedom by establishing a reputation as respectable free settlers. Besides, Elias was tall, fit and, while circumspect, would be well capable of 'managing' his new master, should Baxter not be around when such help was needed.

Only recently released by their previous employers, Baxter had persuaded D'Arcy to secure their continuing support by investing in the construction of a small room attached to the side wall of the wash house. Three months ago, they had moved in with nothing but a double bed, acquired by Baxter from a comrade returning to serve in the mother country, and the clothes they stood up in; the uniforms supplied during their period of indenture having been repossessed by their employer and recycled for their replacements.

The following day, Charlie Wills had arrived at the back gate with a bundle of clothes donated by his Collingwood neighbours keen to give a couple of 'battlers' a fair start. A scrubbed pine table and two mismatched chairs had found their way through the back gate hours later, turning what was little more than a garden shed into a small but comfortable home. Settled sooner and more comfortably than they ever could have hoped, Nellie and Elias had put their hearts and souls into giving back to their new employers – in particular, their charming and gracious mistress.

With her confinement drawing near, Charlotte looked forward to celebrating Dickon's first birthday with the most exciting gift she could think to give him: his very own sibling. Charlotte remembered the joy of her own childhood growing up with the love and companionship of her sisters.

"Just, think," she mused, as she held up a tiny lawn apron she had been hemming for approval by Connie and the two older women, sitting similarly employed at either end of the dining table.

"Just a few, short weeks, now, and my darling Dickon will be crawling around our feet!"

Neither Martha nor Thérèse, who had become a regular visitor since Helen's death, had the heart to disabuse Charlotte of her fanciful notions, concealing their doubts about D'Arcy's response to Dickon's return with assenting nods and smiles.

Such concern was to prove well-founded, for the major and the marriage were now clearly doomed. Sober just long enough to meet the minimum requirements of his duties as a serving officer during daylight hours, as soon as the sun commenced its journey over the horizon, he would head for the gambling dens that lined the docks and wharves hard by Customs House. Such was D'Arcy's reputation for behaviour unbecoming an officer and gentleman, that his earlier investment of charm and solicitude had been recognised by the Chalmondly's circle for what it was: a desperate effort to gain access to easy money and useful connections.

With pregnancy limiting Charlotte's appearances in public to secret visits to the Wills' Collingwood cottage, D'Arcy no longer had access to private homes where money could be made at card tables set up for the gentlemen while their ladies made polite conversation. Nor was he admitted to any of the gentlemen's clubs, where sizeable sums changed hands in rooms specially set aside for games of cards and chance. Now forced to feed his addiction to grog and gambling in the slime and sawdust of establishments catering to a much lower class of players, his wits dulled by raw alcohol and lack of sleep, Charlotte's dowry was dwindling fast.

Routinely, late enough to ensure D'Arcy would be comatose and therefore incapable of disturbing Charlotte upon his return, Baxter would scour the sly grog shops, black jack houses and cock pits until he found the major slumped over a card table or, worse, propped against a wall outside the shack or cellar from which he had earlier been unceremoniously ejected. He would then haul him to his feet, heave him across his saddle, and take him home.

Depending on the hour, Martha might still be up and about, ready with a plate of ham or mutton, a slice of fresh bread and a mug of ale for the soldier and, like as not, would sit with him in the kitchen while he supped, exchanging news of the colony and the family they both had come to regard as their own.

A career soldier, Baxter had put up his hand to serve with 40th Somerset deployed to New South Wales after losing his wife and son in their struggle to survive a breech birth. What he wouldn't give, he told Martha, for the opportunity presented to Major D'Arcy, and how they differed in their regard for the responsibilities entailed. Unwilling, himself, to risk such a devastating loss ever again, this devoted family man had determined to maintain his commitment to his dead wife and child until, God willing, they met up again in the next world. In the meantime, he would do his best to ensure, as far as possible, that the major's family was shielded from the officer's unpredictable behaviour.

With the prospect of Dickon's return, Charlotte felt she had reached the happiest moment of her forced exile. She found herself surrounded by a surrogate family, drawn together by virtue of the circumstances in which they found themselves and a genuine sense of concern for one another.

Across the room, the indomitable Martha, squinting, held a French seam to the fading light before showing it to Connie, who was well on the way to becoming an accomplished seamstress. How close they had all become since boarding the *Chetwynde*. And now there was Thérèse, who would continue to live in the Surgeon General's residence until his term of engagement expired and he returned to England. But with no official position to fill since Helen's death she now divided her days between mornings at the Women's Hospital and long afternoons with Charlotte, Martha and Connie. Together, Martha and Thérèse reminded Charlotte of her maiden aunts, sitting in the parlour at Hatfield Hall, leaning toward the windows to catch the last of the afternoon light while sewing for the anticipated arrival of her younger sisters.

Connie, she had come to regard as a surrogate sister. Younger than her own sisters, Beatrice and Melanie, and unlettered when first taken under her wing aboard the *Chetwynde*, the child had responded eagerly to Charlotte's offer of tutelage. She could now read, write and reckon proficiently, identify countries they had visited on their voyage on the map – a parting gift from Captain Hatfield – pinned to her boxroom wall, and had even adopted Charlotte's measured manner of speaking, softening her broad Irish accent to a gentle lilt.

Then there were the Smallridges, the couple hired to cook, clean and manage the heavier work around the house. Respectful and wary around D'Arcy, once they had recovered from the shock of being invited to join Charlotte, Martha, Thérèse and Connie for tea in the garden, Nellie and Elias had soon filled the place of the loyal and caring family retainers she had grown up with at Hatfield Hall. And there was also Sergeant Baxter. Officially part of D'Arcy's world, he had quietly assumed responsibility for 'managing the major' as he put it, shielding Charlotte and the rest of the household from D'Arcy's worsening behaviour as best he could. Encouraged by Martha, he had allowed himself to be part of a family again.

When Dickon comes home, I must remember to include the names of our Australian 'family' when we play the love-list game, Charlotte thought to herself. Hands on either side of her swollen belly, she caressed the child inside her as she recalled the charming fantasy her nurse had contrived to fill the gap for young Charlotte, Beatrice and Melanie when their parents were summoned to join the Queen's annual progression to Scotland.

After their prayers and before they settled for the night, Nurse would ask them, "Who loves you?" Hands held high, fingers splayed, they would count off the names of every member of their immediate and extended family and, for good measure, their horses, dogs and cats.

Sadly, there had been, as yet, no response to Charlotte's letter informing her father of the circumstances in which she found herself following her not so fortuitous marriage. Unwilling to consider Sir Ian might allow such conditions to prevail, she had chosen to believe her missive had been lost at some point on its long and circuitous journey. A second letter, despatched when Charlotte had found herself, again, with child had, presumably, met a similar fate. Thérèse told Martha she had overheard the Surgeon General, in conversation with Mrs Trowbridge, mention that the *Chetwynde* would put in to Port Melbourne in less than a month. Given Charlotte's imminent confinement, there was no hope of sailing back to England with her uncle on the ship's return voyage, but Captain Hatfield could, and undoubtedly would, safe-hand another letter from Charlotte to Sir Ian when he left.

By the time the *Chetwynde* returned from its next northern run, D'Arcy would have completed his secondment and would rejoin Her Majesty's Royals at Hyde Park Barracks. This would, of course, require him to take rooms in his London club, with Charlotte and her children, accompanied by Martha and Connie, residing happily at Hatfield Hall. In the meantime, thought Charlotte, lulled into complacency by her condition, with the joyous prospect of welcoming a new life into the world and having Dickon home at last, the six months or so left until then would be far less challenging than the time already spent here. Reaching for her journal Charlotte noted:

Such excitement today! Elias returned from a visit to the blacksmith to purchase a new latch for the side gate, with a copy of the Port Phillip Gazette, in which there is an account of the signing of The Act of Assent separating the Port Phillip District from the colony of New South Wales to our north. While my time here has been limited, it is heartening to see the jubilation with which this news has been reported. People who have a vested interest in the community —land owners, shopkeepers, artisans and other free settlers numbering some seventy thousand souls now — have been agitating for the right to govern the region as they see fit for nearly a decade, and at last they have won their independence.

Our friend, Lord Chalmondly, is quoted in the report as saying this acknowledges the contribution the Port Phillip District has made to Australia since settlement, sending two-fifths of the colony's total wool clip back to England off the back of its six million sheep, and signifies confidence in the potential for future growth — particularly in investment opportunities and, of course, the Union Bank.

Dark clouds hung low over the settlement, providing welcome relief from the searing sun of the Indian summer and brief respite from the brilliant, white-hot heat of the day ahead. Later, the cloud would lift, leaving a molten sun to beat down on the unshaded dwellings that dotted the scorched earth, and deplete the energy of those within. But for now, a cool sea breeze blew through open doors and windows, and Martha allowed herself to forego the fear that had beset her earlier in the night when D'Arcy had come home too early to be drunk enough for Baxter to drop him, comatose, on his dressing room bunk.

For Dickon's homecoming had occurred earlier than expected, precipitated by D'Arcy's deployment leading a detail across the northern border, and Dickon had made the transition from breast to cup sooner than most babies of his age. With D'Arcy away, Charlotte had seized the opportunity to bring her son home sooner than planned, wanting time alone with him to settle the boy back into his Jolimont home before she took to bed with the birth of his sibling.

Sergeant Baxter had thought the major's deployment would last for at least three months, and Florence had agreed to keep her own son on the breast long enough to ensure a strong flow of milk for the new baby when it arrived. All had progressed as Charlotte had happily predicted, with Dickon spending his first few days playing on a rug in the garden with Connie or, fatigued to the point of exhaustion by chasing Scamp up and down the back path, nestled in the crook of his mother's arm while he drifted in and out of sleep.

But D'Arcy's mission had been accomplished earlier than expected and he had arrived home that morning. Outraged to find Dickon home in defiance of his explicit instructions, he had ordered the child's return to the Wills' residence the following morning. Wisely, Charlotte had agreed to return Dickon to the Wills' cottage for a little while longer, and the rest of the evening appeared to pass peacefully.

But Martha's fear came flooding back as the silence was broken by the sound of stifled sobs. Stumbling from her bed, she ran swiftly to the boxroom where Dickon slept close by Connie, to see if the infant had wandered from his cot and lost himself in his as yet unfamiliar new home.

But Dickon was sleeping soundly, his tanned and happy face still and peaceful, a rag doll in the image of a long-legged Dalmatian, tucked into the crook of his plump little arm, a thumb resting between his open lips. He carried the doll everywhere, the bell sewn inside one of its feet serving to alert the household to his presence coming and going.

Martha's grimly-set mouth relaxed, and she stepped out of the boxroom into the breezeway to plunge the dipper into the water bucket and salve her dry throat. Somehow, with the need for constant awareness of the major's mood swings, she must have imagined she heard something disturbing. But the dipper slipped from her hand as more muffled sobs sent an involuntary shiver down her spine.

As was her habit when D'Arcy was at home and such a disturbance occurred, Martha moved silently through the doorway to the main house to stand to one side of Charlotte's bedroom door. D'Arcy was careful, as a rule, not to injure his 'investment', as he now referred to Charlotte quite openly when in his cups. She bore the abuse stoically, for the most part, but tonight, with Dickon home, D'Arcy's threats had substance.

So it was not to pry that Martha peered through the narrow gaps between the Victorian Ash panels but to assess the level of risk to Charlotte when she was so close to her time.

Many times, on hearing D'Arcy's raised voice and cruel taunts, she had wanted to burst in and demand he treat his wife with the respect she was due. But she knew she could intercede only once, for there was no doubt in her mind that dismissal would instantly follow unless she could persuade him to stop the abuse for good.

How that might be achieved Martha had no idea but she was resigned to leaving it in the capable hands of the good Lord. She knew only that when the time came that she could no longer contain her outrage, the action she took would have to be extreme, for if the major were to recover sufficiently from the surprise of a servant attacking a master, he would surely and righteously have her locked up. She had been brought to the brink before, however. The closest was early in Charlotte's pregnancy, when the young mother's weeping entreaty to think of the baby was met with threats so vile that Martha had been rendered immobile by shock. What followed had left Charlotte shaking with fear, as it was meant to. Stripping the covers from her body and the pillows from beneath her head, D'Arcy had stepped back as if to admire her form.

"Stand, madam," he had commanded.

Charlotte had reacted warily, raising her shoulders slowly to sit upright and so centre the weight of the infant within her before swinging her feet to the ground. D'Arcy had moved swiftly, grabbing a handful of her silken hair and pulling her roughly towards him. Trembling as she stood before him, Charlotte had flinched from the face held close to hers.

D'Arcy's ice-blue eyes then fixed her with a look of such chilling contempt that Charlotte seemed to shrink in stature, almost swooning at her husband's feet. Maintaining the grip that held her upright, D'Arcy had repeated the act of disrobing her as he had Connie on the only other occasion Charlotte had attempted to dissuade him from forcing himself upon her.

Relinquishing his hold on her hair, D'Arcy had then begun to disrobe himself. Fumbling from the effects of the rum he had consumed while Charlotte had waited, with growing apprehension, for him to join her for their evening meal, he first removed the military jacket and tossed it, carelessly, aside. Next, his belt, placed carefully across the bed, mute warning of the consequences of her failure to please. Then, as he bent to remove his boots, Charlotte had swayed and fallen to a position half sitting, half reclining on the bed. Without taking his eyes from hers, D'Arcy had straightened up to deliver a stinging slap to the side of Charlotte's face. Half fainting from the pain and shock, she had tried to struggle again to her feet. Reaching down with both hands, her husband had then clasped her tightly by the throat until she began to choke for lack of air. In an instant his expression had changed from fury to abject fear.

"Sweet Jesus, what have I done, what have I done?" he keened. "Live, wife, or I will lose everything …"

Charlotte's rapid gasps had eventually slowed to laboured breathing and she looked up, broken and bewildered. Believing the worst of the awful scene being played out before her was past, Martha had moved to creep silently back to her room. Before she could take a step, however, she heard Charlotte beg, again, for respite.

"Husband, please … please, allow me to rest," she pleaded.

"Hush sweeting, hush. You shall rest soon," D'Arcy crooned, his voice at once soothing but edged again with menace as, crouching over Charlotte once more, he eased himself slowly into her. His passion inflamed by the excitement of the assault, his release came swiftly. In seconds he had rolled away to the far side of the bed and exhausted by the effects of alcohol and lust, fallen into a deep sleep.

Safe, for the time being, Charlotte had risen from the bed in search of a fresh gown, and refuge in the sitting room. Silently, Martha had taken her to the stretcher in the major's dressing room where, with practiced hands, she worked diligently to ensure, as far she could, that this pregnancy would not end precipitously.

Now, once again, the menace in D'Arcy's voice held Martha at her watching post outside Charlotte's bedroom door. Charlotte, well into the last month of her pregnancy, was lying back against a mound of pillows, mute and still, bracing herself to endure D'Arcy's all-too-familiar litany of insults. D'Arcy stood at the end of the bed, a patina of sweat gleaming on his hairless chest, making him look, thought Martha, like one of the oiled and well-matched boxers on whom his comrades wagered whole sovereigns in the alleys behind the produce sheds. But this was no wager on well-matched combatants.

"Challenge your husband, will you, madam?" he said. "Your bastard will be returned to the Wills woman's care until I say he may live under my roof.

"And you, my dear, will learn to be a dutiful wife," he said, lurching drunkenly around the bed to fall, heavily, across Charlotte.

In that instant Martha knew the time had come for her to intervene, whatever the consequences. For it was not only Charlotte who was at risk. With her time so near, Martha feared for the life of her unborn child. Reaching into the depths of her work skirt, pulled on hastily to cover her flannel nightgown as she rose from her bed, Martha's questing fingers found smelling salts, a kerchief, her late husband's pocket watch, keys to the front and back doors and to the pantry... and the scabbard of the uniquely shaped knife Tom Newbold had given the day they disembarked from the *Chetwynde*.

Bursting into the room, she sent the door crashing back against the glass sconce shielding a flickering candle. Heedless of the shards of flying glass, she moved swiftly forward on bare, unfeeling feet. Snatching up the heavy silver candlestick from the night stand beside the bed, she swung it in a wide arc, bringing the solid base down on the back of D'Arcy's head.

With a low moan, he fell to one side, crashing to the floor to lie still and silent at Martha's feet. Speechless with shock, the two women watched the fallen figure before them attempt to rise, and then lie still. But to their horror, D'Arcy raised his head, one arm stretched out, eyes darting wildly from side to side, as if searching for something on which to gain purchase and pull himself to his feet. Dropping the candlestick, Martha delved in her pocket for Tom Newbold's knife, ready to drive it down into D'Arcy's back, if needs be, to subdue him once and for all. But with a long, rasping gasp D'Arcy slumped again to the floor, still and quiet.

Lifting her gaze to Charlotte, Martha recognised the signs of imminent birth as the colour drained from the younger woman's face at the pain of the first contraction, and all thought of the consequences of her assault on D'Arcy fled from her mind. Within minutes, Katherine Rose Hatfield D'Arcy entered the world oblivious to the drama taking place around her.

Wrapping the protesting infant in a sheet, extracted from bedclothes strewn across the floor, Martha laid her gently in her mother's arms and addressed the need to staunch the flow of birthing blood. Only then did she turn her attention to D'Arcy, covering him, hastily, with a heavy quilt just as Connie, woken by Charlotte's cries, appeared in the open doorway.

Martha moved quickly to restrict her view before the girl could make sense of the scene before her.

"Much has happened here, this night, child," she said, abruptly. "The major has met with an accident and his wife has just given birth. We must see to mother and child, and then we will attend to her husband.

"Fetch hot water, Connie – two jugs and a large bowl. And fresh towels. We must bathe the infant born this night, and minister to her mother. Hurry, there is no time to lose!"

Connie, responding to the urgency in Martha's voice, turned to run back into the kitchen even before Martha had finished speaking.

"Leave the water outside the door and then go back for my apothecary bag and as much clean linen as you can carry," Martha called after her, stepping out into the hall to watch her run through the curtained doorway and down the steps into the breezeway.

Hardly had the sound of Connie's scuttling footsteps diminished than there was a furtive scratching at the bedroom door signalling her return. Opening the door just wide enough to draw the bowl, water jugs and linen through the narrow gap between plank and architrave, Martha issued new orders.

"Secure young master Dickon in his cot, put on your coat and boots, and run down to the docks. See if you can find Tom Newbold. Sergeant Baxter says the *Chetwynde* was sighted sailing through the heads yesterday. If he is there, tell him Miss Charlotte has need of him.

"Wait!" she called, as Connie knotted her nightgown above her knees, ready to race back to the boxroom for her coat and boots.

Plunging her hand deep into her pocket, Martha pulled out the seaman's knife, still in its ornate silver scabbard, and thrust it towards the wide eyed girl.

"Give him this. And run swiftly, child," she said, thrusting the gleaming object into Connie's hand.

Facing the room again, Martha paused, momentarily overwhelmed by the scene before her. Blood from the wound to D'Arcy's head now marked the damask spread he had dragged from the bed as he slid to the floor. Charlotte had sunk back into the comfort of the goose-down pillows Martha had piled behind her to help her push. Both mother and the babe were lying still, eyes closed, exhausted by the journey they had just taken together.

Between Martha and the bed the floor was covered with shattered glass and bloody footprints. Looking down, she realised the blood came from her own feet, cut by shards of glass, and that she must attend to them before first light.

Taking up D'Arcy's discarded jacket she brushed aside the nearest shards and set down one of the jugs Connie had fetched earlier. Sinking to the boards she dipped her kerchief in the steaming water and worked methodically to cleanse the puncture wounds before applying a salve from her apothecary bag. After she had bound each foot with strips of thick flannel torn from the bottom of her nightgown, she pulled herself upright and stood first on one foot, and then the other, testing her endurance to the pain, throbbing now that the shock had passed. Satisfied that it was not so unbearable that it would disable her in the challenging hours ahead, she turned next to Charlotte and the new baby.

After washing her hands meticulously in more of the hot water poured into the crystal hand-basin decorating the wash-stand, she worked fast to rinse away the risk of infection. All too often, in the excitement following a birth – especially that of a male child – this might be put off until celebrations had taken place, and the consequences were clearly evident in the high number of deaths from childbed fever among otherwise healthy young women.

"Let go, Charlotte, my love," she whispered reassuringly, waking Charlotte to ease the newborn from her mother's grasp. "We must bathe the babe before young master Dickon sees her."

Katherine Rose – the names Charlotte had selected for a girl months earlier, keen to acknowledge Captain Hatfield's many kindnesses by naming the child for his beloved wife and daughter – was fully formed and breathing easily. But as she had with Dickon, Martha ran a finger across Kate's prettily pursed lips and inside her mouth, in search of that tell-tale sign of birth trauma, a cleft palate.

Aware of Charlotte's intense and questioning stare, Martha nodded approvingly, and summoning a smile said, "I think she'll do, my lady. As bonny a babe as I've ever delivered, despite her rapid entry into the world. You must both rest now, and gather your strength. I will attend to everything else."

"Oh Martha, what of Rollo? He is so quiet. Should we summon help?" Charlotte whispered, the euphoria of the safe delivery of a healthy infant evaporating as she reflected on the events leading up to the birth.

"Try not to think about it, my dear. D'Arcy will be taken care of,"

Martha replied, with far more conviction than she felt. "Help is already on its way."

For the next few minutes she gave her full attention to the baby, knowing it was critical to the survival of an infant, even one as sound as Katherine, that it was cleaned and comforted as soon as was practicable after delivery. Experienced midwives also knew that the more a small baby was soothed by the touch of loving hands and soft voices, the sooner it accepted the breast and took nourishment.

Testing the temperature of the water with her elbow, she eased the infant slowly into the large, enamel bowl Connie had used to carry jugs, towels and fresh sheets into the room before, feet flying, she had set off in search of Tom. At first flailing wildly at the new experience, Katherine eventually succumbed to the soothing touch of Martha's hand and allowed herself to be gently lathered, rinsed and patted dry before being wrapped in a fresh binder and returned to the crook of her mother's arm.

Replacing the soiled linen, Martha drew up fresh sheets and covered mother and child with a cashmere blanket taken from the arm of the wing backed chair in which Charlotte had made a habit of writing in her journal before retiring for the night. Before she could clear away the stained water and soiled linens, Tom burst through the front door, Connie hard on his heels. Sending Connie to release Dickon from his restraints, she led Tom into the bedroom, pulling the door shut behind them.

"God Almighty, woman," he breathed, fear constricting the sound issuing from his mouth as he took in the chaos before him. His glance falling on Charlotte, motionless upon the bed, with the baby still and quiet beside her, he turned towards Martha, his eyes wide and questioning. Martha shook her head, reassuringly; gesturing, instead, towards the mound of covered form, lying on the floor.

Holding out his hand, palm up, Tom's eyes travelled from the weapon balanced upon it to Martha's face and back across the room to what was obviously a form hidden under the comforter.

"Tell me, quickly, Martha. What happened here this night?" Tom demanded, his voice low and urgent.

Martha spared him nothing, no detail of the night's chilling events nor of D'Arcy's behaviour since leaving the *Chetwynde*. As she told of her vigils outside the bedroom door and the scenes she had witnessed on the other side of it, Tom's grey eyes alternately flared with anger and filled with tears. When she had finally finished talking, Martha was surprised to find her hands held fast in Tom's own. Releasing them, he wrapped her in his arms and held her close. In the ensuing silence, she was aware only of the comforting warmth of his body through the coarse woollen shirt stretched across his chest. Unprepared for her response to this sudden act of compassion, Martha pulled away to look up anxiously into the seaman's weathered face.

"Tom, lad. Might he still live?" she asked. "I could not bring myself to look upon that evil countenance to see for myself."

Releasing her, Tom strode across the room and pulled back a corner of the cover to expose D'Arcy's ashen features and tumbled black hair. He then leaned forward and pressed two fingers against D'Arcy's throat, finding only a slow and thready pulse.

"He may well be done for, my dear," he said, contemplatively. "Good riddance, too, if he is. And talking of being well rid of this piece of dog's dropping, I'd best get him out of this house before Miss Charlotte wakes and sees the results of your handiwork."

"What will you do with him, Tom?" Martha asked, shaking now the need to remain calm had passed. Her fear was not so much for herself, but for Charlotte, Connie and the children should the army discover that the life of an officer had been extinguished in such a manner – whatever the provocation. The punishment for murder in the colony, she knew, was death; and while Martha would willingly admit responsibility for the act – and accept the consequences – she knew that Charlotte and the children would be hard put to survive the journey back to England without her.

"Leave the major to me, Martha. The pressing question at this moment is what I am to do with you, Miss Charlotte and the babes?" he replied.

"We could not move Charlotte now, Tom," said Martha. "We must give her time to recover before we leave this place. But the major must be removed before the dawn throws light upon the awful events of this night."

"I think I have a plan, Martha," Tom responded. "Listen well, and follow my instructions carefully. Go to the produce store at first light, and announce the baby's birth. Say it was a pity the major was on duty and missed the opportunity to welcome his daughter into the world.

"Whatever you may hear about the circumstances of his discovery, you and Miss Charlotte must put all thought of the actions taken by yourself, or by others, from your minds.

"I will take him away where his discovery can pose no threat to either of you."

As Newbold stooped to test D'Arcy's weight, a soft whinny signalled the arrival of Sergeant Baxter, come to collect the major for the morning ride to the barracks.

Before either Martha or Tom could move, the door opened and Baxter's broad shoulders filled the doorframe. His glance travelling from Martha to Charlotte and Katherine to D'Arcy and then Tom, and the blood and glass, he strode into the room to assume control of what was, clearly, a desperate situation.

"Step aside, Martha," he ordered hoarsely, drawing his sword. "I will deal with this rogue!"

"This 'rogue', sir, is Tom Newbold," Tom responded, the scar running from eye to chin down one side of his face livid against the heightened colour of his ruddied complexion. "First mate aboard the *Chetwynde* under the command of Mistress Charlotte's uncle, Captain Hugh Hatfield. I am also kin to the cousin of the lad she should have wed instead of this ... *gentleman*."

"Martha, will you vouch for this man? And tell me, quickly, what is he doing here?" Baxter asked, lowering the tip of his sword from Tom's

134

throat as Martha told him of D'Arcy's behaviour that night, and her action to diminish the risk to Charlotte.

"He was dead asleep when I brought him home last night, so far in his cups I thought he was no threat to anyone," he replied, moving swiftly towards the bed. "Did he hurt her, Martha? Why is Charlotte lying there so still and quiet – and what of the babe?"

"Dear friend, they are both as well as can be expected no more than an hour since birthing." Martha replied. "They are sleeping peacefully now, which is more than I can say for the major, I fear.

"It is true he was in no state to pose a threat to anyone when you brought him home last night, but he awoke earlier than usual, still fuelled by his demon, drink, and began to torment his wife, regardless of her condition.

"In attempting to defend herself, she provoked him further, and he moved towards her, his arm raised to strike her. She twisted away and caught only a glancing blow on her forearm.

"He then he reached for her again, but the next blow was mine.

"Not expecting to see you before daylight, I sent young Connie running to the docks in search of the *Chetwynde* and Tom – the only man I could trust apart from yourself – to help us decide what should be done with ... the body."

"I planned to haul it aboard the *Chetwynde* and dump it when we are well out to sea," Tom broke in. "I could well use a hand getting him to the docks if you've a mind to help us."

"If an officer goes missing there will be an immediate search followed by a formal enquiry and endless questions, and we could not carry him through the crowded markets and onto the wharf without being seen and remembered," Baxter replied.

"It is better the major is found sooner, rather than later, and in circumstances requiring little explanation. We will dress him in his uniform, and sling him across the saddle of his horse – a familiar sight if we are observed on the way to where I will take him."

Nodding assent, Tom picked up D'Arcy's jacket and together, the two men dressed him in the uniform he had discarded when his assault on Charlotte began. Leaving the room, Baxter returned moments later, with a decanter of port taken from its permanent position on the campaign desk in D'Arcy's dressing room.

"I think the major is entitled to another tot or two," he announced, dousing the body with the contents before the two men, drawn together by their concern for the women each had sworn, separately, to protect, hauled their load out through the front door and up over the saddle of one of the two waiting horses. As they did so, a low moan emanated from the body balanced across the saddle on Charlotte's hunter. Swinging smartly up onto his own mount, the soldier reached down to grasp the seaman's hand; and before turning the horses he touched an index finger to the brim of his cap and lowered it to tap the side of his nose.

A grim smile on his tightly closed mouth, Tom returned the salute, acknowledging both the unspoken assurance, given and received, that the women and children left behind when the *Chetwynde* sailed would continue to be protected.

Retracing his steps along the tessellated pathway as the sound of horses' hooves diminished, Tom stepped up onto the terrace where Martha stood waiting for him to join her. Taking her arm, he seated her in one of the wicker chairs before settling himself in the other. Leaning forward, he placed a hand over hers and began the painful story he had planned to tell her in the presence of Charlotte, in much calmer circumstances.

"Martha, my dear, I had hoped this would be a joyous reunion for us all, with you and Charlotte and little Dickon coming aboard the *Chetwynde* and sitting around the Captain's table to share stories of your new life in Port Phillip Province, and ours on the high seas.

"As things have turned out, events here, this night, and aboard the *Chetwynde* on the run into Hong Kong, have determined otherwise. It is with the heaviest of hearts that I have to inform you of the death of our dear friend and Charlotte's uncle, Captain Hatfield.

"He had seemed well enough and in good spirits at the end of supper, as together we completed his customary tour of the vessel before repairing to his quarters.

"We discussed the weather and the repairs required when we tied up in Hong Kong, and how much we both looked forward to seeing what he called his 'Australian family' again. The Captain told me how he longed to embrace his beloved niece, and hoist young Dickon on his shoulders to view the world he will one day claim as his own.

"At that precise moment, a pod of dolphins broke the surface of the sea to race alongside us, their iridescent bodies reflecting the light from the full moon as they leapt in and out of the water, calling to us with their sweet and soulful song.

"Turning to me, the Captain laughed and said their mood matched his own, precisely. I took my eyes from his face for only as long as it took to glance back at the dolphins. But in that instant I heard a choking sound and, turning back, caught him in my arms as he fell to the boards, holding on to life just long enough to whisper Charlotte's name with his dying breath.

"I am not ashamed to say I wept over the body in my arms. A truer friend, a wiser mentor, no man has ever known. I know I shall never meet his like again."

Shaking his head, the hardy sailor released his hold on Martha's arm to brush the back of his hand across glistening eyes.

"We buried him at sea as he would have wished, with all due ceremony and few dry eyes – for the Captain was respected by crew and passengers alike for the care and compassion he showed to all aboard the *Chetwynde*, regardless of their station in life.

"Hours later, while packing up the Captain's quarters in preparation for the arrival of the new master, Ensign Frobisher and I came across a belted box containing the Captain's personal effects, including a portrait of his wife and daughter, and an envelope addressed to me.

"Inside the envelope there was a letter enclosing another envelope, sealed with red wax holding the imprint of the ship's anchor signet ring which he wore on this left hand, next to the wedding band his beloved

Katherine had placed on his finger, so long ago."

Pulling a crumpled piece of paper from his inside pocket Tom handed it to Martha. Walking back into the house, she leaned towards a candle to read the strong, scrawling script.

Tom, old friend, if you are reading this then I have left you to rejoin my beloved wife and daughter. Grieve not, for I need you to be strong to watch over my darling niece. I fear marrying a man she hardly knew for the sake of propriety may present more problems for her than it was meant to resolve.

Take the letter enclosed to my solicitors, De Villiers, Blenheim & Gaur, in the Temple, when you get home and they will know how to ensure she receives the love and support she so richly deserves.

Take my watch for yourself, as a remembrance of the calm seas and fearsome swells we rode out together on the bridge, and my signet ring, by which my legal representatives and all you meet with on my behalf will know you as my trusted representative.

Give my portraits of Katherine and Rose to Charlotte who will accept them as the most precious gift I have to give her. May the wind carry you safely on the rest of your own voyage through life, my friend. The weight of my wishes may prove a heavy burden but I know you will never falter. Your servant in death, as in life,

Hugh Worthington Hatfield, Capt.

D'Arcy's body was found later that same day, in bushes behind the tanning sheds where, according to a police report, published in *The Argus*, it had been dragged following an attack with knife and club.

There was no money in the major's uniform breeches, and his shirt and jacket reeked of alcohol. The area behind the tanning sheds being recognised as the location of gaming tents and sly grog shops, together with D'Arcy's well known patronage of such dubious establishments, his demise passed unremarked apart from expressions of sympathy sent to his widow, now in seclusion following the birth of their second child.

His assailants, assumed to have been more than one disgruntled fellow

138

gambler, given the number of blows to his head and the deep wound to his throat – from which the army surgeon determined he had eventually bled to death – would, in all probability, never be apprehended.

Tom paid one more visit to the bluestone house, his arrival unremarked among the messengers delivering notes of sympathy to the major's widow from concerned acquaintances, their calls postponed until Charlotte had recovered sufficiently from both his death and her confinement.

The *Chetwynde* would soon have a new master and possibly a new route, he told Martha. He could not say when he would return. But return he would, and he promised, while he was away, to do all he could to see that Charlotte and the children were brought safely home to Hatfield Hall. For Martha, if his plans worked out, there could be another safe haven.

Chapter Eight
STRIKING OUT

Major Roland Wellington Villiers D'Arcy's voluntary exile in Australia ended not, as he had envisaged, on his feet at last, the future master of Hatfield Hall, living in his London club on the income derived from a vast country estate, but on his back in a lead-lined pine box in the hold of the *MS Chetwynde*, destined for burial in the grounds of his father's remote Scottish holdings, far from the life to which he aspired.

The Chalmondlys would also be aboard the *Chetwynde* when she sailed on the morning tide, less than two weeks after she was sighted coming through the heads into Port Phillip Bay. But first, Sir Giles, who had concluded the business of establishing his new bank, had one last piece of banking business to see to before he conceded to his wife's desire to return to London to stand as godmother at the baptism of her sister's sixth child.

Childless, herself, Sir Giles explained when he visited Charlotte the day before their departure, his wife's presence at the baptismal ceremony meant a very great deal to Lady Chalmondly, as she had stood as godmother to the rest of her sister's brood. And now that his bank was operating efficiently under the stewardship of one of the finest financial minds in Europe – a gentleman by the name of Monsieur Louis Roderer – he was delighted to be in a position to indulge her.

"But I have not taken the liberty of intruding upon your recovery from the blessed event of your daughter's birth, and the tragic loss of your unfortunate husband, dear lady, just to talk about indulging my wife or, indeed, my business affairs," Sir Giles explained, so moved by Charlotte's fragile appearance that he held on to her proffered hand for a moment longer than mere courtesy required.

"I promised your father that I would ensure, as far as possible, the viability of a continuing income for your comfort and security based, as we had agreed, upon the interest derived from a capital sum he invested on your behalf in the Melbourne branch of the Union Bank. Here, Sir Giles paused to lead Charlotte to a chair he pulled out for her from a console table, placed to catch the light from a side window. Seating himself on the other chair, he spread open a large, leather bound ledger on the polished surface between them.

"However, dear lady, it is with the greatest regret that I must inform you that your husband's drawings, in the relatively short time you have been in the colony, have depleted that capital sum to such an extent that there is sufficient left in your account only to cover your expenses for the next three months."

Here, Sir Giles looked up from his ledger, more with anger than compassion in his eyes.

"Such is the law which, may I say I and others in my profession, hold in the greatest contempt, that upon marriage, such assets as a wife may hold pass to her husband to be managed at his discretion.

"I am afraid we had no reason to expect your husband would draw down your funds as frequently as he did. In fact, it was only when I asked Monsieur Roderer to prepare a statement for delivery to your father on my return to England that we discovered the extent of the depletion.

"I have since taken it upon myself to ask M'sieur Roderer to personally manage your affairs in so far as my bank is involved in them. I consider him to be a gentleman in every sense of the word, as well as an astute businessman. Consult him as soon as you feel you are sufficiently recovered to venture out again, or send a message to the bank requesting his presence here, and he will advise you in the privacy of your home."

Charlotte, knowing her husband's military stipend could not, by itself, support his addiction to alcohol and games of chance, had long suspected her father's generous contribution to the continuing support of his new son-in-law's wife and family would be unlikely to sustain them for an indefinite period. But she was, nevertheless, unprepared for it to have dwindled to such an extent that it might not last until the *Chetwynde* returned to carry them back into her father's forgiving arms and the sanctuary of Hatfield Hall.

"Sir Giles, I am indeed surprised by your news," she replied. "I am touched that you were kind enough during this busy period preceding your departure to deliver it in person.

"I am grateful, too, for your consideration in placing M'sieur Roderer at my disposal, for I am sure I shall need all the advice and guidance he can provide. I have much to learn about managing my affairs.

"Please rest assured I shall call upon him as soon as I feel I have recovered sufficiently to do so."

Hardly had Sir Giles quit the bluestone house than Elias opened the front door to admit Thérèse. At the sound of her voice, Martha emerged from the dining room where she had been sewing in companionable silence with Connie – her new charge, the infant Kate, in a wicker basket at her feet, while Dickon broke his busy day with a short, sound sleep on Elias and Nellie's bed.

"Thérèse, my dear, welcome," said Martha ushering her friend into the sitting room where Charlotte was seated at the console table, poring over the ledger left by Sir Giles for her detailed perusal.

"Charlotte, look who's come to see us," she said, sending Connie, hovering in the dining room doorway, to ask Nellie to put up the tea tray and bring it into the sitting room as soon as she could.

"Dear Thérèse, how good it is to see you. What news have you brought to brighten this day of unwelcome surprises?" Charlotte asked, gesturing towards the ledger she had just been studying.

But the expression replacing the smile which transformed Thérèse's face from unexceptional to surprisingly beautiful, sent an involuntary shiver down Charlotte's spine. Just then, Katherine reminded them of her presence with an outburst of indignant squeals signalling her need to be nourished. Retiring to the chaise longue, Charlotte loosened the bodice of her dress before taking the infant from Connie's arms and putting her to the breast. For, freed from the constraints of a controlling husband from the moment of the infant's birth, Charlotte had decided to defy convention and nurse this child herself.

"As you can see, Thérèse, we are doing very well," she said, responding to Thérèse's raised eyebrows with a winning smile, before looking down at the infant in her arms.

"And now that Dickon is home for good, I have vowed never to be separated from either of my children again until it is time for them to be sent away to school. But tell us dear friend, what prompts your sad expression?"

Just as Thérèse was about to speak, Nellie bustled through the sitting room door with the tea trolley bearing wafer-thin sandwiches and pastries still warm from the oven. Picking up more from the ensuing silence than she might from a torrent of words, the good woman glanced towards Martha, offering a quick, "I'll leave the pouring to you, ladies, the tea needs to brew just a little longer," before smoothing her apron, and retreating through the open doorway and hurrying back along the hall to the kitchen.

The tea trolley left untouched, Thérèse rose from her chair to stand in front of the empty fireplace, one hand upon the mantelpiece as if bracing herself to deliver the news she had come to share with the two women she held closer than any others in the entire world.

"Charlotte, Martha, I feel myself torn between happiness on the one hand and pain on the other," she said. "My employers, the Surgeon General and Mrs Trowbridge, have decided to remove their precious daughter's casket from the crypt beneath St Peter's where it has lain since she was so cruelly taken from us, and take it back to Buckinghamshire, where Helen can be laid to rest among other cherished members of her family.

"Dr Trowbridge has been given leave to quit his post on compassionate grounds, six months short of his two-year commitment, and he and Mrs Trowbridge will leave on the *Chetwynde* when she sails tomorrow ... and I am expected to travel with them."

Here, words deserted her, causing Martha, lost for words herself, to rise and draw her friend close until she regained her composure.

"The pleasure of returning to my beloved Paris is overshadowed by the pain of having to relinquish my friendship with you, Martha, and you, sweet Charlotte – and Connie and our dear children," Thérèse continued, moments later.

"Truth be told, there is nothing for me to return to in Paris, now. My father, a colonel in the French Army, left for Algiers five years ago, and we heard just one month later that he had fallen in the battle for Isley. I lost my mother, never a well woman, to the grippe less than a year later. And that was the end of my family, for I am their only child.

"When we met aboard the *Chetwynde*, I had been nursing the poor in the Hôpiteaux de Paris to be close to my mother. But when she left this life I was too sad to stay in Paris. Then I learned from the Interne that his colleague, in London, was looking for a nurse to care for his daughter on their voyage to Australia, and you know the rest of my story from there.

"But now, without Helen to care for, my time here has come to an end, and I am sad because in the relatively short time we have known each other, I have come to regard you as much more than just dear friends.

"Dear Martha, you are the sister I never had. Charlotte, you were as a sister to Helen whom I loved as if she were my own daughter. And Connie, Dickon and Katherine are as precious to me as nieces and nephews. That is why my heart is breaking, imagining what it will be like never to see you all again."

Silent while Thérèse described her anguish at the prospect of boarding the *Chetwynde* the next day, Charlotte disengaged her daughter from her breast and, handing the infant to Connie, walked across to the table on which rested the Union Bank ledger. Sitting down, she asked Connie to put Katherine into her crib and wake Dickon for afternoon tea in the kitchen, where Nellie would be sure to offer them sweet treats and fresh milk.

"Martha, dearest, will you pour the tea so that we might take a moment's respite to consider Thérèse's dilemma," she asked, turning the pages of the ledger as she spoke.

While Martha handed around the Minton, filled to the brim with pale, lemon and bergamot scented Lady Grey tea, Charlotte made hastily scribbled notes in her cream vellum, household accounts book, setting aside her pen after five or so minutes, with a satisfied smile.

"Ladies," she announced. "I am confident there is a way we might mend Thérèse's broken heart."

Taking a moment longer for Martha and Thérèse to taste the refreshing tisane, Charlotte unveiled the plan formulating in her head since Sir Giles bade her a regretful farewell.

"Dear Thérèse, let me assure you, at once, that our feelings for you are identical to yours for us. We have come to regard you as one of our own, drawn together by circumstances but bonded by mutual respect and affection, which prompts me to share with you my news, received today, which although disturbing, is at the same time empowering."

Tapping the ledger against which she had placed the open household accounts book, Charlotte explained, "It will come as no surprise to you to learn than my late husband is now revealed as an opportunist and profligate; his interest in me inspired by little more than the prospect of acquiring a comfortable income for the rest of his life.

"Although never remarked upon in my presence, his behaviour, I have no doubt, has been noted by our friends and his colleagues. But it was not until this morning that Sir Giles Chalmondly revealed that the sum my father deposited in the Union Bank to ensure that Martha, myself and my children served out our time here in relative comfort, has dwindled to almost nothing.

"Painful as it must have been for him, Sir Giles revealed the full extent of Rollo's duplicity. His constant drawings have left us in a precarious position. It has become apparent that our lives must take yet another direction."

Obviously, with Charlotte so recently having given birth, there could be no thought of leaving with Thérèse on the *Chetwynde* the next day. Besides, she had Nellie and Elias to think of; abandoned now, they would have no record of employment worth considering to show a new employer.

"To add further to my concern Sergeant Baxter brought more worrying news with him when he called on us last evening," she continued. "This house, like others in this area, is allocated to a serving officer; if, for whatever reason, that officer can no longer continue to serve, it must be offered to his replacement. My late husband's replacement will arrive on the *Argyle* in about four weeks. He was to join the New South Wales volunteers, but will now terminate his voyage here in Port Melbourne to serve in Rollo's stead.

"So you see, Thérèse, it is clear we must move on. And if, after you have heard what I have to say next, you are of a mind to defer your return to Paris, you may choose to come with us.

"If that is your wish, Elias will collect your effects from the Surgeon General's house this very afternoon, and you can move into what was the major's dressing room which has already been cleared of all his possessions."

Her voice clear and calm, Charlotte then went on to recount, in essence, the rest of the conversation she and Martha had had with Sergeant Baxter the previous evening.

Given his knowledge of the frequency of D'Arcy visits to the Union Bank, and being the bearer of news alerting Charlotte to the looming loss of the army residence in which the family was quartered, Baxter had been making inquiries about alternative accommodation. For they would have to live somewhere, he reasoned, until Charlotte recovered her strength sufficiently to attempt the long voyage back to England and, God willing, Hatfield Hall.

But accommodation was now in limited supply. News of the Bendigo gold strike had spread around the world like wildfire, bringing hordes of hopeful diggers and their families to the province in record numbers. And along with the diggers, came the businessmen, bankers, office bearers and spiritual leaders required to service the needs of the rapidly growing population, further limiting the availability of suitable accommodation for a woman of Charlotte's standing, with two infants and responsibility for one older child and three adults – four if that number were to include Thérèse which now seemed likely.

"It was then that Sergeant Baxter drew out a pamphlet from the inside pocket of his uniform jacket," Charlotte continued. "It pictured a country property which, his inquiries led him to believe, could be bought from the bank which now owned it, for a very low sum in consideration of its condition."

Taking the pamphlet from the back of the ledger in which she had placed it following Sir Giles' departure, she unfolded it to show a timber, two-storey structure with a wide veranda shading the ground floor from the worst of the sun.

"The sergeant tells me that although diminished in appearance by peeling paint, shutters hanging forlornly from broken hinges, and wild grass running rampant across what had once been well planned kitchen gardens, it could soon be made habitable.

"While some way out of the city on the road to the goldfields, he assures me the Blackwood Rest Hotel offers more than adequate accommodation for the family and, once refurbished, an opportunity to earn a return on the investment until the time comes when we are able to leave the colony."

The following morning Charlotte put away her mourning gowns and dressed herself, again, in her riding habit, knee-high boots fashioned from durable kangaroo hide by her Collingwood bootmaker, and a wide-brimmed straw hat purchased from the wicker shop next door.

Striding down the front path, she reclaimed her mare standing, ears forward, at the gate. Sergeant Baxter had requested temporary reassignment to help resettle the major's widow, while waiting for his replacement to arrive, and now stood ready to escort the determined young woman wherever she had a mind to go. Their first destination, she informed him was the Union Bank.

Slipping down from her small English saddle into Baxter's careful grasp, she unbuckled the soft leather saddle bag with its hand tooled, Hatfield crest, and strode purposefully up the shallow, stone steps, between the fluted Cathagian columns, and through heavy oak doors onto the vast, vaulted trading floor.

Presenting her card to the liveried porter, Charlotte informed him she was visiting the bank at the personal invitation of Sir Giles Chalmondly, and wished to speak with M'sieur Louis Roderer. Acknowledging the visitor's impressive credentials the veteran employee inclined his head in a courtly half bow, indicating by glance and sweep of arm a large leather settle, set on a Wilton carpet in the Chinoiserie style set behind looped crimson ropes. Once he saw Charlotte comfortably seated, he shuffled off towards the far end of the trading floor to tap respectfully on the new manager's imported mahogany door.

In what seemed no time at all, a Napoleonic figure, impeccably dressed in black tails and pin striped trousers, a white silk stock knotted neatly at his neck, strode the length of the room to brush his lips respectfully across the back of Charlotte's kid-gloved hand.

"*Enchanté, Madame*," he murmured, raising his eyes to engage hers just long enough to plumb their violet depths for character and intellect, instantly recognising the calibre of both.

"Forgive me, Madame," he smiled, releasing Charlotte's hand and straightening to stand less than a half head taller than his diminutive visitor. "Louis Roderer *à votre service*. Sir Giles has apprised me of your

148

position but failed to prepare me for the impact of your presence. If you would be so kind as to accompany me to my office, we may speak *en privé* ..."

"*Merci*, M'sieur Roderer. There is much to discuss,' Charlotte replied, accepting the Frenchman's proffered arm and allowing herself to be guided past the throng of gentlemen and shopkeepers, artisans and diggers doing business at the long, polished counter that ran the full length of the trading room floor.

Once insulated from the noise of raised voices and porters' bells calling for calm but, inevitably, adding to the cacophony, Charlotte seated herself across the desk from M'sieur Roderer, and unbuckled the saddlebag holding the documents she had brought to discuss with him. Before she could withdraw its contents, however, he rose from his high-backed leather chair to pour water from a crystal carafe into two long glasses, handing one to Charlotte. Accepting it gratefully, for the ride from Jolimont had been hot and dusty, Charlotte let the cool spring water soothe her throat and settle her nerves.

"In this climate, water revives the spirit like fine wine," Roderer opined, spreading his elbows wide on the desk and leaning forward to signal that he was now ready to engage in the business at hand.

Placing the ledger Sir Giles had left with her, the previous day, beside the pamphlet Sergeant Baxter had given her describing the proposed sale of the Blackwood Rest Hotel, Charlotte raised her eyes to meet those of her appointed advisor.

"M'sieur, as you are aware of my position – or should I say, predicament – you are obviously aware that it requires me to take urgent steps to ensure the comfort and security of my family until the *Chetwynde* returns in six months time to take us home to England and Hatfield Hall.

"It is my understanding that while my father had deposited a sum sufficient to sustain us for the duration of my late husband's posting to the colony, that sum has been depleted far more quickly than anticipated.

"To add further to my concerns, as a consequence of Major D'Arcy's

149

precipitate demise, the Army has served notice that it requires me to relinquish the quarters in which we are living for reallocation to his replacement at the end of the month.

"However, I believe fate might have intervened to provide us with both available and affordable alternative accommodation, and the prospect of an income sufficient to sustain my household until the *Chetwynde* returns," Charlotte concluded.

The bank manager had listened respectfully as Charlotte told him what he already knew about the circumstances in which she now found herself, his eyes never leaving her face, his mouth compressed, steepled hands held close to his face. Without looking down, he lowered his hands to rest on the pamphlet Charlotte pushed towards him.

"*Madame,* I know this property. Indeed, I was responsible for recovering it for the bank when the couple who lived there walked off the land owing more than they had borrowed to finance its construction.

"I might have been able to help them retain it if they had not had the stronger desire to return to England after their baby passed into God's arms. In the event, they left with only enough in their pockets to book passage for the two of them, leaving these shores three months ago.

"A familiar story, I am afraid. But I regret to tell you, *ma chere Madame,* that the property cannot be leased, it must be sold for the bank to recover its investment," he concluded, pushing the pamphlet back across the desk.

"But M'sieur, that is my intention," Charlotte countered. "I am here today to discuss that possibility. I have looked at the figures in the ledger Sir Giles left with me, and I believe there is enough remaining in the account my father entrusted to the Union Bank to purchase such a property, and still leave an amount for repairs and refurbishment.

"I have the help on hand to achieve both, and I am confident the hotel would not only accommodate my household but pay its way providing shelter for new settlers en route to the goldfields.

"The price of the property is not published in the pamphlet, but I believe that given its condition it must be open to negotiation. Please, M'sieur Roderer, name your price!"

Unused to being confronted by a woman in such a transaction – especially a *gentlewoman* – the banker found himself temporarily without recourse to speech or control of his facial expression. Recovering sufficiently to close his mouth and draw Charlotte's ledger towards him, he made a show of running his index figure down randomly selected columns.

Having been well briefed by Sir Giles, and understanding the underlying instruction that Sir Ian Hatfield's daughter was to be accommodated to the extent that her father, one of the London office's most favoured clients, would have no reason to question his confidence in the Union Bank, M'sieur Roderer allowed his finger to rest on the final figure in the account balance column. Subtracting an amount he estimated would cover the cost of repairs to the building and clearing the land, he then halved the balance remaining to settle on a price which would leave enough on deposit to see the D'Arcy household through the coming months until they could comfortably quit the colony. Any unexpected costs incurred could be carried forward against an amount to be recovered when the property was sold again at a more appropriate price – improvements and the gold-fed, rising market taken into consideration.

Pulling a sheet of pale blue vellum from the top drawer of his leather topped mahogany desk, he slowly and carefully dipped the gold tip of a quill into one of the three inkwells set into a silver and satinwood desk set, and signed his name in the middle of the page. Above that, he prescribed a set of numbers.

Completing the process by blotting his sloping script with even pressure from both his beautifully manicured hands on a soft, absorbent pad, he rotated the document and pushed it across the desk toward Charlotte.

"If the amount indicated meets with the result of your own calculations *madame*, I will have an agreement drawn up between yourself and the Union Bank and delivered to your residence by close of business today," he said, the hint of a smile rising to his eyes.

Glancing down, Charlotte saw immediately that the sale price proposed was far more affordable than she could possibly have hoped to settle for after what she had anticipated would be lengthy negotiations.

"M'sieur Roderer, I am prepared to agree to that figure immediately," she said, hardly able to suppress the quiver of excitement in her voice and, standing, thrust forward her right hand in what she fervently hoped signalled her *bona fides* as a newly established businesswoman.

With gravitas befitting the occasion, Roderer rose to shake Charlotte's outstretched hand. Unable to forsake his heritage, however, he quickly raised it to his lips, allowing his mouth to linger long enough to hide the delight that threatened to undermine Charlotte's newfound status.

Charlotte filled the anxious hours waiting for the contract binding the purchase of the Blackwood Rest Hotel to arrive at her Jolimont home, by responding to Katherine's imperious demands to be fed, after which she joined Martha and Baxter at the dining room table to plan the move to their new home.

Over a midday meal, consumed in the kitchen, Sergeant Baxter revealed he had discovered the Blackwood Rest Hotel while leading a routine detail to relieve the Native Police Patrol as they struggled to maintain law and order among the diggers traversing the many rutted tracks to the goldfields. It was not unusual for fights to break out as tempers flared, fuelled by heat, hunger and exhaustion on the arduous and often ill-prepared journey from the Port of Melbourne. Regular Native Police officers patrolled the route in both directions, to and from the gold miners' Mecca. For as well as skirmishes among the diggers on their way to the goldfields, bushrangers lay in wait for easy pickings from miners returning to Melbourne with knotted calico purses hung about their persons filled with the dust and nuggets for assay and safe keeping in Melbourne banks.

There were also frequent accidents caused by broken wheel shafts when the wooden wheels on bullock carts piled high with furniture, tools, sacks of grain and anything else diggers and their families considered essential to survival in the diggings, bounced and braced against unforgiving rock or stuck fast in oozing, axle high mud.

It was while tending the injured after just such an accident that the sergeant had come across what was to become Charlotte's new family home.

The Blackwood Rest Hotel, although deserted, offered the only available shelter after Diggers Rest along the Melbourne to Bendigo road, and he had ordered his men to stretcher a bleeding woman and her two bruised and shaken children into the building, remaining with them while the rest of his detail recovered the cart, the beasts and their load from the ditch. As the injuries were superficial rather than life threatening, Baxter left the woman and children to rest while he went in search of water and whatever else he might find to revive and speed them on their way. Water he found in plentiful supply from a hand worked pump tapping directly into a bore drilled by the previous occupants. There was even a bucket which he filled and left with the family while he inspected the rest of the building in which his detail might well need to spend the night.

The bones of the structure, he discovered, knocking on walls and testing stairs and floorboards with his full body weight, were strong and secure; the lathe and plaster walls separating high-ceilinged rooms showed no crumbling cracks, and, surprisingly, the breezeway had not yet been plundered for its wood fired stove, the firestones lining the open hearth or the solid pine bench that ran the length of one packing case wall. There was even a cast iron, claw-foot bath in the outhouse whose weight alone made it an immovable fixture.

By the time the bullock team had been reharnessed to the righted and reloaded cart, the family had recovered sufficiently to continue on their way, and Sergeant Baxter had completed his tour of inspection, retrieving one of a number of sales bills describing the property from the floor by the door and stuffing it into his jacket pocket.

Charged with the responsibility of rehousing the late major's family, and appreciating the difficult position in which D'Arcy had left them, it occurred to him that divine intervention might just have presented him with the solution to his problem.

Seated, now, at the kitchen table with Charlotte and Martha, as Charlotte, her pale English complexion suffused with a becoming rosy glow, recounted her conversation with Louis Roderer word for word, he was certain it had.

With Dickon and Katherine both sleeping soundly out of the worst of the midday heat, Connie, too, had been drawn into the conversation about the prospect of the Blackwood Rest Hotel as both a home and a viable source of income.

Nellie was soon persuaded to set aside her preparation for the evening meal, leaving vegetables drawn from Connie's tiny kitchen garden, now lush with the results of Elias' extensive digging and pruning, to soak themselves clean in water drawn from the rain barrel. Elias, concerned about the unaccustomed level of excited conversation, poked his head questioningly around the breezeway curtain hung to keep the flies out, and was quickly beckoned inside to offer an opinion on the planting required to sustain not only the family but the paying guests Charlotte counted on to break their journey to the goldfields at the Blackwood Rest Hotel.

When Thérèse arrived home from the Melbourne hospital where she now spent her mornings, Charlotte reconvened the meeting around the larger, dining room table in the front of the house, where they would be sure to hear the knock on the door when the messenger arrived from the Union Bank bearing the all-important document of sale for Charlotte's signature. They had only just settled in their seats when a tap on the front door summoned Elias, in his butler role, to spring quickly to his feet to admit the document bearer: M'sieur Roderer, himself, stood poised in the doorway.

Greetings exchanged, with each of the individuals present introduced by their name and role within the D'Arcy household, M'sieur Roderer assumed his role as a fiscally responsible executive officer of the organisation which employed him. Accepting the seat Elias had vacated he spread out a set of papers in front of him, and drawing a silver-topped ink bottle from the crested satchel he balanced across his pin-striped knees, he positioned the gold tipped quill pen he had used earlier that day beside it on the shining surface of the table in front of him.

Addressing Charlotte, he began, "*Madame,* it is indeed a pleasure to place this document before you. I am delighted to be able to tell you that Sir Giles, himself, approved the figures presented for your consideration before leaving the bank to join Lady Chalmondly on the *Chetwynde* in time to sail on the evening tide.

"Any concerns I might have had about your capacity to manage such a move into what must be considered not merely a new home but a challenging business venture, were allayed by Sir Giles' assurance that as Sir Ian Hatfield's eldest child, you would have been well-schooled in the running of a large rural establishment.

"In his view you would also have been well-aware of the responsibilities involved in the care and wellbeing of not only your immediate family and retainers, but a continual flow of visitors who may stay a day, a week or longer according to the season and their social commitments.

"So, *chere Madame,* if you care to affix your signature to the page before you, I will then countersign it, and we can celebrate the acquisition of your new home and your first business venture."

Chapter Nine
STAKING A CLAIM

Both Sergeant Baxter and Louis Roderer had recommended the purchase of a six-beast bullock team and a long board, flat-topped cart, rather than hiring a rig to transport the contents of the Jolimont cottage to Blackwood. Reluctant to outlay so much of her precious capital at the start of her new business venture, Charlotte had been persuaded by Baxter's assertion that such an investment could be secured at a very reasonable price from a gentleman farmer who had made his first fortune on the back of his sheep, and his second from the sale of his land, parcelled into claims between gold rich Bendigo and Ballarat. Word had gone round that he would offer his rig for whatever it fetched once it was unloaded on the wharf when he sailed for England. He also pointed out the potential return from hiring out the rig to others on their way to the goldfields, once Charlotte and her household had arrived at their destination.

But it was with some trepidation that she watched the same team of soldiers who had moved Martha, Connie, Dickon and herself into the bluestone cottage on their arrival in the colony, tie down the last piece of blanketed Hatfield furniture onto the long-board tray. Their cheerful assurances that they would be on hand to steady the load every step of the way, prompted her to send up a silent prayer of thanks to whichever God was guiding them to the goldfields for providing them with the resourceful sergeant who would be leading the detail as guide and protector.

By now, Nellie and Elias Smallridge also considered themselves members of Charlotte's growing family and had agreed, without hesitation, to be part of the remove to the new location. In accordance with everyone's wishes to contribute to the success of the new family business, roles were allocated according to skills required to turn the dilapidated hotel into a warm and welcoming country home – for that was how Charlotte intended to encourage travellers to break their journey at the new Blackwood Rest Hotel.

Charlotte would head the household and manage the accounts with assistance from M'sieur Roderer, visiting monthly. Martha would assume the role of Housekeeper, overseeing Nellie as Cook and recruiting local help to take care of the cleaning. Thérèse and Connie would care for Dickon and Katherine. Elias would be responsible for recovering and maintaining the kitchen garden, general maintenance and the stock – so far numbering the bullock team, four caged chickens and one dairy cow with calf at foot, tied to the back of the bullock cart on which Nellie now sat beside Elias in the driver's seat. Elias having managed a heavily laden hay cart pulled by a pair of hard mouthed Clydesdales prior to his arrest and transportation, had been considered the most likely candidate for this position.

M'sieur Roderer had generously loaned Charlotte his own well-sprung carriage and pair for herself, Martha and Thérèse, Connie and the infants – and Scamp, who had refused to be separated from Dickon since they first set eyes on each other. But Charlotte had opted to ride her sure-footed hunter beside Baxter, ahead of the bullock cart, to lead the convoy on their journey to a new future.

In this, they were assisted by members of the Native Police Patrol, trusted indigenous Australians first recruited a decade earlier to resolve disputes between new settlers and the original owners of the land on which imported cattle now grazed. With the discovery of gold, however, they were now deployed to maintain law and order among the diggers. Sergeant Baxter and his detail had ridden in support of William Barrundi's patrols on several occasions, most recently to assist in the rescue of the family he had had taken to the deserted Blackwood Rest Hotel to recover from their injuries just three weeks earlier. He was confident Sergeant Barrundi knew the safest route through the maze of tracks and trails leading from Melbourne to the goldfields as far to the north as Ballarat and Bendigo.

The carriage and pair now followed the bullock cart with William Burrindi's younger brother, Charlie, in the driver's seat. The rest of Sergeant Baxter's hand-picked escort – privates 'Fast Eddie' Jackson, Bill Tiler and Charlie Wills – followed behind, with each man taking his turn to ride up on the box seat, facing backwards to keep an eye out for bushrangers emerging from the scrub to steal whatever they could from unwary new arrivals bound for the goldfields.

Thus Charlotte's well-equipped, well-protected convoy fared far better than most as they progressed through the meandering tracks often ending in impenetrable forest or axle-breaking gullies. Evidence of the fate of other families who had set out with no tracker, and no idea of the hardships waiting for them en route to the diggings, lay all around them. Rain-soaked furniture, bedding and clothing was abandoned where it had fallen from broken down bullock trays, handcarts, wheelbarrows and perambulators piled high with tools and tarpaulins pushed along by men, women and even children, travelling on foot across the unimaginably tough terrain.

The most pitiable sights, Charlotte reflected, later, in her journal, *were the women with infants at breast and children, barely able to walk, hanging on to their mothers' skirts, their faces wet with tears of hunger, thirst and fatigue, their menfolk striding on ahead in search of an unclaimed piece of land on which to throw up a tent – most often just a blanket held up by saplings – to house their families and lay claim to what they had wagered everything would be the mother lode waiting for them in the ground below.*

Having stopped twice on their journey long enough only for Charlotte to dismount, hand the reins of her hunter to Sergeant Baxter, and climb into the carriage to put Katherine to the breast in some measure of privacy, Charlotte's relief was palpable when William Burrindi waved the convoy off the track into a sheltered clearing as the sun commenced its descent. Ahead was a low lying water course and the bullock team, smelling water, had picked up their pace in anticipation of drinking their fill. But as William explained, a tired team would more easily succumb to the churned mud of its well-trodden approach and have to be dug out.

While Sergeant Baxter deployed his men in defensive positions around the women and possessions, Elias skirted the hazardous approach to the water course, seeking sounder footing at the water's edge, where he could fill the two buckets he carried to settle the beasts before they made a run for the wider crossing. Repeating his trip twice in order to settle each pair, he then led the horses, two by two, to the water's edge, returning one last time, with Scamp barking excitedly around his feet, to collect water for the cow and calf at the back of the bullock cart.

Meanwhile, Baxter had turned his attention to the carriage passengers. There was little talk among the women as he handed them down onto the hard, dusty ground, their tongues stilled by shock, as well as thirst and fatigue, by what they had experienced so far. Even Dickon, woken from a deep, heat-induced sleep, stuck his thumb in his mouth and crawled back into Connie's lap as she settled herself on a blanket Nellie spread out over the dried, yellow stubble that passed for grass.

One by one Martha, Thérèse, and Charlotte – with Katherine, well fed and now sound asleep in her mother's arms – took their places beside Connie on Nellie's blanket. The only water carried on the convoy being reserved for drinking, there was none to waste on rinsing the dust from their faces. The precious commodity drawn in measured drafts from a screw topped water bag, passed carefully from hand to hand, had to last until they came across spring water or arrived at their destination – whichever came first.

Glad of respite from the rocking, jolting and jarring of the past few hours, and revived by assuaging their thirst even sparingly, the women thought to visit a tented shop a few yards further on between

159

the clearing in which they rested and the water course up ahead. But William, supported by Baxter, was keen to make camp for the night on the other side of the river, well away from the tent selling utensils, beef jerky, salt, sugar, flour and water. For it also doubled as a sly grog shop. By nightfall, the seasoned troopers told Charlotte, drunken diggers could turn feral and go walkabout in search of what they delicately described as 'entertainment'.

Thanks to Sergeant Baxter's planning and preparation, William and Charlie Burrindi's native skills, the protection provided by privates Jackson, Tiler and Wills and Elias' sorely tested driving ability, the weary convoy arrived at the Blackwood Rest Hotel near the end of the following day: tired, sunburnt and thirsty but otherwise little the worse for wear.

"Sergeant Baxter, we are all too weary to even think about unloading the bullock cart and hauling furniture into the house at this time of day," said Charlotte, sliding down from her horse and tying the reins to the rail along the outer edge of the front veranda.

"Let us take care of the beasts and the horses, and set up camp right here in the courtyard, just as we did last night. It will be far less taxing to set up the tents."

"As you wish, Ma'am," Baxter replied, dismounting and hitching his own horse beside Charlotte's; William Burrindi and the troopers following suit before they set about setting up shelter for the women and children. And while Elias released the bullocks into the post and rail pen at the back of the house, Charlie Burrindi unharnessed the carriage pair to secure them in stalls inside an open, tin-roofed shed which also gave a measure of protection to a few remaining bales of hay. The precious dairy cow they tethered close to the backyard pump, knowing the demanding calf would not stray far from its mother. The chickens and young Scamp were let loose to wander at will, but hovered close in hopeful anticipation of scraps from the evening meal, for which Nellie was already unloading pots and pans.

By the time the animals were fed and the backyard bore had given

160

up enough water through its protesting pump to satisfy both beasts and horses, Nellie had a fire going in a ring of rocks borrowed from the edge of the sweeping drive. Two pairs of bush pheasants, trapped by the Burrindis before any of the others were awake that morning, and hung from the underside of the cart all day, were now plucked and turning on improvised spits over the leaping flames. On the hot stones at the edge of the fire slabs of damper, hastily fashioned from flour and water seasoned generously with bush herbs and salt, rose slowly to catch the juices from the slow-roasting birds.

"Come, Nellie, the meal will cook itself now, let us inspect our new home," Charlotte called from the veranda where she waited with Martha, Thérèse and Connie to discover what lay on the other side of the swinging front door.

Once inside the women went from room to room, exclaiming at the pressed tin ceilings, wide casement windows and sound hardwood floors. The two front rooms, leading off left and right from the wide front hall, would serve well as guest sitting and dining rooms, Charlotte noted. Each featured a large, Adam fireplace and French windows opening onto the shaded front and side verandas. Two more large rooms, whose French windows led onto the veranda at each side of the house, offered more than enough space to accommodate in one, sitting and dining room furniture from Jolimont for the exclusive use of the family; in the other, the large partner desk M'sieur Roderer said he and Charlotte would need to work at together on his monthly visits. Two mahogany bookcases, four high backed leather chairs, a chesterfield sofa and a console table, plundered from the Union Bank's store rooms vault, completed the family library.

"Oh Ma'am," Nellie marvelled on registering the size of the wood fired stove, and the wide, scrubbed pine bench running almost the entire width of the back wall in the iron roofed breezeway. Shelving above the bench provided space for plates, dishes and cooking utensils, while a door opening off the end of the bench led into a corridor with three more doors leading into long, narrow store rooms, each with a high, barred window.

"Like a row of soldiers," said Connie, expecting to be sharing one of them with empty boxes once the family's possessions were all unpacked. Instead, the first was lined with pantry shelves, leaving room between the bottom shelf and the scrubbed pine floor for storage bins and water buckets. The second, with its key-locked cupboards, polished cedar bench, cast brass coat hooks set into the wall beneath a high, wide shelf, beside a numbered bell system, proved to be a butler's pantry.

In the last of the three store rooms, the fading light revealed a flagged, stone floor with an iron-hinged trap-door set against the far wall. Against another, below a wide pine bench, shallow pans held the promise of thick cream, on its way to becoming bright yellow butter, by way of the churn now standing idly in front of a bench. On the third wall, a tall, wire-sided meat safe stood sentinel beside a solid butcher's block. On closer inspection, when raised, the trap-door led down symmetrical stone steps to a cool room built into the bluestone footings. Dusty wine racks lined one wall and hooks for hanging sides of beef, sheep and game, another.

Walking back into the front hall Charlotte noted that the staircase, although every other banister rail was missing – burned, no doubt, when freezing winter rains waterlogged the wood pile – seemed sound in every other respect. Nevertheless, the women trod and tested every stair as it took them up to an open gallery, giving way to sleeping accommodation and a hallway through to the back stairs.

At first light the following morning, leaving Connie in the tent with Dickon and Katherine, the older women tucked their hair into bonnets, wrapped their skirts in calico aprons, and set about sweeping the dust and detritus from the slowly waking hotel.

Outside, while Elias fell naturally back into routine he had known in a previous life, feeding and watering the stock, Sergeant Baxter and his 'lads' – Martha's collective title for Wills, Tiler and Jackson – set about rehanging the front door, repairing shutters and reconstructing the bungalow the Smallridges had collapsed and loaded onto the bullock cart on their departure from Jolimont. Now re-erected against the back of the house, the troopers had cut a door through to it from the hall off the kitchen, giving immediate access to the heart of the house whatever the weather.

Sensing the scale of the cleaning work the women had faced, Charlie Burrindi had walked over the rise behind the hotel to fetch his sister, Assunta, to offer an extra pair of hands in the house and two of his cousins to help Elias check post and rails around the stock pen and the perimeter fences. By mid morning, the floors had been swept clean and every flat surface had been scrubbed and the boys were tying off the last of the wires in the home paddock.

The women unanimously agreed Assunta – so named by the nuns who raised her when her mother died, but soon shortened to 'Sunny' reflecting her disposition – had turned out to be a blessing. After joining the 'boss lady and her sisters' sweeping and scrubbing floors, shelves and bench tops, and polishing the furniture the men unloaded and carried into the big house, she had begun to clear away the dead leaves from the vegetable patch in the kitchen garden, patiently digging out the few remaining carrots and potatoes surviving deep in the rock hard soil. As her brothers had hoped, it was agreed she would join the hotel household as general indoor help, and as soon as she had learned the basics, Nellie's assistant.

With the ground-floor designated guest and family living areas, consideration had to be given to how the bedrooms might be allocated before Wills, Tiler, Jackson and the Burrindi boys heaved the heavy bedroom furniture through the breezeway and up the back stairs.

The first front room off the corridor to the right of the upstairs, central hallway would be taken by Charlotte, so as to be immediately available should circumstances require her presence downstairs when the rest of the household was sleeping. Martha and Thérèse agreed to share the second. The two facing dormer rooms to the back of

163

the house would be given over to Connie, Dickon and Katherine as bedroom and nursery. The corresponding rooms to the left of the central hallway would be held for guests, in order of need and priority. On that side of the house, each room afforded expansive views across the undulating countryside to the goldfields where, if viewed through a telescope, one might make out ant-like colonies of men and women sieving ankle deep in streams and gullies, digging into the blade-breaking earth or chipping away at glinting rock. Two smaller attic bedrooms, built into the high, pitched roof, were to be held, permanently, for Louis on his monthly visits, and Reginald Baxter, whenever he found himself in the area.

The rich elm bunks and marble-topped chests built for Charlotte and Martha on their voyage out aboard the *Chetwynde* would suit the room allocated to Martha and Thérèse. Charlotte's curtained double bed, wardrobes, chest of drawers and wash stand could all be accommodated quite comfortably in her room. The major's stretcher, Dickon's cot and Katherine's crib fitted easily into their bedroom; the campaign table and folding chairs from Charlotte's shipboard stateroom given new purpose in the nursery. In the morning, the bullock team would be turned around and driven back to Melbourne by one of William and Charlie's cousins, to collect beds, wash stands, chests and armoires, purchased by Louis on Charlotte's behalf at one of the frequent dockside auctions, to furnish the guest rooms.

The last items to be unloaded from the bullock cart were the travelling trunks containing the women's wardrobes and the children's clothes. There was also a locked, lacquered box containing a certificate recording Charlotte's marriage to D'Arcy and documents attesting to his commissioning as an officer in Her Majesty's Service. And wrapped in black tissue, the silk flowers securing the veil Charlotte had worn to hide her tears for Richard at her wedding to D'Arcy. Someday, Charlotte knew, she would have to face the fear she felt at the mere mention of D'Arcy's name to share the contents of the box with his daughter.

164

By the end of the day – the third since they had left Jolimont, Charlotte pronounced the house habitable enough for them to move into. With Sergeant Baxter, Privates Wills, Tiler and Jackson and the Burrindi brothers forming a guard of honour, Charlotte, Martha, Thérèse and Connie, Katherine in her arms and Dickon holding on tightly to her skirt, walked in procession up onto the front veranda to the front door. Just as Charlotte reached for the now gleaming brass doorknob, it was opened from within by Elias, having hurriedly changed out of his work clothes into clean moleskins, a white linen shirt and a shiny black waistcoat.

"Welcome to the Blackwood Rest Hotel, Madam," he intoned with due solemnity. Lined up behind him, Nellie coughed, self consciously, before dropping a formal bob, while Sunny's unaccustomed reserve gave way to a fit of the giggles, setting the whole company off as Charlotte, her family and the honour guard trooped in over the threshold.

At Charlotte's insistence, they all took their places around the long, formal dining table – a lucky acquisition along with twelve balloon-back chairs, purchased at a clearance sale the day before the bullock cart was due to be loaded. But before they could raise their glasses to christen their new home with 'Adam's Ale' as Elias described the pump water with which he had filled two large, crystal jugs, there was the unexpected sound of horses pulling up outside, followed by a familiar voice, hallooing through the open front door.

"Your first guests have arrived, *Madame*," M'sieur Roderer announced, as he appeared in the dining room doorway. "May I introduce my brother, Father Claude Roderer, who might be just in time to bless this auspicious occasion, the table, everything on it, and everyone around it."

Clapping her hands, delightedly, Charlotte rose to embrace the new arrivals. "Dear Louis," she cried, forgoing formality and surprising the bank manager by kissing him on both cheeks in the French style. Crossing herself quickly, she turned her attention to the priest.

"*Bienvenue*, Father, please remove your riding coats and share with us this, our first meal in our new home," she smiled, gesturing to Elias who was already holding out both arms for the Roderers' ankle length coats, while Charlie ran outside to hand their horses to his cousins, and Wills and Jackson hauled in two of the high backed chairs from the back office.

Father Claude's grace was mercifully short – for all around the table had been too busy cleaning, unloading and positioning furniture all day or, in the Roderers' case, riding hard to reach Blackwood before sun down, to stop and eat. Gratefully, they were soon devouring more roasted birds caught by the Burrindi brothers, together with Nellie's damper and Sunny's foraged carrots and potatoes, cooked as had been their last meal, on the glowing camp fire at the edge of the driveway.

Her long hair shaken loose from the dust bonnet she had worn all day, wet curls clinging to the sides of her face from the hasty ablutions performed by the women under the gushing pump, violet eyes shining as she glanced at each man and woman seated at her table, Charlotte was more beautiful at that moment than even Martha had ever seen her, a fact not passing unnoticed by Reginald Baxter and Louis Roderer in particular. The spell she cast broken, for the moment, by the need to excuse herself from the table to satisfy Katherine's need for sustenance, Charlotte mounted the stairs to the nursery, content to nourish her baby and reflect on her good fortune as the muted talk and laughter echoed up from the ground floor.

Rejoining the assembled company, the table lighted now by tall, beeswax candles, she inclined her head to indicate the men should resume their seats while she remained standing. Waiting only long enough for a break in the conversation, she held up her hands to ensure she had engaged them all – including Sunny, who had been persuaded to sit in with her brothers.

"Dear friends ..." she began. "I have mourned the joy and community of family gatherings missing from my life since leaving the only home I ever knew to embark on a voyage into the unknown these many months since. But your many kindnesses and unstinting support have shown me that it is not where you live your life that creates a home and a sense of belonging, but how you live it and with whom. I believe I have now found mine and I hope that you will think of the Blackwood Rest

Hotel as your home away from home wherever you find yourselves in the future. For you are all now part of this place, cherished members of my Blackwood family."

Even the redoubtable Reginald reached for his kerchief before pushing to his feet to raise his glass, clear his throat, and offer an improvised loyal toast. "Queen, country and Miss Charlotte – wherever, forever," he intoned, remaining on his feet while the others – even the Frenchmen, foreswearing their loyalty to the *Republique* for the purpose of toasting Charlotte – stood to drain their glasses.

A full moon hanging blindingly bright in the star studded sky, and sputtering candles sending out signals that it was time for them to retire, Sergeant Baxter, speaking for Wills, Tiler and Jackson as well as himself, begged Charlotte's permission to withdraw. With a day's hard ride back to Melbourne ahead of them, the tent, hitherto occupied by the women and children, tonight offered a few precious hours of unaccustomed luxury to the weary troopers.

The Burrindi brothers also scraped back their chairs. Preferring to sleep in the open, they asked to be allowed to set out their swags on the back veranda. They had promised Sergeant Baxter they would remain in Blackwood for two more days to see Charlotte well settled before pushing on to Ballarat to inspect licences held by diggers already well entrenched in the area – an unpopular task added to their role in recent months. On their way back to Melbourne they would call in to the hotel to pick up the bullock team and rig, which Charlie would drive back to pick up the furniture required for the guest rooms. Taking their cue from the soldiers, Louis and Father Claude also rose to take their leave of the women – all but Charlotte showing signs of fatigue after almost eighteen arduous hours followed by a hearty and relaxing meal.

Showing the Roderers to one of the attics furnished, temporarily, with a camp stretcher and a washbowl set upon a small console table, Charlotte offered to sleep with Dickon in the nursery so that Father Claude could occupy her room until the bullock cart returned with more furniture. A true Jesuit, the priest would have none of that, preferring, instead, to throw down the swag strapped to the back of his saddle beside the stretcher in his brother's room.

Persuading Nellie and Elias to store what little remained of the evening meal in the meat safe and leave the dishes, for once, where they sat on the dining room table, Charlotte saw Connie to bed, looked in on soundly sleeping Dickon and Katherine, and went outside to take a quiet walk around the house, exercising great care not to wake the Burrindis, already sound asleep on the warm boards of the back porch.

Chapter Ten

DIGGING IN

Within four weeks of moving into the Blackwood Rest Hotel, Charlotte had lost count of the number of families seeking shelter on the roads to and from the diggings. Exhausted men, women and children who came knocking at her door, desperately in need of respite from the drenching rain turning dusty tracks into a morass of mud that stuck and held fast to cart wheels and poorly shod feet and turned sacks of precious salt, sugar and flour into moulding slime.

All the rooms set aside for paying guests were filled as soon as they were vacated, sometimes accommodating whole families in each one. Often, the best she could offer the spent travellers was cover under the tin roofed shed, up out of the mud on beds of hay bales. Their beasts and stock, such as had survived, stood with their heads down and their hind-quarters turned against the slanting, freezing rain, ankle deep in water in the back paddock.

Nellie kept two cauldrons of opossum stew, the gamey flesh flavoured with onions, carrots and a few small potatoes Elias had found rising from the ground of their own accord as the waterlogged vegetable patch oozed and moved. Twice a day, Nellie and Elias would take hold of a handle on each side of a cauldron and cross the treacherous distance from house to shed to ladle out bowls full of the steaming hot contents to the 'outside guests'. They also took back wet clothes and blankets to dry them around the big wood fired stove, returning them as soon as they could to still the shivering of the men, women and children sheltering among the hay bales.

For this, Charlotte insisted, there was never a charge. But Martha's mantra, *What goes around, comes around*, was to prove true as word soon spread of the kindness encountered at the Blackwood Rest Hotel. Grateful diggers, having welded themselves into a solid community in protest at the government's unrelenting stance on licence fees, took care of their own. It became the custom for those on the road back to Melbourne to deposit their gleanings to stop off at the Blackwood Rest Hotel – paying not only for their own accommodation but, like as not, leaving a contribution towards the cost of caring for the 'outsiders'.

By Louis' third visit to audit Charlotte's books, his brother, Claude, had become a permanent guest, moving up off the floor in his brother's room onto the stretcher while his brother was in Melbourne, and back down onto his pallet when Louis was in residence. Sharing the room in this fashion, he explained, met the strict tenets of his vocation, and would serve him perfectly well until he could move into the cell awaiting him at the mission being built in Bendigo, to the north, for having been given permission to practice in the goldfields until the building was completed, the Blackwood Rest Hotel offered more than just convenient accommodation. Speaking only limited English, Father Roderer had found evenings spent in the company of Thérèse provided an opportunity to converse in his own language and thus learn more about the people in his new parish.

Thérèse, sharing Claude's concern for the plight of the diggers and their families, was keen to contribute whatever she could to help him answer their practical, as well as their spiritual, needs. Growing up in France with a father in the army, she had picked up enough German and Italian to be able to coach him to the point he could communicate with those who had flocked to Victoria from Europe in search of gold.

Riding out onto the diggings from Blackwood on a daily basis, Claude experienced, first hand, the hardships they faced. As well as the drenching rain, freezing cold and searing heat, there was the poverty forcing them to wait, hollow-eyed, until the ground gave up enough of a reward to be able to purchase a life-saving bag of flour or a handful of potatoes. The despair of the diggers who toiled on without reward was even more heartbreaking, reflected in the eyes of their women giving birth and raising children under tents erected over open mine shafts, or in flooding hollows under scavenged boards.

As often as she could, Charlotte rode out with him, saddle bags filled with sacks of flour, sugar and salt and, occasionally, apples and oranges: rare treats to brighten the eyes of starving children. These days, more often than not, Charlotte's journal reflected the suffering of the diggers and their families, rather than the amusing incidents and observations she had first noted to entertain her Hatfield family and friends.

These are simple people, hoping to scratch enough of the fortune hidden beneath their feet, or trapped in the many water courses that run across the countryside, to lift them out of their grinding poverty.

It is not unusual to see a woman with an infant tied across her back working with pick and shovel beside her husband or, similarly burdened, knee deep in a freezing stream, laboriously shaking a sieve to free some speck of gold from the slurry of clay and shale.

And all the while, her other children, sitting silently on the bank nearby, too weak from lack of nourishment to play or tend a fire, under a dripping blanket, while the results of their foraging simmers in a kettle for what might pass for a meal at the end of the day.

Years later, she was to reflect upon the irony of gold being discovered in what was then the south east of the colony of New South Wales, on the very same day as the Port Phillip District was officially recognised as a colony in its own right and renamed Victoria – beginning an era of unimaginable excess built on the back of such poverty and deprivation.

With new strikes reported to the north, east and west of the Blackwood Rest Hotel almost every day, fortune hunters in their thousands journeyed in off farms and sheep stations in South Australia and New South Wales and ships arriving in convoy from Britain, America, Europe and Asia, and Charlotte's hotel and hayshed were soon overflowing. When the rain eased at last, turning the churned tracks to rutted dust bowls, she asked Charlie Burrindi to help Elias fence off a section of the back paddock to house tents, allowing exhausted families – some having walked for weeks to get this far – a safe place to rest for which there would be no charge.

On Louis' next visit to examine the hotel records, Charlotte sat across from him at the big partner desk all day, working on after dinner until the rest of the household had retired.

"Come, Louis, let us ease our aching backs and clear our minds outside," she said. "The air is still and the stars so bright in this part of the world I wish you to see what I see, each night, before withdrawing to the comfort of my room."

Stepping out across the veranda, her arm tucked loosely through Louis', she looked fondly at the man she had first seen as a stiff and formal bank manager and now recognised as a dear friend, at ease with himself as well as with her. Resting her hand easily on his forearm she allowed herself to experience the warmth and comfort of his skin through the sleeve of his white lawn shirt – his own comfort in her presence now allowing him to discard his jacket and loosen his stock the moment he arrived at the hotel.

"Louis, dear friend, all the rooms for paying guests are occupied with such regularity that we hardly have time to change the sheets between departures and arrivals," she began. "And as you can see, the shed is also full, giving shelter to as many as four families on any given night. And look, here we are in the back paddock, now a field of tents put up by weary husbands so that their wives and children may rest a while before they set off on the road again in the morning.

"And here, on the back veranda, are the prostrate forms of the poorest, their tents discarded along the way when they became too heavy to carry, or seized by others as they fell from their cart or wheelbarrow or perambulator, crossing a stream or gulley.

172

"I believe we could, indeed, should, think about extending the accommodation we offer, not as grand as the rooms inside the hotel, perhaps, but available at a somewhat reduced cost. And maybe even a bunkhouse for single men, at no cost at all."

"Ah, *ma chere* ... I see now where this *petite promenade* is leading us," Louis replied, smiling wryly. "But you speak as if you have the time to achieve this ambition. Is it not true that you expect to return to England when the *Chetwynde* calls into Port Melbourne again, next year?

"If that is the case, then it is doubtful the building you contemplate would have been completed by then. Now that returns from the mines are being invested into major building works, shops and dwellings, it takes more time than ever to acquire bricks and boards, let alone the artisans required for such a venture.

"You have built up a successful business now, which would be easy to sell the moment you board ship. But it would be hard to interest anyone in something requiring further work – however well the business has performed in the past."

"Let me interrupt you, Louis," Charlotte responded, turning her face to his. Taking both his hands in hers, she looked earnestly into his eyes, before lowering her own to hide the tears belying her brave smile.

"Louis, I know Sir Giles trusted you enough to reveal the circumstances leading to my arrival in the colony ..." Overcome with compassion, Louis brought Charlotte's hands to his lips and held them there.

"And it is with sadness that I tell you the letters I have sent to my father, begging to be brought home, have failed to elicit a response.

"I tell myself they must have been lost at sea. But in truth, I fear my father is not yet ready to receive me. And with the death of my uncle, Captain Hugh Hatfield, late master of the *Chetwynde*, there is now no-one to intercede on my behalf. So it is likely the *Chetwynde* will set sail for England once more, without me.

"And Louis, this is likely to be the case even if there is a message of forgiveness from my father aboard the *Chetwynde* when she next arrives. For I have lately come to the realisation that I need time to consider whether or not I do wish to return to the life I knew, which places more value on acceptance by a privileged few than one's contribution to life in the real world."

Hope rising unbidden in his heart, Louis took a moment to collect himself, choosing to circumvent the unfamiliar territory of his own feelings in favour of safer ground.

"Tell me what you wish to achieve, dear lady, now that you believe there may be time to complete your plan," he replied, once more the servant of his Union Bank masters.

Leading Louis to a stretch of level ground between the far end of the kitchen garden and the fence separating the front from the back paddocks, Charlotte let go his arm and, striding ahead, stepped out a long, narrow rectangle.

"I want to build a row of cottages, Louis," she said, returning to his side. "Right here. Just small rooms, each with a bed, a table, and floor space sufficient to accommodate palettes for the children; and an outside fireplace the occupants could share to safely build a fire and cook a meal.

"Each cottage would provide only clean, dry, shelter: a place for families to rest before moving on to the diggings. In my experience, they will stay for only one or two nights, such will be the determination of the menfolk to put pick to ground further on.

"So, one long row of six cottages with each family looking after itself, let out at a nominal rate for as long as it takes for the occupants to recover, allowing them to move on with renewed hope and vigour.

"Those who can pay will offer what they can. Those who cannot contribute on the way to the goldfields will most certainly do so on the way back, if they possibly can – as you know from the gold I have asked you to keep for me each time you visit.

"This will leave the hayshed for single men going to and coming back from the diggings until we build the bunkhouse. All too often they are pitiful creatures for whom striking it rich in the goldfields is their last chance to feed families left at home in lands far away. Or worse, broken creatures who have managed to withstand the challenges of climate and conditions, only to lose their meagre gleanings to claim jumpers and bushrangers."

"Charlotte, you are indeed a brave and compassionate woman," said Louis. "Happily, the gold donated by your grateful diggers has grown in value in the time the bank has held it for you, and the return on your investment in the bullock team is now in profit.

"I am pleased to be able to say you now have more than enough in your account to purchase the materials you need for such building and to pay for its construction.

"I will put out the word for labour and supplies when I return to the city, tomorrow."

Back inside the house, Louis bade Charlotte a formal goodnight and retired, reluctantly, to the room he shared with his brother. Thankfully, the priest was stretched out sound asleep on his palette, with no expectation of an explanation for the long delay before Louis joined him. Had he asked for one, Louis knew he would be hard put not to reveal the unexpected change in his feelings for his client and friend.

Charlotte, too excited to sleep, took her journal to bed with her to record her conversation with Louis, and the realisation of a growing sense of purpose she could not imagine sitting well with the role awaiting her if she returned to a life of privilege under the protection of her father.

It seemed as if she had closed her eyes only briefly before a voice, whispering persistently in her ear, dragged her up through thick layers of sleep to find Nellie leaning over her, patting the side of her face.

"Madam. Miss Charlotte, ma'am. Please wake up, you are needed urgently!" Nellie cried. "Mistress Martha said I was to tell you to come downstairs, quick as you can."

Reaching for the robe lying across the foot of the bed, Charlotte rose, immediately, to follow Nellie, who was already through the bedroom door and half way down the back stairs. Running, barefoot, through the back hall and into the breezeway, she was confronted by the sight of Thérèse leaning over what appeared to be a heap of rags piled on the bare, brick floor, and Martha, unwrapping a small mewling bundle on the long kitchen bench. In the far corner, Sunny sat cross legged, calling up the spirits of her ancestors to help her make sense of the situation in which she found herself.

Sunny had been the first to respond to the anguished cries for help from the ragged, barely human figure crawling onto the back veranda where she and her Burrindi brothers chose to sleep. This night, however, she slept alone, for Willie and Charlie were out on a police patrol, hoping to catch the band of bushrangers who stole from travellers camped along the banks of the Lerderderg River. Fearing the unknown, Sunny had rapped hard on Nellie and Elias' door.

When Elias emerged he quickly assessed the situation, and throwing aside the long handled hoe he kept beside his bed for just such unexpected challenges, ran to assist the diminutive figure now struggling to stand without dropping his precious bundle. Guessing what the bundle might contain, Elias sent Nellie running to wake Martha and Thérèse. Sizing up the situation in a heartbeat, Martha had sent her upstairs to wake Charlotte.

The heap of rags was speaking, now, in some unintelligible tongue, but clearly seeking reassurance that the baby Martha had discovered among the folds of blood-soaked cloth wound tightly round its tiny form, was still breathing. There was blood on the head emerging from the rags on the floor, too, seeping slowly from a deep wound on its crown to soak the shining black hair caught into the Chinaman's pigtail.

"Fetch Father Claude, at once." Charlotte said quietly to Elias. "Tell him to bring the Sacraments for I fear the poor soul we see before us will not be with us long."

Kneeling beside the Chinaman, she called to Martha to bring the infant to him, gently placing his dark haired daughter across his chest moments before Father Claude pushed through the heavy curtain screening the breezeway from the back hall. Charlotte rose to her feet at once to give the priest room to perform the sacred rites of passage that would speed the dying man's soul, whatever his beliefs, into the next world in a state of grace. But before he could begin, the Chinaman reached up to grasp Father Claude by his shirt front and pull him close. Whispering rapidly in Claude's ear, he ended his long discourse by reaching his free hand into the pocket of his wide pantaloons to pull out a satin purse, which he thrust in front of the priest's face.

"For Missy," he breathed, hoarsely, flicking his eyes from the priest's to Charlotte, the effort of imparting his story clearly having drained the last of his strength.

"You keep, you keep," he said, holding her fast in his clouding gaze as she reached down for the whimpering infant he thrust towards her in the last conscious act of his life.

Bending low over the lifeless form before him, tears falling unchecked from his closed eyes, the very reverent young priest absolved the soul, anointed the body and gently closed the eyes of the hapless foreigner, silently thanking his God for delivering the orphaned daughter into the arms of a loving mother. For Claude had seen that in the few seconds left to him between life and death, Charlotte had, in silent acceptance of the Chinaman's unspoken plea, accepted the infant he held up to her as her own.

"Charlotte, dear," Martha moved to take the baby from Charlotte's arms. "Let us tend to the infant while Nellie and Thérèse prepare her father's body for burial. She seems to be but hours old and must be cleaned and nourished or she, too, will leave us this night."

While Martha bathed and examined the baby as carefully as she had Dickon and Katherine, Connie, drawn by curiosity to discover the cause of the commotion downstairs, had run back up to the nursery to retrieve Katherine's swaddling clothes from the cedar chest in which they were stored.

Binding the baby in linen and cashmere, Martha turned, unquestioningly, to Charlotte, who was already unbuttoning the bodice of her nightgown to put her adopted daughter to her breast.

The infant eventually asleep in Charlotte's arms, and the body of her

177

father consigned to the cool room until Elias could begin to construct a coffin at first light, the entire family gathered round the dining room table to put the night's events into some sort of order. Taking the Sacraments back to the room he shared with his brother, Father Claude had woken Louis, always a sound sleeper, telling him of the death which had occurred on the premises, and Charlotte's adoption of the infant the dead father had left behind.

Louis, responding to the need for official recognition of these events, rose and dressed hurriedly to join the rest of the household. As a sworn notary and manager of the new colony's premier bank, he was well used to overseeing the execution of legal documents and, automatically, assumed responsibility for ensuring due process.

"Charlotte ... friends," he began, taking the seat left empty for him at the head of the table. "My brother has informed me of the events occurring on these premises in the past few hours, and it is clear steps must be taken to officially record a death by misadventure, and the adoption of the deceased man's orphaned daughter – enacted, as witnessed by you all, by request and consent.

"Father Claude, drawing upon the power vested in him as an instrument of the Church, will sign a certificate of death which I shall draw up this morning; also a deed naming Charlotte as the infant's new parent. As an officer at law, I am authorised to bear witness to the intent of both documents and the signatures of the priest attending the death and the adopting parent.

"I will, in all conscience, be able to assign the orphan child to the long term care of our gracious host, in the sure and certain knowledge that she will be as cherished as Charlotte's two natural children, and on the evidence of the deceased father's intent, as witnessed by you all." Here, Louis paused for confirmation from the others at the table.

"Claude, given your assurance that the Chinaman's story, told to you by the deceased in his final moments, is not bound by the rules pertaining to a deathbed confession, please apprise the rest of the household, if you will, of the cause of this night's tragic events."

178

Rising, slowly, one hand on his small, leather-bound travelling Bible turning his spoken words into a sworn statement, Father Claude began his sad story.

"Dear friends, you may be surprised to learn that I was able to understand the words our late visitor used to convey his desperate message. In explanation I attest that my frequent travels through the goldfields have brought me in touch with a diverse and disparate congregation, among them a growing number of Chinese, arriving in the region to seek their fortunes as diggers or cooks. Most have only a limited knowledge of our language but have learnt to converse with their European counterparts through a combination of mime, pidgin and the few Chinese words Europeans have come to understand through trade and barter.

"In essence, I understood the deceased's name to be Lin Lee Wang, and that he arrived here from Shanghai six months ago, bringing with him a young girl whose family had cast her out in favour of their son as crops died and food dwindled on their drought-stricken farm.

"He had found the girl wandering along the road leading out of their village; like him, in search of work to relieve their families of the responsibility of keeping them alive.

"Together they had made their way along the coast of the Yangtze River to Shanghai. On their journey, they heard about a new land across the sea, where fruit fell from the trees, vegetables grew almost overnight, and willing hands were needed to work on great properties owned by golden skinned, feudal lords.

"The couple signed on as cook and galley hand aboard a crowded vessel en route from London to the Port of Melbourne. On board, they learned that most of the passengers were on their way to a province where gold could be picked up off the ground. Landing in Geelong, they joined the procession of people making their way to the diggings, reasoning that even a small amount of the rich yellow metal might purchase supplies and a handcart with which they could earn a living selling cooked food. The young couple sieved side by side in the freezing

179

water trickling through creeks and gullies, until Siu Lin felt her first birth pains. During the next few hours, while Siu Lin battled to give birth, racial intolerance which had been brewing in the goldfields for months, boiled over.

"Lin Lee was attacked on the river bank where he had gone to fetch water for Siu Lin, and beaten senseless by a gang of white diggers who smashed his sieves and stole his gleanings.

"By the time he had regained consciousness and crawled back to Siu Lin, where she lay hidden in the undulating terrain, he was too late to help her. She had died in childbirth. But their baby had lived.

"Lin Lee had covered his wife's body with branches from a fallen tree and fled with the infant into the bush, fearful the thugs might return and harm their child. Frantically, he had run on through the night, eventually stumbling up onto the hotel's back veranda.

"The rest, you know," the priest concluded, sadly. "I turn now, to Lin Lee Wang's only known possessions."

Here, Father Claude's held up the satin purse Lin Lee had pressed upon him, indicating it should be given to Charlotte in exchange for his daughter's keep. Opening it slowly, he held up the contents, piece by piece, for witness and inspection. The first item was a tightly rolled parchment scroll which, unspooled, revealed a series of indecipherable Chinese brush strokes. The next was a small jade pendant – found, Lin Lee had told him, on the road from their village to Shanghai, and held as a portent of future good fortune. The final item – a shard of mirrored glass – was puzzling until Claude explained how, too poor to commission a portrait, or even a photograph of Siu Lin, Lee Lin had picked it up on the walk from Geelong and held it as a unique keepsake for his unborn child. Convinced Siu Lin would provide him with a miniature replica of herself, he would tell his daughter, when she was grown, that she had but to look in the mirror to see how her mother had looked at the same age.

Receiving the purse and its tokens from Claude's hands, Charlotte passed it, at once, to Louis, for safekeeping in the Union Bank vault until such time as her new daughter was old enough to take possession of it, herself.

"But Louis, surely the document you prepare to sanction the adoption of Lin Lee's daughter should identify the infant by name, should it not?" Charlotte asked.

"Indeed it should, Charlotte. But Lin Lee had not yet named the child when he left us," Louis replied.

"Then perhaps we can do that for him, guided in our choice of names by the artefacts he left behind and the memory of her father's love for her mother," Charlotte smiled.

Rising to her feet, she announced, "I propose we name the child given into our safekeeping this night, Jade Siu Lin Hatfield D'Arcy, sister to Dickon and Katherine Hatfield D'Arcy," she said. Then, turning to Claude, "Will you so name this child for us, Claude, so that her father may finally rest in peace?"

The following morning, with the haze around a rising sun signalling the start of summer, Lin Lee Wang was laid to rest on the side of a hill to the west of the Blackwood Rest Hotel, his daughter's adoptive family gathered around his grave to bid him farewell. When William and Charlie returned from their night patrol, a search would be mounted for the body of Siu Lin, so that she might be laid to rest beside him.

Later that day, spirits were lifted in preparation of not one, but two naming ceremonies. For in the period following D'Arcy's death, such was Charlotte's desire to separate that awful event from the miracle of Katherine's survival that she made a conscious decision to set aside her daughter's special day until she felt the time was right for such a celebration.

Charlotte had never been able to accept the notion of original sin – the basic tenet of the Christian baptism ceremony – offended by what she saw as an affront to parents and children involved in the religious ritual she had witnessed growing up at Hatfield Hall. But persuaded by events surrounding the birth of her first child, Dickon was baptised

181

by the Reverend Stockwell in a secret visit to Charlotte's stateroom aboard the *Chetwynde* as soon as the sea had settled. And after Katherine's life-threatening arrival, she now chose to believe it might apply to the circumstances in which a child found its way into the world, rather than to the child's own state of grace.

In Katherine's case, and now also in Jade's, Charlotte felt the service Father Claude would perform that afternoon would clear away the dark clouds from their beginnings, as it had from Dickon's, and let in the light from whichever source was shining on them now, in this their native land.

Looking around at the congregation gathered in the front parlour for the baptism of her two daughters, their working clothes replaced by their Sunday best, Charlotte experienced a moment of sublime happiness.

Everything seemed to have fallen into place. The ache she carried in her heart since learning of the death of Dickon's father had been eased by the image of Richard, emerging from its rightful place in the sturdy body of his son. The light from Katherine's clear grey eyes and echoes of her father's early charm overlaid dark memories of D'Arcy's duplicity. And the gift of new life bestowed upon her in the form of the orphan, Jade, settled the dilemma facing her with the imminent arrival of the *Chetwynde*. Regardless of whether or not her new master carried with him the longed-for letter of forgiveness from her father, allowing her to pick up the past in the country of her birth, her future, she realised, was here in this raw and strangely seductive new land.

Earlier in the day Nellie and Sunny had disappeared into the curtained breezeway to work their special magic in the kitchen, as evidenced by the sumptuous spread set out on the dining room table. Plundering the cool room they had produced platters of sliced ham, a roasted sirloin of beef, and a slowly turned suckling pig.

The chicken coop had given up a hill of eggs, there were succulent tomatoes, grown by Elias under glass left over from repairs to the windows, fish caught by the Burrindi boys in the Lerderderg River, long batards of fragrant, fresh bread, and a large, frosted christening cake.

Louis had also been down into the cool room to emerge with six bottles of fine French champagne from his personal collection, stored in the cellar of what he had come to consider his second home.

Curiously, although, of course, they had been invited to witness the christening ceremony and join in the celebrations, Willie and Charlie had failed to return from paying their respects to the elders, earlier in the day. There was one other person Charlotte wished could have shared her happiness, but Sergeant Baxter was away settling skirmishes on the northern border of New South Wales, and couldn't be reached.

Glancing through the window, Charlotte saw that a crowd had gathered in the hotel forecourt. 'Outsiders' from the barn and paddock, intrigued by the comings and goings of the night, this morning's solemn funeral procession, and the squalling, in concert, of two demanding infants, sensed disturbance of some sort, and stood about, anxious to see if they might be of help.

Paying guests had come down from their rooms, not to intrude at a time when what they had surmised were significant family events had occurred, but to respectfully offer their condolences on the occasion of a perceived loss and, later, to witness the christening as invited guests.

"Elias, Nellie, Sunny, we have a slight change of plan," Charlotte called out, just as Father Claude took his place beside the improvised font – the sterling silver bowl which had served as a wash basin on top of the chest in Charlotte's stateroom aboard the *Chetwynde*, now sitting on a walnut wine table, covered by a purple silk shawl.

"Let us move everything out onto the front veranda, so that we may share this happy occasion with all our guests."

Laughing happily, Charlotte strode out of the parlour and through the front hall to stand in the open doorway, oblivious to the bewildered glances cast from one to the other by the occupants of the room she had just quit.

Louis was the first to move, carrying the improvised font through from the parlour out onto the front veranda. Elias and one of the inside guests carefully manoeuvred the wide, heavily laden dining table – with puffing, grunting, laughter and applause – out through the front French doors.

Surging forward to catch Charlotte's words of welcome, the travel-worn diggers and their families found the love and happiness in her heart, as well as her words, touched them all. Tears were shed when she told how both babies were now fatherless, especially when they heard how Jade's parents had lost their lives; and there was nodding approval when she read aloud from the declaration of adoption Louis had prepared that morning. Hats were snatched from tousled heads, skirts straightened, and some hurriedly crossed themselves when Father Claude, robed in liturgical vestments, emerged through the open doorway. And audible sighs of delight, tempered with hope, rippled through the crowd as Martha and Thérèse, each carrying a satin wrapped infant in their arms, took their places on either side of the font.

But before the ceremony could begin, two imposing figures strode into the space between the crowd gathered in the forecourt and those taking their places on the veranda. Divested of their uniforms, the Burrindi brothers, their bodies painted and draped in full length opossum capes stood, silently, while the women in their entourage piled bunches of green-leafed twigs on the ground before them.

A young boy, sitting cross-legged in front of the pile, worked up a wisp of smoke and then a flame from a stick rotated swiftly between his hands. Blowing the flame gently forward onto the piled kindling, he started a fire sending off fragrant smoke to cleanse and purify the ground on which the white man's ceremony was about to take place.

Waiting, respectfully, while native dancers wove their way through the smoke and around the fire to complete the cleansing ritual, Charlotte then formally invited them to bear witness to the beginning of Katherine's and Jade's journey through life.

Only then did the Christian baptism begin. Wishing all three of her children to share at least one common godparent, Charlotte had asked Martha, who had stood for Dickon, to stand again, as one of the two godmothers traditionally appointed to girl children. Thérèse had tearfully agreed to stand as the other, calling on the loving spirit of her late charge, Charlotte's beloved friend, Helen, for support.

There was really only one man she would trust to guide her daughters through the complex choices they would face as they grew into womanhood, and Louis had accepted the responsibility unhesitatingly, promising to act *in loco parentis* for the rest of his life.

At the end of the ceremony, as soon as the priest administered a final blessing, hats went back on and the crowd broke into spontaneous applause, and Charlotte sent Nellie, Connie and Sunny out into the forecourt with laden platters for the outsiders.

Exactly one month later, when Louis returned to Blackwood for his regular inspection of Charlotte's accounts, he arrived at the head of a small convoy. Her own bullock team and rig, labouring under the weight of blue-stone footings, bricks, kiln dried saplings, plaster and paint, was followed by a railed cart, drawn by two liver-chestnut horses of doubtful lineage but sound hind quarters and fetlocks sturdy enough to answer all the challenges of the goldfields' terrain. Sitting astride the pile of tents, cooking utensils and building tools in the body of the horse-drawn cart were two broad-shouldered boys, freshly arrived off the blighted potato farms of their native Ireland. Jumping down off their belongings, the lads introduced themselves to Charlotte, Elias, and Nellie, waiting on the front veranda to greet the arrivals, as Michael O'Farrell and Michael Macarthy – more often, 'Mick' and 'Mac'.

Swinging down off his horse, Louis unbuckled his saddlebags, handing the reins to Elias who led the lathered animal to the water trough before walking it into its stall beside Charlotte's hunter. Coming back into the forecourt he waved the Irish lads round to the back of the house to unload the cart and pitch their tent on the site Charlotte had stepped out for the new building. As soon as the cart was in place, he turned the horses loose in the back paddock, leaving the holding pen for the wily, hard to catch bullocks, driven to Blackwood for the first time by a hired driver. Recruited by Louis, he would manage the beasts and the rig

185

from their pen hard by the city stockyards. From there, they would be available to transport supplies to the mines opening up outside Bendigo and Ballarat.

Inside the house, Charlotte and Louis exchanged greetings in the French manner, kissing each other on both cheeks – the closest Louis dared come to the lips he longed to taste – before he noticed his brother was not among those gathered to greet him. And while Martha, Connie and Sunny had hurried to greet him in the front hall, there was no sign of Thérèse with her lilting, "*Bienvenu, mon chere chef du banque!*"

"Claude is still away in the goldfields," Charlotte informed him. "And now that I am required to nourish two demanding infants, it is no longer possible for me to ride with him, so Thérèse is taking my place beside him for the time being.

"There has been an outbreak of violence on the diggings and Claude hopes to encourage peaceful resolution of outbreaks arising, we feel sure, from the growing frustration over the increase in licence fees," she continued, failing to notice the shadow of concern flickering for a moment in Louis' eyes.

"This has happened before, but it now seems to occur with increasing frequency and injuries sustained in these altercations are more serious and widespread, which is why Thérèse rides out with Claude to do what she can for the victims.

"Also, it helps that she and Claude share a common language, for these trips last for several days, and with Therese as his translator he can converse with his congregation without struggling to be understood."

"But, Charlotte, I thought Thérèse was not confident on a horse," Louis replied, questioningly.

"You are right, Louis, dear, but knowing I am unable to ride with Claude, she has made a tremendous effort to overcome her fear and practiced for hours in preparation for this, his longest-ever pastoral visit. Also, Thérèse has a strong sense of the need for her nursing skills; inspired, no doubt, by the many hours she and Claude spend together

186

talking about the desperate situation in which goldfields families find themselves in these troubled times."

Satisfied Charlotte's records were in good order, Louis had left for Melbourne after only two days, anxious to return to the bank to prepare for a visit from the owner's nephew. Charlotte would be sad to hear, he had explained, that Sir Giles had never recovered properly from the stroke he suffered on his return voyage to England, and while he had remained as the titular head of the company, his condition had deteriorated in recent months. It was clearly time for the reins to pass to his successor. The board had approved the move and young Alistair Chalmondly, who had been waiting patiently in the wings, was keen to learn as much as he could about the Union Bank's most distant, and given all the gold now pouring into its vaults, most lucrative asset. So keen, in fact, that he had purchased passage on a brand new, state-of-the-art American clipper the moment the transition was ratified, arriving, fair winds prevailing, the very next week.

While Louis was scrutinising bank transactions back in his city office, Charlotte was hovering anxiously as Mick and Mac dug in the foundations and framed up the new accommodations. Within two weeks, the profile of the wing of row cottages was clearly defined. Within three, floors were laid, dividing walls in place, doors hung, and shutters covered the windows to shield the occupants from storms and prying eyes. By the time Louis' voice echoed once more across the courtyard at the end of the fourth week, beds, tables and benches were also in place, crafted by carpenters only too pleased to pick up paid work on their way to the diggings.

With the cottages completed well ahead of schedule, and building materials to spare, Charlotte asked Mick and Mac if they would stay until she had spoken to Louis about another project she had in mind.

Chapter Eleven

BUILDING ON

L ouis' arrival this time, as always, was eagerly anticipated not only by Charlotte – who, quite apart from seizing the opportunity for discourse his intellect brought to their monthly meetings, found a reason to shake out some of the elegant gowns otherwise relegated to the back of her armoire – but also by the entire household. For Louis brought with him news of the outside world: copies of *The Argus* and the *Port Phillip Gazette*, to be passed from hand to hand and pored over until his next visit, and word of friends from whose company they were now disenfranchised by distance.

But this time, he brought with him an elegant stranger; dashingly handsome – if something of a dandy judging by the cut of his breeches and the swing of his long, loose riding coat, not to mention the length of his lustrous auburn locks, curling over the silken stock knotted raffishly loose round his neck.

"Charlotte, my dear, please forgive our late arrival, we were held up by a commotion on the road from Diggers Rest," Louis said, swinging a leg over the pommel of his saddle and sliding swiftly to the ground to exchange their customary greeting.

"But before I recount that intriguing story, may I present my esteemed friend and colleague, Mr Alistair Chalmondly of the Union Bank in the city of London, who will be spending the next month in the colony, acquainting himself with the business of the bank in our region, and with some of our most valued clients.

"Alistair ... I have the honour of introducing you to Mistress Charlotte Hatfield D'Arcy, proprietor of the Blackwood Rest Hotel and its precincts."

Even before Louis completed his elegant introduction, Alistair Chalmondly had vaulted from the dancing thoroughbred shipped with him aboard the American clipper, snatched the wide-brimmed hat from his head, and raised Charlotte's ungloved hand to his warm, moist lips.

"Enchanted, Madame," he purred, raising his eyes to meet hers as he straightened to stand before her. "Your beauty surpasses even Louis' ardent description of you," he murmured, glancing slyly at Louis who looked aghast at his young colleague's careless indiscretion.

"An unexpected pleasure, Mr Chalmondly," Charlotte responded, noting Louis' discomfiture with surprise and withdrawing her hand from Chalmondly's fingertips.

"We are delighted to welcome you to the Blackwood Rest Hotel, which, as you may know, your colleague and our dear friend, Louis, helped us to establish. Please allow me to introduce you to the rest of the household."

Turning to Martha, standing on the threshold of the wide, front entrance with *I've seen your type before, young man*, spelt out clearly in her sharp and knowing eyes, Charlotte linked her arm through Martha's, and emphasising the prefix, 'Mistress', introduced their visitor.

Recognising, as he was meant to, the esteem in which the older woman was held by his hostess, Chalmondly executed a respectful bow from the waist, murmuring only, "Ma'am."

Inside the house, Charlotte walked him through the group assembling in the front hall. First, Father Roderer and Thérèse, who had arrived back that morning from their most recent sortie into the goldfields; then Connie, coming down the stairs from settling Katherine and Jade for the night, with Dickon bouncing from step to step beside her; and coming through from the breezeway, Nellie and Sunny, with Elias, now attired in his indoor uniform of crisp, white shirt, clean moleskin trousers and gleaming calfskin boots.

Formalities dispensed with, Elias led Louis and Alistair upstairs to their rooms, where Sunny had already left jugs of steaming hot water and fresh towels, and hung up the contents of their saddle bags. As was his custom in anticipation of Louis' arrival, Elias had also left a decanter of Oporto and a crystal goblet on a small silver tray on the wash stand in each of the gentlemen's rooms, to refresh them on the inside, as he put it, as well as the outside.

Dinner that night was a festive occasion, for as soon as Claude had said grace, Alistair stood to raise his glass in a toast to the Queen, to Charlotte – in appreciation of her hospitality, and also to Louis on the occasion of his fortieth birthday.

Shaking his head at yet another of Alistar's indiscretions, Louis laughingly accepted the affectionate congratulations heaped upon him, raising the hand Charlotte placed upon his to his lips in silent recognition of their special friendship.

Such a happy night. Louis is so dear to us, Charlotte confided to her journal, later that night. *Where would we be without his support and wise counsel? But he brought with him disturbing news. Governor LaTrobe has increased the licence fee for the diggers yet again, and there is talk of widespread rebellion. There is also talk of the Governor tendering his resignation to the Colonial Office, in London. His dear wife, Sophie, whom I had the great pleasure of meeting at one of Lady Chalmondly's intimate soirees, is in poor health, and has already returned to England. Louis says the Governor is anxious to follow her. If this eventuates we shall lose a cultured custodian of our colony. A man of many parts, it is he whom we must thank for establishing the Royal Melbourne Hospital, the University and, of course, the beautiful Botanic Gardens.*

An early riser, herself, Charlotte was surprised to find Alistair Chalmondly in the breezeway, standing at the kitchen bench with a piece of toasted bread in one hand and a fork deep into a plate full of shirred eggs in the other, making conversation with Nellie. Close by, Sunny was setting up breakfast for the paying guests, a cauldron of steaming porridge simmering gently on the massive hearth ready for the outsiders.

"Mr Chalmondly, good morning to you." Charlotte said. "Do I assume, from your attire, that you intend to inspect the property?"

"A very good morning, indeed, dear lady," Alistair replied, hastily swallowing the last of the eggs. "And it's Alistair, please. I thought we had dispensed with formality, last night.

"And hardly an inspection, ma'am – one would not presume. Merely a stroll around the grounds, if you will, to avail myself of the opportunity to experience the ambiance of the countryside here about, which is quite different from that of the English countryside, don't you know?"

"Then you might wish to accompany me on my morning rounds," Charlotte said. "I would be pleased to show you what I see when I ride my fences, which will give you insight beyond sight and smells into the life and times of the men and women who trust their fortunes – when they make them – to the Union Bank."

"Delighted, ma'am. You are indeed generous with your time, as well as your hospitality."

"Nellie, please put up a basket with the usual treats for the children, and ask Elias to bring our horses into the courtyard, for Mr Chalmondly and I will be riding out as soon as we have toured the home paddock.

"We will also need fresh water bottles and some cheese and fruit to sustain us until lunch time, or the sun, when it rises, will soon deplete our energy.

"Ah, Louis! Good morning, dear friend," she exclaimed, as Louis walked into the breezeway, dressed, as was Alistair, for the hot weather and rough terrain. "How fortuitous. I thought to let you both sleep, this morning, after your long ride and our very late night. But here we all are, so let us spend the morning together, for I have much of interest to show you both."

Setting down plates with generous helpings of shirred eggs on the kitchen table for herself and Louis, Charlotte looked questioningly at

Alistair who was shaking his head in astonishment as Nellie passed around steaming cups of strong, milky tea.

"Champagne is my preferred beverage at this time of day," he explained, smiling impishly. "But I am willing to try tea if that is what it will take to fortify myself for an experience which will clearly test me to my limits!"

Pausing only to pick up wide-brimmed hats from the stand in the front hall, Charlotte, Louis and Alistair made their way out through the front door to begin the tour of inspection Charlotte had planned to support her plans for a bold new business investment.

Standing in the middle of the forecourt, she addressed herself, first, to Alistair. Turning to face the hotel, she took him back to the beginning of her life in Blackwood. Linking her arm in Alistair's she told of his uncle, Sir Giles Chalmondly, coming to visit her, on the eve of his departure for England, in the Jolimont house she had shared with her late husband. And how Sir Giles had reluctantly informed her that funds, deposited in the Union Bank by her father to ensure her security, had been plundered on a regular basis to cover D'Arcy's gambling debts. And that he had appointed the bank's trusted new manager, Louis Roderer, as her guide and mentor through the difficult days ahead.

Here, Louis took up the story. "Less than a week after the birth of her second child, this brave young woman rode up to the steps of the Union Bank, strode through the doors and sent our ageing concierge running as fast as his cane would carry him to demand my appearance before her in the main trading room."

"Louis, you exaggerate," Charlotte protested, laughingly. "I sought, and was granted, an interview with this wise and compassionate gentleman, who listened to my request for the bank's assistance in managing what little there was left of my dowry, so that I could provide my family with shelter and the means to sustain us – at least in the short term.

"He had faith in my ability to build on my experience growing up on a large country estate to bring this neglected old house back to life, and turn it into an investment with enough of an income to ensure that as a family we can look to the future with confidence."

"And the dear girl has achieved all that and more," Louis smiled, sweeping his arm to encompass a wide view of the neatly edged, circular drive and portico, the repaired, repainted and refurbished hotel, the hayshed now neatly fitted out with permanent horse stalls, and a bunkhouse for single men.

"Before we mount up, we will walk round to the back of the house where we will see a fenced area Charlotte has designated a free and safe camping area; and her latest investment, a row of one-room cottages for families needing low cost respite from the heat, rain and terrain on the way to what they believe to be the promised land," he concluded.

Sweeping his hat from his head, Alistair stood mute for a moment before reaching for Charlotte's hand, all pretence at theatrical formality abandoned, and kissed the back of the rough glove that covered it as respectfully as if he held the hand of Queen Victoria, herself.

"Charlotte, I am humbled by your fortitude in the face of such adversity," he said, looking earnestly into Charlotte's eyes. And, still with Charlotte's hand in his, he turned to extend his free hand to Louis. "Well done, Louis. Wisdom, foresight and compassion. The Union Bank in the furthest outpost of the British Empire is, indeed, in safe hands."

By mid morning, Charlotte had taken Alistair and Louis through the home paddock with its produce garden, now thriving under Elias' care, the holding pen – watched over by two of Sunny's cousins, and the pump house with its two iron, claw-foot baths for the use of outsiders in the cottages, hayshed and campsite.

Mounting up again, she took them out of the home paddock to ride the fences around the property's three outer paddocks. In one of the two bordered by the river, the two Clydesdales, purchased along with the builder's cart, grazed peacefully with three dairy cows, each with calves at foot. Apart from the Jersey cow and calf they had brought with them, astute bartering by Elias had seen two of the neighbouring pastoralist's milkers exchanged for the loan of the bullock cart for a week – the calves, born later, were an unexpected bonus. In the other, a small mob of sheep ensured a goodly supply of lamb for the cool room, supplemented by the occasional side of beef from the same friendly pastoralist, happy to have a new customer on his doorstep.

Charlotte and the bankers then rode out to the top paddock, furthest away from the risk of flooding when the Lerderderg ran high, where she made the men dismount to feel and smell the quality of a fine crop of lucerne, ready to harvest against the long hot summer when the lush, green grass of winter turned yellow, before breaking down into fine, choking dust.

Fording the Lerderderg River, now well below the high water mark burned into a pole recording safe levels for horses and bullock carts when spring rains brought torrents of water roaring down the hills and gullies, Charlotte led them up the hill to a knoll close by the site she had chosen for the graves of Jade's parents.

"From this vantage point, Lin Lee and Siu Lin can watch over their child as she grows," Charlotte said, recounting their story in the moments following a reflective silence. "It is one of the reasons I feel I can never leave this place.

"There is magic here. Although harsh and unforgiving, this land has captured my heart. I am strangely at peace here. My children and the rest of our Blackwood family know it as their home. We have all put down roots here, as surely as the silver gums that reflect the moonlight, guiding our way at night.

"From this point, which I visit often, one can look out onto the goldfields. For they are spreading further and wider every day, as yet more new seams are discovered.

"Soon, I predict, Blackwood will be the centre of a thriving new community. Not as big, perhaps, as Ballarat or Bendigo, but a community of families who, like mine, have discovered the magic of the whispering trees, the roaring winds, and the drenching rain that rewards us with regrowth when the summer heat has tested us to the limit of our endurance.

"And here, gentlemen ... is where I intend to begin, with your support, work on my next project," Charlotte concluded, rising from her saddle to spread her arms wide across the sweep of fields before her.

That afternoon, while the children were sleeping and the rest of the household went about their self-appointed tasks, Charlotte, Louis and Alistair stood around a set of drawings spread out on Louis' large desk in her spacious office. The tall French windows were opened wide onto the shaded side veranda in a vain attempt to catch the capricious breeze swirling lazily around the house. Despite the oppressive heat, there was energy in the room.

"Well, then, Madam Lumberjack ..." Alistair smiled, filling three shallow champagne glasses with a bottle of Louis' best Madame Cliquot, still chilled from its sojourn in the cool room from which the bank manager had retrieved it, moments earlier. "Let us drink to your new venture: the Blackwood lumber yard. The first plank, as it were, in the construction of the town of Blackwood!"

The proposal, when Charlotte had first put it to the two bankers, had sounded preposterous, even to her. But they heard her out with due gravitas, recognising the strengths of the English gentlewoman whom fate had determined should become a force to be reckoned with in her new life.

If either of the two, eminently eligible bachelors had other reasons for hearing her out – damp tendrils of hair falling from the knot at the nape of her neck to rest on the rise of a breast, notwithstanding – neither intimated anything other than professional interest as her scheme unfolded. And both were soon willing to admit that on the face of it, Charlotte's reckoning was sound. Her new venture would supply a growing need in a rising market.

Put simply, Charlotte wanted to retain the services of the two Irish labourers who had built the row cottages to stay on to construct a hip-roofed shed, to stock and sell timber to miners wishing to settle their families in a safe community while they prospected on the rough terrain of the goldfields. Once word spread, she reasoned, shopkeepers would follow. And after the shops, perhaps even a school and a hospital.

The plans on the desk in front of them showed the interior as well as the exterior of the timber shed. Inside, carrels lined both side walls to hold timber of all lengths, widths and weights, and a massive bench for measuring and sawing ran down the centre of the structure from front to back. A mezzanine floor took up the back two-thirds of the space, to be fitted out as accommodation for Mick and Mac, and an office for Charlotte who would oversee the business side of things.

"Judging by the quality of the work they have completed so far, I am satisfied that Mick and Mac are honest, reliable and capable builders," she told the spellbound bankers.

"And as for my vision of building a town, ride out from the hotel in any direction and you will see countless makeshift huts offering little comfort and no sense of community to the families who inhabit them. They must endure winds whistling through poorly joined walls, rain pouring through poorly constructed rooves, and no close neighbours to turn to for support if a dig fails, or a husband is hurt, or a baby is born.

"What I propose would see a cluster of free-standing, soundly built cottages erected within a reasonable distance from the diggings, where families can look to each other for companionship and support.

"Built on my land, they might rent the cottages at first. But eventually, if they strike it lucky in the diggings, they might buy them and put down roots here, in much the same way we did."

That night, their last together before Louis and Alistair were to leave the hotel to return to the bank, dinner was a hurried affair, after which Charlotte, the bankers and the Irish boys withdrew to the office to draw up a list of supplies to be requisitioned in preparation for the construction of the new building.

Once the bankers had approved her new venture, Charlotte had approached Mick and Mac with the proposal they stay on to set up the timber shed and service the needs of new settlers. They had considered long enough only to spit into their palms, shake each other's hand, and doff their caps to the woman who offered them a glimpse of the promised land: free meals and accommodation, and a percentage of the profits.

"God bless you, Missus, for this wondrous opportunity," Mac said, feeling the moment called for a touch of respect and formality.

"Truth tell, we've become more than passing fond of the place," Mick chimed in, his eyes darting sideways to where Connie sat shelling peas on the back veranda, prompting Martha, who missed nothing, to make a mental note to ask Father Claude to talk to the boys about respecting boundaries.

It was decided that Mick and Mac would drive the empty cart back to Melbourne the following day, giving anyone who wanted to travel with them a free lift back to the city with their belongings. Lucky diggers would be glad to speed up the process of getting their gleanings past the growing number of bushrangers waiting to pounce on slow moving foot traffic. And the lads would return as they had arrived, the cart loaded with building materials to stump and frame up the new timber shed. The bullock cart, now resting between hirings in the city depot, would follow on behind, with enough sawn timber to complete the shed and frame up the first two houses – and, perhaps, a small shop.

Louis and Alistair returned to Melbourne the same day that Mick and Mac set out with letters of credit in their pockets to cover the cost of the purchases made on Charlotte's behalf, and Charlotte's routine reverted to its usual pattern, beginning with a quiet breakfast with Martha and Thérèse to chart the day ahead; Connie and the children already outside helping Elias in the kitchen garden or singing along to Sunny's music sticks on the back veranda.

Father Claude, too, had left at first light, setting off in the opposite direction to Louis, Alistair and the Irish lads, his destination the Jesuit mission in Bendigo. Joining Charlotte in the breezeway where she was overseeing preparations for the guests' breakfast, his greeting was unusually subdued, his farewell almost abrupt.

Charlotte was to reflect, later, when trying to help Thérèse come to terms with his departure, that it was as if he were already detached from his Blackwood family – still there in person, but not in spirit. She remembered, too, that she had come upon him deep in conversation with his brother in the moments before Louis and Alistair had left for Melbourne. Their conversation had ceased as Charlotte approached, with both Claude and Louis attempting to forestall any question evoked by their worried frowns by quickly turning their attention to Louis' impatient horse.

It was not until Nellie had finished clearing the plates, flatware and condiments, that Charlotte gave voice to the thought that she might accompany Claude in Thérèse's stead on his next pastoral visit to the goldfields.

"It has been so long since I saw for myself what is happening on the diggings," she said. "I am anxious to meet some of the brave souls whose stories you bring back to us, Thérèse, to see what we might do for them.

"There is also the vexing problem of the trouble over the licences. *The Argus* Louis brought with him carried reports of increasing violence, and the building of some sort of stockade with the purpose of repelling the troopers Governor LaTrobe is said to be sending to silence the miners once and for all."

"Take my place, by all means, Charlotte, dear," Thérèse responded, failing to control the tremor in her voice, at which both Charlotte and Martha exchanged worried glances. "For it is no longer possible for me to accompanying Claude anywhere, ever again."

Instinctively, both women rose to embrace their friend as tears coursed unchecked down her face. Pulling away momentarily to close the dining room door and draw the heavy lace curtains across the French windows, Charlotte returned to the table to wait while Martha poured their friend a cup of tea and Thérèse collected herself sufficiently to reveal the cause of her distress.

Calmly, and with heartbreaking resignation, Thérèse told how, during the months Charlotte had been tied to the hotel while Katherine and Jade were both at the breast, Thérèse's fear of horses had, indeed, been overcome, as Charlotte had predicted, though not by her growing confidence in Charlotte's sure footed hunter, or even by the need for her nursing skills, apparent wherever Claude's ministry took them.

Of course, there was fulfilment in the improvement in Claude's ability to communicate with his predominantly English-speaking parishioners, with Thérèse translating back and forth between them; and there was joy in bringing newborns, birthed in some moulding tent or flooding gully, safely into the world. But over time, under the stars, Claude's and Thérèse's separate tents had been drawn closer together – at first, so they could converse through the canvas and still hear each other over shrill winds and rain falling like shot on a duck pond. As time wore on, though, Thérèse had found the sound of Claude's gentle, even breathing as he slept more erotic than the most sensuous love poem.

There were times, too, when folding their tents Claude's hand might inadvertently brush against hers, and his touch, though brief, had set her senses on fire, the heat rising from deep within her soul.

On the last occasion they had ridden out together, Claude's hand had found hers once again – not by chance, this time, but to draw her to him as they rose to extinguish their campfire and retire for the night to their separate tents. His lips on hers, passion had taken hold of them both. In a torrent of words, the anguished young priest confessed his love for Thérèse, and the torment he had endured over the preceding months, trying to come to terms with his feelings for her in the face of his commitment to his church.

Thérèse had rejoiced in the sense of fulfilment she experienced lying in Claude's arms, held willing captive by the hand – even in his sleep – cupping her naked breast.

But with the dawn had come the reckoning.

Pulling back the quilt drawn over them as their passion cooled, Claude had taken the cloth he used to wrap the holy vessels he carried with him, and poured the hallowed water onto a white linen alter cloth. Tenderly, and with tears falling from his eyes, he had washed the evidence of his love from Thérèse's body, ritually committing the memory of their one night together to the deepest reaches of his heart.

His departure that morning for Bendigo was to seek absolution – not for loving her, but for causing the suffering Thérèse would be forced to share with him as they went their separate ways. For Claude could not forsake his God, nor could he stay faithful to his church if he were to continue on in the company of the other great love of his life. His parting words to Thérèse, as they rode in from their last journey through the goldfields together, offered no hope – but comfort enough, she told Charlotte and Martha, to carry her forward, alone, for the rest of her life.

"Thérèse, I cannot regret my love for you," he said. "I will hear your voice in the sigh of the wind, and the joy of birdsong. I will awake to the memory of your gentle touch every morning for the rest of my life. Even now, the taste of your lips is in every breath I take. May God forgive me and bless us both."

Chapter Twelve
WOMEN'S WORK

B rother Ignatius accepted Charlotte's invitation to join the family for lunch with some trepidation. He had set out from Bendigo with clear instructions to deliver his message, for which there could be no reply, and return, forthwith, to the mission. On no account was he to allow himself to be drawn into discussion about Father Claude's decision to remove himself from the Blackwood Rest Hotel to live within the confines of the mission. Nor was he to reveal the current whereabouts of the young priest, or carry back any message to Father Claude from the Blackwood community, however hard he might be pressed to do so.

But the sun had taken its toll on the nineteen-year-old, fresh off the boat from County Clare where the frost had already settled like snow on the hills behind his mother's hilltop cottage. Brother Ignatius was hot, tired and homesick, and the offer of a glass of crystal clear water, poured in the cool interior of what was obviously a comfortable family home as well as a stopping station for weary travellers, proved too much of a temptation.

Concerned at the young man's flushed appearance, Charlotte insisted he sat for a while until he felt rested enough to start out on his long return journey. Within minutes he was sound asleep on the day bed in the family sitting room, hands clasping the heavy silver crucifix hung around his neck like a talisman protecting him from evil influences.

Waking him, gently, in time to join the family for their midday meal, Charlotte overcame his protestations by pointing out the need to fortify himself for the journey he would be undertaking that afternoon. And it was over lunch, at which he had been pleased to be pressed to say grace, that he naively remarked that Father Claude would have nothing so delicious put before him in Calcutta, where he would be ministering to the poorest of the poor for the foreseeable future.

The message from Bendigo was delivered at the end of Brother Ignatius' visit, rather than the moment he had arrived as had been the intention. But the fact that more than a month had passed since Claude's departure, with no word from him to anyone at Blackwood, or even to Louis, meant Brother Ignatius' message merely confirmed what they knew. Father Claude was already lost to them.

The envelope the flustered young seminarian handed to Charlotte as he prepared to leave contained currency considered appropriate reimbursement for Father Claude's food and accommodation over the past two years. This, she asked him to take back to Bendigo as a donation, on Father Claude's behalf, towards the upkeep of widows and orphans cared for by his Jesuit brothers. And then Brother Ignatius was gone. And with him, the last link with the one member of the Catholic Church with whom Charlotte could find no fault.

Two months later, with the Irish lads hard at work digging in the foundations for the new timber-shed, Charlotte felt she could leave the day to day running of the hotel in the capable hands of Martha, Nellie and Elias, with Connie looking after the children for the two weeks she planned to be away in the goldfields.

She had thought long and hard about being away for so long, but there was much she needed to accomplish on this particular journey, and she would not be travelling alone. Thérèse had agreed to accompany her. Painful as it might be for her to retrace the path she had taken so happily with Claude, she saw it as her duty to continue the work she had begun at his side. But Louis had given his approval only after Charlotte agreed to allow him to provide an armed escort – for the goldfields had now become a dangerous battleground.

Charlotte had thought to hire the Burrindi brothers in their official capacity as members of the Native Police Patrol, but they could not be spared. Lieutenant Governor LaTrobe was mustering police and troops from New South Wales, as well as volunteers from Britain, to put down an uprising orchestrated in protest at the latest increase in licensing fees. The situation on the goldfields was tense; even diggers who were doing well were standing firm with those who were barely making subsistence, and penniless new arrivals who had yet to make their first strike.

The worst imaginable has happened, Charlotte noted in her journal from just south of Bendigo.

After months of warnings by the Native Police Patrol, and troopers who have accompanied them on their tours of the goldfields, the Governor and Legislative Council have employed force to resolve the rebellion by hundreds of diggers, gathered in what they have named the Eureka Stockade, over the unfair imposition of an exorbitant tax on earnings they have yet to make.

I think they are quite brave. And if the results were not so tragic, really quite romantic. They raised their own colours over the stockade, and took an oath to stand by each other and fight to defend their rights and liberties.

The short but bloody battle which followed will be recorded as one of the most shameful episodes in the history of the colony, but I believe it might well prove to be the making of it.

At Charlotte's request, Louis had purchased a gentle-mouthed mare for Thérèse, whom Charlotte had persuaded to accompany her on her journey through the goldfields, as much to help her overcome the melancholy which had overtaken her since Claude's departure, as to answer the urgent need for her nursing skills treating the injured following the battle of the Eureka Stockade.

It was as well the guards Louis had hired to travel with them were trained professionals. Used to surprise encounters with bushrangers wielding knives and guns on their regular bullion runs carrying thousands of ounces of ore from the big mines in Bendigo and Ballarat to the Union Bank, they showed no panic when galloping troopers flew towards them to challenge the women's presence on the battlefield. Once shown, Louis' signature, affixed over his seal of office as a public notary, allowed them to continue their work without question or censure.

Louis' foresight provided more than protection. For the security guards were also strong enough to carry wounded diggers out of the gullies into which they had crawled or fallen, allowing Thérèse to clean and bind their wounds. Those whose wounds were beyond her help they loaded onto the builders' cart Charlotte had thought to bring with them, and transported to the new Melbourne Hospital where their lives might be saved, ironically, by surgeons attached to the troops who had been sent to kill them.

Charlotte's attention was also drawn to women and children, left to fend for themselves as their men fell wounded – or worse. And the most pitiable of all, women giving birth in the middle of the mayhem, with no-one, now, to hold their hand or offer a comforting word.

The two women helped where they could, Charlotte, the guards and the driver, recruited from among the Burrindi brothers' cousins to manage the cart, working as a team under Thérèse's direction. She moved quickly among their constituency, assessing injuries and dispensing treatment where possible, making others comfortable on the builders' cart when she could not; and leaving Charlotte to comfort those whose husbands or wives, father or mothers were beyond help.

What Charlotte found most inspiring was that few of the women railed against the circumstances in which they found themselves. Their will to survive for the sake of their families outweighed the fatigue and even the despair that went hand in hand with death. For although now it was all around them in the wake of the uprising, death was common on the goldfields even in the best of times.

Women died, frequently, in childbirth; with no nourishment to sustain them, their babies following soon after. Whooping cough and diphtheria came for the children. Grown men fell victim to falling rocks, rushing water and narrow mineshafts; a growing number to shots fired indiscriminately by bushrangers and claim jumpers.

Turning off the road back from the goldfields to follow the curving, crushed-rock driveway leading into the forecourt of the Blackwood Rest Hotel, Charlotte and Thérèse reined in their horses to wave a final farewell to the guards, who continued the journey to ensure safe passage for the wounded requiring the special skills of the city surgeons. Some of the injured men's families had packed up their meagre possessions to follow the cart on foot, abandoning hard-won claims in favour of keeping the family together. Others, they knew, after staying to guard a claim, would follow later, when it became apparent their men would never return.

Swinging her leg over the pommel of the stock saddle she had long favoured over the conventional side-saddle she had brought with her from England, Charlotte slid to the ground to watch Thérèse, now completely at home on a horse, follow suit.

How we have changed, Charlotte mused, as the two women stood side by side while their mounts drank greedily from the trough in the courtyard. Gowns had given way to linen shirts tucked into divided, ankle length skirts, copied from a picture of the new French fashion published in *The Argus*; silk slippers and soft kid ankle boots had long been discarded in favour of durable, calf skin, knee-length boots, hand sewn by the Russian bootmaker Charlotte had discovered, on the first of her visits to Dickon in the Wills' Collingwood cottage.

"Just look at us, Thérèse!" Charlotte exclaimed, laughing, as she slapped the thick coating of yellow dust from her wide brimmed hat. Thérèse, stamping the dried mud and leaf mould off her boots, was laughing too, as much in relief at being able to lay aside the horrors of the last two weeks, as at the dishevelled appearance of a once elegant Parisienne and once-fashionable English heiress.

Both horses, startled by the unusual sound of unrestrained laughter, swung their heads up from the trough to look questioningly at Charlotte and Therèse – drenching them both with water falling from mouths and muzzles. The resulting squeals brought Elias and the stockmen rushing towards them, expecting the worst. Shaking their heads, they led the horses away, leaving the two women, saddle bags looped over their shoulders, to try to explain their helpless laughter to the rest of the household gathering on the front veranda to greet them; but interest in their arrival had been tempered by a sobering account of the women's journey.

Over dinner, that night, taken with Nellie and Elias joining Charlotte, Martha and Therèse at table after Connie had taken the children off to bed, discussion ranged back and forth about what might be done to relieve the suffering of some – if not all – the women and children on the goldfields around Blackwood.

Next morning, excusing Connie, Dickon and his sisters from the breakfast table to dress for a spell in the new rose garden, Charlotte raised her tea cup signalling an impromptu toast.

"Martha, Therèse, I ask you to raise your cups to our dear friend and business partner, Louis Roderer, who, although he is yet to learn of this, is to be the patron of the new Blackwood Bush Nursing Hospital."

Much had been accomplished in the months since Charlotte and Therèse had returned from their visit to the goldfields between the Eureka rebellion and the start of the spring rains. The timber shed had been completed, with Mick and Mac installed in their new quarters overlooking the lofted space that held timber, saws, hammers and fixings for the dwellings next on Charlotte's agenda.

The Union Bank, under the signature of its Melbourne manager, had approved a loan to underwrite the cost of materials required to build the first two dwellings and small shop, to be repaid when they were rented or sold, and construction had already commenced on the hospital.

The two Irish labourers Louis had recruited to extend the accommodation the hotel provided for poorer diggers and their families were now very much part of the Blackwood household. They were still working for room and board, bolstered by whatever they gleaned from their Sunday sorties fossicking for gold along the banks of the Lerderderg River. And it was this Irish gold, as Mick and Mac described the modest fortune they had accrued over two years of Sundays spent panning and chipping away at the rocks on the river bed, which would transform Charlotte's plans from a sketch drawn on the breakfast tablecloth, six months earlier, to a two-room structure set on the side of the hill in the far north corner of the hotel property.

For Mick and Mac had dreams of their own. Having lost the means to earn an honest living in their native Ireland, they had arrived in Victoria with little more than the clothes they stood up in, a set of tools, and the will to work their own miracle. Louis had chanced upon them one morning while inspecting a shipment of locks he had ordered to safeguard the transfer of gold from assay tents and the commissioners' pavilions set up on the goldfields to collect licence fees, to the Union Bank. Just off the steamer on which they had shovelled coal to pay their way to Australia, the two lads started out as they meant to carry on, holding a crude, hand painted sign stating, 'Hard Workers'.

A little more than two years later, they had approached Charlotte with an ambitious proposal. Piling half a dozen calico nail bags on the desk in her timber shed office, they offered all the gold the bags contained in exchange for title to the business she had established twelve months earlier. Louis had approved the deal and drawn up a contract transferring ownership of Mt Blackwood Timber & Building Supplies from Charlotte to Mick and Mac, with a peppercorn rent for the lease of hotel land on which the timber shed stood. And Charlotte had been their first customer, commissioning them to build not only the cottage and shop but the Mt Blackwood Bush Nursing Hospital with the proceeds of the sale of the timber shed.

Walking up the gently sloping incline at the eastern end of the hotel property to inspect the progress of the new hospital, Charlotte paused a moment to take stock of the elevated structure. French windows opened wide to allow beds to be wheeled outside to catch a cooling summer breeze on a sweeping veranda, shaded by the overhanging, high-pitched roof; a wide portico at one end would allow patients brought in by horse and cart to be unloaded under cover from the merciless sun and drenching rain. Thérèse, as usual, was inside the building, directing the positioning of every shelf, cupboard, bench, hook and hinge.

Standing there, looking up at the almost completed building, Charlotte reflected on the enthusiasm with which Thérèse had seized upon the project, making it her own. As Charlotte had hoped, it had lifted her out of the melancholy into which she sank following Claude's departure. Now, while Claude did what he could to relieve the spiritual suffering of the poor in Calcutta, Thérèse had a mission of her own, relieving the suffering of the poor in Victoria. For despite the enormous wealth to be found in the fields all around them, mining families who were yet to earn as much as subsistence from the diggings were struggling to survive the effects of starvation, isolation and accident in the strength-sapping heat or freezing cold.

Women and children now outnumbered men camped along the water courses or on the scorched or sodden plains, and a growing number of mothers were dying while giving birth alone and unaided, leaving orphaned children to fend for themselves as best they could.

"Martha, the sights we saw while we were away would break the hardest heart," Charlotte had said, introducing the idea of building a hospital to Martha and Thérèse over breakfast, months earlier.

"Thérèse saved the lives of many on the very brink of death after giving birth exposed to the elements, and without so much as a sip of water to ease their pain, or a sheet between them and the bare earth beneath them.

"While the injuries sustained by their menfolk in the rebellion were every bit as deserving of her special skills at the time, they were occasioned by events outside the norm. The suffering and death of women during childbirth are seen as part of life's natural cycle, and will continue unabated unless there is somewhere for them to turn for help when their time has come."

Addressing Thérèse, Charlotte continued, "With your experience at the hospitals for the poor in Paris, and the Women's Hospital in Melbourne after we lost our darling Helen, I believe there would be no-one better placed than you, dear Thérèse, to take charge of our little hospital in the bush ... if you should feel inclined to do so."

"Oh Charlotte, how could you doubt that for even a moment?" Thérèse had responded. "But we don't have to limit the help we provide to birthing mothers. No-one knows more than Martha about bringing mothers and babies safely through that journey, and if we had enough space we could open a small *clinique*, like the one we had in Paris, where we could clean and bind wounds to prevent infection, and set broken bones to save arms and legs."

Martha, who had been as worried as Charlotte by Thérèse's decline, began at once to make lists of the sheets and pillowslips, nightgowns, binders and birthing cloths they would need to support four beds in the birthing room, while Thérèse wrote a list of prescriptions to give to Louis on his next visit to stock the emergency clinic. Meanwhile, Charlotte had gathered up the crisp linen table cloth on which the women had sketched a rough plan of the proposed hospital building, and taken it across the courtyard to the timber shed for Mick and Mac's consideration.

Pleased to be able to consider a commission so soon after starting up in business for themselves, the boys had refined the plan and presented a costing within the hour. Charlotte had signalled her approval of their detailed specifications and speculative quotation with a firm handshake.

Turning back towards the house she saw a band of troopers wheeling into the driveway. Sweeping the wide-brimmed hat from her head, she waved it high above her head, running down the slope as fast as her flying feet would carry her.

"Reginald!" Charlotte cried as she pulled up in front of them as they tethered their horses. "How wonderful to see you! And Charlie, Eddie,

Jack, too! It has been far too long since you called in to see us. Let us hope you can stay long enough, this time, to share a meal with us and perhaps rest your weary horses here overnight."

"Mistress Charlotte, ma'am," Sergeant Baxter replied, laughing as Dickon, Katherine and Jade rushed out to swarm around the tall soldier they knew as Uncle Reggie, who could always be relied upon to carry a toy or a comfit tucked inside his uniform jacket for each of them whenever he called in to the Blackwood Rest Hotel.

At the sound of the men's voices, raised in a chorus of greetings to Charlotte and the children, Connie, Martha and Thérèse gathered to welcome their long time friends.

"Can you find room in the back paddock for four weary soldiers to pitch a tent, ma'am?" Baxter responded in answer to Charlotte's invitation. "We have ridden hard all day and hoped we might find a billet here before pressing on to Bendigo in the morning."

"Oh Reginald, of course we can. But you must stay in the house, and the boys can enjoy a decent night's sleep in the new bunkhouse we have built onto the hay shed. But first, let us provide refreshments. Please, come inside, all of you. Let us hear your news."

"We are hot and dusty, ma'am," piped up Charlie Wills, sweeping Dickon's hat from his head and ruffling the unruly red hair springing free from restraint.

"We'd best stay on the veranda or your guests might think they have been invaded by bushrangers!"

"Then we shall all stay on the veranda," said Charlotte, clapping her hands. "Connie, would you run inside and ask Nellie and Sunny to put up the big trolley with plenty of lemonade, iced tea and some of her wondrous pound cake. That should hold us all until dinner time."

While Nellie and Sunny saw to the refreshments, the troopers unsaddled their mounts and turned them loose in the back paddock, and Elias, after a whispered conversation with Martha, disappeared into the house on a mission of his own. Within minutes, the whole family had gathered on the veranda, pulling up chairs, moving tables and piling up cushions on the weathered jarrah boards for the children to nest in. The tea trolley arrived, wheeled in by Nellie, shaking her head as Elias struggled along behind her, carrying a keg of ale he had hauled up from the cool room on the fair assumption the troopers might prefer a mug of ale to a cup of tea or a glass of lemonade.

Dressing for dinner, Charlotte thought back to the first time she had encountered Sergeant Baxter and 'the lads' as he still referred to troopers 'Fast Eddy' Jackson, Charlie Wills and Bill Tiler, five years ago when D'Arcy had left his wife and family on the doorstep of their new home after a long and eventful voyage half way round the world.

Still recovering from Dickon's premature birth on board her uncle's ship, the *Chetwynde,* Charlotte had risen from her bed, a day later, to find the bluestone house filled with familiar pieces of Hatfield furniture, rugs and pictures, carefully unpacked and carried in by Sergeant Baxter's 'lads' working tirelessly under Martha's direction. Later, as her husband's behaviour deteriorated under the influence of grog and gambling, she was to come to know Sergeant Baxter as a valued friend and protector.

Charlie Wills, new father of twins at the time they first met, had happily played the role of surrogate father to Dickon for the first twelve months of the child's life when his wife, Florence, had been recruited as Dickon's wet nurse; and a lasting friendship had been formed between herself, her son and the Wills family – as evidenced by Charlie's affectionate greeting to Dickon on his arrival that day, and the child's happy response.

With the benefit of time spent in the bath house, the troopers presented at the family dining table as smartly as if they were on parade at the Governor's mansion. Martha, Thérèse and Connie – now close to seventeen, had put away their workday skirts and shirts in favour of gowns, now somewhat out of date but still elegant enough to draw admiring glances from their guests that night. Not that the troopers would know a hooped skirt from a starched petticoat, or a crinoline from a bustle; to them, the women just looked beautiful, their soft conversation and gentle laughter a welcome relief from the onerous duties and rough company of army life.

With the meal served, Nellie and Elias filled the last two seats at the table, leaving Sunny and one of her 'aunties' to look after the rest of the inside guests – the outsiders having been catered for, as always, before tables were set in the inside dining rooms.

It was not until Elias had set the port in front of the men that Sergeant Baxter's mood turned sombre. Exchanging glances with the troopers, he stood, swiftly followed by Eddie, Charlie and Bill, to propose a toast to the ladies in appreciation of the hospitality they had provided so unstintingly.

A second toast followed, prompting much laughter, to Elias, for aiding their recovery from their long and tedious journey that afternoon, with a medicinal draught of ale.

Still standing, the Sergeant surprised Charlotte and her household by raising his glass for a third toast. "To the *Chetwynde*," he said, solemnly, "and all who sailed in her."

Glasses drained, one by one, Charlotte, Martha and Connie sank back into their seats to absorb the full portent of his words. In the silence that followed, Sergeant Baxter and the troopers resumed their places, reaching to pour water and wine to comfort, as best they could, the three women with particular ties to the vessel and crew lost at sea three weeks earlier.

At the mention of the *Chetwynde*, Charlotte was reminded of the loss of her beloved uncle, Captain Hugh Hatfield, the ship's master on the voyage which had brought Charlotte, Martha and Connie out from England. He had died at sea, on a subsequent voyage, in the arms of his trusted friend and first mate, Tom Newbold. Tom had become Charlotte's self appointed protector from the moment she stepped aboard the *Chetwynde*, and later, together with Sergeant Baxter, had absolved her from the responsibility of dealing with the consequences of her late husband's last assault.

212

Eventually, with the *Chetwynde* sailing under a succession of new masters, in different waters, contact with Tom had been lost. Had it not been for Reginald's sad news, Charlotte might never again have given the *Chetwynde* more than a passing thought, other than to hope that, someday, it would bring Tom Newbold back into their lives.

Across the table, Martha's face had lost all colour. Appointed by Charlotte's father to accompany his daughter on her voyage to Australia in position of companion, the two women had soon become close friends, with Martha supporting Charlotte through the most testing moments of her young life. Through those difficult years, Martha had drawn strength from her friendship with the *Chetwynde's* first mate, who had assumed responsibility for the women's welfare from the moment they attempted to board the rocking vessel on a rising tide. And although she had not heard from Tom since they left the city for the goldfields, Martha had never relinquished the expectation of resuming the special friendship that had developed between them when time and tides brought them together again. But it seemed Tom was now lost to her forever, claimed as cruelly by the sea as it had claimed the cottage in which she had intended to spend the rest of her life, safe and secure in the rolling green hills of her native Somerset.

Thérèse, attuned to the suffering of others since her separation from Father Claude, gripped the older woman's hand and held it tightly in her own as Reginald read aloud from an account of the shipwreck published in *The Argus*. Not an easy task, the bond between the two men, forged on the fateful night of D'Arcy's demise, making the telling much harder than it might otherwise have been.

"The ship had completed its contract for the Atlantic run, and was *en route* once more for the Antipodes," Sergeant Baxter continued, softly. "Port Melbourne was their ultimate destination. But they had deviated from their usual route to drop off supplies to a whaling station at Freemantle, off the coast of Western Australia.

"Quoting from the Freemantle *Enquirer*, the report states the *Chetwynde*, unfamiliar with local weather conditions, sailed into a fierce storm and was blown onto one of the many reefs off Rottnest Island, breaking up and sinking swiftly in the raging waters.

"Whalers waiting out the storm on nearby Dyer Island watched helplessly as the ship went down. A passing naval frigate retrieved the ship's colours after the storm had passed. With no word of survivors it is presumed all hands went down with the ship."

Hardly had the troopers left the following morning, than the sound of galloping horses again brought the occupants of the Blackwood Rest Hotel hurrying out onto the front veranda. This time a large, four-wheeled coach and four flew towards them, the driver leaning back, feet up on the buckboard against the pull of the reins slotted between the fingers of his leather-gloved hands. Amazingly, the lathered horses drew to a halt with the coach aligned with the hotel's front door.

Leaping down from the driver's seat, Jedediah Mansfield swept his sweat stained hat from his head and, taking the two steps up onto the veranda on the run, introduced himself to Charlotte as the Victorian agent for the Cobb & Co, "America's most safe and reliable passenger-carrying, long-distance transport company, ma'am."

Brilliant blue eyes, a hard body and a deeply tanned face marked Jed Mansfield as an outdoorsman. A wide smile exposing perfectly even, brilliant white teeth, and a lazy drawl delivering each syllable emerging from his mouth like a measure of molasses spilling off the back of a spoon, had given him an advantage over other equally proficient drivers when the owners were looking for someone to open up Australia for them.

At twenty-eight, Jed had travelled the length and breadth of the United States of America, loved two women other than his mother, and had yet to find the one who might persuade him to settle down and raise a family.

"With your permission, ma'am, it's been a long journey and I need to rest and refresh my passengers, if you get my drift," he said, with a wry smile.

"We are always pleased to welcome visitors to the Blackwood Rest

214

Hotel, Mr Mansfield," Charlotte replied, moving forward to greet the two women and three men walking towards the veranda.

With the rain clouds gathering the party moved quickly indoors, assembling in the guests' sitting room while their bags and boxes were unloaded and deposited in the front hall and rooms were hastily made ready upstairs. The travellers, with the exception of Jed and his co-driver, unused to the pace and sway of the new form of transport, were keen to take advantage of the opportunity to rest overnight before continuing their journey on the long and rutted road to Bendigo – especially now, with the prospect of having to get out of the coach and push the vehicle out of potholes as rain turned the rutted roads into rivers of mud.

"Ladies, gentlemen, I am afraid we have only four inside rooms to offer you," Charlotte informed them. "So, unless some of you are prepared to share, the only alternative would be for one or more of the gentlemen to accept a bed in the bunkhouse, entailing crossing the courtyard in heavy rain."

The two women, Mistress Grace Lichmore, governess, and Mistress Eliza Fitzwalters, dressmaker, agreed, at once, to share one of the rooms, allowing three for the gentlemen. Commissioners George Williams and Henry Blake, destined to spend the next two weeks under canvas in licence commissioners' pavilions out in the middle of the wet and windy goldfields, were more than happy to double up, leaving one room for the drivers should they, too, agree to share and one remaining for Dr Theo Anders, a physician from the American frontier town of San Francisco.

Blue, recruited to ride shotgun beside Jed as a deterrent to the many bushrangers lying in wait among the trees and gullies along the roads to Victoria's frontier towns, was a man of imposing stature but few social skills. The prospect of an evening spent inside the hotel in the company of women, he knew, carried with it the obligation to engage in small talk. Growing up as the only child of a western district widower, Blue had never had to suffer that impost. And when his father passed away he realised he was far better suited to a quiet and contemplative life on

215

the road than the rigors of social intercourse required to find a wife he would have to talk to for the rest of his life.

"Bunkhouse," he said, in response to Jed's questioning glance, picking up his bag and heading for the front door.

While the stagecoach party repaired to their rooms to deal with the damage done by dust and distance, Martha oversaw preparations for high tea. Platters of cold lamb, bush pheasant terrine, soft creamy cheese, warm bread and jugs of ale and lemonade were set out on a large console table for the guests to serve themselves according to their taste and appetite.

Charlotte, Martha and Thérèse joined the new arrivals as they gathered in the front dining room. Adopting the relaxed form of address now creeping across the colony, they were all soon on first-name terms, circumventing the more cumbersome conventions that might otherwise have interrupted the flow of conversation. When everyone was seated, Charlotte persuaded Grace and Eliza, who had arrived from England the previous day, to entertain the assembly with an account of their journey out on one of the new iron screw steamers taking the great circle route, under steam and sail, through the rarely seen icefloes off the coast of the Antarctic land mass.

"It was an incredible journey, a voyage of discovery, if you will," Grace began, her impeccable English and attention to detail identifying her, immediately, to those who might have failed to ascertain her vocation by her mode of apparel: grey serge, floor length skirt, plain white blouse unrelieved by any embellishment other than the small pendant watch that hung from a black enamel mourning bar pinned high on her left breast.

In contrast, Eliza's proficiency with needle, silk and thread was immediately apparent from the cut and quality of her silk bodice and the froth of petticoats appearing, intermittently, from beneath the hemline of her artfully draped, ankle length skirt.

"It was fantastical!" Eliza interjected. "There was unbearable heat and such a to-do as we crossed the equator, and then wind and snow and such cold as we ventured into Antarctic waters, that we feared to go up on deck in case we became frozen to the very boards on which we stood."

"It was, indeed, a voyage of such contrasts, I believe we might fill a book with the stories we could tell," Grace agreed. "There were, regrettably, as many deaths on board from heat as from cold, with infants faring the worst; all four children in the one family being committed to the deep as each succumbed to the bronchitis sweeping the ship as we sailed from the equator into the Antarctic waters."

"Worse to witness than even the tragic committal of children were the floggings," said Eliza, taking up the story. "Trials were held in the forward salon, with first class passengers summoned to attend so that justice could be seen to be done. Within minutes the unfortunate offenders were hauled up on deck and tied to a crossbar affixed to the mast, whereupon a burly fellow was appointed to administer a number of lashes upon the poor man's back commensurate with the nature of his offence. As if that were not enough for him to bear, a bucket of stinging vinegar was thrown at his bleeding back to ward off infection."

"Indeed," said Grace, visibly upset by the memory. "Eventually, on the last such occasion, at the point at which the punishment was to be administered, the prisoner was untied and his sentence commuted to time to be served in the brig, with only bread and water to sustain him. We heard later that was because several gentlemen among the first class passengers had protested to the captain that the barbarity of the floggings was profoundly upsetting for the ladies.

"I think we were both pleased and relieved to see land, at last. We were told it was Australia but, in truth, all we could see was a long stretch of sand with some rather unimpressive vegetation stretching away in the distance. But then the ship swung round to anchor off Williamstown, whereupon a succession of small boats surrounded our vessel and took off a number of passengers before the pilot came aboard to bring us through to Port Melbourne."

"But the sunset, Grace, the sunset!" said Eliza. "In all my life, and throughout our entire voyage, I never saw a sunset so glorious as the one we witnessed as we stood on deck waiting for the pilot to come aboard.

"All the passengers came up from the salons, standing in awe of the brilliant hues, changing like a child's kaleidoscope as the sun sank into the sea, giving way to an indigo sky decorated with stars glittering like diamonds."

But it was not until the evening meal, with the children asleep in their beds and the outsiders fed and made comfortable for the night, that friendships were forged between Charlotte and her guests that were to influence the future of the growing number of diggers and their families working the river banks, hills and gullies around the hotel, and the determined women who lived there.

Grace, Charlotte learned, was but one of a number of English women who had responded to an advertisement, placed earlier in the year in *The Times* of London, inviting unattached gentlewomen in good health to consider migrating to the new colony of Victoria. There, fortunes made in the goldfields had created a demand for governesses to prepare the daughters of newly affluent parents for the opportunities presented by enormous wealth. The stipend a governess with the right background might expect to receive in the young and prosperous colony could be as much as double the expectation of a similar position in an English house.

Along with the financial inducement – attractive enough on its own to warrant the attention of young women dependent on the good will of the families who employed them for what amounted, in most cases, to little more than subsistence – was the lure of adventure, a chance to change the course of their uneventful lives.

Grace, now twenty six, had loved and lost the young soldier to whom she was betrothed when he fell at the battle of Boma Pass – one of a number of British regulars fighting on behalf of their Sovereign in South Africa, five years earlier. A succession of unfulfilling positions engaging with other people's children, when she longed for her own, had influenced her to seek change. Bendigo, on the other side of the world, had seemed as far away from the tedium of the life she sought to leave as one could possibly get. But the condition of the road, and the sights she had seen from the coach window, thus far, offered little to encourage her to believe she had made a change for the better.

Taking advantage of a lull in the conversation as her companions worked their way through a sirloin of beef, a leg of lamb and three chickens, complemented by Yorkshire pudding and garden fresh, green beans, later that night, Grace sought reassurance from Charlotte.

"Grace, my dear, although I, myself, have not yet ventured as far north as Bendigo, I understand from those who pass through our doors on their way back from your destination, that it is growing fast in size and stature, and that there are shops and dwellings to rival anything to be found in Melbourne," Charlotte responded, placing a hand, reassuringly, over that of her visitor.

"Indeed, we are told the owners of the big company goldmines established thereabouts are pouring considerable fortunes into public buildings and great houses meant to make a lasting impression on those who chronicle the development of Victoria in years to come."

Close in age, both women had experienced a moment of instant rapport on their initial meeting. Grace sensed by her manner and accent the quality of Charlotte's upbringing and education; Charlotte recognised tragedy and resilience behind Grace's outward demeanour of carefully measured calm.

"Grace," Charlotte continued, "it is my belief that we share elements of the past and a sense of hope for the future. Bendigo is no further away from Blackwood than you already travelled from the Port of Melbourne. If the situation to which you have committed in Bendigo fails to meet your expectations, you will always find a welcome here. In fact, before you leave, I would appreciate your advice on a project I have in mind."

Before Grace could reply, the two commissioners, their professional reserve relaxed by the contents of a bottle of Bordeaux, disengaged themselves from Eliza's charming defence of expenditure on fashionable attire as antidote to what she termed 'marriage woes', to attest to the pace and scale of Bendigo's growth on the very land from which the gold

219

that funded it had been mined. There were, indeed, homes and shops as elegant as any in Melbourne or, for that matter, English county towns.

Eliza, her attention arrested by the mention of shops, listened intently as commissioners Williams and Blake described the tea rooms, frock shops and milliners patronised by the wives and daughters of newly wealthy mine owners and pastoralists who were making their own fortunes victualling the tens of thousands of diggers now populating the goldfields as far west as Stawell and Ararat and as far to the east as Wangaratta and Beechworth.

The favoured goddaughter of a titled ageing relative, grateful for the young woman's attention as a child and, later, a creative needlewoman who had listened attentively to the older woman's dissertations on style in her London salon, Eliza had been the beneficiary of a generous bequest when her godmother passed away. Transferred from the Union Bank in the City of London to its Melbourne office, a sizeable sum now sat waiting to be invested in a suitable property that Eliza had determined would establish her as the director and creative genius behind Bendigo's first *Salon d'Haute Couture*.

She had selected Bendigo for her directorial debut, she informed the assembly, on the advice of Mr Alistair Chalmondly, Chairman of the Union Bank, whom she had met at her godmother's funeral. Over canapés and chilled Pouilly Fuissé, he had revealed he, too, was one of Lady Eloise Cadogan's many godchildren, although not a beneficiary. Lady Cadogan, it transpired, had been a close friend of his uncle, the original chairman and owner of the Union Bank.

Although promised to another, Sir Giles had generously supported Eloise's ambitions to leave the theatre and set herself up in a reputable business. In a very short space of time she had become the proprietor of a highly fashionable Bond Street boutique, patronised, mainly, by her fellow artistes. Soon after wedding bells had sounded for Sir Giles, they rang out again for Eloise and Sir Charles Willoughby Cadogan, one of Sir Giles' young friends. But Eloise and her benefactor remained close for the rest of their lives. How piquant, then, was their meeting, Alistair

220

had mused. Would it not be a lark if history were to repeat itself?

In time, the ambitious young woman informed them, if all went according to plan, she would open a second salon in fashionable Collins Street. At twenty two, she was still young enough to risk all in the name of adventure, old enough to know what she wanted, had no husband to impede her progress, and supreme confidence in her talent and tenacity.

Theo Anders had so far kept his ambitions – and his reasons for exchanging one frontier town for another – to himself. But hearing Thérèse's account of Aborigines she had met on her expeditions into the goldfields with Claude, and later, with Charlotte, setting simple fractures – straightening the broken bone, binding it with soft bark and applying a mixture of blood and beefwood gum – loosened his tongue, too.

Encouraged by Thérèse's story, Theo told how his career as an army doctor had been cut short by his refusal to amputate the badly damaged arm of an infantryman mown down by a Mexican cavalry unit in a skirmish on the southern border of the newly won American state of California. Against orders, and over his patient's agonised screams, Captain Anders had reset the bone and sewn up the gaping wound through which it had protruded. Following a procedure he had only read about in a paper published by an orthopaedic surgeon from London's Guy's Hospital, he then soaked strips of linen in a stiff mixture of corn starch and spring water. Splinting the arm straight, he wound the coagulating fabric around the restraints, where it set hard and had remained for the next six weeks.

During that time, the arm healed and, once the plaster cast in which it had been encased was removed, the soldier found he was able to hold and aim his rifle once more. Also during that period of time, and despite the success of Theo's ground-breaking procedure, the court martial process cashiering the brilliant young army doctor for disobeying the order of a superior officer ground through to completion.

Thus dishonoured and discharged, he made his way to England, where he applied for specialised training as an orthopaedic surgeon at Guy's

Hospital. Once certified, however, he found the cold weather and social structure too constraining for his liking. Looking for an environment more suited to his casual style of dress and conversation, he found his interest engaged by an advertisement in a medical journal, seeking surgeons to work in the new Royal Melbourne Hospital. But when he arrived, a little over a week ago, he found the hospital fully staffed, and was now on his way to Bendigo where, he had been told, a doctor with battlefield experience might feel right at home in a private practice treating axe wounds, snake bites and broken bones occasioned on the goldfields.

Jed had contributed little during the course of the conversation ebbing and flowing around the table throughout the evening, waiting for the woman at its head to enlighten them as to how and why such an obviously well educated woman of significant social standing, not to mention beauty, had chosen to bury herself in an isolated hotel at the back of beyond.

But Jed's curiosity would remain unsatisfied – at least for the time being. As the last of the wax dripped down the sides of the candelabra in the centre of the table, Charlotte rose, smiling, to thank her guests for their fine conversation and bid them a good night.

Chapter Thirteen

WIND AND FIRE

T he Spring rains had given way to unseasonable warmth before Charlotte was to meet up again with her new friends, Grace Lichmore, Eliza Fitzwalters and Theo Anders. Commissioners Williams and Blake had been regular visitors during the intervening weeks since Cobb & Co had started their weekly runs from Melbourne to Bendigo and back again, breaking the journey both ways to rest passengers and horses overnight at the Blackwood Rest Hotel.

Jed and Blue had become more or less permanent fixtures since Charlotte had agreed to provide permanent cover for their coach and horses, and hold two rooms in the main house, for two nights a week, for 'passengers of quality'. Diggers and their families fortunate enough to be in a position to purchase seats on the express run to and from the goldfields would be accommodated in the cottage wing; single diggers, Blue, and occasionally Jed, if there was no accommodation left inside the house, were put up in the bunkhouse.

Blue had become a firm favourite with the family, especially the children, for his willingness to turn his hand to any project once he had seen to his horses and washed down the stagecoach. Pitching in to help Elias and the stock boys dig in a fencepost, tighten fence wire, help the children build a tree house or scare out the occasional brown snake lurking behind the bins in the feed shed, was all in a day's work to Blue.

At night, he would pull out the mouth organ he kept buttoned in his shirt front pocket, and teach Dickon and the girls songs he'd learnt at his father's knee in the shearing shed. And some nights, when the work around the property was done, Blue would take off with the stock boys, Sunny and the aunties, and walk over the hill, round the edge of the Black Forest, onto clan land to listen to stories of the dream time.

Jed had become indispensable for another reason. The way Nellie put it to Elias, with his easy good humour and southern charm, Jed 'balanced Charlotte out'.

And then there was the way young Dickon had taken to him. The boy dogged Jed's every step, standing by his side in the middle of the ring Jed had set up to exercise Charlotte's hunter and Therèse's hack when the women were too busy to ride them. He taught the seven year-old to rope a horse the cowboy way, with a rope thrown from the ground or, riding up in front of Jed, from the saddle. Eventually Jed introduced him to Rocket, an undersized, overweight, ageing brumby he'd spotted in a paddock, half way to Bendigo. Outgrown by a pastoralist's daughter and left, untended, to wait for its end, Jed had bought it for a guinea on the way back to Blackwood. In the run up to Christmas, he had seen to its neglected feet and clipped out the last of its winter coat; and when he judged it fit enough, had bunked up the overjoyed boy on his first, very own, mount.

Standing with Jed in the centre of the ring as he worked horse and boy on the end of a lead rein in the exercise ring, Charlotte smiled at the pony's slow gate and asked, "Why 'Rocket', Jed?"

"Well, Miss Charlotte, ma'am, it's like this," Jed replied, with a slow grin. "A boy's gotta be able to ride, and to learn right, he's gotta be able to sit safe before he gets fancy. And I figured you'd have to put a rocket under this here mount before he'd make a move that'd surprise even hisself."

Watching from the veranda as Jed and Charlotte stood laughing together, Martha and Therèse exchanged knowing glances. "It's about time, my friend," Martha said, smiling as she turned and walked back into the house. Therèse, inspired by the memory of true love, sent up a

224

whispered parody of Claude's sacred affirmation, *"Bendictus qui venit"*... blessed is he who comes.

It had been many months since Cobb & Co had brought the first of its regular stream of passengers to Blackwood. In the meantime, livery stables had been added to the growing collection of buildings on Charlotte's property. Large enough to accommodate the Cobb & Co coach and four, Charlotte had made provision for up to a dozen more horses needed, she predicted, to meet the increase in traffic following the discovery of gold at nearby Ballan Flats and the quartz vein at Simmons Reef.

Since then, the population of Mt Blackwood, as the area around the hotel between the river and the Black Forest had become known, had risen so rapidly that Mick and Mac were hard put to keep up with the demand for dwellings to house the families prepared to stay. So hard put, in fact, that they had taken on two young Scots who had answered an advertisement the lads had placed in *The Argus* calling for qualified carpenters to oversee casual journeymen.

Now wealthy young businessmen, Mick and Mac had built themselves handsome brick homes with pitched iron rooves and bullnosed verandas, leaving their accommodation in the timber shed for the Scottish lads. Jobbing journeymen who came and went, working for room and board during the week and fossicking for gold on Sundays, as they had done, themselves, were accommodated in 'the seminary'. So named by Mick and Mac for its cell-like design, the self contained structure was connected to the timber shed they had purchased from Charlotte, five years earlier, by an open breezeway housing an iron bath and a wood-fired stove.

The business had since more than doubled in size, with the addition of a hardware store fronting the main street Charlotte had envisioned, with shops and dwellings facing each other in two straight lines. There was also a collection of outbuildings behind the seminary holding enough sand, shale and bluestone to meet the demand for grand-scale, commercial structures required by the mining companies moving into the area.

The hospital, too, had grown, with a children's ward and a consulting room added to the birthing room and surgery. While necessary, to accommodate a growing community, this had created something of a crisis. For even with Martha's overseeing the birthing room, and two of Sunny's cousins to help with the treatment of minor wounds, Thérèse was exhausted by the end of the day.

All my grand plans seem to be turning out so well we are overwhelmed by success! Charlotte confessed to her journal. *Today, we are at the end of a particularly busy day at the hospital – coinciding, as it did, with the arrival of a coach full of passengers looking forward to a fortifying meal, and fresh linen.*

Then there are the children. Although Connie and I can teach them their letters, I have less time to spend on their schooling each day, what with the hotel and the hospital demanding my attention from first light to nightfall. And it is not only my children growing up unlettered. More and more families are moving permanently into Mt Blackwood, most with children too young to be sent away to school even if their parents could afford to board them out.

Clearly, someone needs to set up a school, even if only a preparatory institution.

The house was full, with her visitors happy to double up as they had the first time Jed had brought them to the Blackwood Rest Hotel a little more than twelve months earlier. Fortunately, Christmas Day had fallen on a Saturday, allowing them all to spend two wonderful days together at the Blackwood Rest Hotel.

George Williams and Henry Blake, Dr Theo Anders, Grace Lichmore and – looking very prosperous, indeed – bowed and beribboned Eliza Fitzwilliam, sat comfortably interspersed with members of the hotel family, all talking together at the top of their voices to anyone prepared to listen.

The family, as Charlotte would always describe the people she had gathered around her since leaving England, had continued to grow, now numbering twelve, not counting herself. There was Martha, of course, dear friend and companion, and Connie, the orphan girl she had taken to her heart aboard the *Chetwynde*, now a young woman; dear Thérèse, nurse-companion to Charlotte's late friend, Helen, and now matron of the little bush nursing hospital Charlotte had built in the bloody aftermath of the Eureka rebellion; and Nellie and Elias, hired as cook and general hand while Charlotte was still married to the late Major D'Arcy. Also, the redoubtable Sergeant Baxter and dear friend and advisor, Louis Roderer. And now, too, builders and Councillors, Michael O'Farrell and Michael Macarthy and, by virtue of his continuing presence, Jed Mansfield – who had, it was blatantly obvious to everyone but Charlotte, lost his heart to the laughing woman in the blue dress at the head of the table.

"The solution was staring me in the face," Charlotte said to the friends she had gathered around the table in the family dining room to celebrate Christmas.

"I thought to myself, I will simply lay my cards on the table and see who picks up," Charlotte continued.

"Tomorrow morning, Thérèse and I will take you on a tour of our hospital. As you will see, the building itself is sound, our equipment has been purchased from the suppliers to the Royal Melbourne Hospital, but we believe the standard of treatment we offer falls short of a growing community's need for a qualified physician-surgeon."

Here, the entire company turned to look at Theo Anders. His face remaining carefully composed, he reached into his inside breast pocket and drew out a sovereign. Reaching forward, he placed the coin in the centre of the table, leaning back and folding his arms, waiting for Charlotte to play her next card.

"Later in the day, when the heat has gone out of the sun, Mick and Mac will take us to a site at the other end of the main street which I have purchased for the purpose of building a small, preparatory school. They have advised me such a project would meet with the full approval of our local Shire Council, should we be able to assure them a suitable principal could be appointed when the building is completed."

Heads now turned in Grace's direction. Glancing sideways at Theo, she unpinned the fob watch she habitually wore over her left breast, and with a mischievous smile, laid it beside Theo's sovereign.

"Of course," Charlotte continued, "we shall need an exceptionally skilled seamstress to oversee the work of two of Sunny's girl cousins who have demonstrated an aptitude, in Martha's opinion, for sewing straight seams, and could be brought on to sew school uniforms.

"Such a person would also have to be skilled enough to be able to dress the wives and daughters of the owners and managers of mines being set up to the west of us at Simmons Reef. She might not wish to spend the whole of each week in Mt Blackwood if she has a flourishing business elsewhere ... but a second shop with a couple of apprentices to take orders and complete set tasks in her absence, perhaps ..?"

By now, the entire table was smiling broadly, and Eliza drew off one of her fingerless, black lace gloves, and tossed it on top of Theo's guinea and Grace's watch.

Then Henry Blake rose to his feet, cleared his throat and, with a half bow in Charlotte's direction, said, "Charlotte, dear lady. You have played your hand well. It would appear the house takes all. But without wishing to trump your tricks, so to speak, George and I planned an announcement of our own tonight.

"This would appear to be an appropriate moment to inform you that we have both resigned from our government positions to go into business for ourselves. We have decided with so many localised strikes, and the availability of safe transfer of assets from Mt Blackwood to Melbourne with Cobb & Co on our doorstep, to set up an office on Main Street, between the hardware shop and the new Cobb & Co office.

"Councillors O'Farrell and Macarthy have approved the concept in plan, and put a team of carpenters and journeymen together to build it for us. So we, too, are here to stay."

Sitting down, flushed, at the spontaneous round of applause his news evoked, Henry gave way to his partner who, rising to his feet, raised his glass and proposed a toast, "I give you Mt Blackwood, ladies and gentlemen," he said, joining in the chorus of 'Hurrah! Hurrah!' that sent the flames flickering lazily in the candelabra into an instant frenzy.

Before the party had a chance to sit down, Charlotte called the company to order with a winning smile. "Ladies, gentlemen, I believe the house is still ahead. For tonight, I am delighted to inform you that Councillor Michael O'Farrell came to see me last week, on the occasion of Connie's nineteenth birthday, to seek my permission as her guardian to ask our dear girl for her hand in marriage.

"I am reliably informed she might be disposed to answer such a request in the affirmative. Perhaps you would like to put the question to her now, Councillor."

Leaping to his feet, Councillor Michael O'Farrell, reverting to his roots, was once again the laughing Irish lad who had arrived on top of a cart full of building supplies, with nothing to offer but the bluest of blue eyes, a shock of shoulder length black hair, and effortless Irish charm.

Walking to the end of the table where Connie stood, one hand over her open mouth, the other gripping the arm of her chair for support, Mick dropped to one knee and, holding out a small velvet box in the palm of his hand, declared his undying love.

"Connie, darlin' girl. You are the fairest thing I've ever seen. When you walk past, me poor heart starts beatin' so fast I fear it will fall apart, me eyes are blinded by the light from yours, and I am sick with fear you might fall for some useless heathen who'll take you away from here, and then I might never set eyes on you again – in which case I will surely die. I can chance the fickle finger of fate no longer. Marry me, sweetheart, before I take me last breath here on the floor at your feet!"

In the breathless silence which followed, Connie gave him the answer he so desperately sought.

"Yes, Michael O'Farrell, I will marry you. Now get up off your knees and stop making a spectacle of yourself and me both."

In the kissing and laughter, toasting and applause that followed, Jed lifted Charlotte's hand to his lips, turning it over and kissing the palm. Visibly shaken, Charlotte looked, as she always did, for support from Martha.

But the older woman avoided her glance, hiding a delighted smile behind her napkin. "You don't need me to tell you what to do this time, my girl," she whispered into the stiff, white linen.

Later that night, when Charlotte stepped out alone onto the front veranda for her customary walk around the hotel grounds, Jed fell into step beside her – as he often did, casually assuming the role of companion and protector.

But, this time, there was a tension between them that distracted her, causing Charlotte to misjudge the depth of the step from the veranda to the ground below. In a second, Jed's arm was around her waist, her wrist caught in his steadying grasp.

"Charlotte," he breathed, as she turned to thank him and, wrapping both arms around her, held her close.

"Jed ..." Charlotte began, but the rest of her response was lost as his mouth covered hers.

"Let us walk," Jed whispered, releasing her from his embrace and propelling her gently forward into the deep shadow of the hayshed where, turning her towards him, he held Charlotte's face in his hands and sought, again, the lips that had surrendered so completely to his own, just moments before.

Slowly, deliberately, his mouth moved down, his lips brushing her neck and coming to rest on the swell of her breast. Raising her hand from Jed's arm, Charlotte reached for the damp curls at the nape of his neck.

Wordlessly, Jed turned away, leading Charlotte by the hand, back across the forecourt, up onto the veranda, through the open door, on up the curving staircase and over the threshold of Charlotte's softly-lit bedroom.

Closing the door behind them he stood watching her as she let her bodice fall back from her shoulders, exposing her naked breasts to the flickering candlelight. Lifting her hands from the hooks at her waist, Jed released them to let the silken fabric of her skirt slide down over her petticoats and pool at her feet. Untying the drawstring that held the petticoats in place, his breath caught in his throat as they foamed around her ankles, leaving her standing naked before him.

Lifting her easily into his arms, Jed laid the love of his life on top of the white cotton quilt, his eyes never leaving hers as he cast off his soft cambric shirt, boots and moleskins to lie beside her, raised up on one elbow to take in the full wonder of the gift she was offering him.

For a fleeting moment, the humiliation of lying naked before D'Arcy flashed across Charlotte's mind, and in that moment she was able to smile, knowing she had laid the ghost of her dead husband to rest forever.

Reaching up, she drew Jed's face down close to hers, and whispered so softly that she thought he could not hear the words, "I love you, Jed."

But he did. Easing himself gently into her, he gave her his response.

Looking back, in the long, dark days after the fire, Charlotte knew she had fallen in love with Jed the moment he leapt from the driver's seat when the Cobb & Co stage pulled up in the forecourt of the Blackwood Rest Hotel for the first time. She tried to think what it was that set her senses on fire, quickening her heartbeat and awakening, unbidden, a long-forgotten need for a man's tender touch. She remembered having to make a determined effort to speak; her response to his effortless smile and confident greeting clipped and formal as she had struggled to subdue the sensation coursing through her mind and body.

Perhaps it was the smile, or the clear blue eyes that seemed to look straight into her soul; or his arm grazing hers as she led him through the rooms his passengers would occupy that night.

Whatever it was, even though Charlotte had managed to collect herself by the end of their tour of the hotel, the damage was done. She had succumbed to the fantasy of lying in Jed's arms that night, alone in her four-poster bed.

Unwilling to trust even her journal with the conflicting memories raging through her heart and mind, she had learned to shut them down as soon as they surfaced. But they waited for the still, immeasurable moments before dawn to rise, unbidden, confronting her again and again. The loss of Richard, her first love – so right and yet so wrong; the brutal consequences of her marriage to D'Arcy; what might have been with

Louis had she not made a decision to eschew that sort of love forever.

But then Jed had walked casually through the walls she had built around herself. Fearing the consequences, she had fought her feelings for him, even in the face of Dickon's growing reliance on him for the companionship he might have found in the father he had never known. But watching the boy and the man together filled Charlotte's heart with happiness for her son ... and walls came tumbling down.

Blue, a complex character with the rare gift of sensing the real value of those with whom he came in contact, had opened up to Connie about the man who had taken a chance on a young drifter, hiring him as a driver when Blue had quit his father's farm to make his own way in the world. Blue, in turn, watched out for his boss, sensing his feelings for Charlotte and keen to see good things happen between the lonely young woman and the worthy young man whose apparently effortless charm hid the pain of love lost under the most tragic and brutal circumstances.

Blue had learned something of Charlotte's past from Connie, always present with the children when they gathered on the steps of the bunkhouse to hear his music or listen to his stories about bushrangers, wild boar and tiger snakes encountered in the bush. He soon realised Connie's regard for Charlotte matched his own for Jed and that they both shared the hope that the two most important people in their lives might recognise a need in each other which the other would fill.

And so it was that sitting on the edge of the back veranda one evening as the sun went down, he tipped his hat to Charlotte and patted the warm boards beside him. Well used to Blue's casual approach to conversation – on the rare occasion he had something he wanted to say – Charlotte put aside the plant she was potting, and drawing off her gardening gloves, sat down beside him.

"About Jed," he began, without any preamble. "Good man. Has feelin's for you. Don't need to get hurt no more." So saying, he pulled on his boots, got up and walked off, back towards the bunkhouse, leaving Charlotte momentarily lost for words.

Connie, who had overheard the one-sided conversation through the

232

open kitchen window, hurried outside to sit beside Charlotte in the spot Blue had vacated moments before.

"Charlotte, dear, don't be offended, Blue means well, it is just that he has no conversational skills, and blurts things out straight from the heart."

"I know that, Connie, but what did he mean about Jed having feelings for me, and not wanting him to be hurt more that he had been? You are closer to Blue than any of us; what has he told you?" Charlotte asked.

Taking Charlotte's hand Connie replied, "Charlotte, Blue is only telling you what everyone else knows. It has been over a year since Jed and Blue first came to stay with us, and it was apparent from the start that Jed had eyes only for you. But we all wondered why it took so long for him to reveal his feelings.

"One morning, I saw Jed leaning over the fence into the back paddock, just staring into space, with such an intense expression on his face that I held the children back from running up to greet him, as is their habit whenever he is here.

"Instead, I took them on to the livery stables, where Blue was getting the team ready for the run back to Melbourne. Worried, I asked him if Jed was unwell, for I had never seen him without his customary warm smile and easy good humour.

"It was then that Blue told me of Jed's feeling for you. And his concern that loving you as much as he did, he could not survive losing you. His anguish that morning had been caused by his indecision over whether or not to declare his love and risk the consequences of refusal, or worse, loving and losing you.

"Neither Blue nor I intended to share the story of Jed's past life, and the pain which prompted him to abandon his country of birth to live on the other side of the world.

"But I feel you should be prepared for your response when Jed does declare his love for you, as I am sure he will, someday, so that if you feel you cannot accept him, you will reject him as gently as possible."

Softly, compassionately, Connie told Charlotte how Jed had fallen in love but twice in his twenty-eight years. At twenty, a woman he had met at a Town Hall dance asked him to walk her home at the end of the night. She had invited him inside to rest a while before undertaking the long walk back to the spread where he had worked as a wrangler since a hurricane had ripped his home apart killing his parents and younger sister. Believing he had found true love, Jed had spent three months in heaven, plummeting to earth when his lover left him for a sixty year-old banker with better prospects than a poor farm boy. He had then quit his job and gone to work for Cobb & Co, determined to make something of his life so that he stood a better chance of holding on to the next woman with whom he fell in love.

At twenty-three, he met Salome, a young Creole girl singing in a bar in New Orleans. It was true love on both sides and there was talk, long into the night, of saving up enough to set them up on a piece of land somewhere. Their plans were accelerated by the joyful news that Salome was expecting his child. But racing home to New Orleans after a week away on the southern run, Jed walked into the bar where Salome worked to find another girl singing Salome's songs. A gunfight had broken out the night he left, a stray shot finding Salome's heart as she stood up to sing. Claiming her body from the city morgue, Jed laid his love to rest in the coloured's cemetery on the edge of town, and left New Orleans, never to return.

In time, after travelling the length and breadth of America, Jed had come to terms with his loss. Hoping adventure might fill the void in his heart, he volunteered to take on the challenge of opening up Australia to Cobb & Co, offering premium travellers a fast and relatively comfortable alternative to bullock carts and horse-drawn drays. Within a month of arriving he had set up the goldfields run from Melbourne to Ballarat and Bendigo and come face to face with the love of his life.

A year later, in the laughter following Mick's declaration of love for Connie, Jed had finally found the courage to reach for Charlotte's hand, offering his heart along with the kiss he placed on her open palm. Life had changed for both of them, since then. As it had for the hamlet of

234

Mt Blackwood, now a broad sprawl of homes, shops, churches and new hotels. The hospital had grown again in the twelve months since Theo threw a golden guinea onto the table at Charlotte's seminal Christmas lunch, signifying acceptance of the role of resident physician-surgeon.

There was now also a school, built in record time by Mick and Mac, exchanging their cutaway jackets, striped trousers and top hats for moleskins and flannel shirts to work alongside a dozen new carpenters and journeymen recruited especially for the purpose. The two-room, wooden school building stood at the opposite end of town from the hospital, surrounded by a neat, white picket fence with a notice proclaiming, MT BLACKWOOD ELEMENTARY SCHOOL over the double front doors.

The fact that the hospital and school were situated at opposite ends of the town had proved something of a problem for Dr Theo and school principal Grace Lichmore, severely limiting the opportunity for them to call in to each other's place of work, to confer on the question of children's health. These meetings seemed to require increasingly long and involved discussions, seriously infringing upon the amount of time Theo deemed necessary to commit to his patients, and Grace wished to devote to her pupils. In the end, they had solved the problem by building a solid brick house midway between the hospital and the school, moving in on their wedding day, one year to the day since Grace, too, had thrown in her lot at Charlotte's table.

There had been another Christmas wedding a week later, when Louis had walked Connie up the aisle to save the life of Councillor O'Farrell, who had spent the intervening months since he proposed to her telling anyone who would listen that if she didn't turn up on the day he would give up the Ghost right there on the altar steps.

Eliza Fitzwilliam had dressed both brides, bridesmaids Katherine and Jade, and all the women present at both weddings. She, too, had accepted Charlotte's Christmas Day challenge to establish a presence in Mt Blackwood, spending two days a week in the elegant, bow-fronted salon Mick and Mac had built for her in the centre of town.

235

The dwelling behind the shop had become a dormitory and workroom for two more of Sunny's cousins that Charlotte had recommended as Eliza's first Blackwood apprentices. The wife of one of the new settlers, herself a skilled and experienced dressmaker, arriving fortuitously in the weeks before the salon was completed, now came in daily, to teach the girls and manage the shop when Eliza was in Bendigo.

While still a permanent resident of that elegant city, Eliza was successful enough, these days, to be able to afford to hold a room at the Blackwood Rest Hotel for her exclusive use. For, losing none of her spontaneous charm, Eliza had shown a natural talent for making money – developed no doubt, during long, evening sessions with Louis – who now helped Eliza, as well as Charlotte, to maintain faultless records and grow her business.

With things running routinely now, Charlotte had persuaded Martha to relinquish some of her more onerous duties overseeing the household, and spend more time doing what she loved best – sharing with Thérèse the joyous events taking place in the hospital birthing room with increasing frequency as more settlers arrived to stay.

Two live-out wives had been hired to manage the day to day running of the hotel while an assistant cook now gave Nellie respite on weekends. With Elias' back becoming a problem, a full time gardener was engaged to look after the kitchen garden, now supplying enough fruit and vegetables to ensure fresh produce and preserves sufficient to keep the hotel well supplied across all four seasons.

There was also a new face in the nursery. Sunny had moved inside to oversee the children when Connie left to become mistress of her own house. Not that there was a lot to do for Dickon, Katherine and Jade now that they spent the best part of the day in school, but encouraged by Charlotte, Sunny made the best of her free time by concentrating on her letters and improving her spoken English. In time, she confided to William and Charlie when her brothers came back in off patrol, she might ask Grace if she could help out at the school. There were black children attending classes now, as well as the whites, and it would be useful to have someone on hand who could speak both languages.

Jed and Charlotte had exchanged vows in a simple ceremony conducted on the hotel's front veranda. Father Ignatius had become a regular visitor over the years since Claude left for Calcutta. Neither Thérèse nor Father Ignatius had spoken of Claude again since the day the then Jesuit brother had unwittingly delivered the news of his exile. But having learned of the couple's impossible love for each other, and fighting his own doubts, the younger priest was mutely sympathetic. He burned with the injustice of far more sinful relationships being swept under the rug while the union of a loving man and woman could not go unpunished.

Having come to know both Jed and Charlotte well, he was delighted to be invited to bless the young couple now before him – even if he would have preferred to conduct the ceremony in one of the two new churches crowning the hill above the township. But Charlotte would have no part of that. She had insisted on the banns being read on the front and back verandas where they would be heard by everyone inside the house, across the courtyard in the bunkroom, cottages and the tents pitched out in the back paddock.

This was where her new life had begun. The hard times she had shared with them all were at an end. Holding the ceremony in the open, she could share this with them, too ... the happiest time of all.

On the morning of her twenty-sixth birthday, four weeks to the day since that seminal moment when Jed had first held her in his arms, Charlotte descended the curving staircase in a simple, muslin gown, fashioned by Eliza and lovingly stitched by Martha, Theresa and Connie, and carrying an armful of perfect blooms from Elias' rose garden.

Jed stood waiting for her in the open doorway, Blue by his side, both men spellbound by the vision coming down the stairs towards them. Reaching him at last, Charlotte placed her lace gloved hand on the sleeve of Jed's buckskin jacket and together they walked out to joyous applause from family, guests, diggers and townsfolk gathered in the forecourt to wish the popular couple enduring happiness.

As Father Ignatius pronounced them man and wife, a magnesium flash sent a puff of smoke drifting up into the eaves above them. Looking to each side of her, Charlotte saw the laughing faces of Dickon, Katherine and Jade, Martha and Thérèse, Connie clinging to the arm of her besotted husband, Nellie and Elias, Sergeant Baxter, Blue, and, of course, dear Louis, frozen in the act of showering the newlyweds with rice and rose petals.

"We will have this moment forever," Charlotte murmured, smiling at the photographer before turning to Jed for the traditional wedding kiss, prompting cheers and laughter from those on the veranda and the crowd milling in front of them.

Looking beyond the assembly gathered in the forecourt, Charlotte could see the rooves and steeples of the town sprawl spreading up the slopes of the surrounding hills, and she reflected on the change the discovery of gold had brought to what was once no more than a place to find a meal and a bed for the night.

In little over five years, the abandoned hotel she had seen as a place to house her family and, perhaps, provide enough of an income to just sustain them, had become the hub of a thriving community, with a hospital and a school, and even a bandstand where the townsfolk congregated for tea dances on a Saturday afternoon. In short, life was progressing with comforting predictability in the burgeoning town of Blackwood.

And for the first time since she set eyes on the Blackwood Rest Hotel, awed by the amount of work that would have to be done before anyone could even begin to think of making a living from it, Charlotte felt she was able to leave it to look after itself for a while.

While their guests were enjoying the sumptuous wedding breakfast it had taken Nellie, the two new housekeepers, the assistant cook and Sunny's aunties the whole morning to set up on long trestle tables, Blue, William and Charlie slipped away to the livery stables. Within minutes, the stagecoach came into view, the horses tossing their plumed heads and stamping their blackened hooves impatiently, as excited by the celebrations as were the children squealing and spinning in front of them. Flowers framed the doors and windows, satin wedding cushions covered the seats, and ribbons flew from the luggage rack.

"Let's be having you, then, Mistress Mansfield, ma'am," called Blue from the driver's seat, to more laughter and applause. Next to him sat William Burrindi, riding shotgun, with Charlie bringing up the rear for reinforcement if required. Sweeping his wife up in his arms Jed made a run for the stagecoach, pausing only long enough to plant a kiss on each of the three children before leaning out through the window to call, "Let's roll, Blue, my wife needs kissin' again!"

Melbourne had changed almost beyond recognition in the years Charlotte had spent in the goldfields.

I never saw so many people in one place, Charlotte noted in her journal, seated on a velvet settle in the lobby of the Grand Hotel while Jed signed them in. *When I first set foot on these shores Melbourne was a very different place. The roads were quagmires in the winter and dustbowls in the summer. The buildings were mostly wooden with only the churches and banks giving any indication they were here to stay. There wasn't even a proper bridge across the Yarra.*

Now, with the countryside giving up so much gold, the city is as elegant as any I believe one would see in England or Europe. There are buildings four storeys high, luxurious hotels and horse drawn vehicles seating as many as sixteen passengers – men, women, rich and poor, all in together.

And the shops! I am sure we shall soon see dear Eliza's fashions in Collins Street, where all the wives of wealthy businessmen flock to shop. And this night we are to accompany Louis to a reception at Bishopscourt, the architectural masterpiece everyone is talking about. It was designed, I am reliably informed, by a convict!

We are to end our week away with a visit to The Melbourne Mechanics' Institute and School of Arts, which has just had gaslight installed, to attend the first of two concerts to be performed there.

The week Jed and Charlotte spent in Melbourne was among the happiest she was to know. Wondering, wordlessly, at the gift they had been given, never out of reach of each other's touch, they gave themselves over to the sheer joy of tender discovery.

Lying among the goose-down pillows in the pastel silks of the Grand's bridal suite, or strolling, hand in hand through falling leaves in the beautiful Botanic Gardens, for a few precious days it seemed time had forgotten them.

Blue didn't need to sound the horn as they reached the sweeping approach to the hotel to announce their return. Members of the Native Police Patrol had met them on the road at Diggers Rest and ridden on ahead to wake the new driver and alert the livery boys to ready the team that would take the stagecoach, now stripped of its wedding finery, on to Ballarat and Bendigo.

By the time they drew to a halt in the forecourt, the whole family was lined up on the front veranda to welcome the newly-weds home, and before Jed could open the door Dickon, Katherine and Jade had broken free from the grownups and run towards them.

"Children, children," Charlotte protested, laughingly, as Jed handed her down the steps to be clutched and squealed at by all of them at the same time.

"One would think we had been away for a year instead of a week!" she said, kissing them each, in turn. "But dark clouds have been following us all the way from Melbourne; let us go inside before the storm breaks, and you shall see what wonderful surprises we have brought back with us."

Jed slept first, still holding Charlotte in his arms. Lying awake, not yet willing to let today's events become tomorrow's memories, Charlotte waited for the next flash of lightning to illuminate her husband's face, smiling in sleep as it had when he lifted himself off her, just minutes earlier.

Tracing the curve of his mouth with the tips of her fingers, she felt the beginnings of his morning beard, recalling how she had laughingly complained when he drew his face across her naked breasts when they began to make love.

The storm had been rolling around the skies above Mt Blackwood for most of the evening; every now and then a short stab of lightning, a lazy roll of thunder, but as yet, no rain. *We could do with rain to settle the dust*, Charlotte thought as she finally drifted off to sleep.

A clap of thunder breaking directly overhead woke her with a violent start, moments later. It took her a few seconds longer to smell the smoke. Jed was on his feet, into his moleskins and pulling on his boots as Charlotte reached the window. Outside, the forecourt was lit with a strange, orange glow. Among the hazy figures running from the bunkhouse she could see Elias, racing for the horse trough.

"Out, Charlotte, we are on fire!" Jed shouted, scooping her skirt and shirt up off the floor and throwing them towards her across the bed. Pushing her bare feet into her boots, she struggled into her clothes and reached the bedroom door at the same time as Jed. Tearing it open, they made for the nursery, snatching the two girls from their beds, and finding Dickon's room empty, headed for the stairs with Sunny following close behind.

Hurrying down into the front hall, they could see the glint of shattered glass and fragments of flaming curtains falling onto the smouldering brocade sofa as they passed the sitting room. To their left, the dining room was already well alight, a river of flame flooding across the Persian rugs to pool around the ornate feet of the solid mahogany table.

In the time it took Jed, Charlotte, Sunny and the girls to reach the shelter of the hayshed, its few remaining bales dragged away by outsiders who had been sleeping there, it seemed the whole of the ground floor was alight.

The only overnight guests, both men, were already clear and running for the pump. Counting heads, Charlotte was relieved to see Martha, Thérèse and Nellie standing close by, wrapped in their bed quilts. Elias was where she would expect him to be, in the centre of the action, working the pump, with outsiders from the bunkhouse, cottages and tents lining up with buckets, bowls and whatever else might hold water to stop the flames reaching the livery stables. It was clear, now, that the hotel could not be saved and Blue and the stockmen were racing the wind to free the horses.

"Dickon!" Charlotte screamed, realising her son was not among the people at the pump or huddled in front of the hayshed. Pausing only long enough to meet her anguished glance, Jed set down Katherine and turned back towards the burning hotel.

Through the open front door Charlotte watched in horror as he bounded up the front stairs, the flames following close behind him. Through the exploding front windows she saw him run from room to room, searching for his stepson. Disappearing from view he pushed down through the thick white smoke billowing up the back stairs; she saw him, again, in the back hall as the front of the building fell away. Over the roar of the fire and the crash of falling timber, she caught the sound of his voice ... "Dickon, lad ...Dickon?"

Mesmerised by the scene unfolding before her, Charlotte failed to register the sight of her son riding towards her on Rocket until he appeared in front of her. Laughing, crying, she reached up to stop the horse by its tangled mane as the boy slid down into her arms.

"I was sleeping with Rocket, he's scared of thunder," he said.

Looking beyond Dickon, expecting to see Jed, she realised there was no-one between the boy and the inferno behind him.

And then the roof opened up like a glorious flower, only to fold back on itself in a breathtaking display of sparks and flying embers, and crash through to the ground floor. Falling to her knees, Charlotte looked into the heart of the fire to see her beloved husband, his arms reaching high above his head, sink down slowly into the flames

Chapter Fourteen
CHINESE NUMBERS

Councillors Michael O'Farrell and Michael Macarthy surveyed what was left of the Blackwood Rest Hotel as dawn broke over the smouldering ruins. They had arrived dressed as the builders they were and always would be, with their entire team of bricklayers, carpenters and journeymen ready to clear away the debris as soon as the embers had cooled.

Charlotte, Martha, Thérèse and the girls were already settled as best they could be in Mac's house. It was large enough to accommodate them all with space to spare and conveniently situated next door to Mick and Connie's, built in its mirror image, where Louis and Reginald could stay when they heard of the disaster. Dickon had refused to be far from the horses, choosing to spend what was left of the night in the hayshed with Blue.

Theo and Grace were with Charlotte and the girls. Father Ignatius had been sent for, and Nellie and Elias, despite having lost everything but the clothes in which they stood, had insisted on preparing breakfast for everyone still on site in one of the open fireplaces servicing the row cottages. Blue was there too, grey faced with grief at the loss of his one, true friend, but needing to be there when his body was retrieved from the ashes. He wanted to tell Jed that although the coach was gone he and Dickon had managed to save the horses, running them two by two through the flying embers that eventually ignited the straw in which the Cobb & Co coach was housed overnight and sent the two-storey building up in flames.

"It all happened so quickly," Elias told Mick as he handed him a plate of eggs and a mug of coffee. "Every able bodied man, woman and child passed buckets from the trough to the edge of the fire while the stockmen took turns to keep the pump handle swinging. But it was no use. Only the wind changing direction turned the flames away from the hayshed, bunkroom and cottages.

"Ever since the fire burnt itself out we've been throwing water on what was left of the hotel, trying to cool the smouldering embers enough to retrieve Jed's body – God rest his soul.

"Blue got the team away, and ran them through to the back paddock. Dickon rode Rocket out and we found the dogs under the water tank out back."

"My men will get Jed out, Elias," said Mick as Elias took a soot-stained rag to his eyes.

"We need to do that before Charlotte comes back, as I know she will. She's not a woman to wait at home to be told what to do. She'll be here as soon as the sun is up, and she can't see Jed the way he'll look when we find him.

"He went down in the front dining room, I'm told. Let us pour as much water as we can carry there, so we can move the roof trusses and see what's underneath them. It's my guess we'll find him, felled and finished off fast beneath one of those, pray God."

Running his fingers through his ash streaked hair, Elias trekked back across the gravel courtyard to issue new instructions to the men huddled hopelessly around the horse trough. Their eyes red ringed with smoke and fatigue, they reached again for their buckets without a moment's hesitation, glancing up at the lightening sky to gauge how long they might have to cool the fallen timber and find Jed before his wife arrived. From the hayshed came the sound of sawing and banging and each man there recognised it as a carpenter already at work on a coffin.

Within minutes, men were venturing into the ruins, boots soaked in standing buckets, long-handled hayforks, hoes and crow-bars poised to prise apart the fallen beams. As one they moved forward, a line four-abreast of weary men throwing down buckets of water before them as they took another step forward onto the steaming embers; behind each man, a bucket line ready with a filled bucket to pass forward until the moment all movement ceased when, up front, one of them wordlessly raised his arm.

It took six of them to raise the beam that had taken Jed down and held him there while the fire consumed his broken body. A woman ran from the tents to thrust a blanket at one of the men on the end of the nearest bucket line, and stood back to watch as it was passed swiftly forward to cover the charred body, so full of life the day before. The bunkroom door, quickly taken off its hinges, heaved from hand to hand along the bucket line and slid beneath the blanket-covered body, served as a stretcher.

Blue and Mick, regardless of the heat still rising from the debris underfoot, kicked through the embers to lift the stretcher and carry Jed silently out through the smoking ruin, across the courtyard and into the hayshed. Hats were snatched from heads as they passed by. No-one spoke. There was no sound at all except the crunch of booted feet on hissing coals and loose gravel, and a long drawn out sob as Blue helped manoeuvre the misshapen figure into the raw pine box, hastily placed on a trestle table stripped of the breakfast plates it held moments earlier. Before he could nail the lid into place, Father Ignatius arrived with his satchel full of vestments and holy oil, to say the words that would see Jed's soul pass through purgatory to its rightful resting place.

"Holy Mother of God," he whispered, hastily crossing himself as he pulled back the blanket to find a place to anoint the remains. Murmuring the rest of the litany as speedily as he could, while still showing the deceased the respect he deserved, he finished in time to allow Blue to drive the last nail into the lid just as Charlotte walked through the open shed door.

Not looking at the coffin, she went straight to Blue who had pulled away, standing resolutely erect beside the makeshift bier. Silently she embraced him, reaching up to kiss the young man's cheeks, now wet with tears.

"Be strong, Blue, for I have need of your strength just now," she said. "Together we must farewell a loving husband and a true friend. Come now, stand beside me as we wish him God's speed on his final journey."

Turning, at last, to look at the coffin, Charlotte reached for Blue with one hand, and rested the other upon the lid over the place where her husband's heart might be.

"Dear Jed, sleep well, for you have earned your rest. You will live on while those who knew and loved you live. We will talk of the love and laughter you leave in your wake as you walk through our memories. We will shed no tears for you, for then we must acknowledge we have lost you."

So saying, Charlotte took her wedding shawl from her shoulders, spread it carefully across the coffin, and walked resolutely from the darkened barn into the sunlight to thank each member of the bucket line, each man with a rake or hoe or crowbar, each woman with a broom, blanket or bowl, for their effort to contain the fire and, failing, find her husband. And for the rest of the day, while Father Ignatius sat with Jed in the barn, comforting those who queued to pay their respects, Charlotte saw to the comfort of the outsiders – for diggers and their families, unaware of the catastrophic events of the previous night, were still arriving on their way to and from the goldfields.

Martha and Thérèse appeared when the sun, as if to spare the men toiling in the midday heat to clear the site, withdrew behind a solid band of blue-black cloud, giving way to drenching rain. With Connie and Sunny caring for the children, they set about assessing burns and wounds that went unnoticed while the fire was being fought and ignored while the fire fighters searched for Jed.

Some they dressed on site, others had to be treated by Theo and the nurses they had trained to cope with such emergencies, under tents

246

hastily erected with blistered hands and streaming eyes.

The Burrindi brothers and the rest of their Native Patrol unit, alerted to the fire by the smoke drifting five miles away, had ridden like the wind to do what they could, working tirelessly throughout the day to ensure the site was safe. At sunset, they climbed wearily up on their jumpy mounts to report the fire to their superiors in Melbourne – William promising to first deliver news of the disaster to Louis and leave word for Sergeant Baxter, away on duty across the northern border.

Louis had dressed with particular care for dinner with Alistair and Isabella Chalmondly in the Bank's splendid apartments at Bishopscourt. While he wished to impress his employer – and being French, also the lovely Isabella – as an *homme du monde*, his partner for the evening would be Eliza Fitzwilliam, the delightful owner of the new *haute couture* establishment opened three months ago at the top end of fashionable Collins Street.

Louis had seen much of Eliza over recent months. She had taken rooms in the Alonquin, a small but elegant apartment building close by St Patrick's Cathedral on the crest of Eastern Hill. She loved the lofty view but had never known complete rest since she moved in. Her sleep was interrupted intermittently by the ringing of bells calling the faithful to worship when, in her opinion, God-fearing people should be resting from their worthy labours. She now wished to purchase one of the elegant terrace homes built in East Melbourne on the back of the gold rush; still close to the booming central business district and with a view across the lower reaches of Eastern Hill, but far enough from the bells to allow her to lie undisturbed between her silken sheets.

But while her salons in Bendigo and Blackwood were both doing well, and anyone who was anyone had queued for admission to the grand opening of the Collins Street Salon, the income from these enterprises on deposit at the Union Bank was not yet sufficient to enable outright purchase of such a property. The lady, quite reasonably, looked to her bank to lend her the difference.

However, the fact that the house on which Eliza had her heart fixed happened to be next door to the one Louis, himself, had purchased some twelve months earlier, together with Louis' feelings for Eliza – which had grown surprisingly over the months she had spent in Melbourne planning her city business venture – had presented the high principled bank manager with a moral dilemma. Although the projections for Eliza's future income, based on his scrupulous stewardship of her accounts over the past three years, more than stood up to the challenge of meeting repayments on a loan of such scale, Louis could not, in all conscience, authorise such a loan himself.

Presenting Eliza to Alistair this evening in a social setting would give the Chairman an opportunity to renew his acquaintance with the young woman he had first met in London, years earlier, and judge for himself her candidature as a borrower of the Union Bank's money.

With Alistair and his new bride, Lady Isabella Chalmondly née Wilmington Fyffe-fyffe Smythe, and their thirty-two pieces of luggage finally unpacked, Isabella would no doubt wish to visit the salon on everyone's shopping list, during her visit to Melbourne. An invitation would lead neatly into a brief history of Eliza's spectacular commercial success and, hopefully, endorsement of the loan by the Union Bank Chairman, himself.

Turning to assist the beautiful young woman from his carriage on arrival at the elegant mansion, Louis caught his breath at the sight of auburn curls drawn back into an elegant chignon and creamy breasts glimpsed tantalisingly above swirling silk, as Eliza stepped down into his arms

Although he had fallen in love with Charlotte when she first strode into his office all those years ago, the responsibility of ensuring her recovery from the degradation of her finances by her profligate late husband had made it impossible for him to declare himself. Over time, his passion had mellowed to a warm and respectful friendship. He found he was content to become her adviser, confidante and, by virtue of his position as godfather to all three of her children, a privileged member of the family.

248

There was nothing impeding his love for Eliza, though, and with her lively wit and ready smile, she brought lightness to his life such as he had never known in all his forty years.

Tactile and intelligent, she would sit with him for hours while he pored over papers at night, interrupting his reading with a hand laid gently upon his shoulder, a murmured, "Louis, dear," as she leaned down to set a glass of claret on his desk. Yes, Louis was undoubtedly in love – and if he was not mistaken, his love was reciprocated.

Patting the inside breast pocket of his black velvet cutaway tail coat, he reassured himself that the diamond hoop he had secreted there as he set out to collect her earlier that evening, was still in situ. If all went to plan, he would place it on her finger in the privacy of the coach before they arrived back at the Alonquin, later tonight.

Alistair and Isabella had heard Louis' coach pull into Bishopscourt's gravel driveway and were waiting under the portico to greet their guests.

"Louis, my friend, what a dashing figure you cut tonight. One might be excused for thinking you had come a-courting!" Alistair, no more subtle or discreet now than he had been on his first visit to the colony, slapped his friend on the shoulder and burst out laughing as the hapless banker cast a horrified glance at Eliza, regretting his rash decision taken earlier, in the office, to confide in Alistair his intention to propose that night.

"Do introduce us to your charming partner, Louis," Isabella intervened, saving Louis from more torment.

Introductions completed, with both women performing reciprocal social bobs, Isabella linked arms with Eliza to lead the men into the spacious interior of the building. As things turned out, no business at all was conducted that evening. Alistair had glanced over the ledgers recording Eliza's profits and losses in the office after Louis had indicated his interest in the young woman, and found nothing at all in the latter column to occasion concern. He could justifiably recommend approval of a credit limit far in excess of the amount required to purchase the East Melbourne investment. He knew from personal experience that a woman of Eliza's undeniable good taste would need sufficient funds to furnish such a property stylishly – and no doubt, extravagantly.

Besides, if a marriage took place as soon as one could reasonably expect, the house might become available to accommodate visiting bank executives, such as himself, when the lease on Bishopscourt ran out. An important consideration, as notice had been given, already, of the Archbishop's intention to make it his official residence by the end of the year.

Following the succulent rack of lamb, resting in a concentrated jus with just a hint of port and garnished with sprig of mint, served with *pommes duchesse* and fresh English peas, Alistair stood to propose a toast. But not before startling the butler by ordering him to ensure a double helping of crème fraiche on his wife's strawberry fool when dessert was, eventually, served.

"Dear friends," he began, a smile teasing the corners of his carefully composed mouth. "As you may have observed, my darling Isabella has been eating enough for two, tonight. So there is little to be done to preserve her genteel reputation other than to share our joyful news. Please join me in a toast to my beautiful wife, the loveliest mother-to-be in the entire world – Isabella!"

"Alistair, you are incorrigible," Isabella protested, collapsing helplessly in her chair as her husband raised his glass, and after emptying the contents, covered his blushing wife's lips with his own.

But Alistair was not done with his mischief yet.

"Let us take a turn in the garden before dessert is served," he said, pulling Isabella to her feet and making for the open French windows. "I think another kind of 'fool' has to be served up before the strawberries, don't you, Louis?"

When Alistair and Isabella walked back into the house, dessert was forgotten altogether as Eliza lifted her left hand to reveal Louis' diamonds decorating the third finger. Whooping delightedly, Alistair sent the butler for a magnum of, "La Veuve Cliquot-Muiron's finest!"

The rest of the evening was given over to plans for an elaborate wedding, hosted by the visiting Chairman of the Union Bank and his beautiful wife, with the reception at Bishopscourt, of course, and the ceremony held in respect of Louis' religious affiliation (with his brother – not, necessarily, the church into which they were both born and educated) at St Patrick's Cathedral. With no reason to delay the ceremony, and with Alistair and Isabella having booked passage back to England at the end of the month, the date was set for the day before the Chalmondlys' departure.

News of the disaster had reached Louis the morning after the happy evening he had proposed to Eliza. Now, happiness was tempered by shock and sadness. Advising his assistant manager he would be away for at least a week, Louis had called for a hansom cab to take him to Bishopscourt to advise Alistair of his proposed journey and the reason for it. He then went on to the Alonquin, to break the sad news to Eliza.

"Charlotte will have immediate need of me," he said, holding her close. I must leave for Blackwood immediately.

"I will go alone, my love, for I can travel faster by horse than by coach. My return will be determined by the time it takes to satisfy myself that she and the children are appropriately cared for until her intentions are known about their immediate future."

"Oh, Louis, poor Charlotte. She loved Jed so dearly, and now she is alone again. Ask her, please, if she would like me to come to her. Send a rider with the answer, and if it is in the affirmative, I will leave immediately.

"But she might prefer to bring the family to live here while she decides what to do next. The purchase of the East Melbourne house will be finalised any day now. Tell her it is hers for as long as she wishes for I shall have no need of it once we are married."

Charlotte was never so pleased to see anyone as she was Louis, when he pulled up his horse in what was once the grassed forecourt of the

Blackwood Rest Hotel. Now, it was scorched and scored, covered with workers sawing timber and barrowing shale, making ready to begin to rebuild the Blackwood Rest Hotel as soon as ashes had been raked over and carted away. Her glistening eyes belied the tears she had vowed not to shed, and she clung to Louis in silence until she could trust herself to speak.

"Louis, dear Louis," she whispered, eventually. "I knew you would come."

Nellie had seen Louis wheel into the drive and appeared with a tray on which she balanced a plate of bread, cheese and slices of ham, a carafe of water and two goblets which had materialised from who knew where. Elias followed behind her, uncorking a bottle of claret retrieved from the bluestone cellar running under what had been his and Nellie's quarters. Blue, now never far from Charlotte's side, moved forward to take Louis' horses – the one he rode, and the changeover led to be able to complete his journey before nightfall.

"As you can see, we have no livery stables left to house your horses," Charlotte said, as Louis nodded a silent greeting in Blue's direction. "But Blue and the boys have built stalls out of straw bales, thankfully stored in a tin shed behind the bunkhouse for want of space in the stables."

"God love you for coming so quick, sir," said Nellie, blinking furiously. "Things need doing properly and Miss Charlotte will not leave here except to go back to Councillor Macarthy's house at the end of the day to tuck in the children. First light she will be back here again."

Before Louis could reply, Martha joined them. She had set off from Mac's house, minutes earlier, to walk Charlotte back with her when the workers went back to their homes and families. All formality long forgotten between them, the older woman held Louis close, knowing what awaited him in the process of enacting the formalities necessary to record Jed's death and the disposition of his remains.

"Mick and Connie have a room set aside for you in their house, Louis, which is joined by a common wall to Mac's," she said. "Mac has kindly given his over to Charlotte and the children, Thérèse and myself, and moved in with his brother for the time being."

Fortunately, Louis had taken the books for the hotel, hospital and school back to Melbourne with him on his last visit, in preparation for the bank's annual audit to be conducted, this year, in the presence of its new Chairman. So he was able to quickly assess Charlotte's capacity to rebuild and re-establish herself at the Blackwood Rest Hotel.

Charlotte and Louis had walked together from the twin houses in which they had each spent a sleepless night, to the Blackwood branch of the Union Bank the following morning. Unpacking the ledgers from the saddle bag slung over his shoulder, Louis came round the desk between them to hold Charlotte's hands in his own.

"Charlotte, dear, the hospital and the school have absorbed most of your capital over the past two years. We must think, carefully, where the money will come from to rebuild the hotel and fund the running costs until you get on your feet again.

"Then there is the question of wages. You have a considerable number of men and women working for you now. They have families to support and will expect to be paid.

"And, my dear, although it pains me to distress you further, I must remind you that you no longer have the unpaid support of your husband. Jed was able to manage the livery stables, the stock, and the stockmen – not to mention earnings he brought in by way of Cobb & Co's passengers. Who could you afford to take over that role?"

Before Charlotte could answer, Louis' clerk put his head round the door to ask if Charlotte would receive a visitor.

Even with the rain, it had taken almost a week for the ground to cool enough to begin clearing the site. In all that time, Blue, who still lived in the bunkhouse, had quietly taken on the responsibilities Jed had assumed over the two years since the Blackwood Rest Hotel had become Cobb & Co's gateway to the goldfields.

With their stagecoach lost in the fire, the company had sent a new coach, team and driver to cover the route, operating from one of the new hotels established in Mt Blackwood since the mines had opened up. The horses Blue had saved would be rested until such times as surface burns healed and the fear settled in their heaving chests and rolling eyes.

His own future with Cobb & Co was made clear when word came from the American owner of the Australian franchise that he was selling the operation to a Victorian investor, and Blue should seek employment elsewhere. In that instant, Blue grew into the man Jed saw in him from the start. Telling Dickon to stay close to Elias, he went looking for Charlotte.

On hearing Blue's news Charlotte looked at Louis and said, "I think we have found the answer to your question, dear friend."

"Dear Blue," she said, "Louis and I have been wondering who to approach for the position of station manager for the new Blackwood Rest Hotel, livery stables and outside accommodations.

"Elias will have enough to do restocking and maintaining the cellars, the produce garden and the gas lighting we will install in the new hotel. We shall need a younger man, with experience, to oversee the maintenance of the buildings and the management of stock and horses.

"He would have to be capable, and known to us as a true and trusted friend. It would appear Cobb & Co has released you at exactly the right time.

"If you will accept the position, we are prepared to offer you double the wage you received from Cobb & Co and a dwelling attached to an office of your own.

"Please say you will stay with us, Blue, for I cannot bear the thought of losing you too."

It took Blue a moment or two to process the offer being set out before him. Twisting his hat in his hands, he looked first, at Louis, and then at Charlotte.

"Sorry, Mistress Charlotte, ma'am," he began, slowly. "Afraid I can't do that."

Seeing Charlotte's reaction, Blue was quick to explain, "I came to see you today to ask if I could stay on at Blackwood, doing anything, for room and board alone.

"I couldn't accept no more until you are back on your feet – and then I wouldn't feel right about you paying me more than what Jed did.

"Excusin' manners and all, ma'am, but maybe I could make you an offer," he continued.

"My ma passed away when I was born. There was only me and pa after that. When he passed on there was nothing to keep me on the farm so I sold it and hooked up with Jed. It wasn't a big place, but I reckon there'd be enough to make Cobb & Co an offer for the team healing in the back paddock, and maybe even a new coach.

"And I'm thinking the new Blackwood Rest Hotel could then have its own rig to bring outlying diggers in to meet the stage going on to Bendigo or back to Ballarat and Melbourne. Passengers back to the hotel again, too."

Neither Charlotte nor Louis – nor anyone else, for that matter – had heard Blue utter as many as two sentences, consecutively, in the whole of the time they had known him, and both were, themselves, quite speechless for a moment.

Then, "Where is this money, Blue?" Louis asked, gently.

"In your bank, sir," Blue replied. "Jed put it there for me."

There were other unexpected investors in the rebirth of the Blackwood Rest Hotel. Over dinner at Mick and Connie's, Theo revealed he had inherited a considerable sum on the death of his godmother the previous year. It was just sitting in Wells Fargo Bank while he made up his mind what do with it. And, if Charlotte was amenable to the idea, he would like to make her an offer for the hospital. He and Grace had found each other in this little frontier town and felt they had put down roots here. Grace's work at the school was rewarding, and Theo felt he was able to make a real difference to the health of the local community.

He also had a wonderful working relationship with Thérèse, and together they were trying to put an end to detrimental common practices such as purging as a treatment for everything from constipation to diarrhoea – often resulting in patients arriving at the hospital dying of dehydration. They had also introduced the idea of isolation for typhoid and diphtheria, common scourges in Europe imported with devastating consequences into the goldfields. Three tents now stood ready within walking distance of the hospital to accommodate any man, woman or child who presented at the clinic door with a fever, until they could be properly assessed and diagnosed.

There was much more to do for the growing community and if Charlotte would only name her price, Theo would transfer the money held in San Francisco to the Union Bank in Melbourne, immediately. The interest on the balance would be more than enough to cover the cost of wages and supplies.

"Do say yes, Charlotte dear," said Grace, sitting beside her husband, across the desk from Louis. "Theo will need to keep himself fully occupied during the coming months, for my time will be totally taken up with the school and... and the baby."

Charlotte looked questioningly at Grace, then rose swiftly to embrace her friend, the prospect of a new life lighting the darkness of the hour prompting handshakes and embraces all round.

There was also the pastoralist who had supplied the hotel with beef and lamb over the past five years. He told Martha, who told, Louis, that he had been thinking about running a few more sheep, and wondered if Charlotte might be interested in an offer for the paddock that ran alongside the Lerderderg River. And later the same day, Blue revealed he had been approached by the owners of the new Leviathan coach company about space for their carriage and team when the hotel, coach house and stables were rebuilt.

When Louis looked again at the figures, back in his Melbourne office, the estimate submitted by Mick and Mac for the cost of supplies to rebuild the hotel and the livery stables balanced very favourably against the sums pledged for the hospital, land and stabling – particularly as the Councillors had refused to put in a price for the actual labour, seeing it as an opportunity to repay their friend and patron for the start she had given them when they needed it. The only cost that wasn't covered, as far as Louis could tell, was the amount required to furnish the new Blackwood Rest Hotel.

Given the high standard Charlotte had set in its first incarnation, expectations of comfort and style would be high. Unless another investor indicated interest, he would have to talk to her about raising a mortgage to cover that very necessary expenditure.

But then Louis remembered Charlotte's deed box, buried deep in the bank vaults. Might it still hold some of the miners' gold?

Calling for the Vault Master, Louis followed the officer down a flight of granite steps to an underground labyrinth of bluestone cells, each with a six-inch steel door and a series of Smith & Co locks with individual keys.

There were gold vaults containing dust, nuggets and quartz; silver vaults with whole shelves given over to separate, family depositors. And there were vaults containing tier upon tier of steel deposit boxes containing quantities of jewellery, legal documents and, very possibly, sizeable undeclared nuggets, secreted away to escape the gold tax.

Louis knew Charlotte had such a deposit box but was fairly certain that the gold it had once held – donated by successful diggers in return for the generosity they had encountered on their way out to the diggings – had been used to build the hospital and the school. Still, as a banker, he was obliged to check, and as so many transactions were now delegated to members of his ever expanding staff, he might have missed a more recent deposit.

Standing to one side, he allowed the Vault Master to turn each key in the door of the Box Vault, and as the heavy metal door swung open, stepped forward into the chill, stale air. Taking a moment to adjust to the thin light from the lamp the Vault Master had placed on a bench along one side of the windowless room, Louis called out a series of numbers identifying the box belonging to Charlotte. Placing it on the bench, the officer then turned the lock and stepped away to allow his employer to examine the contents unobserved.

As Charlotte's legal representative, Louis had no qualms about sorting through the unlocked box before him. But lifting the lid, he was disappointed to find it held nothing more than the deeds to the hotel, land and holdings which made up the Blackwood Rest Hotel estate, a scattering of newly minted golden guineas, and Jade's father's yellow satin purse.

Collecting the coins from the bottom of the box he stacked them in towers of ten to come up with the total of two hundred and thirty guineas. A small bag of gold dust had lain hidden under the deeds, which might add another few guineas, leaving only the contents of the Chinese purse.

Sighing, Louis loosened the drawstring and took stock of the contents for the second time, remembering his brother, Claude, holding up the purse Lin Lee had given to Charlotte to help with his daughter's keep.

The first item Louis retrieved was the tightly rolled parchment scroll with its indecipherable Chinese characters; the next, the small jade pendant; and last, the shard of mirrored glass – to capture the living likeness of Jade's mother, Lin Lee had said, in the reflection of her daughter's image.

Pulling open the spooled scroll, the banker's practiced eye now recognised a rhythm to the indecipherable brush strokes. A code, perhaps. Or maybe a column of figures. He had seen something like it when the Chinese bankers, working with chop and abacus on the goldfields, had brought in wicker baskets full of calico bags to be held for safekeeping in the Union Bank. He remembered that in 1853, when resentment of the Chinese was at its height, so many bags were brought in that a whole vault had been given over to the Chinese bankers.

"Vault Master," he called, turning and beckoning to the officer now standing, respectfully, by the vault door. "Ask Mr Shen Moon to wait upon me here, if you please."

Within minutes, the officer in charge of Chinese deposits and withdrawals hurried into the room, adjusting his gold rimmed *pince nez* on the bridge of his nose with one hand, the fingers of the other curled around the frame of a rattling abacus.

"What do you make of this, Mr Moon?" Louis asked, pointing to the scroll he had placed back on the bench.

Setting down the abacus beside the deposit box, Shen Moon picked up the scroll and drew it open. Fixing one end under the edge of the deed box, he held the other in one hand while the fingers of his free hand flew over the abacus, his mouth moving wordlessly. Repeating the process, he rewound the scroll and turned to face his employer.

"Well, Mr Moon, what does it all mean?"

A smile spread slowly over the accountant's face. "This is a record of investment, sir. Very common on the goldfields in the early days. The Chinese diggers were, for the most part, unable to speak English and banked with those with whom they could communicate in their own language.

"Almost anyone with an abacus became a banker to the Chinese diggers. They set up tents on the goldfields and devised a system of accounting recorded on individual scrolls.

"Each time a Chinese digger came in with a handful of gold dust or nuggets it was weighed, assayed, and its value recorded on the investor's personal scroll. The records were duplicated when it was bagged and taken to Melbourne to be deposited ... here."

"So we can match the characters on this man's scroll to our records for the period?" Louis asked.

"Yes, M'sieur Roderer, sir. And if my calculations are correct, whoever this belongs to holds the key to a small fortune."

"And that amounts to ...?"

"Eighteen hundred guineas and a few pence, sir."

It had taken less than three months to clear what was left of the Blackwood Rest Hotel and build again. The first load of burnt timber, dead embers and ashes was hauled away, the day after Jed's funeral, in a convoy of drays, carts and hand barrows, by silent townsfolk. They came to pay their respects to his widow in the best way they knew how; giving something back to the young woman who had given them a hospital and school, and for many, also a meal and a place to lay their heads.

But before anyone set foot in the ashes the first day, Charlotte had walked alone to the spot where Jed had fallen, scooped up a handful of ashes and placed them in a small metal box. When the land was cleared, before the footings were dug, she stepped over the plumb lines and buried the box in the freshly raked earth. Stepping back over the taut string, she watched as Mick and Mac, who had withdrawn respectfully to one side, led a line of labourers forward to dig in the stumps that would support the floor of the new hotel.

Jed had been buried at first light, the morning after the fire that claimed his life. There had been no time for Louis and Reginald to reach Mt Blackwood in time for the funeral, such as it was. The Burrindi brothers had rounded up the other members of the Native Police Patrol checking licences nearby, and ridden at full gallop to render assistance. Too late to do more than bucket the smouldering ruins, they had dug Jed's grave in the tiny hillside graveyard consecrated by Father Claude for Jade's parents. They had lowered the coffin into the earth as Father Ignatius said the words no-one could bear to hear; standing back as Charlotte, supported by Blue, dropped wildflowers into the void.

Sombre as it was, the mood at dinner on the night of Louis' arrival a day later, was lightened by the news of his impending marriage to Eliza. Theo and Grace had arrived at the house Mac had given over to Charlotte earlier that day, bringing with them a basket of pies and pasties prepared for them by Grace's cook, the west country wife of a local farmer. She had been a regular visitor to the Blackwood Rest Hotel, bringing eggs, butter and cheeses to subsidise the income from the wheat crop her husband was bringing along on their nearby smallholding. The soft burr of her voice and her matronly figure – not to mention the basket of wholesome, comforting food – had reminded Martha of the cook back at Hatfield Hall, waiting in the front hall to farewell Charlotte with just such a basket for their journey into the unknown.

Grace had also brought an assortment of her own skirts, shirts dresses and undergarments for Charlotte until the girls in Eliza's Blackwood frock shop could fashion new garments. Katherine and Jade were fitted out from the school's clothes library – hand-me-downs donated by parents whose children had outgrown them. Therese and Martha were perfectly comfortable in their hospital uniforms for the time being, and Nellie had gratefully accepted garments the farmer's wife had told Grace might do her friend a turn as they were both, "about as round as each other".

"We will now, of course, delay our wedding plans until the end of the mourning period," said Louis, after he had received the spontaneous expressions of surprise and congratulations from everyone seated at Mac's long, mountain ash table. Charlotte, at its head, smiled for the first time since she had fallen asleep in Jed's arms the night of the fire.

"Dearest Louis, there will be no delaying such a happy occasion. There will be no period of mourning for Jed, no widow's weeds for me, for Jed is not lost to us but continues on in the memory of those who loved him. We will all attend this joyous occasion, and he will be there among us.

"Besides, dear Grace will not be in any condition to travel if you delay beyond the end of the month, and you know how important it is for her to have something of interest to tell her pupils about when school resumes after the holidays."

Charlotte also declined Eliza's offer of accommodation in Melbourne, explaining she felt compelled to return to Blackwood, where she belonged.

"Being close to Jed gives me comfort. I feel the children will benefit, too, from continuing their routine as best they can, being with their friends, at school, and riding their ponies with Blue at week's end. And Mac has made us welcome, here, until the hotel is rebuilt.

"Tell Eliza that while we would all love to see her, she will be far too busy now to travel all the way to Mt Blackwood and back within the little time left until the wedding. We will see her in all her splendour on the day!"

But by the time Louis returned to Melbourne, having completed the formalities required by the fire and Jed's death, Eliza had set her army of seamstresses to work on silk, taffeta and muslin cut to measurements recorded in her client register, to create new gowns for her Blackwood women friends, and for her bridesmaids, Katherine and Jade.

She arrived in Blackwood a week later, barely able to fit herself and one of her Collins Street fitters into a coach filled with their wedding wardrobes, protected from the elements by clouds of black tissue and calico bags, each with a different name embroidered across the foot.

After a final fitting, the gowns they chose to wear at the wedding would be taken back to Melbourne and left in Eliza's new house, which the women and girls would occupy while Theo and Elias went next door to Louis' to wait on the nervous groom.

Alistair had claimed the right to give the bride away, proclaiming a tenuous relationship through a shared godmother.

Returning to his seat in the magnificent Cathedral overflowing with dignitaries – including the new Governor, businessmen and their wives, and other loyal customers of the Union Bank gathered to wish the happy couple well, Alistair reached across his wife for Charlotte's hand, knowing that however happy she was for Louis and Eliza, she would miss the close and easy companionship of her long time friend.

Chapter Fifteen

REVISTING THE PAST

hen Reginald Baxter cantered up the sweeping drive to the Blackwood Rest Hotel twelve months later, he wondered if the stories he had heard of the fire that razed the hotel, taking the life of Jed Mansfield with it, had been exaggerated. For the building in front of him was the one he knew well. True, the paint hadn't yet been scored by the sun and the shutters hung straighter that they had when he had first found it, abandoned by its previous owners, all those years ago. But it was still, unmistakably, the Blackwood Rest Hotel.

He had ridden out to Mt Blackwood as soon as his unit returned from a year-long posting to New South Wales. With gold running out in the Victorian goldfields, diggers who had yet to strike it rich had set off on the long march across the border to Lambing Flats. A new strike there offered what they saw as a last chance to make their fortune. Many, already resentful of the number of Chinese diggers in Victoria, saw them as intruders on the goldfields of New South Wales, too. As sporadic episodes of violence increased, the outnumbered New South Wales Police had called for military reinforcements from Victoria. Sergeant Baxter and his men had answered the call, taking much longer to quell the battle of Lambing Flats than had been expected. News of the fire and loss of life had appeared in the handbill that passed for a broadsheet in Lambing Flats. As soon as he rode back into Victoria Barracks Reginald had put in a request for a three-day furlough, picked up a spare horse, and ridden hard to reach the family he had come to regard as his own.

Martha saw him first, as she walked out across the veranda on her way to the hospital. Calling to Dickon to run and tell his mother to come quickly, she stopped in the middle of the forecourt.

"Reginald, is it really you?" Martha asked, as he drew close. "We have missed you, dear friend. Charlotte will be so happy to see you again. We have much to tell you."

Dismounting, the soldier clasped Martha in his arms and then thrust her away at arm's length.

"Let me look at you, Mistress. I was afraid you might have been hurt, or worse, in the fire they said completely destroyed the old hotel – although that seems hard to believe as I stand here today."

"Ah, Reginald, it did happen. What you see before you is a replica of the old hotel – at least on the outside. Inside there are some differences, but you will notice other changes, as well." Before she could go on, Charlotte came running from the newly built stables, her face flushed with excitement at seeing the trooper she had relied on so much in the past, standing before her.

"Reginald! You are back!" she cried, taking both his hands in hers. "We knew you had been sent north but you were gone so long we thought the posting must have been permanent.

"Come inside, dear man, there is so much to tell you but, first, you must be in need of refreshments after such a long ride. Let Dickon take your horses and cool them down while we make up a room for you. We have new livery stables with water tanks supplying troughs in every stall, and room enough, now, for twenty horses when the coach is out."

Handing the reins of the lathered mounts to the lithe young boy who was already unbuckling the girths to let the panting animals breathe more easily, the weathered sergeant slung his saddle bag over one shoulder and followed Charlotte and Martha into the familiar front hall. Pausing, Charlotte turned and looked up into the trooper's clear, blue eyes.

"You have no doubt heard the home you found for me burnt to the ground a little more than a year ago, Reginald. But as you can see, I insisted its replacement reproduced every feature of the place we had come to love – as much for its memories as for the space and scale of the rooms.

"I feel I never really thanked you for everything you did for us during the dark days with Rollo, and for the many kindnesses you showed us when there was no-one else to turn to.

"But the greatest was to see us settled in this place. Had you not found the Blackwood Rest Hotel, and helped us acquire it, who knows what might have happened to us.

"You are part of our family, Reginald. This is as much your home as ours. There will always be a bed and a place at the table for you in the new Blackwood Rest Hotel, just as there was at the old one. Welcome home, dear friend."

Over dinner that night the trooper learned the full extent of the damage the fire had done, destroying the hotel, the livery stables, and something inside Charlotte, as well. Losing Jed had extinguished the incandescent light behind her eyes; her radiant smile was more measured now, and the defiant set of her jaw, lifted in response to any challenge that came her way, was more inclined to tilt in contemplative appraisal, these days.

But this was not a woman defeated by the suffering she had experienced, Reginald thought, seeing Charlotte with fresh eyes after such a long absence. Nor was she the disillusioned young bride struggling to build a life for her family in a harsh and unfamiliar environment. The woman who sat at the head of the table, now, was wiser for the sum of her experiences. Confident she could face any challenge, having lived through the very worst, she had found some measure of inner peace. This, as well as the gaslight which illuminated every corner of each room as candles and spirit lamps had never done, was the change Martha had known he would see when he remarked upon the reincarnation of the hotel in its original image.

The gaslight, Blue had told Reginald as they smoked their after-dinner pipes outside, was something Charlotte had insisted on when the hotel

265

was rebuilt. At first, it was thought the fire had been started by a lightning strike igniting the shingle roof. But on sifting through the ashes, while clearing the site, Mick had come across solidified pools of red glass where the French windows in the dining room had stood open to catch the cooling night breeze. Ahead of the storm, the gentle breeze had quickly turned into a wildly gusting gale. It was now considered likely that the wind had whipped up the heavy tapestry curtains, knocking over the ruby glass lamp, left burning to light the way through to the kitchen for guests in search of a cooling draught of water during the night.

There were changes outside the building, too. With the gold rush all but over the tents set up in the back paddock to accommodate early diggers and their families had been packed away; stored in the stables against need for relief in the aftermath of future bushfires and floods. The row of cottages still stood, but two had been opened up as one, giving Nellie and Elias a sitting room as well as a bedroom. A similar arrangement had been made for Blue; the last two left empty for the occasional overflow of guests from the main house.

The bunkroom, built onto the back of the hayshed, had been dismantled and re-erected against the back wall of the new livery stables, affording changeover drivers on the runs from Melbourne to Ballarat and Bendigo a bed and a bath – for with two large tanks supplying the stables alone, there was now water enough to supply a bath house at one end of the bunkroom.

The 'outsiders' as Nellie had dubbed those who could afford neither a room nor a meal inside the hotel but who were never turned away, were now mainly single men – last-chancers looking for the leavings early diggers had missed or considered not worth the effort to prize from the earth or river bed. A loft had been built into the roof of the hayshed with space enough for up to a dozen to roll out their swags after a bowl of Nellie's ever-ready, pot-luck stew.

When the men had finished their pipes, Blue left to make sure the livery stables were locked down for the night, and Charlotte and Martha joined

Reginald on the veranda. This was the women's favourite time of the day, when the children had gone up to the playroom, dinner had been served, and what guests there were had retired to the sitting room or their beds. While Nellie and her helpers cleared the tables, Charlotte and Martha would spend a quiet hour together, going over the events of the day, planning the future, or reminiscing about times past.

Tonight, although neither Reginald nor Charlotte and Martha were aware of it, a letter the trooper held in his jacket pocket would bring all three elements together in the person of Tom Newbold, who was to arrive in Port Melbourne at the end of the week.

Standing as the women walked towards him, Reginald waited while they took their seats before resuming his own. Darkness had descended on Blackwood, relieved by myriad stars. Looking up, as they often did, Charlotte and Martha searched for the Southern Cross, and took comfort in reassuring themselves the constellation was still there, fixing, as it did, their place in the universe. The full yellow moon threw up the trees at the edge of the Black Forest in bold relief, and turned the dams, lying still while the stock slept, into shimmering mirrors. And the night was so still Reginald could hear Charlotte breathing, the rhythmic rise and fall of her breast at once soothing and erotic.

But the trooper was not aroused. Instead, the moment teased him with the memory of the only woman he had ever loved, lost with the son she had struggled so valiantly and for so long to give him. Drawing Tom Newbold's letter from his tunic pocket, he stood to adjust the gas lamp to one side of the front door, and begged the ladies' attention.

"Miss Charlotte, ma'am, Mistress Martha, This morning, upon my return to the barracks, I was handed a letter which had been held for me these three months past.

"The author is well known to you both, a faithful friend we thought lost to us when the *Chetwynde* went down off the coast of Western Australia, some three years past.

"I speak of none other than Tom Newbold. He was thought to have gone down with the ship, but was taken by a fast running current driven by wild winds, well away from the wreck, to be deposited on a sandbar several miles to the north of Whalers Bay where the ship ran onto a reef.

"The pounding the poor man took from being buffeted against the rocks had rendered him unconscious," Reginald continued, informed by the letter. "He lay on the sandbar until the incoming tide took him forward onto a long, white beach. I will read you the story, told in his own words."

Sergeant Baxter, Sir,

I write to you as a true friend of Miss Charlotte Hatfield, as was, and wife to the late Major Rollo D'Arcy, God rest his soul. You will be surprised, nay, shocked to hear from this old seafarer after these many years, but I am back from the dead and, by the time you read this, will not be far from your side.

It is true the ship in which I sailed foundered off the coast of Western Australia, and it was thought all souls were lost. Indeed, all were, but for me. I was found by natives, washed up on a beach some eight miles from where the Chetwynde went down, my body broken and my mind gone.

Those noble savages took me to their camp and cared for me as if I were their own. When my bones mended and my memory returned, I trekked along the coast, back to Whalers Bay, where I joined the crew of a steamer sailing for Hong Kong. From thence, I signed on to a sailing ship bound for Southampton.

On arriving in that fair port, I travelled, on foot, to Hatfield Hall, where I would find shelter and sustenance from my family, who still live on the estate. I hoped, while there, to collect a letter from Sir Ian Hatfield, father to Miss Charlotte, in answer to one I had delivered on her behalf some three years earlier.

I know you will have honoured our bond to look out for the dear lady, her children and her companion, Mistress Wootten, and look to you to take me to them when the Shiraleen, my new vessel, ties up in Port Melbourne at the end of April in the year of our Lord, 1859.

Your Respectful Servant, Sir,

Thos. Newbold, Seaman.

Tom Newbold stepped off the stagecoach just four days later. Reginald had turned his horse around the morning after he had satisfied himself Charlotte, Martha and the children were safe, to be in Melbourne when the *Shiraleen* sailed through the heads – for there was less than a week left before the month ran out.

There could be no mistaking the trooper, standing straight and tall in his bright red jacket, oblivious to the chill wind that whipped along Coles Wharf. He had taken that position at first light every morning since his return from Blackwood, waiting until the pilots congregated in the Dock Master's office to check the shipping news. But Reginald had not immediately recognised his friend. The seaman's shoulder length hair, beard and moustache, once black as coal, were now stripped of colour. It was only the swinging gait and steely eyes that marked him as the strong and resourceful seafarer Reginald had first met that fateful night, when a chance meeting served to bind them together forever.

Over a draught of ale in the Queen's Arms, a short walk from Customs House along Flinders Lane – now but one of a carefully planned grid of intersecting streets and lanes in the city visitors already hailed as equal to its European counterparts – each man listened intently to the story the other had to tell.

The seaman learned of Charlotte's journey from the bluestone cottage in Jolimont to the isolated hotel in the goldfields, her struggle to purchase a foothold in the unforgiving countryside, the ultimate success she had made of her life and of the happiness she had found and lost.

Over a second pot, the sergeant heard of the seaman's promise to the *Chetwynde's* late master, Captain Hugh Hatfield, brother to Charlotte's father, Sir Ian, to watch over his beloved niece and do all he could to reunite her with her father. On the *Chetwynde's* final Melbourne to Southampton run, he had carried a letter to the Temple chambers of solicitors, De Villiers, Blenheim & Gaur, from Captain Hugh to Sir Ian, begging his brother to rescue Charlotte from her unfortunate situation.

It was not until he visited Hatfield Hall after his lost years recovering from the shipwreck, that Tom understood why Sir Ian had not replied, forgiving Charlotte's youthful transgressions and bringing her home.

Looking down into the creamy froth topping the rim of his half pint pot, Tom shook his head and sighed deeply. "Reginald, my friend, I fear it is my sad duty to deny the poor lass that happy end to her exile. For I must tell her that if she wishes to see her father again she will have to sail for England as soon as possible.

"Even so, it is doubtful he will know her or be able to speak the words she longs to hear. The poor man has suffered a stroke and can neither speak nor recognise those with whom he was once familiar. Her mother, the lady Margaret, is long dead. And it has fallen to her younger sisters to provide an income for their father.

"My nephew, Luke Barker, footman as was in Miss Charlotte's time at Hatfield Hall, is now raised to the position of butler, and having taken pity upon his employer, has appointed himself also Sir Ian's manservant.

"Luke does all he can for him, for despite his concern for the family's social standing which has cost him so dearly, Sir Ian is a good man and has treated the people on the estate most kindly.

"But Luke says the physician gives no hope at all of him continuing his existence upon this earth beyond a half-year at most."

The first thing Tom noticed about Charlotte was that the apprehensive young girl he had first met, boarding the *Chetwynde*, was now a strong, confident woman. The second thing he noticed was the pain in her eyes that belied the smile on her face. Although more than a year had passed since Jed died, it was clear she had not yet come to terms with the loss. And here he was, Tom Newbold, sworn friend and protector, come to deliver more sad news.

Thankfully, Martha Wootten, Charlotte's trusted companion, waited to greet him on the veranda. He would find a quiet moment to talk, first, to her about the time and telling of his story, as he had so long ago, aboard the *Chetwynde*.

Only then would he talk to her about his own lost years, and how when his memory finally returned, hers was the face and the voice and the touch he thought of before all else. He would tell her he was done with the sea; that he had signed off when the *Shiraleen* tied up at Port Melbourne. But had she remembered him as fondly?

When she stepped towards him and whispered, "Tom," the catch in her voice answered his unspoken question.

Beside Martha, two young girls hid smiles behind their hands as a tanned, long-limbed boy stepped forward to greet the weathered seafarer.

"Good day, sir, I'm Dickon. If you will hand me your swag, I will take it to your room."

"Pleased to meet you, I'm sure, young man," Tom replied, as seriously as he could. "And this here is a kitbag, sir, not a swag – a term with which I have yet to become familiar.

"I have had the pleasure of meeting you before," he continued. "Although I doubt you would remember the occasion, for you were but minutes old, and we were in the midst of a fine old storm on the open sea. I am pleased to see you are grown into such a fine young man."

Dickon had heard the story of his birth, mid-typhoon many times before, and stood even straighter as the man his mother and aunt Martha credited with his survival stood before him a decade later.

Tom turned to the girls, whom Martha had pushed forward to meet the grizzled old man who spoke so strangely. He recalled the start of the fair skinned, dark haired girl's life – every bit as threatening as her brother's – but chose to leave the memory buried with her father, bowing low in response to the child's perfectly executed bob.

"And you would be Miss Katherine, would you not?" he asked. "I would know you instantly for you are the image of your lovely mother."

He then turned his attention to the almond eyed child waiting to be introduced to the man she thought looked very much like the one in pictures mama had shown her to explain the sudden appearance of gifts under the tinselled spruce in the front hall, each year.

Reginald had told Tom about Jade's birth and adoption, so he was well prepared as Charlotte, stepping forward and placing a protective arm around the girl's shoulders, smiled and said, " And this, dear friend, is my younger daughter, Jade."

"I am honoured to meet you, Miss Jade," Tom replied, responding to the child's giggling bob as formally as he had to that of her more serious sister.

It was not until high tea had been cleared, and Charlotte had gone over to Blue's office to make sure he came to dinner, that night, that Tom and Martha found themselves alone. They had moved onto the front veranda, and while Tom filled his pipe, Martha poured herself another cup of tea. Their companionable silence held until Tom had completed the ritual of tamping the tobacco down into the bowl, striking one of the new sulphur matches on the sole of his boot, touching it to the tobacco and drawing on the stem until the flame settled and the leaf glowed gold, then red.

"Come Martha, let us walk," he said then. "I am unused to sitting about and my sea legs have not yet settled enough to stand for long in one spot."

Rising, the couple stepped down off the veranda and set off across the courtyard, side by side, arm in arm, as if they had been walking together, thus, through all the years they had been apart.

"Martha my dear," Tom began as they reached the stables. "There are things I must tell you that will disturb the peace I see our dear Charlotte has found in this place, and I am truly sorry for the upheaval I am sure will follow.

"But the news I bring cannot wait, and I fear courage will desert me if I have to face the poor girl, alone. As before, I need your help in the telling. . .

"But first, I have something to say to you of a more personal nature. Whatever your response, I know in my heart we will always be friends. So, please, give an old sailor a minute to make a fool of himself, for I've thought of nothing else on the long voyage out here."

Seeing Martha's questioning frown soften to a smile, he found the will to continue, telling her how, being at sea since he was a lad, he

272

was never in one place long enough to engage the affections of any woman who might put up with him. As a consequence, he had saved up a sizeable nest egg, thinking to purchase a little cottage for himself, somewhere on the coast, perhaps, against the day the sea might prove his master instead of the other way round. But then, late in life, as fate would have it, he had met a woman who seemed to see some good in him, trusting him with safety of a young woman she had come to love as dearly as a daughter.

"I have stood on a rolling deck for too many years to go safely down upon one knee to do this properly, my dear," he said, "But tell me you will take pity on an old salt who has held the memory of that woman in his heart for almost a decade."

Taking a moment to search for the clean white handkerchief she kept in her deep skirt pocket, Martha dabbed at her eyes and gave Tom her answer to the question he had waited so long to ask.

"Yes, Tom dear, I will marry you, if that is what you are asking. For you have never been far from my thoughts. I grieved for what I thought would be a lifetime, when Sergeant Baxter brought us news of your demise.

"We have shared the darkest of times together. You have shown yourself to be a true friend to me and to those I love.

"But you should know I cannot leave Charlotte after all this time, and I believe Charlotte now belongs here.

"So if you are prepared to unpack your kitbag in this place, I can think of no happier ending to my life than to spend the rest of the time I have left as your wife."

Tears rolling down his weather-beaten face, Tom reached inside his vest pocket and pulled out a wide gold wedding ring, inscribed on the inside, in flowing script, *For Martha.*

Placing it gently on the third finger of Martha's left hand, he confessed, "I had this made in London, before I set foot on the ship that brought us back together. If you had refused me it would have stayed in my pocket, travelling with me wherever I went, a lasting memory of what might have been."

Walking back to the hotel, Tom told Martha the news he had carried half way round the world to deliver to Charlotte. Martha listened intently, and by the time Tom had finished, knew that there was only one course of action she could advise him to take when they returned to the house. Charlotte had to be given the opportunity to make peace with her father before it was too late. They would tell her, together, that night.

After dinner, when the children had been excused, Martha took Charlotte by the arm and, asking Nellie to put up a tray of strong tea and bring it out onto the veranda, led the woman she still regarded as her young charge, out through the French doors to where Tom waited in one of the wicker chairs, set around a marble topped table.

Under a darkening sky, he gently described his findings when he went to Hatfield Hall to deliver the long-delayed letter from Charlotte's uncle to her father. By the time sombre black clouds had sealed in the night, Charlotte had made the decision Martha knew was the only one possible for her.

On hearing of Tom's proposal, and the decision he had made to stay in Blackwood, Charlotte knew she would be leaving the hotel in safe hands. With Nellie and Elias continuing to manage the kitchen and cellar, and Blue overseeing the stock and stables, there was nothing to prevent her going home at last.

But was it her home? For so long she had lived with the hope of being accepted back into the family to live out her life among the people she loved. But as time passed with no word from her father, hope faded, to be replaced with the realisation that she had grown to love the land from which she had been expected, in due course, to return.

"I shall leave for England at week's end," she said. "And I shall take the children with me."

Chapter Sixteen

GOING HOME

Sunday lunch was a time-honoured tradition faithfully upheld where families of English ancestry gathered together on the last day of the week in the Queen's dominions around the world. Australia, and Charlotte's Blackwood family, was no exception.

The three days between Charlotte's decision to return to Hatfield Hall and this notional day of rest had involved hurried meetings with Nellie and Elias to ensure household accounts, due each quarter, had been settled with produce suppliers, with Blue to see if anything was owed to the farrier and feed merchants. Theo would take care of the hospital now that he owned it, leaving only the school, and Grace and the schools governors – Councillors O'Farrell and Macarthy and the Manager of the Union Bank – could manage those accounts.

With Tom by her side Martha had no qualms about running the hotel for as long as it took to resolve past and present issues with Sir Ian and ensure the future of the Hatfield estate. The Native Police Patrol had been briefed to keep a special watch on the hotel during her absence in case bushrangers, whose pickings were slim on the roads now that Victoria's goldfields had been all but exhausted, saw the well-patronised Blackwood Rest Hotel as a new target.

With time running out before Charlotte and the children set off in the coach driven by Blue – who trusted no-one else to transport its precious passengers – to Melbourne, this Sunday lunch was to be the last they would spend together for the foreseeable future.

Louis and Eliza and Sergeant Baxter would be waiting to meet and farewell Charlotte and the children on their arrival in the city. Today, Tom and Martha, Theo and Grace, with little Theo, Mick and Connie and baby Harriet, Mac (*still looking for a wife as fair as my brother's*), Thérèse, Blue, Nellie and Elias and Sunny would be sitting around the family dining table with Charlotte and the children. Father Ignatius – who had other duties to perform later in the day – would also be there and although any gathering among the group was usually a happy occasion, the mood, this day, was sombre. But Charlotte knew just how to lift it.

"Dear friends," she began. "Thank you all for coming with so little advance warning. I would have left Blackwood with a much heavier heart had I not been able to carry with me the memory of you, gathered around my table.

"You all now know the reason for my precipitous departure. I have no concerns about leaving the hotel, the hospital, the school and all the other enterprises we have embarked upon, together, as I know they are in safe hands. And I have no doubt that under the watchful eyes of Councillors Macarthy and O'Farrell, my beloved Blackwood will continue on as an orderly, caring community in which to raise happy, healthy, children.

"But there is one outstanding matter we must take care of before I leave. It is my great pleasure to announce the forthcoming union of my dearest friend and companion, Martha Wootten, and Tom Newbold, without whose selfless support, my son and I might never have survived the voyage out from England – or indeed, our beginnings here in Victoria."

It was the first time anyone had seen Martha blush. But her colour rose with the level of applause as the women left their seats to kiss her smiling face, and the men stood to pump Tom's hand and slap him on the back.

Tapping the bowl of his wine glass, Father Ignatius called for attention as he, too, had a special announcement.

"Ladies and gentlemen, yesterday, upon my arrival, Tom and Martha informed me that they are anxious to be married as soon as possible, feeling they are too old and set in their ways to live under the same roof without God's blessing.

"As something of an authority on goldfields marriages, I can state, with confidence, that the church allows an 'irregular' marriage, doing away with the reading of banns, if a priest is sure a couple are entering into wedlock in full understanding of the commitment they are about to make, and there is no prior commitment by either party to prevent their lawful union.

"I therefore propose we proceed with the ceremony without further ado!"

Adjourning, the assembled friends gathered under the spreading fig tree Elias had planted when they had first moved into the rundown hotel, to witness Tom and Martha exchanging the time-honoured vows, with Dickon stepping up as Tom's best man, Thérèse standing up as Martha's maid of honour, and Jade and Katherine as beaming bridesmaids.

By the time Blue delivered Charlotte and the children to the door of the elegant, East Melbourne home of the banker and his wife, Louis and Eliza had been hovering on the balcony for more than an hour before their expected arrival, hoping for an early sighting through the long glass they had acquired on their honeymoon in Florence.

With Bishopscourt now owned by the Church of England for the purpose of housing Victoria's Archbishop, the Union Bank had, as Alistair had predicted, taken over the house next door to Louis' for their visiting dignitaries. A permanent housekeeper, butler, lady's maid and below stairs staff had been retained, and rooms had been prepared there for Charlotte and the children to ensure that during their last few hours in Melbourne they would want for nothing.

They would, of course, dine with Louis and Eliza that night. Blue had been invited and Sergeant Baxter would also join the party gathering to farewell the family each had come to regard as their own. But there were two calls Charlotte wished to make before that. Declining Louis' offer of the bank's open landau, she set out with the children, on foot, to retrace the steps she had taken so often during the first twelve months of Dickon's life.

She had remained loyal to Mishka, the Russian bootmaker, bringing him to Blackwood once a year to measure and fit her children's feet and those of the rest of the hotel family. He still worked on a bench at the front of his tiny Collingwood shop, next door to the basket weaver's with its wares strung from the eaves. His welcome was effusive when Charlotte and the children appeared in front of him. Dusting off the wooden bench, as he had a decade before, he called to Iris to bring sweet Russian tea for Charlotte, Babushka dolls for the girls, and a Georgian kite with its distinctive black and white tails, for Dickon.

They bought fresh bread and a large Eccles cake from the bakery along the road, and ended up in the lane where the Wills' house was easily recognised by the pot of geraniums perched on the front step.

"Charlotte, dear girl, how wonderful to see you," Florence cried on opening the door. Wiping her hands on her apron, she pulled Charlotte close and held her tightly before releasing her to brush away the tears streaming down her face.

"And Master Dickon, let me look at you. What a fine young man! And this would be Katherine, and this, Jade. Such beautiful young ladies."

Interrupted only by the need to settle a squabble breaking out among her own children, Florence led her visitors along the narrow hall into the crowded kitchen. In seconds, it seemed, peace was restored, and the Wills' children, Charlie, Mollie and Alby, were soon chatting animatedly with Dickon, Katherine and Jade over fresh bread and strawberry preserves – put up from fruit in their own garden, Florence told them, proudly – and slices of sugary Eccles cake.

"The sergeant told Charlie and the rest of the lads you were leaving the colony, and the reason why," Florence said, sadly. "I'm that sorry for you, lass. But it has to be done.

"Come back as soon as it's all sorted, though. This is where you belong. You are a true colonial now, Charlotte. Like us, your children were born and raised here – even Dickon can claim that, seeing as he was born at sea, on a ship bound for Australia."

Charlotte stood at the rail of the *SS Bellarossa*, a new, five hundred ton iron steamship, rigged as a three-masted barque with two funnels, until she could no longer distinguish the faces of Louis, Eliza, Reginald and Blue from the blur of buildings behind them. A pilot had just come aboard to guide them out through the heads; after that they would be on their own, facing weeks now, instead of months, on the open sea, with only three short stops for refuelling, fresh food and water, before reaching England.

I suppose we will get used to the noise and the vibrations from the engines and screw, Charlotte thought sitting on the end of an elegant, rose velvet day-bed in her first class-stateroom, but finding she was too tired to rest. Recognising that her fatigue stemmed from the uncertainty of leaving the place in which she and the children had built a future, to revisit the past, she determined to rise above her doubts. Pulling herself to her feet, she reached for the door separating the children's stateroom from her own.

"Come children, set aside your squabbles, we are going to explore the ship."

Dickon looked up expectantly from the chore book Blue had given him when he took on the position of property manager *(no man sits around like a girl when there's men's work to be done, boy)*, glad to have something to do rather than reflect on the loss of the life he loved. Katherine and Jade clapped their hands, delighting in the prospect of a promenade – anything, really, that might present a brighter picture than that of a moping boy with no-one and nothing to engage him other than teasing his sisters.

Although rigged as a barque, the *Bellarossa* bore little resemblance to the *Chetwynde*. Built to carry more cargo than passengers, the fittings were utilitarian, and without the privileges afforded to a captain's niece,

279

the standard of service left much to be desired. Still, the children found enough to interest them when they were allowed on deck. Outgoing and confident, they soon made friends with the crew and the children of other families located on their deck. Egg and spoon races, deck quoits and skittles got rid of the fidgets all young people experience left in their quarters for too long; morning observational walks, with one eye shut and the other pressed against the near end of a long glass, opened up a vista of green sea and foam crested waves with dolphins leaping alongside the ship while big white birds blundered aloft in the rigging.

Charlotte, too, spent as much time as light and wind allowed on deck. Walking from bow to stern and back again, she replayed the vision she had kept locked behind a wall in her memory. In her head, again, the lonely departure from Hatfield Hall with no farewell from family and friends, the marriage to D'Arcy on board the *Chetwynde*, when all hope of being reunited with Dickon's father was lost, and the humiliation which followed. When the scenes played out in her head became too painful, she returned to the journal she thought she had closed forever upon Jed's death.

Untying the crimson ribbon with which the covers of the leather bound volume were held together, she would turn to the last entry – an account of the happy time they had spent in Melbourne immediately following their wedding. Between the page capturing their last week together, and the empty one facing it, she had slipped the photograph taken on their wedding day.

For too long now, I have looked only at what is happening before my eyes, she wrote, now. *It was ever my intent to record the things I saw on my journey out from England, and my experiences in the year or two I expected to stay in what I saw, then, as an alien land, so as to amuse my family and friends on my return.*

In retrospect, I tricked my mind into thinking of what was, in reality, my exile, as something akin to the Grand Tour I might have taken had fate allowed me to remain untouched by love at so early an age. Instead of walking along the rutted roads of Port Melbourne upon my arrival, I might have been promenading on boulevards in Paris or Rome; instead of riding out into the goldfields to deliver infants born in freezing gullies, tilting my parasol against the glare of the sun stepping down the hilly paths in Positano.

But as the weeks and months and years went by, the grand tour I was destined to embark upon became the life I lived, transforming me from the sheltered, shallow girl I was to the woman I have become: stronger, surer – wiser, even – in the role thrust upon me when Dickon was but a concept beyond my comprehension.

Now, with three children and two families to care for, the only fear I face is deciding which family I will, in the end, return to. Do I look to the past or to the future? Will my children, knowing nothing of one, and everything of the other, challenge that choice when they are of an age to choose for themselves?

The port the *Bellarossa* tied up at after standing off for two days, waiting for the fog to lift, was Portsmouth – *the very same point at which my journey began,* Charlotte noted, later.

The day had dawned as cold and wet as it had on that fateful day, and a chill wind again whipped along the walkway in what passed for the beginning of Spring in the northern hemisphere. The children shivered, despite the merino knits and ankle-length oilskins Martha, remembering the cold she said creeps into your bones, had insisted they took with them. Even Charlotte, wrapped in one of the fur-lined travelling coats Eliza had brought back from a buying trip to Europe, thanked British bureaucracy for insisting all passengers stay on board until Customs officers were satisfied the *Bellarossa* carried no illegal imports or undesirable immigrants.

Thankfully, a portly figure, resplendent in the livery of the shipping line which owned the *Bellarossa*, came bustling towards them. "Begging your pardon, milady, Algernon Babcock, Engagement Officer with Gilmore and Gregory, at your service.

"Might I venture to suggest that you and your party follow me to the end of the walkway where a carriage awaits you. It is, of course, a closed carriage, and will afford protection from the elements while I see to your trunks and travelling bags."

281

Turning away, he snapped his fingers at a group of porters, huddled around a glowing brazier awaiting such a summons. Two ran forward and, after a hurried briefing, sprinted up the crew gangplank, leaving Algernon Babcock to lead Charlotte and the children to one of the Gilmore & Gregory carriages reserved for the convenience of first-class passengers.

As the horses entered the familiar, tree-lined drive that wound its way through acres of parkland, Charlotte was surprised to see weeds growing through the white gravel, and last season's leaves banked up in drifts against the sturdy trunks of the English oaks that edged the approach to the red brick mansion she had once called home.

Alighting from the carriage, as if replaying the memory of her departure from Hatfield Hall in reverse, she was aware the courtyard was deserted. It had always been the hub of the Hatfield estate, with gardeners busily sweeping, clipping and trimming, footmen scurrying back and forth carrying letters for the post or a hamper for the poor, and maids polishing the ornate brass bell push. And above the buzz of exchanged greetings and debate about the pruning of a tree or the shaping of a hedge, her father's booming laugh floating through the morning room window as he dandled one of her little sisters upon his knee. Now all was still and silent.

Dismissing the carriage, Charlotte led the children up shallow steps to stand before the imposing front door. No running footsteps could be heard signalling a front hall maid hurrying in response to the sound of wheels crunching on gravel, to alert the butler. But as she raised her hand to the bell, now hanging dull and tarnished, the heavy door swung wide enough to allow cautious scrutiny of the unexpected guests. Then, flinging it open wide, Luke Barker reached for Charlotte with both hands.

"Charlotte!" he cried, then, "Cook, come quick, it is Charlotte, come home at last!"

In the moments before the comforting figure of the only person to speak to her on the morning of her departure appeared, Charlotte

282

looked, again, at the face of the man standing in doorway.

"Oh, Luke, is it really you?" she whispered.

"Yes, it's me, Charlotte. Leicester took his pension and I took his place, five years ago this Michaelmas past. Hatfield Hall has seen many other changes since then," he said, shaking his head, sadly.

Just then the brave woman who had risked her position by coming up the front stairs to push a basket of wine and pasties into Martha's arms for the long journey to Portsmouth, rounded the banister at the top of the front stairs. Risking nothing now, she ran through the hall to push past Barker, tears streaming down her lined face, and held Charlotte close for a full minute before she found her voice.

"Charlotte, dear girl. Those of us still left here have longed for this moment. All these years, and no word of your whereabouts; we did not even know if you had survived the voyage until Tom paid us a visit a few months ago.

"But you are back now, safe and sound, thank the good Lord – and with a parcel of bonnie children too!"

Dickon, Katherine and Jade, standing silent and wondering behind their mother, now stepped forward to make their bow and bobs and were each, in turn, held close against a warm apron smelling of cloved apples.

When Cook had taken the children down to the kitchen to sit around a blazing hearth with servings of apple pie, fresh from the oven and topped with clotted cream from cows clustered conversationally around the milking shed, Charlotte asked Barker to take her to her father. Calling upon the privilege of their childhood friendship he took her, instead, into the morning room – one of the few rooms that had not been closed off in recent months. Leading her to the sofa, he pulled up a footstool and sat before her.

"Charlotte, first, I must speak frankly," he said. "Much has changed over the decade you have been away. The estate has suffered greatly from the growth of industry, in particular the number of mills built in the north of the country.

"Many servants and farm hands, ours among them, have deserted the land and big country houses, lured north by the prospect of higher wages, working in the mills.

"Only the older men, and women with too many offspring to find accommodation in the overcrowded mill towns, are left to manage the estate. And even though the numbers of those who rely on the estate for support are, as a consequence, much reduced, we are now unable to care for them in the manner Sir Ian would have wished.

"We have shut down most of the rooms in the house in an effort to conserve money better spent elsewhere. Only Cook, Balfour and myself live in these days, and we manage the whole house ourselves, with just two of the estate wives coming in to clean and launder."

Here, Barker stood to pour a measure of Spanish sherry into one of the finely etched glasses set out on a silver tray atop a box piano, reminding Charlotte of her mother playing the instrument with one or other of her daughters sitting on the stool beside her.

"My mother," she began, before the glass reached her lips. "Please tell me the end was peaceful. And where are my sisters? Why are they not here to greet me?"

"We loved the Lady Margaret as we love you," Luke replied. "And take comfort in the knowledge that, so weakened by the consumption she had fought so bravely the whole of the previous winter, her weary heart simply gave up the struggle. The end came peacefully in her sleep.

"Your father, I fear, suffered greatly from the loss of his dear wife. Within days of consigning her to her grave, he suffered a stroke which has left him unable to walk, speak or care for himself these five years past."

As the afternoon light faded into early autumn dusk, Barker went on to tell Charlotte how, without Sir Ian to oversee accounts, the estate had been allowed to run down by a new steward, appointed to take the place of a man her father had regarded more as a partner than an employee, when a fall from his horse ended his life.

"The new man had neither the wit nor the will to manage the estate efficiently and soon left to join the exodus to the north.

"Although his replacement, promoted from within, has done his best to slow the decline, we are in dire straits, as you will have no doubt ascertained on your arrival from the neglected appearance of the house and gardens.

"We have been forced to sell off most of the stock just to survive, and must rely on the support of Miss Melanie and Miss Beatrice for your father's special needs. They, too, are in the north, employed as governesses by wealthy mill owners who aspire to having their daughters marry up.

"They have yet to learn of your arrival, and when they do, will have to seek leave to travel such a distance to see you.

"I do the best I can between managing the house and caring for your father, holding things together for the little time the physician says Sir Ian now has left to him."

Setting aside the wine, Charlotte rose to her feet and took Luke's hands in hers. "I am here now, dear friend, and will lift the burden of caring for my father from your shoulders. Please take me to him; it is time we made our peace."

Although now aware of her father's condition, Charlotte was unprepared for the sight of the mindless old man huddled into a hill of pillows who had replaced the tall, distinguished gentleman she remembered. Willing herself to walk forward, Charlotte sat on the edge of the bed and took the fragile spectre in her arms.

"Father," she whispered, "It is Charlotte. I am come home."

The children settled quickly into Hatfield Hall, and into the local schools: St Anne's for the girls, Westchester for Dickon – driven there and back each day by Balfour, who had driven the same route with their mother and her sisters.

The Hatfield schoolroom, long unused now that Charlotte, Melanie and Beatrice had outgrown it, was opened up to provide a place for Dickon, Katherine and Jade to play in as the northern winter closed in. The large round table, around which the Hatfield girls had gathered with their governess, now held lead soldiers and board games. But the walls were still lined with their books, and the polished floors were still covered with colourful rag rugs, pulled up close to the glowing coal fire. The girls loved this room, but Dickon, never happy cooped up indoors, however inclement the weather, spent as much time as possible outside.

He could usually be found helping Arthur Trevorrow, the new estate manager, elevated to the position when the fleet of carriages he had maintained in times past had been reduced to one. The boy told Arthur about the coach and four his family owned in Australia, and how he was learning to drive under Blue's expert tutelage, hoping to become a driver, himself, when he went home.

He also told Arthur how much he missed riding. Rocket was now too small and too old for the long limbed lad who, nearing twelve, was an experienced rider. Blue had put him up on Jed's mount after the fire, and he was doing well on the big red stock horse. But with the Hatfield stables empty, save for the carriage pair, kept for collecting Beatrice and Melanie from the train station on their occasional visits, and now the school run, he was afraid he would soon forget all Blue had taught him about handling the big horse.

Arthur thought for a moment, then led the boy out of the stables and into open parkland reaching all the way to a stand of elms that crowned the hill behind Hatfield Hall. Once a fitting backdrop to the stately home, a rising vista of disciplined walks, carefully pruned trees and planted gardens, it was now given over to four goats, two Clydesdales and a silky black colt, just to keep the grass down. The goats took no notice at all of the man and boy approaching the fence, put up to contain the occupants of what had become just another field. The Clydesdales looked away, avoiding eye contact and a possible call to work; but the colt, half way up the hill, threw up its head and whinnied expectantly. Leaning forward over the fence, Arthur whistled, softly, his face breaking into a smile as the gleaming black animal streaked towards them, mane and tail flying, head tossing with the sheer thrill of running.

Dickon was over the fence before the horse pulled up in front of them. Arthur took a little longer. When he caught up the boy was already running sure hands over the animal's trembling withers, all the way along its back and down its legs to feel each fetlock.

"He's a fine animal, sir," said Dickon, laughing as the colt pushed its velvet muzzle into his neck. "What's his name?"

"I called him Midnight on account of his colour and being sired by my son's horse, Night Sky, before that brave animal met his end – ten years to the day after my boy went away. A tree Night Sky was sheltering under in the height of a summer storm took a lightning strike, killing the horse instantly.

"My son loved that horse, and because of that, I have held onto this one. But he needs to be ridden and my bones are too set, now, to risk a fall off a frisky young fellow like this. You remind me of my son, Dickon, and if you can ride Midnight as well as he rode Night Sky, he's yours."

Grabbing the colt's mane, Dickon swung himself up on its back before Arthur could take his next breath; horse and boy wheeling in one fluid movement and racing off up the hill at full gallop. Bareback, holding on with his knees like Jed had first taught him on Rocket, Dickon was in his element. Returning at a canter, the boy slid to the ground and threw his arms around the horse's neck.

"I guess he's yours, son," said Arthur, smiling, taking a rope halter from over his shoulder and tossing it to Dickon.

While the children were at their lessons, Charlotte was at her father's bedside. She washed him, fed him, and talked to him about her life in Australia and how, now that she had children of her own, she understood how heartbreaking the decision to send her away must have been for him, too. She brought out her journal, turning the pages to recount her first impressions of her new home, and show him the sketches she had drawn to illustrate them. While he followed her pointing finger with vacant eyes, she hoped that hearing her story, he might give some sign that he had forgiven the upset she had caused by eloping with Richard. But when he turned his face to hers, there was no sign that he knew who she was; no hope, now, of the words she longed to hear.

On his most recent visit, Dr Millswyn, Sir Ian's physician, had respectfully suggested Beatrice and Melanie should be summoned forthwith. Despatching a messenger to the post office, Charlotte realised decisions about the future of Hatfield Hall could no longer be delayed. Walking downstairs to the kitchen, where Cook, Balfour and Barker would be meeting for morning tea, she joined them at the fireside.

"Friends, the time has come when we must look to the future," she began, helping herself to a cup of the hot amber liquid from the pot set to brew on the hearth.

"Luke, I would like to meet the new estate manager. I can wait no longer to meet my responsibilities. I am not the sheltered girl you knew before I went away. I manage a property twice the size of Hatfield Hall at home, and decisions I make, daily, have influenced the lives of countless families.

"My sisters will soon be home and I wish to have a plan to put before them which will see them living back in their home again, with Hatfield Hall generating an income sufficient to ensure a future for everyone on the estate."

"Yes ma'am," replied Barker, smiling, slowly. "As soon as you have finished your tea."

Opening the door to the estate manager's office, Barker stepped to one side to allow Charlotte to enter. A grey haired figure of medium height and familiar frame rose to greet her. Positioned as he was, his back against the window, no light fell on his face to help Charlotte recognise him.

"Hello, Charlotte dear, we have missed you." The voice, so like that of his son, sent Charlotte's senses reeling.

"Mr Trevorrow, sir, is it you? I have pictured myself at your table, with Richard by my side, so many times since I was sent away," Charlotte whispered, tears welling.

"Indeed it is, my dear. Come, let me kiss your pretty face." Walking around the big oak desk standing between them, Arthur opened his arms to enfold the young woman.

"The boy ..." he began, looking deep into Charlotte's eyes. "Your son – a fine lad, if ever I saw one – bears an uncanny resemblance to my own. Could it possibly be ...?

"Yes, Arthur. Dickon is Richard's son. Your grandson," Charlotte replied, gently.

"It is my greatest wish that he should know of his true beginnings. But out of respect for my own father, even though he was the cause of my separation from Richard and, ultimately, Richard from his son, I beg you to withhold this truth for just a few more days, until..."

Here, Charlotte found she could not form the words that foretold her father's death. Arthur nodded, kissing Charlotte's face, again, and murmuring, "I know, child. I know."

Barker, who had waited outside until the emotion of the moment had passed its peak, now stepped forward, placing a package on the desk beside Charlotte and the estate manager.

"This was brought to me by young Danfield," he said. "He was clipping the hedge facing the house when a messenger galloped up to the front door. Failing to elicit a response, he charged the boy with its safe delivery.

"As you see, it is addressed to your father, Charlotte, but in the present circumstances, the responsibility for responding to its contents must fall to you."

Breaking the red wax seal, Charlotte tore apart the paper enclosing a letter to which a number of legal documents were appended. Her cheeks, flushed with happiness moments before, lost every vestige of colour in the minute it took her to read the contents of the letter.

"I fear we have lost Hatfield Hall before we have even begun to save it," she whispered, handing the letter to Arthur.

Reaching for his spectacles, the estate manager glanced quickly over the letter and loosened the documents from the crimson tape that bound them together. He then read the letter again and, spreading the documents out across his desk, scrutinised each one, thoroughly.

"It would seem your fear is well founded, Charlotte," he said, guiding her to the leather armchair Sir Ian used when he came into the estate office to peruse the stock records and sign off the wages. It was not for Charlotte's comfort that Arthur ensured she was seated, but for fear she might faint when she learned the full import of the news the solicitors' letter had conveyed.

Barker, moving across the room to stand beside her, waited tensely for Arthur to continue.

"These documents confirm the contents of the letter from Mr Rawlinson, partner with De Villiers, Blenheim & Gaur, Sir Ian's solicitors," Arthur began, going on to explain that repayments of a loan secured against, first, parcels of land, and then the house known as Hatfield Hall, had fallen so far in arrears that with compounding interest added to the principal, it now exceeded the value of the entire Hatfield estate.

Letters alerting Sir Ian to the risk of allowing the problem to continue had gone unanswered until two years ago, when one Wilfred Dyson wrote to the bank over the title Estate Manager. His letter respectfully informed De Villiers, Blenheim & Gaur that Sir Ian had instructed further loan repayments should be drawn down from the family trust account until further notice. Dyson had departed and the bank now advised Sir Ian that the trust fund was exhausted at the end of the last quarter, and in order to recover its money, the Board had had no option other than to offer the estate for sale.

"Fortunately – or so it says here – the bank contacted Sir Ian's solicitors to acquire the deeds to the estate at the same time one of De Villiers, Blenheim & Gaur's other clients wrote to them enquiring about substantial country estates that might be available for sale.

"With Sir Ian's condition in mind, they had invited an offer on Hatfield Hall which would satisfy the bank and still leave a sizeable margin for restoration, putting in an offer on behalf of the family to lease back the property from the prospective new owner.

"Holding the power to act on Sir Ian's behalf, De Villiers, Blenheim and Gaur executed a deed of sale to their overseas client which satisfied both parties, and wish to advise Sir Ian that the new owner will be arriving within the week to inspect his new acquisition," Arthur informed Charlotte, sadly.

"You are not expected to vacate, nor will you need to remove any of the contents of Hatfield Hall. As soon as he is satisfied the estate can be made to support itself, the American gentleman will return to his home in the Carolinas."

Standing at her father's graveside as the priest intoned the litany that would consign Sir Ian to his earthly resting place, Charlotte allowed her thoughts to wander across the wooded hills that surrounded the churchyard in which she stood.

Through closed eyes she saw a laughing girl, hair flying, muslin gown floating above a carpet of bluebells, running towards a dark haired boy, his arms held wide to catch her.

Opening them again she witnessed her father's remains being lowered into the earth and Beatrice and Melanie stepping forward with posies of early Spring violets to cast into the darkening void. The grandchildren Sir Ian had known only as strangers who had gathered at his bedside each evening to kiss him goodnight, paused uncertainly at the graveside to drop rosemary on the polished lid of his coffin for remembrance.

Slowly, Charlotte led the family, followed by Barker, Arthur, Cook and Balfour, back to the Hall, pausing only long enough to accept the condolences of Hatfield tenants who had come to honour the landlord who had never asked them for rent. Today, she thought, she would thank them all for coming. Tomorrow she would gather them together again, to break the news that Hatfield estate had passed into the hands of a new owner.

The next morning, as Dickon, Katherine and Jade stood on the front steps, waiting for the carriage to take them to school, a lone rider

291

appeared through the trees edging the winding drive, approaching the house at full gallop.

Charlotte, waiting in the doorway to see her children into the carriage, felt the stirring of some distant memory as the rider reined in his horse and slid to the ground.

Dickon, used to welcoming visitors to the Blackwood Rest Hotel, stepped forward to meet the tall, dark haired newcomer, and as her son and the rider faced each other she saw them together as if locked in a frame forged more than a decade earlier.

"Sweet Jesus," Barker murmured by her side, turning to catch her as Charlotte slipped, wordlessly, to the ground.

Later, alone in the morning room, his eyes never leaving hers, her hands held fast in his, Richard told Charlotte how he had discovered, by chance, that she and her children were in England.

His solicitors, De Villiers, Blenheim & Gaur, had written to inform him that as the late Captain Hugh Hatfield's executors, they were pleased to advise him that he had inherited the Captain's entire estate, with the exception of a bequest to be paid to one Thos. Newbold; and that they awaited his instructions on its investment in England or transfer to his bank in America.

There was also a letter, in Captain Hatfield's hand, containing information the solicitors were certain Mr Trevorrow would consider of such importance they respectfully suggested he attended their chambers in London as soon as possible.

"I did not receive the solicitors' letter until a month ago," Richard said, "I had been away from my office for half a year, selling cotton to the mills in Europe for a group of growers in the Carolinas, where I have lived since I was removed from the Bristol Assizes, all those years ago."

Here, tears spilled, again, from Charlotte's eyes; Richard, raising her hands, briefly, to his lips, continued. "It lay there, on my office desk, until I returned. As soon as I had absorbed its contents, I booked passage for London.

"It was in De Villiers, Blenheim and Gaur's Temple chambers that Elliot Rawlinson, the partner who looked after my affairs, advised me of the imminent sale of Hatfield Hall, offering it as one of the choices I might consider for investing the inheritance I had received from my late benefactor.

"Purchasing Hatfield Hall seemed the right thing to do, for Beatrice and Melanie, and for you, dearest, if you ever came back. And it meant my father and the other tenants living on the estate would be able to stay in their homes for as long as they wished.

"It was only after the documents of sale were exchanged with the bank that I was told you were here, caring for your father. I came, at once."

Rising from the sofa on which they both sat. Charlotte walked towards the bell pull. "Richard, dearest, I know there is much more to your story, and you must hear mine, but your father needs to see his son. He was away from his office when you arrived, and must, by now, have learned of your return."

Luke came back into the room minutes later, and the two men, childhood friends, exchanged the joyous greeting delayed by their concern for Charlotte's recovery. Richard's father had, indeed, been located, Luke told them, and was waiting in the front hall.

"We will be in the kitchen, Richard," said Charlotte. "Go out and greet your father. Bring him back in here, where the fire burns brightly, and when you are ready, join us downstairs."

Over a midday meal which reminded Charlotte of many such family gatherings over which she had presided at the Blackwood Rest Hotel, Charlotte, together with Beatrice and Melanie, Arthur, Luke, Cook and Balfour heard, for the first time, what had really happened to Richard after he was taken away to Bristol Assizes.

Thought to have died in the typhus epidemic which took so many in the holding cells at Bristol Assizes, he had, in fact, been released into Elliot Rawlinson's custody days before the sailor who carried the disease was remanded. Rawlinson, acting on instructions from his client, Sir Ian

Hatfield, was to hold the boy in London, until further notice.

Sir Ian had never intended to pursue the charges he had brought against his daughter's lover, instead charging Rawlinson with keeping him in London until after Charlotte had sailed for Australia. Sir Ian's brother, Captain Hugh Hatfield, had learned of this deception when he returned to London after leaving Charlotte and her new husband in Melbourne. De Villiers, Blenheim and Gaur acted for both brothers, and it was while sitting across the partner desk from Rawlinson in their Temple chambers, that Hugh made the decision to place Charlotte's future in Richard's hands.

Rawlinson had told him how, on meeting Richard, he had taken to the boy, providing a bed for him in his own house and finding a place for him clerking at De Villiers, Blenheim & Gaur.

Eventually, the charges had been expunged from the records, but Richard, having been advised of the annulment of his marriage to Charlotte and her subsequent marriage to an officer in Australia, said goodbye to his friend and mentor, thanked him for his many kindnesses, and signed on as a stoker on a steam ship bound for America.

Arriving in New York, he had lived rough for weeks before riding the rails south to find work picking cotton on the big plantations in the Carolinas. He learned to live with the pain of losing Charlotte by working among slaves and criminals for shelter and sustenance. His luck changed when, weighing in at the end of another gruelling day he made a mental calculation of weights the manager was trying to total with pen and paper, blurting out the answer as the owner walked past.

Intrigued, the gentleman in the white linen suit and wide panama hat paused to ask Richard where he learned to reckon so quickly, and if he could also write. Learning of the young man's time clerking for a firm of London solicitors, the owner took him out of the fields and into his office. Mr Piers Lascelles had never remarried after losing his wife in childbirth. Their child – a son – had clung to life for only a matter of days thereafter. Gradually, he had come to see Richard as the man his son – had he lived - might have become.

As the issue of slavery took a hold on America, Lascelles persuaded a group of his fellow growers to adopt a new plan for future growth based on paid wages and wider distribution. Richard did the projections and drew up agreements which would later be ratified by governments in Britain and Europe. As sole agent for the group, he travelled frequently across the Atlantic Ocean and made his American growers wealthy men. The commission he earned he sent to Elliot Rawlinson to invest as he saw fit. Wealthy now in his own right, the purchase of the Hatfield estate was easily affordable – even without the Hatfield inheritance.

Glancing at the clock as it chimed the third hour past noon, Belfour rose to collect the children from their respective schools. The drive to Bristol would take an hour, there and back, giving Charlotte the time she needed to tell Richard the rest of her story. Most importantly, as it concerned the birth of his son.

Arriving home cold and hungry, Dickon, Katherine and Jade pegged their coats in the back porch and ran down to the kitchen where they knew a hot pie and a cup of sweet, milky tea would be waiting for them. After kissing their mother and making their bobs to Arthur and Richard, the girls perched on footstools in front of the fire, plates warming their laps, cups steaming on the hearth. Dickon kissed his mother and lingered, his arm along the back of Charlotte's chair.

"Sit with us Dickon, we have a story to tell you," Charlotte said, waiting for the boy to take his seat and Cook to set his food and drink in front of him before beginning.

Lying awake in her bed, Charlotte ran over the hours spent with Richard after everyone else had retired for the night. Exhausted by the events of the day she was relieved when Richard had left Hatfield Hall to sleep in his father's house. Tomorrow would be time enough to consider the prospect of living out the promise they had made to each other before convention tore them apart, as both had hoped that, one day, they would.

But while the sight and sound and touch of him stirred Charlotte's soul, as they had so long ago, would the consequences of lives lived separately, ever since, conspire against them as they sought to build a future together?

Walking along the gravelled path, through the churchyard in which her mother and father rested, to the weathered Norman church on the hill behind Hatfield Hall, Charlotte paused at the door to say a final, silent farewell to Jed. She had told Richard about Jed, of course, walking hand in hand across the moors as they talked more about their lives away from each other. It was important to Charlotte that Richard understood she could never forget the only man she trusted with her love after D'Arcy. She had told him about D'Arcy, too, sparing him nothing because she knew that only by facing the despair she had known during her time with him would she finally be free of the memories that still came unbidden in the night.

Dickon had told Richard a lot about Jed, when they rode together on Midnight and Melody, another of Night Sky's progeny. He learned how Jed had taught his son to ride on Rocket. How he had taught him to rope a beast and build a fire out in the open, under the stars. And he saw how the boy still grieved for the man who lost his life searching for the boy he loved like a son.

His feelings about D'Arcy he kept to himself. Unable to confront the man whose brutality had left such a scar on Charlotte's soul, he spared her his own anguish.

He learned, too, about Louis Roderer, the banker essential to Charlotte's recovery after her marriage to D'Arcy ended; and Sergeant Baxter, the trooper who did so much to shield her from the worst of D'Arcy and see her safely settled in Blackwood. And Theo and Grace, and Mick and Mac, and the lovely Eliza, and of Thérèse and Connie – the Irish orphan Charlotte took in on the *Chetwynde,* now a mother, herself. And, of course, of Tom and Martha ... who waited to welcome her home on the other side of the world.

296

During the preceding weeks, Charlotte and Richard had talked long into the night about how their future together would affect the lives of those they loved on both sides of the world.

In consultation with Beatrice and Melanie, and with Mr Rawlinson on hand to advise on the establishment of a trust to fund the decision they had reached, Hatfield Hall would stay in the family as a preparatory college for girls, with provision for day students and weekly boarders. The sisters, as joint principals, would recruit teachers, set the curriculum and maintain standards. As trustee of the fund Charlotte and Richard had established to support the school, Elliott Rawlinson would oversee the administration. Arthur had been persuaded to continue to manage the estate which could now be expected to pay its way supplying the necessary produce to feed its growing family of teachers, students and resident staff.

What to do with the tithed cottages on the estate had been the easiest of their decisions. Tenancies having been handed down through generations, they would be gifted to the present occupants who, with continuing employment on the estate assured, could now expect to earn sufficient income to maintain them.

From his travels across America, and through Europe, on behalf of the co-operative he had helped to establish for the cotton growers in the Carolinas, Richard told Charlotte he thought an opportunity existed for someone to do the same for Australia's wool growers. The English mills had an insatiable need for wool to meet the demand for military uniforms, in particular. The demand for wool was growing across Europe, too, as French, German and Italian processors realised the benefits of industrialisation.

Given what he had read in the newspapers and journals, Australia was now the world's leading wool producer, and an enterprising trader might do as well with wool as he had with cotton.

Taking Arthur's arm, recalling how moved Richard's father had been when she asked him to stand for her father on the day when she and his son were to finally fulfil their destiny, Charlotte stepped slowly forward. Behind her, Beatrice, Melanie, Katherine and Jade; ahead, Richard, Luke and Dickon.

The sadness of parting from Hatfield Hall, this time, was sweetened by the knowledge that she could now return as often as she wished.

Standing at the rail of another Gilmore & Gregory vessel with her husband and children, she watched the receding land mass she once called home fade away in the mist.

The next time she saw it, she would be returning just as her father had planned – a respectable, and very happily married woman.

End note ...

The Blackwood Rest Hotel which provides the setting for most of this story was inspired by the story of the real Blackwood Hotel – now in its third incarnation after bushfires destroyed earlier weatherboard constructs.

Intrigued by persistent rumours of ghosts claimed to have been heard, seen or experienced as a cold, cloudy presence, I felt compelled to learn more about the history of the Blackwood Hotel and found that all three incarnations have been run by women.

The first was widowed Bridget Cruise (1839-1903), buried with her second husband, Joseph Cruise (1833-1867), in Blackwood Cemetery. Four of her six children, Mary Anne (1856-1861), Kathryn (1858-1862), Joseph Peter (1859-1861), and Ellen Cecilia (1861-1887), were also buried in the Blackwood Cemetery. Joseph Francis (1863-1913) and Mary Ann (1865-1921) who outlived their mother were laid to rest elsewhere.

Although A Respectable Married Woman *is not Bridget Cruise's story, she did take over the Blackwood Hotel to provide a home and a living to support her then four surviving children. It was, however, written as a tribute to Bridget and all the goldfields women who showed such courage and fortitude in their efforts to ensure, as best they could, that their families survived.*

I am grateful to Blackwood local historian Robin Zanon for her interest in my research and for providing details of Bridget Cruise and her family and records of their burials in the Blackwood Cemetery.

Glenda Banks is now working on a sequel to *A Respectable Married Woman* which takes Charlotte and her family forward through her children and grandchildren to Federation and on to the beginning of WW1.
